Now and Eternity

By

Kathleen Whittam

ISBN: 0615927157
ISBN 13: 9780615927152
Library of Congress Control Number: 2013921922
Kathleen Whittam, Keizer, OR

This book is dedicated to my friend and mentor, Peter Rogers, my former boss who was happy to share his business knowledge with everyone. When I retired he asked my plans and then encouraged me to follow my dreams, no matter what my fears, because one only fails if they don't try. Thank you, Peter, for your wisdom and encouragement!

Acknowledgement

I would like to thank those individuals who have encouraged and helped me along the way.

Sue Miholer who help with editing and who answered millions of my questions on writing.

My children, Noelle, Rob, and Patrick, who patiently listened as I read portions of the book as I wrote and re-wrote sections.

My friends who supported me with encouragement and unending enthusiasm. God bless you all.

Last, I would like to thank, Weasley and Willow, my two dogs, who sacrificed hours of play time while they waited for me to finish writing for the day.

Contents

Prologue

Nate stood in the shadows of the trees watching the woman throw the tennis ball for her small dog. He listened to the peal of her laughter at the antics of her dog. The small creature tossed the ball back into the air only to chase it down as if it had escaped and made a dash for freedom. He was certain from her laugh that she was the one he'd searched for these many years.

This small city in Oregon drew him because of the annual rainfall. Rain meant greenery, an abundance of wildlife, a combination that he needed. He'd lived in much drier climes and found the recent drought had decreased available wildlife.

In checking out the town he found a reasonably large city park bordering the Willamette River. The river accessed a wider hunting range than most parks in the area. He enjoyed watching the various activities available in the park—activities that ranged from walking, disk golf, volleyball, and evening concerts. Here he could walk in anonymity through crowds of people and observe them.

The silence the trees provided along the dirt trails along the river brought calm to his soul. Perhaps silence was not the right word, although the human sounds were muffled. The forested trail was alive with the songs of birds and the skittering in the underbrush of the small creatures that inhabited the area. Larger animals also inhabited this forested area—animals on which he could feed: deer, coyotes. He'd even smelled a cougar and seen its scat, if not the cat itself.

He wasn't sure when he first spotted the woman, but there was something in the set of her shoulders and the tilt of her head which stirred memories. He wondered if he'd found her. He hardly dared hope. She disappeared from his life long ago and this town was many miles from where they'd met and fallen in love. He came to the park daily since the day he first saw her. Watching and waiting, though she'd not been consistent in coming. The time of day she came varied by several hours. No matter. Time was not important. What difference was a few more days? He could afford to watch and to wait.

His initial impulse was to run directly to her and surprise her. He realized that was foolish. She could be a complete stranger; a look alike. He held back, determined to be prudent. He'd find a way to get a closer look without frightening her by acting like a demented stalker.

He moved south through the filbert orchard and strolled the loop back to the amphitheater. From there he ambled, hands shoved in his jeans pocket, down the black-topped path toward the fenced dog enclosure. He sank to a bench of a nearby picnic table—a casual observer watching people and their canine friends.

As he watched, eyes shadowed, she lurched on the uneven ground. She'd always been sure-footed—almost always. He chuckled at a memory of her sliding down a trail on her backside.

She called her dog, put it back on a leash and the two of them came out through the double gates of the off-leash enclosure. She smiled in his direction. Not a smile of recognition, rather one of friendly acknowledgement one might give a stranger. He tipped his hat as she strolled past.

He watched out the corner of his eye as she went to her car and lifted her reluctant dog, Rocky, inside. She kept up a familiar banter with it. She expected the little fellow to understand every word she spoke. Nate smiled in remembrance of the earlier time, the way she'd talked to another small dog.

There was no doubt. It was Kara. The years changed her—no surprise there. Her once honey blond hair held silver streaks. There were smile lines around her eyes, of course, she was always smiling. Her face bore a hint of fine line from time and care, but none of it mattered. He had found her at last.

He nodded in acknowledgment as she backed out, but didn't try to make contact. Not yet. He'd be gradual in his approach, let her come to her own remembrance. She might have forgotten him, he didn't think she could. Memory of him might not be in the forefront of her mind after all this time. But it didn't matter; he had time to wait for her memory to awaken. After waiting almost fifty years, a few days more would hardly matter.

He'd hang around at the park, close enough to be noticed in an activity. Playing volleyball or walking would do. Check to see if she came to any of the concerts and casually show up. Let her get comfortable seeing him and hope familiarity allowed occasional greetings. Maybe he'd find where else she spent time, casually bump into her shopping.

It would be easy to track her and listen to her conversations with others at the park. His hearing was far superior to humans. If he concentrated he could hear across the park.

Josh knew about his search. His brother could advise him, though he thought he was a lunatic. Of course, Josh thought he was a lunatic when he first met Kara. He'd think of some way to meet her with or without Josh's help.

He grimaced thinking of the past. He'd wanted to give her everything and would have—if only she'd agreed. They could have shared their lives, but she refused and sent him away. Her refusal boiled down to two reasons: her belief in a different eternity and his lifestyle. Ultimately, she held to her beliefs though separating caused them both sorrow. He understood and accepted her reasons for her sake, but it still hurt. She should know he was a different man.

The woman glanced in the rearview mirror at the handsome young man as she drove away and laughed softly at what her daughter would say. "Mom, you're such a cougar!" She wasn't though. She appreciated beauty in all its forms. The young man was beautiful in the way Michelangelo's David is beautiful. He had the grace and quiet strength David had in the statue. And, she admitted, an equally beautiful face.

On her drive home, she compiled a list of what she hoped to accomplish. Most days her lists were longer than her stamina, but she made the lists anyway. Today her garden needed attention. She *had* to weed—an endless task she hated. Why did God allow weeds? The weeds grew faster than her herbs and vegetables. Yet she had plenty of produce to eat and share with her friends.

Gardening spoiled her for canned foods. One simply could not compare freshly picked tomatoes or green beans with those in cans or even those from the grocery store. The *fresh* produce suffered from being shipped in from God knows where. Fresh herbs made an amazing difference in the taste of food, too. She laughed at the rabbit trails her mind took. She must have ADD, considering the twists her mind could take.

Later, she sat in her backyard reading a new book as a reward for completing her weeding. Except for the weeds, she loved to garden. There was something soul-satisfying in planting a garden and watching it grow. As she sat in the shade, her eyelids drooped as the hum of the bees and the songs of the birds relaxed her in a way little else did. As her mind drifted toward sleep, a picture of the young man popped into her mind. Her eyebrows drew together before sleep pulled her away. A distant memory of a beautiful, dark-eyed young man stirred in her mind. It couldn't possibly be him.

Chapter 1

1963—As she stood in the middle of an empty bedroom the girl recalled her fourteenth birthday. She'd spent the weekend with her grandparents and came home to re-done bedroom. The childish room she'd left on Friday held new French provincial furniture, fresh paint. A beautiful "grown-up" room. She sighed. *At least the furniture and bedspread would make the move with her, along with the memories of that wonderful day.*

"Kara, get the cat in the carrier right away; we don't want Fosdick to sneak out. We'll never catch him if he gets outside. You know how he is ... Oh, be sure to put water bowls in for both Fosdick and Don José," Her mom didn't need to remind her.

"Okay, okay, I've got it covered." Did mom think she'd forget to take care of her pets? Hardly. They were the only friends who'd make the move with her. She needed her cat for moral support. The dog had the heart of a lion, albeit a cowardly lion. His clownish antics made her laugh on the worst of days. Their names fit their personalities. Don José had loads of personality; he wasn't just a dog. A Chihuahua, he acted as if he were a guard dog. Fosdick, her large orange tomcat, her brave friend and confidant. He listened to her most private thoughts.

Moving from Phoenix was the last thing she wanted. Every street held memories. Downing Drugs was where her dad took her for a surprise sundae or milkshake; where she bought comic books as a child, then movie magazines, and makeup in more recent years.

There was Cactus Stables where she learned to ride on the beautiful desert trails. The early morning desert air was fresh with the scent of creosote bush and sage. The grandeur of the saguaro cactus and graceful ocotillo. In a perverse way, she loved the doggone cholla, the jumping cactus with vicious thorns, which she'd learned to avoid at a young age.

She also loved her friends, most of whom had gone from grade school through high school with her. Last week's graduation meant she'd never see many of them again. No more cruising Central, no more slumber parties, no more sneaking out to meet boyfriends.

"Mom, I have to say good-bye to Bridget and her family before we leave and to call Karl before we go."

Bridget, her best friend since fifth grade was a year behind Kara in school. They spent summer afternoons at the park laying in the sun, giggling about the boys. They'd dampen their swim suits in the pool on occasion. Bridget's fair skin and strawberry blond hair never failed to draw the attention of the boys.

Brig went to the local Catholic girl's school. During the school year they make do with an hour or so after school and weekends after chores were done. They shared books; they read all of the *Anne of Green Gables* books, plus many others.

After reading *Cherry Ames*, she decided to be a nurse—before she realized not everyone recovers—people actually die. She spent three years working as a Candy Striper at Good Samaritan Hospital, the same hospital where she'd been born, before she figured it out. She wasn't usually that slow.

She hadn't known her current boyfriend since they wore diapers Karl, was from New York. She found him attractive because he was different, not to mention he was a great kisser. He'd gone to radical things like integration rallies. No one else she knew had gone to one or cared to go.

To her parents' dismay he was outspoken about civil rights. They'd come from the South. Prejudiced, she guessed, but it was something she'd never thought about much. It was a simple fact of life. Since she'd never met any black people, it was a moot point—at least until those girls were killed in the bombing of that church in Alabama.

When it was reported on the news, she cried. "What kind of people would bomb a *church*?" Her parents tried to soothe her angry tears, but she continued to wail. "They sure should be able to go to a decent school and be safe in a church at the very least, for Pete's sake."

Somehow she'd overlooked the beatings the Freedom Riders endured and the murders of black adults. Karl shook her out of blind acceptance of the status quo. She came to the painful discovery he was right and her parents were dead wrong. They'd said *coloreds* weren't clean and they weren't very smart. Karl suggested given an equal opportunity were as clean and smart as anyone.

Karl forced her to think about uncomfortable social issues. It was easy to believe what he said when she gazed into his soulful eyes.

She lived in an environment where the majority of the people thought the way her parents did. Their neighborhood was totally white. In fact, in Phoenix it was easy to tell by an address what race lived in a particular neighborhood. It was easy to accept prejudice at face value since her friends thought the same way. Maybe that was why her parents were happy to move her as far from Karl as possible. They didn't want him to corrupt her thinking with more of his radical ideas. She was forced to move to a tiny town. Barely a spot in the road, from what she knew. There wouldn't be any *radical* thinkers there.

While her friends basked in the sun pool-side, she'd be twiddling her thumbs in Podunk-Ville. College and the military was drawing all of the class of 1963 in different directions, so she'd never see them again. A few chose to marry after graduation. *Why would anyone make a choice like that? Tied to your parents then tied to a husband and kids before you had a chance to live. Not her, she had plans for her life.*

Her saving grace was she'd only be in Payson for the summer, then off to Arizona State College in the fall. Flagstaff was nowhere as big as Phoenix, but the campus setting was beautiful. She visited it the previous year. It was small enough to know most people, yet a whole new world to explore. It was a place she could grow out from under her parents' vigilant eyes. While there might be other kids from Camelback who planned to attend Arizona State, the playing field would be level. The "big fish" would begin as fry right alongside of her. She could become her own person. And she could hardly wait!

But first was her good-bye to Bridget. Always welcome to walk in the O'Brien home without waiting, she called, "Hey Brig, are you here? We've got the car packed up and I want to say good-bye before I leave."

"I was hoping you'd have time to come over," Brig bounced into the room, her enthusiastic nature at full force. "I'm going to miss you so much. I can't wait until we get to be roomies next year. We can spend lots of time together."

She grabbed Kara in a bear hug, a cloud of her soft hair billowing around her face. "You better write me about the campus." (Translate "campus" to "boys.")

Her mom chuckled at her enthusiasm. "All she's talked about is joining you next year. Just think, both of you studying to be teachers."

"Believe me, I can't wait, either. Right now, the only person I'll know is my cousin. He'll be a freshman too. No doubt, we'll stumble around lost. By next year, I'll know my way around so I can help Brig find her way. We're going to have loads of fun, but don't worry," she amended guilelessly, as she turned to Mrs. O'Brien. "We're going to study hard."

Mrs. O'Brien, eyebrows raised, smiled. "You'd better. I wouldn't want either of you to flunk out."

A horn honked announcing her parent's anxiety to get on the road. After more hugs, she sadly left the O'Brien's comfortable home—her second home—and crawled into the back seat with her animals. She'd miss the entire O'Brien family. Bridget and even her crazy little brother. She chuckled as she thought about all windows he'd broken and the time he got a fish hook caught in his head. He was a regular Dennis the Menace.

As they drove away she mused she might never see Karl again, the ninety mile drive might as well have been a million. He didn't return her call and she wasn't sure what his plans were for the summer. He'd applied to an east coast college, but like most of them, he hedged his bets applying to ASU in Tempe as well.

They drove through the Pima Reservation, A desolate part of the desert, with nothing but scrub brush and litter. She sighed and slumped down in the seat.

As they climbed in elevation, the landscape began to get interesting with huge boulders strewn about and amazing vistas. They passed spots in the road named Rye and Sunflower

The landscape changed as the elevation rose with ever increasing signs of piñon pines, junipers, and the ever-present prickly pears. Her mind wandered over trivia until scattered shacks appeared close to the road. "Who lives there, Dad?"

"That's part of the Tonto-Yavapai Apache Reservation,"

When she thought of Apaches, the infamous Indian chief, Geronimo, came to mind, even though he was a Chiricahua Apache.

"Are they friendly?" Her diet of old cowboy movies had Apaches scalping helpless settlers. Surely things changed.

"If by friendly you mean nice, of course, they are. They tend to keep to themselves. They're more taciturn than the ranchers around here. But once they get to know you, they'll warm up. The Apaches are like anyone else. Some are good workers, some aren't, but overall they want to improve their lot. I have a fellow working for me who's a member of the tribe. I think you'll like him."

He changed the subject with a wave of his hand. "This part of the highway is paved clear to Strawberry, but when we take you to Flagstaff next fall, it's a dirt road over the top of the Mollogon Rim."

Prone to carsickness, climbing the huge escarpment on dirt roads would be no picnic even if she didn't get sick. Her dad described the logging trucks they'd meet on those roads, too. There were plenty of tales of them losing loads, smashing cars, killing the drivers and their passengers. Something else to look forward to. At least the trip would get her out of this town. She'd face it when she must.

Rubber-necking she tried to get an idea of her summer home. They passed a grocery store, a couple of cafés, two taverns and a liquor store. Not exactly exciting. Dad pulled into a drive-in and ordered burgers and fries for a quick lunch. She slipped Fosdick a bite of burger and a couple of fries to Don José without her mom catching her. She wasn't supposed to feed them from her plate. *"Technically, this sack is not a plate, so it shouldn't count."*

Next stop, the house where they'd live. She dreaded the after-noon because she had a good idea what was in store. *Overall, her mom was a nice person, but when she wants a job done, she turns into a martinet. Nobody gets a break—not even dad—until everything is done to her liking. Oh well, like they say: "There's no rest for the weary." Drat!*

When they pulled up in front of a very small, very plain brown house, she gazed about in dismay. The house had absolutely no person-ality. No landscaping, unless you counted the natural vegetation made up of scrubby plants and a couple of small juniper trees in the front—and it wasn't fenced. *How would they keep Don José in the yard? He'll go exploring and lose his way.* She tried to hide her dismay from her parents. This was a hard move for her mom, too, and she didn't want to make it harder.

The pepper tree in the backyard of the house in Phoenix came to mind; along with the beautiful magenta bougainvillea which grew up the side of the house, and the passion vine that grew along the fence. There were always loads of beautiful annuals in bloom and grass—beautiful green grass. Here? Scrubby plants and dirt. Make that gravel—crushed granite.

She gritted her teeth. The interior was as much a shock as the out-side. The house was new—a plus—but there was only *one* bathroom. She hadn't lived in a home with one bathroom since she was eight. The living room was small, but a pretty stone fireplace graced it. The kitchen was way smaller compared to the kitchen in Phoenix. No formal dining room. She tried to be positive, but it was hard to find many pluses about this house.

The furniture arrived before they did, but the beds had to be put together and made. None of the furniture was where the martinet (aka Mom) wanted it, so they shifted it this way and that until she was happy. Then *all* the boxes had to be unpacked, everything put away. They had to wash the dishes before they could be put away. Thank goodness for a dishwasher.

When they stopped to have dinner—more burgers from the drive-in—the only chore left was to hang pictures on the wall. They were allowed to put that off until tomorrow. Big. Fat. Hairy. Deal. Okay, she was more than a little cranky by that time.

Before they ate, Mom told her to put Don José outside. Sure enough, when she went to call him inside, no Don José—and it was getting dark. Now Donnie is a big Chihuahua, but still a very small dog. With his dark brown coat, she feared he'd be impossible to find in the growing darkness. She hated being right.

"Don," She called. "Donnie-boy, where are you?" It wasn't like she expected him to bark or anything; she just hope he'd come running. The fact that he hasn't meant he was wandering in the dark! "I'll look for him," she called to her parents.

"Grab a flashlight and don't go too far. You don't know this area. While I'm sure he'll be able to find his way back, I'm not so sure you could."

Geez, a little trust would be nice. Dad handed her a flashlight. *He was laid-back guy, but when he said something, he meant it—no exceptions.* She promised she'd go down to the end of the block and no farther.

It was black as pitch. No ambient light from every corner cast a friendly glow as it had in Phoenix. It was hard to define a block under these circumstances. The flashlight was of little help, but if she shone it at her feet, it kept her from tripping in a pothole. There was a lot of trees and underbrush in this direction. She heard noises from the underbrush. She called grumpily, "Don José, is that you?"

His familiar bark was frantic. He raced toward her as fast as his little legs would carry him. She bent and grabbed him up into her arms and almost dropped the flashlight in the process. "What's wrong, Donnie?" She spoke in a soothing voice. "It's okay; I've got you. Are you all right?"

"There are javelinas in the area," A deep voice came from the trees. "That's most likely what scared him. You'd best be getting along home, Miss. Javelinas are dangerous if they have young'uns with them. Like they do now. You need to be careful."

She jerked around at his voice. The flashlight clattered to the ground. She grabbed it up and shone it toward the voice. Her mouth dropped open. If a man was beautiful, he was. He stepped from the shadows. While lanky, he was muscular. He dressed in the standard dress for this area—jeans, boots, a western shirt, and of course, a cowboy hat. She couldn't be sure of his hair or eye color without shining the flashlight directly in his face. He also carried a rifle.

"I startled you." He bit back a laugh. "Sorry, I didn't mean to scare you, Miss, but it isn't safe out here right now. It might be best if I walk you home, to make sure you and your little dog get there safely." He lifted the rifle to emphasize his meaning. He had a slow, easy smile.

"Oh, umm, ah, that would be nice." She stammered. She tried to close her gaping mouth. *He'll think I'm the village idiot. So much for first impressions.* Don José continued to whine anxiously. Her head swiveled, as she watched for a javelina to charge out of the underbrush.

He gave a reassuring smile. "Don't worry. I think they've moved on. I don't reckon I've seen you here. Are you visiting?" The young man glanced over at the frightened dog, and tried to distract the girl with questions.

"No, we just moved in today. At least my mom and I did. My dad's been living in a motel for a couple of months. Mom and I waited until I finished high school to come up. Our house was on the market and it sold at the perfect time. Dad found a house to rent here. He came to Phoenix to sign the final papers and move us up here." She realized she was babbling, so decided to ask him a question. "What about you? Have you lived here long?"

"I've been here about a year," he said as he escorted her the last few feet to the door.

The young man didn't need better light to understand he wanted to know this girl. She held an aura of innocence that intrigued him. She was different from most girls he met. What they wanted from him didn't require conversation. They weren't worth the time and effort like this one was. Was it her innocence that attracted him? Maybe. He found her fresh-faced look appealing. *Some girls plastered on makeup so thick you can't see their faces.* He saw hers, and liked what he saw. His eyes darted her way every few seconds.

"Please come in. Meet my parents," She hoped to prolong his visit—to see in full light if this guy was as handsome as she thought.

He'd turned away, but turned back with a wistful look. It was a big chance going in a human's house, but he wanted to, if for no other reason than to spend more time with her.

"Are you sure it won't be an imposition—with you trying to get settled and all?" Could he get this lucky? He tried to maintain a casual expression.

"My parents will want to thank you for my rescue," She remembered belatedly, she hadn't thanked him either. She felt like an idiot.

"If you're sure it won't be an imposition, I'll stop in for a couple of minutes to introduce myself," He leaned his rifle next to the door.

At his smile she tripped over the doorsill. "Mom, Dad," She yelled as she set Don José down, in an effort to cover her embarrassment. "Come meet ... uh, I didn't ask your name," she finished in a small voice. Her face turning red.

He was a little over six feet tall. She was partially right about his eyes—oh goodness, his eyes were dark—deep, dark coffee brown, almost black—eyes in which she could easily get lost. His eyes were rimmed with gold, with lashes long enough so any girl would die for them. Her face flushed a deeper red as she stared into those eyes, unable to look away.

He grinned, "It's Nathan Whitworth, but most folks just call me Nate."

"Come meet Nate Whitworth," she blurted as her parents walked into the room. "He just rescued Donnie and me from javelinas!"

"What?" her parents exclaimed in unison. "How far from the house were you?" Nate assured them they were a short distance down the road. "Sometimes they run right down the middle of Main Street."

"Good grief. I never expected they'd come this close to town," Dad continued anxiously. "Thank you very much, young man!"

"Glad to help out a young lady in distress. It gave me a chance to meet your pretty daughter and the two of you." He smiled. "I haven't met many of the town folks."

"I was just serving some ice cream. Would you care to join us?" Her mom gestured toward the kitchen.

"Thanks very much, but I, uh, just ate. I don't think I have room left. I'd like to sit a spell, though, get to know you all." He wondered, *what kind of people parented this extraordinary girl?*

"Sure, Nate. Join us in the kitchen and tell us about yourself. Do you live nearby?" Her dad pulled out a chair for Nate before he sat down. She grabbed bowls for her father and herself while her mom fixed a bowl for herself.

Funny, the jamocha almond fudge didn't have as much taste as it usually did. She spooned a bite into her mouth, but forgot to swallow it. What was the matter anyway? She'd been around handsome guys without making a fool of herself. But there was something about him; he made it hard for her to remember to blink.

"My brother, Josh, and I have a cabin a little way from here. I came out to do a little hunting earlier and ran into your daughter and the little dog as I finished up. The little dog was terrified, so I decided I'd better walk them home. I didn't want them to have a chance meeting with any of the javelinas—especially this time of year."

"It's lucky for Donnie and Kara you were there. I am so grateful. Any luck with your hunt?" Dad asked, always interested in details.

"Yeah. I mean, yes sir. I bagged a couple of javelinas." He had to watch what he said.

"Great. What did you do with them? Did you leave them out there?"

"Not exactly sir, I bled them out," A shadow crossed his face. "I left them hanging. I'll go back and get the meat when I leave. Josh and I live off the land right now. We hunt and fish, sell the spare meat and hides to the Apaches. What brought you all here?" His change of subject was smooth. So practiced at turning attention away from himself, no one noticed.

"After I lost my business in Phoenix, I had an opportunity to start over with a related business, a hardware store. It was too good a chance to pass up. My wife will be my bookkeeper. That'll keep it all in the family while the business gets off the ground—keep overhead low. Kara is one of my cashiers—until she leaves for college in the fall."

"I wish you luck." Nate stood to leave. "If you don't mind, I'd like to come around to see you folks again." The urge to leave—to stay grew stronger. Humans made him nervous. He was afraid they'd see the evil in him. He didn't want her to see that side of him.

"See us or see Kara?" Her dad teased as he stood to shake Nate's hand.

He ducked his head in embarrassment. She thought he whispered her name; he raised his eyes and said, "All of you, of course."

"Any time, son, any time." My dad chuckled as he clapped him on the back. "Kara, why don't you see Nate to the door?"

"Twist my arm," she thought. Smiling, she jumped up from the chair and walked him to the door. "Thanks, Nate, for getting me home safe. I really do hope you come again. I don't know anyone here except a cousin. It would be nice to have another friend." She hoped she didn't sound desperate.

He smiled down and whispered, "Don't worry, I'll be watching for a chance to see you again." He walked swiftly down the driveway and disappeared into the dark.

Darn. She hoped for a kiss. She blushed at the thought of wanting a virtual stranger's kiss. Karl was far from her mind in the presence of this tall, dark, not to mention, handsome man. Poor Karl deserved better treatment, but he was in Phoenix. Who knew if she'd ever see him again? He didn't get her last call, so he may have assumed she wasn't interested enough to tell him good-bye. Nate was here and he gave this summer interesting possibilities. She could hardly wait to see him again. At least she hoped she'd see him. Soon.

"He's a polite young man," Mom said as she came back inside. A pretty and petite woman, so people had a tendency to underestimate her because of her size. Kara learned early on not to ever make her mad.

She was an iron hand in the velvet glove sort of person. She could go for the proverbial throat or any other body part as well as any man.

"These cowboy types all have a sort of old-fashioned courtesy that I like," dad responded.

Me too. She smiled to herself. She like it—him a lot. She went to her room to think about what transpired and what this summer could bring.

11

Nate went back, picked up the two dead javelinas, and tossed them over his shoulders. *Drained of blood,* he thought wryly, *drained of blood indeed.* He'd drained them both in a matter of moments. It never took him long to drink blood and he never made a mess when he drank. He'd been a vampire long enough to keep himself clean when he killed.

He and Josh would gut these and sell the meat to the Apaches—no questions asked. The meat wasn't as tasty as corn-fed pork, but it filled empty bellies.

He and Josh never bothered the Apaches on the reservation either. If they found a man, Indian or otherwise, alone, away from the population, they were fair game. That particular meat they left for the cougars and coyotes. They'd leave enough blood to attract predators. Then there were no questions asked if the bodies were found.

She pulled off her tee shirt and slacks and grabbed her pajamas from the drawer. It'd been a long day. She was positive she'd fall asleep the minute her head hit the pillow. Fosdick padded in behind her. He waited in his accustomed spot on the bed. Her mom didn't like the cat on the bed, but she accepted it as a lost cause long ago. She pretended not to know the big orange cat shared Kara's bed as his nightly routine.

Fosdick's purr usually lulled Kara into a relaxed sleep. Tonight, however, sleep refused to come. With the light out, the darkness was absolute. All she heard were strange noises—crickets chirping, coyotes howling, and were those frogs? The noises, unfamiliar to her ears, seemed louder than the hum of the cars and the wailing sound of distant trains in Phoenix. Cripes, how would she ever sleep? Her entire body was tense with the strangeness of it all. Quiet tears soaked Fosdick's coat His purr got louder, lulling her to sleep.

Chapter 2

Nate couldn't tell the Carson's he avoided the town's people except for business. Each transaction was as short as possible. He'd rather the town folks think he was a visitor. There were fewer questions that way. Too much familiarity was dangerous for the vampire brothers.

Nate said his cabin was nearby. It was for him. It was roughly twenty-five miles—as the crow flies—in the mountains up in a remote canyon. A nearby stream provided water and heavy vegetation concealed the charming cabin with its wide covered porch. Several windows let in the light if the shutters were open. The high-pitched roof, covered with hand-hewn cedar shingles, gave it a timeless look. The Franklin stove was unneeded for heat or cooking. No smoke would disclose the spot where they lived in secret.

It took Nate ten minutes to trot up the mountain carrying the two javelinas. He seldom used his pickup truck while hunting. Never positive if he'd hunt humans or animals; the pickup made him too easy to spot. He dropped the javelinas to the ground.

"Josh, I'm back. Come on out and help me gut these. I have something to tell you."

"Hey, man. Looks like you've been living high on the hog." Josh punned, then chuckled at his own bad joke. "You bagged two. They should get us a few extra bucks!"

"Yeah, they should, but what I really wanted to tell you was I met this girl ..."

"And did she taste good?" Josh interrupted.

"No man, listen. This one's different." Nate didn't try to hide his irritation. Josh was seldom serious about anything.

"She's special. She just moved up here. She is the kind of girl I actually want to get to know."

"And then kill her," Josh snickered.

"Shut up. Be serious for once. This is different. I *like* this girl. She's sweet, innocent, and unconsciously funny. I walked her home and met her parents, like an ordinary human would do."

"What? Are you crazy? What the hell do you think you're doing? You know how *dangerous* that could be for us. We can't afford to be around people and get to *know* them." Josh snapped, angry with Nate. "You know that. You're the one always preaching to me."

Nate set his jaw. "Mind your own business. I *will* be careful."

"So ... what? You think you're going to date this girl? Maybe marry her? Ha." Josh sneered out his words. "What kind of a relationship do you honestly think you can have? If she finds out what you are, you'll have two choices: You'll have to kill her or we'll have to leave. Be realistic, man. It isn't going to happen!"

"I don't know if I can have any kind of relationship with her. But I want a chance to know her better. See what happens. You're my best friend. I want your support on this. Please. Let me try,"

"I think you're completely crazy! I don't know ... I guess you can try. So what is this *special* girl like?" Josh's disgust permeated his every word.

"She's about five and a half feet tall. Pretty honey blond hair, brown eyes, and the sweetest smile I believe I've ever seen." His eyes took on a faraway look. "She's crazy about her parents and her cat and dog, so you can't kill any of them either."

"When I met her I wanted to put my arms around her and protect her. I would have kissed her, but she doesn't seem the type to rush. She's so innocent. I don't want to scare her and ruin any chance I might have."

"You think she's still a virgin—that innocent?" Josh asked skeptically.

"Maybe. All I can say is she's nice and a shy."

"Ha. You are wasting your time. If you're going to pick a girl, why didn't you pick a fun one? You know, a girl you could use, abuse and then kill." Josh couldn't help throwing water on Nate's dream.

"That's not what I want this time. I want to spend time with her, let her get to know me. If things turn out, I'd want her to join us. We could always be together. A family," Nate said wistfully.

"You are living in fantasy land, aren't you? You're supposed to be the smart one." Josh shook his head. "So when do you want me to meet this paragon of virtue?"

"Not yet. I want to get to know her better. Soon." It was important Josh understand. While the two of them weren't biologically related, Nate thought of Josh as his younger brother since they were changed. He guessed he loved Josh because neither of them had any living family, human or vampire. They took care of each other.

"Okay, but I think you're out of your ever-lovin' mind." Josh was doubtful. He knew it could end badly for the two them. He'd seen his brother suffer remorse for having to kill a human. It hurt to see him suffer.

The two finished gutting the javelinas, packed them up in burlap bags and took them to the reservation. The Indians weren't picky where they got their food—as long as it was fresh and a reasonable price. Buying from Nate and Josh saved them the worry of getting caught poaching in off-season. A deal was readily made. Nate and Josh headed home.

"Let's take a side trip by Kara's house," Since it was the middle of the night, Nate was sure she'd be sleeping. He wanted to know which room was hers.

"Are you sure you want me to know where she lives? What if she tempts me and I can't control my hunger?" Josh teased.

Nate growled. "Ha. Ha. You really don't want to go there. You know I'd stop you, one way or another."

"Jeez, man, cool it. I'm just joking." What was going on with his big brother anyway? Nate was usually sensible. Now he was going off the deep end over some silly, human girl. He shook his head in confusion. When he wanted to *know* a human girl, it was strictly in the biblical sense—then he'd kill her.

As they approached the house, all the lights were off. They moved with soundless steps to the side of the house where the bedrooms were located, listened and sniffed the air. Two people who breathed deep in sleep and a dog who growled were in the front bedroom. The dog gave a sharp bark. A sleepy voice quieted it. The boys ghosted to the back bedroom. The sounds of crying and the purr of a cat was all they heard.

"Something's wrong!" Nate whispered anxiously. "Maybe I should check—" Before he could finish his sentence, Josh grabbed his arm.

"Cool it, man. Think it through. You said she just moved up here. She's in a new area away from her friends—everything familiar. She may need a good cry. Leave her alone. You may find her dad isn't so friendly if he finds you trying to climb in that window." For someone who joked his way through life, Josh occasionally made good sense.

"You're right. I hate to think she's upset about anything. We should head back to the cabin unless you need to hunt." He glanced doubtfully back at the house.

"No, I got enough blood earlier. There was this girl ...," he smirked. He had just enough time to dodge the blow Nate threw his way.

Monday morning was a whirl of activity trying to get ready for work. The one-bathroom issue meant planned times to shower. Hers was after work. It meant she put her makeup on in the bedroom instead of the bathroom. She selected a clean blouse, a pair of slacks, and a pair of comfortable shoes. As she dressed she wondered what she should call her parents at work. "Mom and Dad" didn't sound businesslike. They decided at breakfast she could call them by their first names at work. But at home, they'd be Mom and Dad. No surprise there.

The storefront fit her idea of what a store in a ranching community should look like. It had a wide covered porch and hitching posts on both sides of the front steps. Locals still rode into town on occasion. The porch boasted two long benches on either side of the door. All it needed to complete the picture were cracker barrels and a checkerboard!

She'd worked part-time as a cashier in a drugstore, but this was a different register and different merchandise. She was nervous she'd mess up.

"Quit worrying, Kara. The merchandise is well marked. Most registers aren't too different. I'll show you how to use it and you'll see." He gave her a quick demonstration and had her try it. He was right—it was a snap. "Now that you've got the register handled, dust the shelves to familiarize yourself with the stock.

She was glad she listened to him, because an hour later the doors of the hardware store opened. It was time to face the strangers who'd come to shop. Since this was a ranching community, many women wore western gear, too. Their skin tanned a deep a leathery brown. Dark as any man, from helping their men with ranching chores. The men got into friendly arguments, joshing over whose wife was the best cowhand. They boasted their wives could ride and rope as well as any man. "The bonus is I don't have to pay her wages," one rancher joked.

His wife snorted and saying, "Huh. You may not give me any money, you ornery cheapskate, but I make you pay just the same."

"She got you there, Sam." The store dissolved in laughter.

Everyone made purchases, but she was reminded of her earlier allusion to the old country stores used as much for visiting as shopping.

She met Daniel, the Apache man who worked at the store. He was well educated, friendly, and jocular. He looked every inch an Apache except that he wore his black hair short and dressed like the rancher's in jeans and western shirt—all the Apache men did. She understood how foolish she'd been in prejudging the Apache's by old movies.

The day was busy enough to keep her from boredom, but slow enough to chat with people who came to shop. She'd never remember everyone's name, but she was entertained by their tall tales.

Every time someone opened the door, her head snapped up, hoping Nate would come by. A few minutes before closing, he ambled through the door. He smiled her direction. Her stomach erupted into a flurry of dancing butterflies. He walked past her straight to where her dad stood.

"Hi, sir. I wondered if I could take Kara to get a Coke and bring her home afterward."

Dad grinned and stuck out his hand. "I thought I'd see you in here today, Nate. First, call me Pete. Second, it's fine with me if you take Kara out, but she has to be home by seven for dinner. Of course, you have to ask her, too." Pete chuckled.

"Thanks, Pete." Nate gave an uncomfortable grin. "I'll ask her now. Then I'll wait outside so I don't distract her."

She said yes and struggled to focus on her work. She danced out the door moments later.

Nate waited on a wooden bench, his legs stretched out before him. His eyes sparkled as she came through the door. Jumping up, he took her hand, and led her to his truck. Polite, he opened the passenger door of the small pickup truck.

"There's not much choice in drive-ins—two to be exact," he said, his dark eyes boring into hers. "Your dad said you have to be home early, so I thought we'd go to the nearest one. We can go to the park after we get our drinks. There's more privacy there. Is that okay with you?"

"Sure. It's not like I know where things are, so whatever you suggest is fine." As she gazed at his slow smile, her heart skipped a beat. She felt a momentary pang of guilt over Karl, so fast, it was gone in an instant.

In less than ten minutes, they had their drinks and were on their way to the park. Nate pointed out the local sites. "The town paid for the jail with fines on the drunk and disorderly, rodeo week. The majority of them were from the valley."

"Tell me about your life, your family and your friends. What was living in Phoenix like?"

She did her best to describe her friends. She'd begun to tell him about Phoenix when he jumped up.

"It's almost seven; I have to get you home. I may not be allowed to see you again if we're late."

Wow. He planned to see her again. It was a good thing because she never asked a single question—there was so much she wanted to know about him.

"There's a movie at the Ox Bow on Saturday." He pointed to a large log building across the street. "Would you like to come with me?" He asked, doubt in his eyes.

"Sure. What's playing?"

He brightened as he answered, "I don't know yet, they bring second or third run movies up in the summer. They're usually old movies, but it's a chance to get out and have some fun."

"I'd like that. Let's check with my folks, but I'm sure they won't mind." His face lit in a big grin as he escorted her to the truck and opened the door for her. Saturday was her turn to find out about him.

They pulled in the driveway at 6:55, a mere five minutes prior to deadline. A jolt of pleasure shot through her as he took her hand.

Mom welcomed him inside and invited him to stay for dinner. "It's nothing fancy. Meatloaf, scalloped potatoes, and green beans, but there's plenty." Moms "nothing fancy" was always delicious.

"Thanks. That sounds good, but Josh expects me back at the cabin. He'll have dinner waiting. We usually eat together, but maybe another time?"

Her parents okay-ed the movie plans for Saturday. Kara walked him back outside. He dipped his head to hers and his soft lips brushed her cheek. She tingled clear to her toenails. What was it that made her heart race with a simple kiss on the cheek?

He smiled as if he knew a secret. At the open door of his pickup he whispered, "Sweet dreams tonight, Kara." Sweet dreams wouldn't be a problem. Not after the way she felt from his kiss. She wouldn't dream about Karl either. It was shallow to forget Karl so fast. How would she feel if she found out, Karl never cared for her?

Nate's absent the next few days depressed her. She cheered herself up with the thought of the coming weekend. In the meantime, she kept busy at work. The job was sort of fun. She met all sorts of characters right out of the old west. Ranching towns were quite different from Phoenix.

An element of earthiness entered into conversations, which included everything from branding cattle to castrating calves. Nothing was sacred. She regretted a question about the local *treat* of mountain oysters—the current topic of conversation.

"Why honey, don't you know what they are? They're the gonads from castrated calves. We'll bring you a mess of 'em. Just flour 'em and fry them in hot bacon grease. You're gonna love 'em" The ranchers guffawed at her appalled expression Ugh! She wanted to barf at thought of them.

Many of these same ranch families dated back to the Pleasant Valley Wars. She vaguely remembered reading about the wars in the Zane Grey novel *To the Last Man.*

Though the war was long over, there was no love lost between the two factions. These cattlemen swore sheep destroyed the grazing lands. "Those woolly varmints should stay out of cattle country." Of course, anyone who raised sheep vehemently disagreed.

The ranchers said Zane Grey built a cabin nearby, where he lived while he wrote several of his novels, including *To the Last Man.* The cabin would be fun to explore. Maybe Nate would take her there for a picnic.

⤳

Nate popped in the door Saturday afternoon long enough to say he would pick her up at six. "We'll grab a burger before the movie. It's scheduled to start at seven-thirty. But I make no promises about the starting time."

When he picked her up, he greeted her parents. "I promise to have Kara home before midnight." As he put a careless arm around her to lead here outside, heat rose in her face, but she beamed at the pleasure of his touch.

"Where do you want to go for a burger?"

"The Burger Hut again?" mentioning the place where they'd gone for cold drinks previously. The Burger Hut was like a lot of the older drive-ins. Metal awning covered two picnic tables and benches. After ordering at the window, one had the option to use a table or eat in their vehicle. They opted to eat in the truck, since the sun was beginning to set and the temperature had dropped. The choice proved best by the arrival of a group of obnoxious teenagers, who shot straw wrappers and threw French fries at each other. She was disgusted before she remembered doing the same thing a few weeks ago.

As they left the drive-in, they turned on Main Street to head for the Ox Bow Saloon. This old building was built with huge ponderosa pine logs. Nowadays its wood floor sagged, but she felt the ghosts of the past when she walked through the doors.

It was a saloon and a dance hall—past and present. The smell of sawdust and spilled beer wafted through the hall. As she closed her eyes, she imagined the sound of a tinny piano and heard the laughter of those long dead. It wasn't as if she thought it was haunted, though Nate told her that was the rumor. But the past eked out of every board in the room.

Now this historic place served as a part-time movie theater. Rows of metal folding chairs were set up. Its usual tables were shoved against the wall waiting until the movie crowd left. Modern touches—the chairs and the popcorn machine—struck a discordant note in this piece of the past.

Nate and Kara picked seats in the back, near the outside aisle. Whispers wouldn't disturb anyone nor would a make-out session. They'd sneak out early if the movie was boring. Nate put his arm around her and pulled her close to his side as the lights dimmed. With a tentative smile, she turned her head to face him. She met his eyes. His eyes glowed in the flickering light of the projector as the opening credits rolled. He bent his head, their lips barely touched in a gentle kiss. She responded with an unexpected surge of heat.

She'd seen the movie before, so if her parents asked, she could give them a passable rundown. It was a good thing. Her entire focus on was her lips fully involved in Nate's. All she'd remember was the feel of his arms around her.

They left before the movie was half over. In the park, she shivered in the evening chill. He removed his jacket, with gentle hands placed it over her shoulders. He asked more about her childhood, but she held a hand in the air.

"Enough about me. I want to know about you. Where are you from? Why did you pick this area to live?"

He ducked his head to hide a frown. There were questions he couldn't easily answer. "There's not much to tell. Both Josh and I lost our families a long time ago. We lived in the same, um, foster home and became friends. We call each other brother because we are more brothers than friends. After we left the foster home, we traveled together. Like I told you, we've been here in this area a little over a year."

"What happened to your parents? How old were you when you lost them?" She was full of questions.

"Our parents were lost in a flood when we were fairly young. I don't remember much about them or exactly what happened. Neither of us was with our parents the day they died." His eyes looked at his feet. He frowned.

"I'm so sorry." She sandwiched his hand between hers. She couldn't imagine living through such a devastating loss. How would she handle the same situation?

"It's okay," As she began to loosen her grip, he held on. He took a hold of her chin and forced her to look at him. "It's like another life—like it didn't really happen."

Firmly, he held her and pulled her to her feet. His eyes bore into hers. "When I'm with you, the past doesn't matter. I'm happy."

She turned her head unable to meet his eyes. "You've made this move bearable." Her words were inadequate for what she felt. "I hated moving away from my friends, but I've hardly thought about them. I almost feel guilty for the way I've forgotten them." He gently kissed her cheek; took hold of her chin and returned her face to his. Kisses as soft as a breath of air covered her eyelids and trailed her face to her lips. Her body ignited with internal flames.

He pushed her away in sudden distress. "Look Kara, I want you, but I have to be honest. There are complications in my life. Perhaps we shouldn't date. If you decide you don't want me around, let me know. I'll back off."

He read the questions in her mind and laughed. "Enough of this serious stuff. We're supposed to be having fun tonight. Shall we go chase javelinas?"

"Uh, I'll pass on that." She snorted a laugh. "We could go bowling or something. Or ... we could go back to my house dig out some cards or play Monopoly."

"Cards, it is. Monopoly takes too long. Think about what we can do tomorrow and next weekend, too."

"Have you ever been to Zane Grey's cabin? Some of the ranchers told me it's up in the mountains near here. Maybe we could go on a picnic there," she said, enthusiastic over the idea.

"Ah, you like Zane Grey?" His expression turned thoughtful.

"Yeah, I've read several of his books: *Riders of the Purple Sage, The Hash-knife Outfit,* and *To the Last Man.* I guess I'm a tomboy, but I especially like his stories about Arizona. I never realized he actually lived here when he wrote his stories."

"He was definitely an interesting guy. A little weird, though, a bit of a recluse. I've seen the cabin. I'll be happy to take you to see it. You'll find it interesting. Should we take a picnic tomorrow?"

"I'd love to. I'm meeting my cousin for church. It gets out at noon. Will that give us enough time?"

"I guess so, but why do you want to go to church? Isn't it a waste of time?" His look of disgust shocked her.

"Hardly a *waste*. My beliefs are important to me. They're a big part of my life." She frowned as she considered his choice of words—*waste*?

"That's cool, if it's what you want, but it would be nice if we could spend the whole day together." He tried to mollify her, realizing his tone of voice and choice of words upset her.

"You could come to church with me," she suggested.

Nate gave an ironic grin. "I don't think so. I'll pick you up afterward. I'll get food for the picnic. We won't have to waste more time."

When they got back to the house, her mom and dad were ready for bed. Kara could tell they didn't want any late night company. Apparently, Nate got their non-verbal message as well—though they were welcoming. He shared their plans for the picnic, inviting them along. Kara hid her laugh. If there was anything her dad hated, it was picnics. He always said if he wanted to eat with ants and bees, he'd invite them in the house.

"On second thought, Kara, let's call it a night. It's late. Tomorrow will be a full day. I don't want you too tired to enjoy yourself." He held out his hand as he turned to her parents. "I'm sorry you won't be joining us. It's in a beautiful area and the cabin is full of history."

"I'm sure it is," my mom said, "but I've got laundry to finish and I have a hunch Pete is will be watching a ballgame."

Dad chuckled as he held his hands in the air. "Guilty! The Sox are playing. You two have fun. Monday's a work day, so don't be late getting home." Excusing themselves, they went to their bedroom. "Come on, Donnie." The small dog trotted behind to his bed.

She walked Nate outside. He touched the side of her face with his feather soft touch and repeated his "Sweet dreams, Kara" from earlier in the week.

Oh yeah. Sweet indeed.

She closed the door to her bedroom and began to undressed. Fosdick patiently waited for her on the bed. She laid her pajamas down, hugged the cat to her chest, his coat silky smooth against her body. She whispered her private thoughts in his ear as the rumbling began in his chest. She got the uncomfortable feeling she was watched. While the curtains were closed, there was a sliver between them. She peered out at the blackness.

"I'm an over-imaginative idiot." She sat Fosdick back on the bed and quickly pulled her pajamas on. As she crawled into bed, she whispered secrets about Nate to Fosdick.

Out in the darkness of the backyard a voice whispered so softly only Nate would hear. "Peeping Tom?"

Nate started. "What are you doing here?" Upset Josh caught him as he watched Kara, half-dressed, through to slit in the curtain.

"I'm waiting for you to quit mooning over that girl. She does have a nice body, though," Josh whispered thoughtfully.

"Were you spying on her?" Nate spit angrily.

Josh held his hands out in front of him, placating Nate. "No man, I came to see if you were ready to hunt. I saw you standing here so I came over to check out what was so interesting. No harm intended." Josh grinned an impish grin.

Nate growled low in his throat, "Yeah, I'm ready. Let's get out of here." While Nate was angry at being caught watching Kara, he was furious Josh watched her too. Josh might be like a brother, but he didn't want to share her with anyone.

His movements were stiff with anger. But the anger didn't interfere with his senses. Tonight he didn't want an easy kill. He wanted a fight, even if it would be a short one.

Josh was fifty feet to his right when the scent of a cougar caught Nate's attention. He was off like a shot, Josh at his heels, when he caught the cat. It spun around half screaming, half growling. As it leapt toward him, he leapt and took it down midair—its spring incomplete. Josh caught the scent of a lone camper a mile away. He reached the camper and killed him before Nate finished drinking the cougar's warm blood.

When Nate reached him, Josh had a self-satisfied smirk on his face. "It looks like this guy met with an unfortunate accident. I think he may have tried to fend off a cougar. What do you think?"

"Did you leave enough blood to make it look real?"

"No, we'll have to carry him to where you took down the cougar. Add a few stab wounds to the cat and blood from small critters along the way. It's not like anyone is going to check."

"You carry; I'll catch the critters." Nate's anger was slowly cooling, but he wasn't ready to forgive Josh.

Nate caught cottontails and a small deer to spread their blood over the body. His mind wandered to his earlier conversation with Kara. It was true his parents and Josh's had been killed in a flood. The Great Mississippi Flood of 1927. It flooded huge areas of seven different states. Almost two hundred and fifty people lost their lives. The death toll would have been that high if he, Josh and two other people hadn't been pulled from the river by his "foster family." He'd been twenty-three at the time and Josh just nineteen.

What else could he tell her—*we were pulled out of the river by a few nomadic vampires who decided to turn us rather than kill us?* He couldn't do that. It was far too soon to reveal the truth. He had to figure out the best way to tell her the man who'd fallen in love with her was a monster. Yeah, *that* was going to be easy.

He and Josh became like brothers through the shared pain of loss and in joining this strange new life. Where they differed was in how they took to the desire for human blood. Josh was of a practical nature. He didn't have any qualms in drinking human blood. Nate couldn't bear the thought of killing a human and avoided feeding on them.

The day came when overcome by overwhelming need, he attacked and killed a young woman who was out feeding chickens. When he finished draining her blood, he realized she couldn't have been more than thirteen or fourteen—a mere child.

Her mother called from the house. Her name, Grace, was forever burned into his mind, as was what happened next. Her mother came outside wiping her hands on her apron. She called for Grace again, when she saw him. A look of horror covered her face. He stood over the body of her daughter, blood dripping from his chin. He had no choice. To avoid detection, he grabbed the mother, bit her neck, and drained her blood as well. He'd killed two innocent people.

Filled with remorse, he turned anxious to find Josh. He realized Josh must be inside the barn where the farmer was doing his early morning milking. He took two steps toward the barn when he heard the sound of a baby wailing inside the farmhouse. He stopped, foot in the air... *No, oh God, no. No.*

In slow motion he turned and went inside the house. Sitting in a wooden highchair was a chubby baby, his face wet from tears. The baby's wails turned to smiles as Nate approached. It stretched its dimpled arms up to him, wanting to be held. With self-loathing, he picked up the smiling baby. As he held the baby close to his chest, he closed his eyes, took the baby's head in his hand and snapped its tiny neck. He remembered the feel of his baby brother in his arms. Born a few short months before the flood, he was lost before he had a chance to live. Nate felt the pain of that loss along with this one. Pain sharp enough to make him cry out and double over.

There was no other option. This farm was remote. He couldn't leave the baby to starve, nor could he take it with him. His only alternative was to kill it as humanely as possible. But to kill an infant was like a knife in his own heart. He took the baby, wrapped him in a blanket and laid him in his crib. He bent and kissed the chubby little cheek—fast turning cold. Sick at heart, he stumbled outside to find Josh.

Josh was leaving the barn as Nate exited the house. He wore a self-satisfied grin. "There were two men in the barn. Man, I'm full." For a moment, Nate wanted nothing more than to knock Josh on his backside. So many dead. It wasn't Josh's fault he was like that. It was in the nature of a vampire. The others in his new family were the same—human life was meaningless.

He was the odd one, with his disgust over the diet of human blood. Now, he was as guilty as them all. 'Good', was the only word he managed as they left, weighed down by remorse.

The two boys continued to do everything together for the next several years. Before dawn one rainy morning, they left the cabin where their coven lived. They planned to hunt game on their own. Josh always tried to support Nate's strange habit of drinking animal blood. That morning they doubted anyone else was out in the downpour. They were wrong.

A group of farmers became suspicious of the family. Perhaps a coven member was careless and seen feeding. Whatever the reason, the farmers came after sunrise while Nate and Josh were out on the hunt.

The two returned as the flames exploded around the cabin. They ducked out of sight watching the fire as it burned bright and hot. It consumed the dry wood of the shack with their vampire family trapped inside. Sometimes he could hear their screams in his head as they begged for mercy. He could smell the thick, black smoke from the kerosene and oil fire in his dreams.

The farmers hadn't seen Nate and Josh. They must have thought they killed the entire coven since people believed vampires couldn't be out in the daytime. In fact, it was their own reticence which kept them inside during the day. Vampire hunted at night to avoid being seen. Fearfully, the boys ran for their very lives. If they were spotted, the farmers would hunt them down and kill them, too. They learned from the elder vampires, there were few ways a vampire could be killed. A broadsword, which could decapitate them, anything that pierced their heart—knife, pitchfork, or bullet, each provided quick deaths. The last was the most terrible. Fire. Death by fire was slower and pain-filled. Nate and Josh saw the truth of that slow death played out before their eyes. It was the day Nate no longer hesitated killing humans. It was the day Nate Whitworth learned to hate.

While he and Josh were on the run, they never worried about their food supply. The depression was in full swing. Many people were on the road as they left the dust bowl hoping for greener pastures. Their trucks piled high with necessities of life or the personal items they most valued.

A family broken down or camping by the side of the road made for easy pickings for the two vampire boys. By the time anyone found the bodies, most of them were desiccated. The authorities never wasted time trying to establish a cause of death. Nate never felt guilty anymore. He was an avenging angel, albeit a fallen angel.

They hadn't fed in a few days when they came across a small Hooverville by the railroad tracks. Since it was night time, they surreptitiously approached the edge of the camp ready to enter the nearest shanty to kill the inhabitants. The man inside the cardboard shack was awake. He yelled, leapt up and went after Josh with a butcher knife. With a quick slash, he opened Josh's chest. The wound was deep enough to kill a human, however, it missed his heart. It merely stunned Josh.

Nate lost all control. Humans killed his vampire family and now this man tried to kill his brother. He wasn't going to let that happen. Screaming profanities, he ripped the man's arm from his body, then savagely tore at his throat. People from other shacks came running to help the man, but Josh recovered enough in that short time to join Nate in the melee which followed. By the time they were through with their rampage, not a soul, man, woman, or child, was left alive in the camp. Most of the shanties torn down and the meager contents scattered. Sated, but shaken following the attack, the boys figured they needed to make tracks and get far away from the remains of the camp.

They hopped the next freight train not caring where it took them. At the first stop, a bull, railway security, attacked them with a Billy Club. His body was found days later, bloodless, and with the Billy Club rammed down his throat.

～⊙

As they returned to the cabin, Nate decided to forgive Josh. "Tomorrow Kara and I are going on a picnic up to Zane Grey's cabin. Wanna come along?"

Josh raised his eyebrows. "You mean you're actually going to let me meet her?"

"If you can behave, yes. I mean it though; you have to act human every second of the time. You have to be a gentleman," Nate warned.

"Geez, that's no fun," Josh teased, but seeing Nate's expression, he quickly added, "Okay, okay; I'll be a good boy."

"Keep in mind that this is important to me. I'd like to have you both in my life if I can."

"I know, man, I know. I'll try. I promise." Josh was sincere. He loved Nate who always looked out for him. He wanted to please him. *But Nate takes things so serious. Life's too hard to take so seriously. I want to enjoy myself—have fun. Nothing wrong with that.*

Chapter 3

As she dressed for church, she thought about the previous night. The feel of Nate's arm around her—his tender kisses—the loss of his family. It must have been hard for Nate to lose his family at such a young age. She couldn't imagine the pain of such a loss. Thrust into the home of strangers on top of that. Her heart broke to think about it.

An unbidden thought came to mind. Nate spoke of complications in his life. What kind of complications would make her not want to date him? Make him leave? Could it be his way to prepare her that he was moving on?

Of course, she'd leave for college in the fall, but she'd be home on occasional weekends and holidays. He had his truck, so he could drive to Flagstaff to see her. Did he see the relationship as a summer romance? Convenient for now, but not worth the trouble to continue in the fall? They we're barely getting to know each other. The thought of his casually dumping her at summers end made her weak in the knees. She sat abruptly on her bed. *Wasn't that what she'd done to Karl? Perhaps this was Karmic justice. Maybe, she deserved to be treated like that.*

She heard the slam of a car door followed by a knock on the door. Her mother called, "Kara, Geoff is here to pick you up."

"On my way," she yelled back, "as soon as I find my Bible."

"You set it on the table last night so you wouldn't forget." Mom's reminder ended on a note of impatience.

She grinned at her cousin as she skipped out of her room. "Hey, Geoff thanks for picking me up." Geoff graduated from Payson High and would be going to Arizona State College in the fall, too. He was her favorite cousin, partly because of their closeness in age and partly because she saw him more often than her other cousins. It would be great to have his familiar face around next fall.

"It's okay. I couldn't let my favorite cuz down, now could I? I figured it would be hard to walk into a church without knowing a soul. I'll introduce you to my friends who go to the same church. They're a good group overall. You might enjoy having friends here."

⌒〇

The small white building was easy to overlook. A steeple rose from the east side of the building, but other than that it was non-descript. Several cars were parked in the gravel parking lot.

A far cry from the Phoenix church, which was considerably larger and much prettier than this. Her opinion didn't change as they went inside. No carpeting graced the floor, no polished pews, no raised pulpit, and no carved communion table. Metal folding chairs and a stack of hymnals by the door, and a picture of Jesus, so small it was lost on the wall. Oh, there was a piano—an ancient upright. But at least they'd have music.

It turned out there was no minister either—at least not a regular one. Geoff explained the situation as they arrived at the church. The ministers alternated weekends. The one this week came from Phoenix. Another minister came from Mesa to cover the other two Sundays. If there were five Sundays in a month, there was no sermon—just singing! She was forced to remind herself that she hadn't come for the building. She's come to worship God and to make friends.

Geoff's friends were a lively bunch, but they all settled into their seats as soon as the first bars of the opening hymn began. If she remembered the names correctly, there was the vivacious twins, Lois and Linda Lawrence; Bob Bennett, with the crew cut and horn-rimmed glasses. Next was funny Freddy Jacobs, a tall, gawky boy who liked to joke and tease. Last ... was Joyce ... Joyce Anderson. A bleached blond. She'd have been pretty if she didn't have such a hard look about her. Glad she didn't have to like them all, because Joyce had no interest in trying to be friends. She was resentful to the point of rudeness at Kara's being there. She could think of a word that described the girl, but she *was* in church.

The minister preached on Romans twelve, focusing in on verses seventeen and eighteen. King James did not make for easy reading, but the message was clear enough. The minister must have read her mind— at least her thoughts about Joyce. If she understood the text correctly, even if Joyce was hateful, which she was, she should be nice to her. She'd have to work on that. Hopefully, Joyce was paying attention, too.

Church ended with the singing of the Doxology. The minister greeted everyone with a handshake as they left the church. As they exited, the twins bounced up to invite her for a barbeque at their house. "Oh, I'm so sorry, but I've already made other plans ... I'd love to come over another time."

A small, familiar pickup pulled into the parking lot. Nate jumped out of the truck and ambled over as all eyes turned his way.

"Who is he? He's gorgeous." She heard one of the twins whisper. She smiled but didn't answer.

"I asked your mom and dad where the church was so I could pick you up. I hope you don't mind."

"Of course not. Everyone, this is Nate Whitworth. Nate, meet Linda and Lois, Freddy, ah, Joyce, and Bob. This is my cousin, Geoff. Did I get everyone's name right?"

"Close, I'm Lois; she's Linda," one of the twins teased. "If you get it right next time you get a gold star. Almost no one can tell us apart," she giggled. No one noticed Kara's hesitation in saying Joyce's name

"Nice to meet you all. I hate to rush Kara off, but we have a picnic planned. We have an hour's drive to get there. I promised to have her back early. Since she needs to change clothes, we ..." He took her shoulders and turned her away from the group as his voice trailed off.

They approached the truck to a chorus of "bye for now" and "have fun." In a sour voice Joyce ask, "Where did she meet *him*?"

Kara didn't miss the jealousy in the girl's voice. In spite of the sermon, she smirked.

They drove back to the house so she could change into pair of shorts, and take off her heels for comfortable shoes. With a quick hug and a "See you later" to her mom and dad, she scooted out the door and into the truck. Nate drove to the outskirts of Pine, turned east on a dirt road. The road steadily climbed in elevation. Nate assured her they'd not reach the top of the eight thousand foot escarpment that made up the Mollogon Rim. But they'd be high enough, nevertheless.

Nate leaned her direction and said, "I invited Josh to meet us at the cabin. I wanted the two of you to meet and have a chance to get to know each other. I hope that's okay."

"Sure. After all, you've met my family; it's only right I meet yours." He flashed a smile, but kept his eyes on the road. In spite of its being a dirt road, she loved the fantastic view. She focused on it view and ignored the dust and the ruts. At one point, they forded a small stream, passed an old neglected apple orchard and a few rustic cabins.

One narrow cabin, built next to the water, had a porch that dangled precariously over the stream. The owners must really love to fish! On second thought, it was a fishing shack. A sense of wonder came over her as she thought about those who lived there in the past. Who'd planted the orchard? Did they live anywhere near? Did a family use the fishing shack? Did they come for weekend outings? She continued to speculate as the road continued upward.

As they neared the top of the mountain, the cabin came into view. It wasn't the half-fallen down ruin she imagined. Instead, a charming painted cabin with a wide front porch and broad steps leading up to it sat in front of her. The cabin was raised above ground with a lattice enclosure around the base. She guessed the lattice kept animals—like skunks—from going under the house. Though skunks were cute, she was well-aware of their potent spray.

Nate explained the cabin was falling down when a local business-man bought it and rebuilt it, keeping to its original integrity. He wanted it to be what it became—an historical attraction.

As they crawled out of the truck she noticed a boy standing under a tree watching them. She tipped her head his direction and asked, "Is that Josh?"

"It is indeed." He smiled, reached into the truck bed, and grabbed the picnic basket. "Hey, Josh, make yourself useful. Grab the blanket for us."

The boy who sauntered toward them was almost as good-looking as Nate. He was shorter and stockier than Nate, but very well-muscled. He had dark blond hair, hazel eyes, and a smile that quirked up in a mischievous way.

"You must be Kara, the girl I keep hearing about," he drawled as Nate elbowed him in the ribs.

"And *you* must be Josh, Nate's brother." She smiled as he nodded in agreement.

"And *we* are hungry, so spread the blanket so we can eat," joked Nate.

"That's what I've been waiting for—eating." Josh smirked.

"Remember," was Nate's one-word reply.

She had the vague feeling she missed something, but the conversation switched to historical facts about the cabin and Zane Grey, then included hunting in the area. Finally the focus changed to the food they were eating.

Josh was funny in a quirky way, saying things that didn't quite make sense. He laughed at Nate when Nate frowned. "Nate thinks you're quite special, good enough to *eat*. I think he wants to marry you."

Nate had enough of his teasing. "Josh, shut it. You're obnoxious to say stuff like that. Kara and I barely know one another. You promised to behave."

"Sorry, big brother. I'll be good." He said what Nate wanted to hear, but his expression was recalcitrant.

In spite of that, they had a good time. After they finished the picnic lunch, they disposed of the food. No unwelcome guests of the furry variety were welcome. Food disposed of, they went to the cabin to look at the artifacts. After an hour of looking at all the historical accumulation, they decided to wade in the stream and snitch apples from the abandoned orchard.

The water in the stream was so cold it took her breath away, and the rocks were slimy with algae. Nate came up behind her, and wrapped his hands around her waist so she wouldn't fall. When Josh splashed them, a water fight began in earnest. Soaked and out of breath from laughing, they lay in the sun to warm and dry themselves. Nate smiled and pulled her head to his chest as they lay in the sun. Pulling strands of wet hair back, he nuzzled her ear, his breath warming her from the inside.

Josh cleared this throat. "I think that's my signal to leave you two lovebirds alone."

"See you back at the cabin," Nate mumbled, not bothering to look up.

Driving down the mountainside, she rested her head against Nate's shoulder. There was little need for talking. Being together was enough for now. A relaxed contentment stole over her as she thought about the day. It was a very good day. If she could have wished for one thing; she'd wish for more time.

"I'm going to miss you this fall," she said.

Nate stiffened at her words. "What do you mean?" He turned, his eyes focused on her.

"When I leave for college," she half-questioned his response.

Nate pulled to the shoulder of the road. "Kara, I hoped you'd change your mind and stay here."

She put a hand to his cheek. "It's like you said to Josh, it's premature to think of getting serious. We need time to get to know each other. It's not like we won't see each other. I'll be here for some weekends, for holidays and semester break. I'll be back next summer. You can drive up and see me there, too."

"That's not enough, Kara. I want you here all the time." His growl was unmistakable.

It angered her. "Wait a minute, Nate. I want to get my degree. It's important to me. You knew I was planning to leave, so why are you upset?" She straightened and pulled away.

His face grew hard as he looked away. "I hoped I could convince you to stay."

"What, and work at my dad's store forever? I want more than that," she snapped. Her anger had nothing to do with working at the store. She enjoyed the work. But who'd want to work for their dad forever at a minimum wage job? Who'd want to work for their dad forever at any price? Not her.

"You wouldn't have to work. I could give you anything you'd want," he stated, hurt.

She snapped, "Doing what? You can't make all that much money hunting! Look, let's not worry about it now; we have lots of time to enjoy this summer. We don't need make future plans—at least not yet," She tried to placate him, but when she reached out to touch his arm, he jerked away.

When he started the truck, he growled a begrudging affirmative reply, his face a thundercloud. The day lost its warm glow of contentment. Nate dropped her off without coming inside.

"I'll see you soon." She waved as he sped away. He didn't answer and he didn't wave back.

Glad for the excuse to shower, so she didn't have to talk to her parents—yet. She wanted time to collect herself before she answered any questions. She was ready to face them after the shower.

"By the way, Kara, while you were out Karl called. He wants you to call him back. I wrote his number next to the phone."

"Oh, thanks mom, umm, I'll call him later," She didn't look forward to that conversation, but she owed Karl an explanation when she broke up with him. If he had a new girlfriend, she wouldn't feel so guilty.

No sign of Nate over the next couple of days—not in person, and not a phone call. Was he going to dump her because she wanted to go to college?

She was so distracted at work her dad called her on it. "Kara, you're supposed to be working, not staring off into space. Pay attention to what you're doing. Just because you're my daughter, don't think you can get away with shirking." Her face flamed with embarrassment at his criticism.

She tried to focus on work. She owed it to her dad to give her very best efforts. He didn't have to give her this job. He gave it to her to earn spending money for college. Plenty of other people in town wanted work. Her thoughts turned to Karl. She hadn't reached him, not that she'd made an effort.

Geoff called on break. Bless him. "There's a barbeque and dance at the twins' house Friday night. They've invited you. Usually there's plenty of excellent food." She hadn't heard a word from Nate, so she told Geoff she'd love to go to the party. It should be fun—a group party. Fun and entertaining, but it wouldn't allow too much intimacy.

During the afternoon break Daniel approached. "I saw you at the movie the other night with Nate Whitworth. Are you dating him?" He knit his brows.

"Oh, do you know Nate? We've been out a few times. Why?"

"I met him once, but I've heard some strange stories—about him and his crazy brother. They're probably silly rumors, but be careful. At least until you know him better. I know for a fact, the brother is a hot head, always ready for a fight. I know it's none of my business, but be alert, okay?"

He reached over and patted the top of her head with his large hand, grinning in such an ingratiating way she couldn't be mad. He was like the big brother she always wanted. She was about to ask what he'd heard when more customers came into the store.

Thursday afternoon, Nate ambled into the store. She didn't have a customer, so he walked directly to her station. "Look, Kara, I'm sorry about the other night. You were right. We need to enjoy the time we have now. So ... do you want to go out tomorrow night?" He sounded hopeful. She panicked.

She choked out her reply. "Nate, I'm sorry, but I've made plans."

"Wh-what?" He stuttered his reply.

Mom picked that moment to yell from the office, "Kara, Karl's on the line. Can you take his call now?"

"*Karl*? Well isn't that just fine." He growled sarcastically as he stomped out the door. He ignored her when she called his name.

Great. As if things weren't bad enough, now Nate, who was mad, was madder than ever. She sighed, as she walked to the office to talk to Karl.

⌒◯

So Kara was going to a party, huh. Nate burned with anger. He wanted to see the guy she was dating. No doubt he's a loser. He'd watch the party and see how she behaves. Struggling to keep under control, he thought, *I can't kill everyone she sees, that would scare her off. I want things to work out between us, even if I have to be patient and wait for her.* He wanted her so much it hurt. He'd never wanted anyone the way he wanted her.

⌒◯

Kara showered, dried her hair, and pulled it into a ponytail for a quick hairstyle. She'd barely finished the final touches of lipstick when Geoff announced his arrival by beeping the horn. To her chagrin Joyce sat in the front seat next to Geoff.

"*No* boy, Kara?" she laughed in a saccharine sweet voice. "My, my, what a shame."

Geoff's whispered, "Shut up, Joyce. Be polite for once."

Mortified, she tried to put on a brave face. When they arrived at the party, Geoff took her around to make the introductions. The twins' home sat at the top of a hill, so it had a 360-degree view, except for the surrounding trees. From what she could tell in the dark, though, the view was impressive. They sat outside on a huge patio, half of which was covered. Perfect for entertaining—especially for a large group of noisy teens.

The party was fun. Everyone, with the exception of Joyce, welcomed her to the party. They ate grilled chicken and three different salads as well.

When dinner was cleared away they moved the tables aside so they could dance. She hadn't danced since she left Phoenix. Funny Freddy, the skinny boy with the dark soulful eyes and brown hair, asked for the first dance. The song was "The Peppermint Twist." One of her favorites, it was a fast and a non-touching sort of dance, so she didn't feel awkward dancing with a virtual stranger.

Freddy didn't act like she was a stranger; he grinned as he promised his undying love and devotion. She couldn't stop laughing.

The fact she came alone didn't matter, as it would back home. In Phoenix, you came with a date and you danced with your date exclusively. The policy here was everyone danced with everyone else. It didn't matter she came alone.

After they danced for more than an hour, the twins' parent brought out homemade peach ice cream. She'd never eaten homemade ice cream before. It was delicious. Everyone had seconds. They laughed about brain freezes and wiped ice cream off each other's mouths. After they put their empty bowls in the sink, she got the high sign from Geoff. It was time to leave. Freddy hurried up, "Can I drive you home, Kara?" Geoff gave a nod. Freddy offered his arm and escorted her to his car. It was easy to talk to him. Alone in front of the house, Freddy leaped out and opened her door. "Have a good night, Kara." He bent forward and gave her a chaste kiss on the cheek.

"Thanks, Freddy. I enjoyed the party." He hopped back into his car and with a quick wave, drove away. She waved and turned to go inside.

"Kara," a voice whispered from the dark. "Kara, can I talk to you? It's important I talk to you. I apologize for being seven kinds of a fool— for the way I acted." Nate walked slowly forward, his hands out in supplication. She nodded, afraid to speak.

"I knew you planned to go to college, but I thought I could get you to change your mind."

She opened her mouth to answer, but he said, "Please let me finish. When I had time to think, I realized it was completely selfish. You should follow your dreams—as long as they can include me, too. Thursday when I came to ask you out and you told me you had plans, I imagined the worst. When you mom said Karl was on the phone I was sure he'd take you away from me or worse—you were never interested in the first place. I worried you were using me for summertime entertainment. All my good intentions went right out the window. I'm sorry. Before you forgive me, you need to know everything. I followed you tonight and watched you at the party and just now, I listened to your conversation. I'm not exactly sorry for that. I heard what I needed to hear." He gave an apologetic smile.

She shook her head, with a slight smile. "I'll work on forgiving you, but you can't sneak around listening to all my conversations."

He took her in his arms and pulled her to his chest. "I don't deserve you, but I will try." He bent his head and kissed her. It was such a sweet kiss her eyes fill with unshed tears.

She put her hand against his chest and pushed him away. "Come over tomorrow, okay?"

"More than okay." He grinned and kissed her again before he turned away. "Kara, sweet dreams."

She smiled at his ritual remark. She was fortunate the weekend turned out this way.

There was so much to tell Fosdick, but before she finished, his familiar purr drew her into a peaceful sleep.

When the sun rose the following morning, so did she. She bounced out of bed with all the fears of the previous week dissipating in night. She made the bed, dressed, and skipped, smiling to the kitchen. Mom and Dad sat at the table, coffee cups in hand.

"How was the party?"

"It was great, Mom. The Lawrence's home is beautiful and has an amazing view. The food was great. And guess what? They made peach ice cream. We really should get an ice cream freezer, Dad. I danced with everyone there and had a lot of fun! Oh, and guess what else? I forgot to tell you Karl got accepted to George Washington University."

They laughed when she stopped chattering long enough to draw breath. "It sounds like you did have a good time! That *is* good news about Karl. Didn't you tell me he wanted to be a doctor?"

"Yes, he's leaving for Washington, DC next week. His semester starts in a month and he has to be there early for freshmen orientation. I won't get a chance to see him before he leaves."

"Have the animals been fed?" She continued in a manic manner. Receiving a negative response, she grabbed the bowls and poured kibbles into them. She appreciated how calmly the dog and cat waited for food. They never pushed or shoved trying to be first at the feed trough. They never tried to eat the other's food either. Not common behavior among animals. It's one of the traits she loved about her four-legged friends. They were polite, furry people.

"What time is it?"

"It's a little after 8:00. Time for everyone to be out of bed. You know what they say 'Early to bed and early to rise ...'"

"Auuggh, Dad," she moaned. "Not that again!" Privately, she thought her dad was funny. She loved his unfailing sense of humor, but she didn't want him to know it.

"Your dad and I ate cereal before you got up. I'm leaving to get my hair cut and go grocery shopping, so if you want breakfast you'll have to cook it and promise to clean up the kitchen, there's plenty of food here. You'll have the house to yourself, so behave."

"Mo...om." She stretched out the word, pretending to be insulted. "It's okay by me to cook. I'll even clean up," she joked.

The smell of fresh coffee and frying bacon caused her stomach to growl. The sound of the doorbell caused her to jump since she didn't expect anyone this early. Frowning, she dried her hands. Her eyes widen in surprise as she opened the door. She questioned "Nate?"

A slow smile crept across his face "Is this too early?"

"No, I was fixing breakfast. Care to join me? There's plenty."

"I'd love breakfast. I haven't eaten and I'm famished." Grinning, she stepped aside to let him in.

Chapter 4

When her mom returned from her errands, Kara helped put away the groceries "I love your hair. It looks really cute styled that way." She raved on about the new hair salon when a knock at the door interrupted them. Nate was back.

"Hi, Mrs. Carson. Can Kara come out and play?" He grinned impishly.

"Of course, Nate. Would the two of you mind taking Don José for a walk? I want to vacuum the living room and you know how he gets."

"Yeah," Kara chuckled visualizing the dog's antics. "He attacks the vacuum like he's going to kill it. It's really funny!"

She grabbed the dog's leash and picked him up to carry outside.

Mom gave a long-suffering sigh. "I guess you could call it funny, but it makes it difficult to get any work done. Thanks for getting him out of my hair, kids."

As they walked Don José, she turned to Nate. "Speaking of hair, I was thinking about getting mine cute short, similar to Mom's. What do you think?"

Nate turned, he stared at her with an oddly hungry expression. "I think your hair is beautiful as it is. I'd hate for you to change it." He fingers ran through a strand of her hair.

He turned away, his face blank, his voice husky. "I liked the guy who brought you home. He was a nice guy. Good thing or I would have ripped his throat out." He chuckled as if it was joke. It wasn't, he was deadly serious. "I know it's too soon to say, but I have never felt surer about anyone, Kara. Simply put, I love you." He rubbed his hand over his eyes, avoiding her expression.

As she opened her mouth, he put his fingertips to her lips. "I know. I should slow down. I've told myself the same thing, but it doesn't change how I feel—I love you." He put his arms around her and pulled her to his chest. "I don't know what I'll do when you leave. You may find me up outside your dorm more than you want." His lips touched her forehead.

Overcome by his outpour of emotion and her own confusion, her eyes misted. "I can't imagine that would be possible. Leaving will be hard for me, too. When I'm not with you, all I see is your face, your eyes, and I feel the touch of your skin. Nate, I think I love you, too. But I'm not sure what to do with those feelings."

"Marry me."

"No, I can't. First, I'm not ready for marriage. I need time to decide what I want in life ... to decide if you're the right person to share my life. Second, all my parents ever talk about is my going to college. It's their lifelong dream. The Depression and then the war prevented them from going. My dad in particular suffers from that loss. It's why he's so set on my graduating. I can't let him down. No matter what, we'll have to wait."

"I'll wait for you through eternity, if that's what it takes. But waiting is hard." Nate hesitated then questioned, "Why would you think I might not be the best person to share your life?"

"It's why I need more time. I thought, Karl, my old boyfriend, was the one. But when I met you, you turned my world upside down. I want to get my head on straight. When you're around it's hard to think rationally."

In a secluded spot, they fell on the dusty ground, wrapped in a fervent embrace. Beginning to fear she was losing control, she tried to push Nate away when a wet tongue washed across her face. She startled.

"Oh, Donnie-boy! Poor guy." With a nervous chuckle, she pulled away. "We forgot you. We have to finish your walk." Reluctantly, Nate let go and helped her to her feet, brushing the dirt off their clothes as he stood.

Nate reached over to pick twigs out of her hair. "Instead of cutting your hair, you could shave your head. We wouldn't have to worry about picking stuff out of it." She swatted at him as he laughed, jumping out of reach. Don José joined the romp, leaping and barking. He ran in a circle as far as his leash would allow, entangling them.

They laughed until they couldn't laugh any more. Freed from the leash, they strolled, hand-in-hand, back to the house. Don José led the way, his tail a happy banner, a flag in a breeze.

"I suppose you're going to church tomorrow." Nate's words were a statement rather than a question.

"You suppose right. Wanna come along?"

"I'll take a pass. But I want to see you afterward. Can I pick you up? We can do whatever you want—picnic, go exploring, go out to eat."

"Okay. Let's both think about it and be spontaneous."

"That's me: Mr. Spontaneous!" he chuckled.

"What about tonight? Do you want to do something tonight?"

"I don't think your parents would approve of what I *want* to do." She swatted at him, red-faced. "How about we have an early night tonight and recover from the past couple of days. We'll focus on tomorrow."

"Okay." She turned her face up to receive his kiss.

"Sweet dreams, Kara," He stroked her cheek with the back of his fingers. "I know mine will be."

Nate stood and watched as she and the dog entered the house. As he drove back to the cabin he deliberated how to handle Josh. Josh resented Kara and he wasn't sure how to handle his brother's resentment. Maybe if he didn't bring it up, Josh would come around. Time was all he needed, and all Nate needed too.

He desired Kara by his side every possible moment. She could change her mind. She didn't understand what he offered. How could he tell her what he was without scaring her? He could offer eternity—to always live—to always be young and beautiful. After all, vampires were like ordinary people. Some were good; some bad. He didn't kill people often. He didn't go on wild killing sprees. At least, not lately. He killed in order to feed himself. He killed when someone deserved to die. How was that evil?

Nate shook his head to clear it. Maybe an idea would come to him in the morning. Maybe he could be 'Mr. Spontaneous' after all.

⤸⟲

When Geoff picked up Kara on Sunday morning, they rehashed the party. "I don't know why Joyce is such a brat," he offered. "I think she's jealous. You have a boyfriend and all the guys were eager to dance with you. Her last boyfriend dumped her. That's no excuse for her being snotty, though. I hope she behaves in church."

Ugh, she thought, *I forgot she'd be at church.* "Maybe she'll get over it," she said hopefully.

"Huh, if she does, it'll be a first." She read the disgust Geoff's face. "It usually takes her a while to start needling someone, but she's like a bulldog once she starts in on them."

"Thanks for the heads-up. How do you think I should handle her? Should I be my usual charming self or should I say what I'd like to say?" She hoped the humor hid her ire at just the mention of Joyce's name.

"Ha! That would be fun. I've seen you smile while you verbally rip someone to shreds." Geoff knew her all too well. She was like her mother in that respect.

"I know," she groaned. "I don't want to be that person, but if she keeps pushing me ..."

"You'll kick her butt!" Geoff suggested. They burst into laughter.

The rest of the crowd arrived at the church exactly when they arrived. All turned toward the two of them with friendly smiles and waves—except for Joyce. In a falsely sympathetic voice, she asked, "Oh Kara, no boy on your arm today?"

"Not yet. However, the boy you drooled over last Sunday will be here to pick me up. I wanted to warn you so you'd have time to get a napkin to wipe your chin. I wouldn't want you to embarrass yourself."

Joyce's eyes narrowed; she turned and stomped away. Fred burst out laughing as did Lois and Linda. Everyone else smiled broadly. Geoff elbowed her as he stage whispered. "Game on!"

The minister from Mesa preached that Sunday. He was younger than the one from Phoenix. While nice enough, he had the disconcerting habit of rocking back and forth, his waving hands as if shooing flies. It was distracting.

It was impossible to concentrate on his message. She wore glazed look and a sideways glance proved she wasn't the only one. Geoff stared at his feet frowning. The twins wrote notes to each other. She struggled to keep a straight face, wanting to laugh, but she controlled the urge.

The service ended as they sang the Doxology. Relief filled her as they filed out. She grappled for something nice to say to the young minister—settling for a "thank you for driving up here." She smiled. Lame, but it was the best she could do.

Nate sat on the hood of his truck. He beamed when he saw her. At that same moment, Joyce turned with a scowl. As Nate strolled toward her, Joyce stepped in front of him, cutting him off. "I hope to get to know you a lot better since you're hanging around Kara." That syrupy voice made Kara want to puke.

Nate's eyes widened in surprise. "Um, yeah, maybe some time." He stepped around her and grabbed Kara's hand. "Sorry to rush off again, but we have things to do." He wiggled his eyebrows suggestively and grinned. "We're going fishing!"

Fishing? She hadn't fished since she was a child and she'd never baited a hook. The thought of impaling worms made her cringe.

"Nate? I don't know how to fish."

"Don't worry, I'll help you, it's fun, and you get to eat your catch!" He smiled at her reluctance.

After Nate drove her home, she sprinted inside to change into an old pair of jeans and a tee shirt. With an expression of doubt, she got into the pickup. At least they'd spend the time together.

They drove for an interminable amount of time over the bumpy dirt road until Nate pulled over to the side. He jumped out pulling her out behind him. He reached into the back for two poles and a tackle box. She looked around for water. "Where are we supposed to fish?"

"It's a little way up this trail." His idea of "a little way" was way out of line with hers.

She was irritable by the time the trail turned downward into a picture postcard vale, complete with a pristine stream. She gazed in awe at its beauty. The trees cast dappled shadows over the grass and water. Where the sun touched the water, it sparkled more beautifully than any precious gem. Nate set the tackle box down, and handed her a pole. Then, bless him, he baited the hook and showed her how to cast a line. The line barely hit the water when she felt a gentle tug. "Nate, I think I've got one!"

"Reel it in. I'll help you get it off the hook and on a stringer." She didn't bother to ask what a stringer was—grateful he'd take the fish off the hook. She reeled in a small pan-sized rainbow trout. Its iridescent colors were so beautiful she wanted to throw it back. Only the thought of eating the trout stopped her.

Nate put the fish on the stringer, re-bated the hook. Within minutes, they'd caught three fish. Half an hour later, they limited out.

"Okay, now I'm going to teach you how to clean fish." He pulled a knife from a sheath on his belt. Taking the knife, he deftly sliced open the belly of a fish, took his thumb and ran it up inside the fish as its innards fell onto a newspaper he'd laid out.

"That is gross and disgusting," She emphasized with a slightly green face. "I'm not doing that."

His brown eyes focused on hers. He said, "If you fish, you clean. You may be hungry sometime and have to do it. Now is the time to learn. I'll help, but you've got to try." He spoke firmly. "Come here."

With reluctance, she moved forward and he placed the knife in her hand. He handed her a fish, belly up, and guided her hand as she made the cut. That part didn't seem too bad; then he took the knife and grabbed her hand forcing her thumb out, sliding it up the interior of the fish. It wasn't as bad as she expected since his hand wrapped around hers, but it was gross.

"Okay, try this one on your own." Nate tried not to laugh.

She grabbed the knife and the fish. *Since he thought she was so funny, she'd show him! She could gut a stupid fish if she wanted.* In a couple of quick moves, she'd successfully gutted the fish. "Ha! I did it!" She cast a look of superiority.

He reached over and hugged her as he chuckled. "Go wash your hands in the stream and I'll finish up. You did good." A big grin lit his face. "Now we can tell everyone you're a real fisherman! You think your folks would like a fish fry tonight? I'll cook the fish."

They packed the fish on ice in the chest he'd brought, wrapped the innards for disposal in the Forest Service garbage cans. He bragged about her until she smiled. She could do it again, if only to show him.

Before they headed home they stopped at a store where, he picked up spices and a couple of lemons for the fish.

⟳

"You actually took Kara fishing and caught enough fish to feed us? I wish I'd been there to watch her clean a fish," her dad guffawed, but he also beamed with pride. His obvious pleasure at her accomplishment took the sting out of his teasing.

"Are you sure you know how to cook trout, Nate?" Her mom was skeptical, but when he assured her he did, she agreed to let him. While he prepared and cooked the trout, Kara and her mom fixed the rest of the meal to go with it. Nate showed her how to fillet the cooked fish so there were almost no bones. It was delicious. Fragrant with spices and so tender, it fell free from remaining bones. The squeeze of lemon provided the perfect finishing touch.

After dinner, Nate stayed to help with the dishes. It was one of the few times she enjoyed cleaning the kitchen. Everyone shared stories—dad included the embarrassing story of trying to get her to catch crawfish with him. They called them crawdads. Excited to help until she saw the creepy thing that looked like a bug as it scurried along the creek bottom. In her childish mind, a crawdad was a bird, not comparable to something from a nightmare.

When it came time for Nate to leave, he thanked her parents for sharing the evening with him. "Sometimes I forget what having a family is like," he said wistfully. "It was nice to be part of one again, even for an evening."

Mom actually hugged him before she had a chance. Dad slapped him on the back and invited him back any time ... especially if he brought the fish. Even Fosdick went over and rubbed against Nate's leg, purring his tacit acceptance of Nate into the family circle.

It was an almost perfect day—barring Joyce, it was perfect. Kara slipped a tiny bite of the fish in a napkin for Fosdick when they went to bed. He'd enjoy the covert treat. Her nighttime ablutions complete, she crawled into bed with the cat whose purr was louder than usual, thanks to his treat. He curled around her head as she told him about the day. Long before she finished the story, her voice trailed off into a sleepy murmur then her breathing deepened in sleep.

Nate stood outside her bedroom window as he waited for the light to go out. In a voice too soft for her to hear, he whispered, "Sweet dreams, Kara."

Chapter 5

If the weekdays were long—the weekends were too short. She thought about skipping church the next time the minister from Mesa was due to come. But the reason she went to church wasn't about entertainment.

Nate and she spent their days hiking, fishing, and exploring. Nighttime they were wrapped in each other's arms in a secluded spot. On one exploration they found a site which contained an abundance of arrowheads and pottery shards. After the adventure with finding the arrowheads, she considered becoming an anthropologist or an archeologist instead of a teacher. The beauty part was she didn't have to make up her mind yet. There was plenty of time to explore her options.

Nate knew about so many different things. He evaded her questions when she asked where he'd gone to school and if he'd gone to college. When she asked his future plans, he smirked. "My only plans are waiting for you to marry me."

"I don't understand why you won't answer me, especially since I spill my guts about my entire life."

"I know where we should go next weekend; to the Tonto Natural Bridge. It's not far—before we get to Pine. Let's go Saturday. We can spend the entire day exploring."

"I'll check with Mom and Dad, but I doubt they'll have any objections. Tell me about this bridge."

"Supposedly, a miner hid from the Apaches in the caves under it. It's not very deep and there's a trail to the bottom. We could spend time exploring a few of the caves." Nate's excitement was catching. She was eager to see this wonder with him.

"I don't want to go too far into the caves." The thought of being lost in a cave frightened her since she read Tom Sawyer. She shivered, claustrophobic at the thought of Tom and Becky Thatcher lost for days in that cave in Missouri.

"Don't worry; I'll bring rope to mark the way."

Her mother would ask, if someone said, "Let's go jump off a bridge," would she do it? Of course, the answer was supposed to be *no*. If Nate asked her to jump off the proverbial bridge, she'd grab his hand and say *okay*. She'd tell her parents where they were going, but on the pretext it was picnic, with no mention of caves. It wouldn't be a lie, but it wouldn't be the whole truth either.

"I'll pack a picnic hamper. We won't not show my parents the ropes and flashlights we're taking."

His brows drew together as he gave a questioning look. After a pause he said, "If you're sure that's what you want to tell them, I guess its okay. By the way, if you have hiking boots, wear them. They'll help with the climbing."

Plans confirmed, they drove toward Pine the following Saturday morning. Dawn broke as they left her house. The sky was filled with shades of pink and gold. The scent of the junipers and pines filled the air. It would be a glorious day, not only because she was with Nate. Breathing in the air, she thanked God for the day.

The drive to the turnoff only took about fifteen minutes. They followed the dirt road for a mile. She wasn't good at distances, especially when it came to dirt roads and being forced to drive at a slow rate of speed. With Nate by her side, it was even harder. How could she pay attention to distance while watching his perfect his profile?

When Nate pulled to a stop, she was confused. There was no bridge in sight nor any apparent need of one. "Where's the bridge?"

"Have a little patience," he grinned. "I thought we could eat our breakfast here; then I'll show you where the bridge is hiding. Remember, we have the whole day. There's no point in rushing it."

When he raised his eyebrows and gazed from under his lashes she forgot her argument. Besides, he was right. They had the whole day and she planned to make the most of it.

She spread a blanket under a scrub oak and laid out paper plates and cups. She'd packed breakfast with a thermos of hot chocolate, hard-boiled eggs, and donuts. The hamper was half-full with sandwiches and chips for lunch.

Nate opened the thermos, poured cups of the hot chocolate. She grabbed the hard-boiled eggs and Nate the donuts. The look on his face was comical as he bit into a jelly-filled donut. He'd never tasted the sweet treat before. They ate two eggs and two donuts each. As she bit down on her second jelly-filled donut, the jelly squirted out on her chin. She gasped with surprise when Nate leaned over ran his tongue over her chin.

"Nate, wh ...what are you doing?"

"Hey, it was too sweet to waste ... and the jelly was pretty good, too," was his mischievous response. Her face flamed. "Let's leave the basket here and come back for it later. We'll need the ropes and flashlights before we eat again."

They picked up the gear and began to walk. She wondered how far they'd needed to go, when the earth fell away at her feet. She staggered back in surprise, but Nate's arms encircled her, offering support until she caught her balance. He smiled into her wide eyes—safely guided her around the opening to a steep trail.

Glad he warned her to wear boots, because even with them, she slipped and slid on her backside down the trail. Nate never once lost his footing. The trail was quite steep and it would be a struggle to climb up the trail.

When they reached the bottom, she took a good look around. It was a mind-boggling structure open to the air on two sides of the bridge with the back walled with innumerable smaller caves.

"Where do you want to start—top or the bottom?" Nate asked.

Overwhelmed, she waved her arms. He took her hand and led her to the nearest cave. "Let's start at the bottom and work our way up."

Over the course of the morning they found an old wooden bucket, a pickax, and an old lantern. The cave had been mined at some point in time. The stuff they found appeared to be old, but she had no idea how to determine the age of the artifacts. Not knowing didn't make it any less interesting, though.

In her imagination, she pictured an old bearded miner who worked in the cave. She visualized him in heavy work pants and a dirty flannel shirt. Nate laughed as she described her image of the man and hugged her.

They checked out several more caves when they found one that showed signs of recent campfires, broken beer bottles and cans littered the ground.

"Hmm ... this must be a where the local kids have their boondockers."

"Their what?"

"You know, out in the boondocks—like out away from everyone— where they party without fear of parents or the police."

"Oh, I get it." They picked their way back out of the cave through the detritus of the parties.

"Are you hungry yet? I'll run up and get the basket if you are."

She looked at her watch; surprised at how much time had passed. "Now that you mention it ..." She smiled, letting her words trail off. It was more interesting to explore these caves than she'd have guessed. Maybe she found it interesting because Nate was with her.

He bounded up the steep trail like a mountain goat. *He must be hungry, too.* She turned to look back at the caves. *Maybe they'd have time to check out the caves at the top.*

As her eyes drifted upward, a pair of large golden eyes stared down at her. She screamed, turned to run, but stumbled over the rocks and fell as the huge cougar leapt toward her. She rolled into a ball expecting the slash of its vicious claws—its teeth rending her flesh. As time froze, she caught a flash of movement. The cat and another animal shrieked, then all went silent.

Fearful, she turned her head to see Nate with the cougar pinned to the ground, its movements feeble. Was Nate biting its neck? She must have hit her head and be in a bizarre dream. She shook her head back and forth in confusion and denial at what she'd witnessed.

Nate stood slowly, wiped the back of his hand across his mouth. "Kara, are you okay? Are you hurt?" His voice faded in and out, like a badly tuned radio.

"It's all right, Kara. Let me see your scrapes; I'll bandage them." She heard a strange noise before she passed out; someone was screaming.

When she woke, she lay on the blanket under the scrub oak. Vaguely, she wondered how she'd gotten there and why her hands were bandaged. Nate held a cold, wet cloth to her head. In a flash her thoughts cleared. She sat up quickly and scooted away from him as a wave of dizziness hit her.

"Kara, Kara, it's okay." He spoke soothingly, as if trying to quiet a frightened animal. "I'd never hurt you—you know I love you. Don't be afraid. I promise, I will never hurt you."

"How did you do that? How did you kill that cat?" A voice—hers, at least she thought it was hers—barely whispered. She shook with shock.

"I never wanted to tell you like this. I wanted to wait until you knew me better. But I don't have a choice now. There's just no easy way to tell you." His shoulders slumped as he lowered his eyes. He took a deep breath. "Remember when I told you my parents drowned in a flood? They did; they drown in 1927. The people who pulled Josh and me from the water weren't exactly your everyday people. They were vampires." He paused at her sharp intake of breath. As he gazed into her terrified eyes, his own dark eyes held the sorrow of the ages. "The vampires saved my life. Well, they sort of saved it. They changed me. On one hand, I'm dead, but on the other, I'm going to live forever. I know it's confusing, but try to understand. I never had a choice. This life hasn't been all bad, the living forever part anyway."

"Vampires are monsters that kill people—suck their blood. So you and Josh must kill people ..." She let the question dangle, but her revulsion was unmistakable.

He closed his eyes, avoiding the horror on her face. "We kill what we need to survive. Josh and I kill more animals than people. We don't go around wiping out villages or anything like that, at least not any more. We try to keep it to an occasional hiker out in the desert." She winced at his confession. He pleaded for her understanding, but she understood all too well.

"Oh, dear sweet Jesus," she moaned. "It's wrong. I can't believe you could do such a thing. Killing innocent people is just plain wrong. How can I trust you won't kill me? Kill my parents? Kill my friends?"

He reached for her, but she pulled away in fear. "Please Kara, you've got to understand. I would never hurt you, your family, or any of your friends. I *like* them. Vampire don't have friends. You've made it possible. As for your parents... I wasn't kidding when I said it felt good to be part of a family. The people I kill are nameless faces. They're not missed by anyone."

Tears fell silently from her eyes. "How could you possibly know that? They may have had family waiting for them at home. I know you have been sweet to me, but this is too much to take in. I don't know what to do. I want to go home. I need to think."

Nate reached for her again. Although she cringed at his touch, she let him pull her into a hug. She sobbed as if her heart would break. Nate felt his heart would break, too.

He held Kara until she'd cried herself out and fell asleep from exhaustion, cradled in his arms. He let her sleep until the sun hung low in the sky. He stared at her face—memorizing every feature—tracing her face with a touch as light as the brush of a butterfly's wing. He was afraid to lose her. He knew he must take her home, but he had to get her promise not to expose him—at least not yet. He stroked her face with a firmer hand, kissed her swollen eyes, her nose, and her mouth before she stirred.

"Nate?" she murmured softly, jerked awake, and pulled away from him. Her eyes filled with terror.

"It's okay, Kara, it's going to be okay," he whispered softly. "I will do anything you ask. I want to stay with you. I want you by my side. We could be together for eternity. I'd make you so happy." Nate spoke of his great hopes and desires.

"But if you want me to leave you alone, I will. I'll give you all the time you need to decide, but please, I beg you, don't tell anyone what I am. If Josh and I are exposed, we'd have to leave immediately. I know what people will do if they find out what we are." His face twisted in pain. "We saw what happened to the ones who rescued us—the hate in the faces of the farmers who burned them to death. I can't stand the thought of your parents and friends hating me, wanting to kill me. They will if you expose me."

Nate dampened a cold cloth again to put it over her swollen eyes. He attempted a smile. "I can't take you home looking like that. Pete would shoot first and ask questions later." He managed a weak chuckle.

She gave a small smile in return. "Okay, I won't tell anyone, but I need time to think this over. Will you promise to give me a week before you come over?"

He nodded and said, "A week—I can do a week." He nodded his head in consideration. "Now I suggest you keep the cold cloth over your eyes." He picked her up and carried her to the truck. He returned for the supplies and leftover food. He sat in the truck in thought, turned toward her and gently touched her cheek. He tried not to react to her flinch. "Remember how much I love you and how I can give you eternity."

"I have eternity," she snapped with conviction. She knew where she stood with God.

"No you don't! Humans get old, get sick and die. I don't want you to go through all that." Frustration filled his voice.

"That's the way life is, ups and downs, and after death, eternity. Please don't pressure me, Nate! I need time to think ... to figure out the best thing to do." Her face in her hands, she pushed trying to squash out the day's revelation.

He turned the key on the truck and drove home in virtual silence with only an occasional word spoken. When they reached her house, she didn't hesitate. She jumped from the truck, grabbed the basket and ran to the door. When he got out of the truck to go with her, she turned to face him, her hand out to stop him. "Leave, Nate, go home now. Remember, I have a week."

Nate looked like she'd struck him, he backed away, got into the truck and drove off. She felt terrible for hurting him, but what else could she do?

She burst through the door, threw the basket down in the middle of the living room and raced for her room, obviously in tears. Her parents sat on the couch stunned.

⟿

"What do you suppose that was about?"

"I suspect it was a lovers' quarrel, Pete. I'll give her some time then see if she wants to talk.

Kara's sobs could be heard through the door. Fosdick waited outside, yowling his distress. He frantically pawed at the door. It opened a crack—wide enough for the cat to squeeze through—and slammed again.

After waiting for the crying to abate, Joann decided to take the bull by the horns. She knocked on the bedroom door. "Kara, can I come in?"

"No, go away! I don't want to talk to anyone." She sobbed in misery.

"Can I get you something—tea, toast, a bowl of soup?"

"No! I'm not hungry. I want to be left alone." She knew her mother wanted to help, but how could she? How could she make her understand something she couldn't understand herself? Especially, since there was much of the story she could never tell—if she gave Nate the silence he'd requested.

"Okay, honey. I'm right here if you need me."

Joann look toward Pete, shrugged her shoulders as she whispered in his ear. "I think they may have broken up."

⟿

Nate drove as slow as he could until he reached a point where the road ended. He pulled the truck under a tree; sat on the bumper and watched the stars come out one by one. Sighing, he sluggishly walked to the cabin, hoping Josh was off on a hunt. All he wanted to do was to crawl into his bunk, put his face to the wall and sleep. He didn't want to explain his anguish to his brother. Maybe all this would go away by morning. But he was afraid that was wishful thinking.

Josh was in the cabin and heard Nate come in. As he turned, he spoke teasingly "Hey, Nate, did you and Kara have a good time today?" When he saw Nate's face, he hurried to his side, concerned. "What happened, man? You look like you just lost your best friend, but since I'm here ...," he joked weakly, his voice trailing off.

"I don't want to talk right now." Nate's voice was husky with emotion he struggled to control.

Josh was immediately angry. "It's that girl, isn't it?" Josh snapped. "Little miss perfect. What did she do to you? I told you she would be trouble. You don't need her kind of trouble. You should kill her or dump her!"

"I'm not going to kill her. I know you mean well, Josh, but you're not helping. Leave me alone." Nate turned away.

"Come on, man. Tell me what happened," Josh pleaded with Nate.

"I killed a cougar in front of her, so I was forced to tell her what we are. She was *so* scared." His voice a monotone, he struggled to control his shaky emotions.

"What!" Josh shrieked his response. "Well, damn. Now we're screwed; she'll tell everyone. We need to get out of here. You *know* what will happen when she tells! You've seen it happen before."

"She isn't going to tell anyone—at least not yet. Now leave me alone. I don't want to talk." Nate stretched out on the bunk, rolled to face the wall, and pulled the blanket over his head.

"Fine—just fine! I'm going hunting. I hope you come to your senses—before we're both dead!" The slamming door shook the cabin walls as Josh stomped out.

She didn't know what she'd do without her cat. He was the only one she could safely tell her fears—her sorrow. She told the cat what Nate was, and asked what to do. Her mind was jumbled; it was hard to think. No matter what she whispered to the cat, he continued to purr and to knead the pillow next to her head in his best comforting manner. As she continued to cry, her thoughts slowly untangled and become clearer.

Fosdick shifted his position licking the salty tears from her face with his sandpaper tongue. Her thoughts raced. It's only fair to talk with Nate—ask a few questions. She'd write them down as she thought of them. Since they were certain to fly out of her head when she faced him.

She snuggled Fosdick away from her tender face and into her arms. Slowly, she drifted into an uneasy sleep, while the cat kept watch.

Even though she hadn't slept much, she woke early. Grabbing a pencil and a pad of paper from her desk, she jotted down a few words, chewed on the eraser, and wrote a few more. A shower should clear her head.

Church would be a comfort—though she didn't want to face her friends, but she wanted to connect with the best friend of all. Besides, if she was gone, her parents couldn't question her

She pushed the pad beneath the mattress before making the bed. She didn't expect her parents to pry, but she couldn't take the slightest chance they'd see what she'd written.

As she grabbed the first outfit she touched from the closet, she dashed for the shower. After the shower, she dawdled with her hair and makeup. Finally brave enough to face her parents, she walked into a vacant kitchen. The table held the empty picnic basket and a partial box of donuts. Propped against the box was a note:

Kara,
  We've gone out for breakfast and we'll see you later.
Go ahead and feed yourself.
                                    Love, Mom

Good, more time. She poked around the kitchen looking for something to eat, but nothing appealed—especially the donuts. She thought of Nate licking the jelly off her chin and her eyes welled with tears. "No, I am not going to cry."

Glancing down and realized she wasn't completely alone. Patiently waiting and staring up at her, sat Don José and Fosdick. "I'll bet you want breakfast." She smiled sadly at her two small friends and dug out their bowls and the pet food. Patting them both, she set the bowls on the floor, and refilled the water bowl. Performing the ordinary tasks calmed her.

She wandered listlessly until the sound of Geoff's car drew her attention. Church was something she needed. Even snotty Joyce would be better than facing her real problem.

Geoff took one look at her and asked the dreaded question: "What's wrong?"

She scowled. "Nothing I want to talk about."

"Okay, I get it. Boy problems. Hey, you don't have to talk if you don't want to. I've been through it too ... well ... not exactly boy problems." He stumbled around trying to clarify what he meant. She giggled at his discomfort.

"Atta girl! Don't let it get you down. There's plenty of fish in the sea."

"Now you sound like Daddy," she grumbled.

"He's a good man, if you ask me."

"You're right. He is a good man." She wasn't sure exactly who she meant.

Chapter 6

Church *was* the perfect place to take her mind off problems. Her friends were warm and expressed concern when Geoff told them not to bug her because of boy problems. Joyce smirked, but Kara refused to rise to the bait, instead she focused on her prayers.

Before the service began, Fred grabbed her hand. "Since you don't have any plans, why don't we go bowling after church? Isn't it time you gave some of us other guys a chance?" He teased with a grin.

"If you'd seen me bowl you wouldn't ask. But if you're not afraid to retrieve my ball from the next lane, I'm game." He laughed. Fred was the perfect person to be around. He was always cheerful.

Fred turned to Geoff. "I'll take her home so she can change. That's okay, isn't it?" She noticed Joyce's consternation and gloated—just a little.

Geoff got a stern look on his face. "Do you think you can behave like a gentleman, young man?" Everyone laughed, including her.

It was odd to leave, with no Nate leaning against the bumper of his pickup—a side-ways grin on his face. More than odd, it was gut wrenching.

Fred took her elbow, escorted her to a beat-up green sedan, and opened the door. He bowed at the waist. "Your chariot awaits, Madam." Who wouldn't be cheered by his antics?

Her parents were home when she and Fred pulled up. As he came inside, she quickly introduced him. "Mom and Dad, have you met Fred Jacobs? We're going bowling."

Fred's presence dispelled any unwanted questions, but didn't stop the questioning look her parents exchanged when they came in.

Dad laughed. "Has he seen you bowl? Good to meet you Fred. You're a brave man if you're taking our Kara bowling!"

"Have a little faith, Dad. I might have improved," she groused. But her parents were delighted at her improved mood.

The bowling alley had all of nine lanes—a lot smaller than the 24-lane alley where she'd bowled in Phoenix. She had to stop comparing everything to Phoenix. Otherwise, what was she going to do in Flagstaff? Would she continue to make comparisons instead of embracing the change she claimed to want?

Fred made the perfect companion for her dark mood. While he loved to laugh and tease, he proved to have a deeply serious side. "I've enlisted in the Army. I want to go to college, but there's no way I can afford it working part-time."

"Can your parents help you?"

"It's just my mom and she barely makes enough to get by as it is. She's searching for a better-paying job, but they're few and far between in a town like this. The Army recruiter promised I could go to college on the GI Bill after I finish my enlistment. If I stayed on for a second tour, I might be able to begin my education while in the Army. Then my mom wouldn't have to worry about my future. I'll be set." He was so earnest. She knew he'd thought it through.

"You're a good son."

"I try to be, but sometimes it's not easy. So you're going to ASC?"

"Yes, did Geoff tell you?" He nodded. "My parents planned for my college education since I was small. Neither of them went, so it's doubly important I graduate. I can't let them down."

"So you're going to please them?" a crease formed between his eyes.

"Yes and no. I do want to please them, but I want to be a teacher." It was amazing they could have a serious a conversation amidst the laughter over her abominable bowling. She'd never think of him funny Freddie anymore. He was simply Fred, her friend.

After bowling, he suggested they get a burger before going home.

"Can we go somewhere other than the Burger Hut?

After a thoughtful look, he said, "Of course. There's the other burger place, or we could get pizza. Do you like pizza?"

"I love pizza! That would be perfect." Fred didn't question her, but understood why she wanted to avoid the Burger Hut. He was a kind, thoughtful guy. She was glad she'd agreed to go out with him. He had a way about him that made her relax.

As they ate pizza, she paused to question Fred. "You've met Nate. Can I ask your impression of him? I know this isn't what I should ask on a date, but I'd appreciate a third-party impression."

Fred chewed his bite thoughtfully. "Overlooking the fact all the guys hate him because he looks like a Greek god and the girl's moon over him for the same reason, I'd say he's a nice guy." He hesitated, another bite of pizza gave him time to think.

"I have to add, I do have questions about him. For instance, where did he come from? None of us remember seeing him around before he picked you up from church. It's as if he popped into existence. Does he hold down a job? If so, where? We've never seen him at work. In a town this small it's something hard to hide." She nodded her head, but didn't interrupt.

"Then," he hesitated, "why doesn't he ever come to church with you? It's obvious he's nuts about you, so why is church the one place he never takes you? He must know it's an important part of your life. I don't know; he might go to an early mass or something. It could mean nothing."

Fred was willing to minimize the importance of the questions. But she noted his comments and questions include everyone—at least all the boys. Apparently, Nate had been a hot topic of conversation among them.

"Thanks Fred, I appreciate your honesty and the questions you brought up. You see, I have to decide whether to continue our relation-ship. I want to be fair. I want to base my decision on logic, not emo-tion. You've helped a lot." While she knew the answers to some of the questions he raised, it helped to know others noticed, too. She often wondered why he wouldn't go to church—at least occasionally. "Okay, enough of this," she concluded.

"Now I have a question for you," Fred grinned impishly. "Do I get a chance to take you out again?"

She returned his grin, "I'd say it is a distinct possibility." They continued eating the pizza. It was better pizza than she'd expected. She usually limited herself to no more than three slices—two on a date. Now she grabbed her fifth slice. "I usually don't eat this much. I'm embarrassed I'm eating so much, but this is sooo ... good."

"Don't worry, I won't count how many slices you've eaten if you don't count how many I've eaten!" They agreed, chuckling.

The door opened as Fred took a napkin, reached over and wiped pizza sauce off her chin. She didn't see who'd come in, but they must have decided the place was too busy or too noisy. They spun around and left.

"So when can we go out again?" Fred asked.

"I can go out any day during the week as long as I'm home by nine—I work in the morning. I'm not sure about next weekend. Maybe Sunday, but I'll have to let you know."

She couldn't answer. She expected to talk to Nate Saturday. His answers to her questions would determine if she could go out with Fred Sunday.

"How about if I call, say Wednesday, and see if you'd like to go out. I don't want to disappoint you, but we can't go bowling," he said soberly. "League night, you know." He sighed with a sad shake of his head.

"Doggone it," she said with a mocking laugh. "We'll have to settle on something else."

As they walked to the car, Fred turned serious again. "Could I ask a favor from you, as a friend? Will you write to me when I leave for boot camp?" She turned and took his right hand in hers, squeezed it once and let it drop again. "I hear it can get lonely for a guy like me who's never been away from home for more than a weekend."

"I'd be happy to write, Fred. I might even break down and send a box of cookies or something." She smiled at his look of pleasure.

When they pulled into the driveway, Fred took her hand. "I'll pray you make the best decision possible, okay?" She smiled and nodded in response. Her throat was too tight to speak. He lifted her hand to his lips and kissed it. "See you soon."

Chapter 7

She stood in the driveway waving until Fred turned the corner. Without warning, a hand covered her mouth. Jerked off her feet, the surroundings blurred as someone threw her over his shoulder and carried her away.

Shocked into silence until she was unceremoniously dumped to the ground. She screamed as he jerked her up by one arm. Spinning around; she half-expected to see Nate. Instead, it was Josh she saw. His face was feral rather than the cocky boy she'd met. Without warning, his fist hit her jaw, hard. The coppery taste of blood filled her mouth.

Before she could react, his fist landed a second blow to her stomach, hard enough to knock the wind out of her. She crumpled to the ground. As she gasped for breath, she was jerked her to her feet and shaken. Her head snapped back and forth.

"Who do you think you are?" he roared. "You think you can cheat on my brother? Nate's back at the cabin upset and you're on a *date*? You hurt him!" Spittle sprayed her face as he screamed. "I don't know why he wants you, but if he does, you'd be lucky to have him. You're nothing but a spoiled bit ...."

His words trailed off as he knocked her to the ground again. He kicked her in the stomach. Instinctively, she rolled in a ball to protect herself as he continued kicking. As he reached for her arm again, he disappeared. Something hit a solid surface with a grunt of pain.

"If you *ever* touch her again I will kill you," a low voice snarled. Through her foggy brain it was hard to comprehend what happened.

"You might be the nearest thing to a brother I have, but I mean it, Josh. Get out of here. Leave now, I don't want to see your face again tonight or I won't be responsible for what I do." Nate's voice—her head cleared enough to recognize it—was quiet; a deadly quiet.

"I'm trying to make her see sense. To help you." Josh pleaded.

"By trying to kill her? Leave!" The screamed command left little doubt of the threat behind it.

"Kara, Kara, Kara." He crooned her name over and over as he squatted next to her. "Are you all right? Dear God, how badly are you hurt?"

She heard him and tried to answer, but all she could do was moan.

"I'm taking you to the hospital." He picked her up as if she weighed nothing and loped through the woods. There's an expression, "as the crow flies." Now she understood what it meant. It was the route he took. They didn't travel on regular roads, they traveled overland. His pace smooth, but the country around them blurred. She closed her eyes to keep from vomiting.

Everything was surreal. Was the blurring part of a nightmare or real? They reached the entrance to the emergency room in moments— at least it seemed that way to her.

"Help her!" Nate pleaded as the first of the emergency room staff appeared. "She's been hurt, but I don't know how badly. Her name is Kara Carson. Her parents Pete and Joann Carson. Please call them."

An orderly hurried out with a gurney. Nate laid her down with gentle care and kissed her brow.

Casting a suspicious look, the orderly said, "Stay for any questions we might have. The police will want to talk to you."

He knew what the questions would be. He admitted he saw her attacked, but he couldn't reveal Josh had done it. He'd have to lie. His worry for Josh almost matched his worry for Kara. *When would Josh learn? If he didn't, he was going to get them killed. His thoughts turned to Pete and Joann. What could he tell them?* He didn't have time to decide because they ran through the doors.

"I'd like to know just what the hell is going on," Pete bellowed, his hands balled into fists. "Where's Kara? They told me someone beat her up. Did. You. Hit. Her. Nate?" His hands fisted, Pete delivered his words in a gruff staccato fashion.

Nate understood for all his friendliness, Pete would be a merciless enemy if his family was threatened. While Nate expected the question, it hurt to hear it anyway.

"No sir. I would never hurt her." He hadn't hurt her, but he was responsible for what happened. He should never have told Josh.

Pete's eyes softened. "Sorry I cursed at you. I'm upset and worried, but that's no excuse. I would have been surprised if you had hurt her. What about that Fred—do you think he'd hit her?"

Fred? Nate frowned, confused.

"The boy who took her bowling tonight. Him." Pete clarified.

Nate felt he was the one with the wind knocked out of him. "Fred?" His voice squeaked. "The only Fred I know is the skinny guy who goes to her church. He doesn't seem the type to hurt her." *She'd been out on a date? A stab of anguish went through him. Why would she go out so soon after their argument? Hadn't they postponed decisions until next weekend? Had she made her choice and not told him yet?* Head in his hands, he waited for news.

A police officer showed up to question him. The hospital reported Kara's suspicious injuries, so the police were going to question Fred, too. A no nonsense man he asked, "You found her?"

"Yes sir."

"Where did you find her?"

"Off a dirt road about a mile and a half from here. I could show you, but I can't give a better description."

"Why were you there?"

"I needed time to think, so I went for a long walk."

"Did you see her attacker?"

"Only a glance of him as he ran off."

"I understand she was out on a date. Do you think the attacker could have been Fred Jacobs?"

"I don't think so, sir. Fred is tall and skinny. I'm sure the attacker was short and stocky."

"We have to figure out what time she got home and why she was so far from home when the attacked took place. Did Fred really drop her off? If so, did she leave the yard of her own volition, or had she been forcibly taken?"

After ordering Nate to show up at eight in the morning for further questioning, the officer left. He left a card for Pete and Joann with the incident number and the duty officer's name.

A nurse came to take her parents to Kara's bedside. Nate paced up and down the hall. Another nurse suggested he go home to rest. "You won't be able to see Kara tonight—they're keeping her for observation." He shook his head and continued to pace.

After an hour of waiting, her exhausted parents came out. They weren't surprised as Nate rush to meet them. Despair written across his face. "Her x-rays look okay, but they want to watch her. She has a concussion and bruised ribs. The doctor wants to make sure there are no other complications. It's possible she could have a ruptured spleen. Although no symptoms have shown up; just all the bruising, but the doctor wants to be sure. She's in room 132. You can see her tomorrow." Joann patted his arm.

Nate walked outside with them, pretending to leave. As soon as he was out of their field of vision, he ghosted back to the hospital and down the hall to her room. A murmur of voices came from inside her room, so he slipped into another room until he heard them leave. Two orderlies walked down the hall. He peered out of the partially opened door to make sure the hall was clear, and then crept into Kara's room. At first he thought she was sleeping, but he heard a smothered sob. He was at her side in an instant. "Do you need something for pain?" he whispered.

She shook her head and closed her eyes again. She opened them trying to focus on his face. "I'm afraid to sleep. What if he comes back?"

"Josh won't be back to hurt you, Kara. I'm no Fosdick, but I can try to take his place—at least until they throw me out." He managed a grin, hoping to cheer her up.

To his surprise, she nodded her head. He crawled into the narrow bed careful to avoid the IV line and pulled her head to his shoulder. "It's okay, Kara, I'll keep watch. You'll be safe."

Slowly her eyes closed and her breathing deepened into asleep. It felt right to lay next to her, one arm cradling her neck, the other thrown across her waist. When he took a deep breath and let it out, it sounded very much like a sob. Later, Nate heard the soft steps of the nurse returning to check Kara's vital signs. He slid soundlessly from the bed and stepped behind the curtains.

The nurse used a small flashlight to check Kara's vital signs. Apparently, all was well because the nurse left to complete her rounds. He slipped back in the bed and stroked her cheek with a feather-light touch.

Sick at heart over what happened, he questioned how Josh justified hurting her. Had Josh seen her out with Fred? He must have. Did he plan to attack the human boy as well? It would be like Josh. He'd have to break his promise to Kara to make sure Josh didn't attack Fred.

He slipped out of bed without disturbing her. After a quick check on the hall, he left. With luck, he'd be back before she missed him.

Since he had no idea where Fred lived, his only choice was to return to the cabin. He could track Josh if he was gone. No matter what, he'd find him tonight. Nate was sure the police would have questions for Josh, too. He'd have him to hide where the police would never find him. Kara's friends knew he had a brother even if they'd never met him. But plenty of people in town knew Josh and would identify him as a troublemaker. It would be better if Nate could claim Josh left after an argument earlier this summer.

Josh sat on his bunk, head in his hands. He looked up as Nate opened the door. "How is she? Is she going to be all right?"

"No thanks to you, she is," Nate growled. "She has a lot of internal bruising and a concussion, but they expect her recover." He paused. "What in the world were you thinking when you attacked her?"

"I'm sorry, man, but I saw her out with that guy ..." He held out his hands imploringly. "I knew how you felt about her. It was like she spit on you. I lost it, like you did when I was attacked in that Hooverville. I wanted to hurt her like she hurt you."

His explanation stabbed Nate in the heart. He was no better than his brother. They both has anger issues. "What about Fred? Did you attack him, too?" Nate asked wearily.

Josh gritted his teeth. "Not yet."

Nate's head snapped in Josh's direction. "Not at all. Not now—not ever. You have *really* opened a can of worms. The police are investigating Fred and me. Right now, we're the suspects. How long before they hear about you and your hot temper. I have to report to the jail in the morning for further questioning. I can't deny I have a brother. You're going to have to hide out while I try to convince them I sent you away after an argument with me. There are plenty of witnesses to your temper. The police will know you're a troublemaker ... I'll find you after things cool down. Don't show up here until I come for you. Not under any circumstances. Do you understand?" Nate's voice softened. "Josh, I don't want you hurt either."

Josh threw his arms around Nate's shoulders and tried not to cry. "I'm sorry, man. I didn't mean to cause you trouble. I mess up everything I do. You'd be better off without me around."

"You're my brother, Josh—no matter what. But you need to think before you act—talk to me first. When you act rashly, you get us both in trouble. Remember ... wait for me to find you, okay?" Nate's voice softened even more and he hugged Josh.

"I have to get back to the hospital. I promised Kara I'd be there when she woke. You need to leave tonight. If the police come looking for you, make sure there are no signs you've been here." They hugged good-bye and Nate left.

Nate ran to the hospital and to Kara's room. One of the advantages of being a vampire was the stealth with which he could move. Speed was another major advantage. While hunting prey, vampires could outrun virtually anything they hunted. Now both traits were advantageous for another reason—he could return to Kara's side before she missed him—sneak in without anyone noticing.

He crawled into bed without it shaking. He lowered his arm over her protectively. He felt peace steal over him. Maybe Kara's God was looking out for her, too. Neither one of them had done such a hot job of it earlier. He allowed himself to doze, knowing his predatory senses would hear anyone coming toward Kara's room. Before the morning shift change, he slipped out of her bed and pressed a kissed her forehead. Her eyes fluttered open. He put a finger to her lips to silence her.

"I'll be back later. I have things to take care of and the nurse will be in shortly. I'll be back during visiting hours." He bent and kissed her again before he sneaked outside.

He went to the cabin to make sure Josh had gone and to change his clothes. He didn't sweat, but his clothes got plenty dirty, especially when he hunted. *Or when I fight with my brother*, he thought wryly.

Josh was gone. No damning footprints around the cabin or the surrounding area showed he'd been there. Josh had done a good job covering his trail.

Once dressed, Nate rushed back to town. His first stop was the Carson's to hear news about Kara. He'd plead ignorance to cover the fact he spent the night in her bed. His next stop was the jail and the inevitable questions.

The Carson's invited him inside and offered breakfast. "No thanks, but I'll take a cup of your good coffee." He smiled at Joann, who managed a tired smile as she poured the coffee.

The Carson's looked like they hadn't slept all night. "Have you heard anything from the hospital yet?" Nate asked.

Both shook their heads distractedly. "Not yet. I expect them to call soon. We'll head over right after breakfast to check on her."

Don José and Fosdick paced anxiously, sensing something was wrong. "Can I feed the animals for you?" Nate asked as he jumped to his feet. "I know where the food is kept from watching Kara."

At the sound of her name, Fosdick let out a yowl of distress. Not waiting for an answer, he got the bowls and filled them with food. As he placed Fosdick's dish on the floor, he whispered, "She'll be home soon, don't worry, old son." The cat looked up and gave a grateful meow as if he understood every word Nate said.

"Thanks, Nate. I can't keep my mind focused this morning." Joann shook her head. Pete reached over and patted her hand.

The phone rang and Pete leapt out of the chair to grab it. "Yes, this is Pete Carson. She is? Well, that's good news. How soon can we see her? Okay, we'll be there."

Both Nate and Joann focused their attention on Pete as they listened to the one-sided conversation. Nate forced himself to allow Joann to ask the questions while he waited for the response. He knew Kara looked fine, but an official confirmation was welcome. She'd be hospitalized two more days, but he could see her visiting hours. Right.

"The police want to see me at the jailhouse today. I guess I'll head on over. Tell her I'll see her later. I'm glad she's is going to be okay. Thanks for the coffee." He bent to scratch behind the cat's ear and whispered, "Stay outside tonight."

He arrived at the jail as a battered green sedan pulled up. Fred. "They called you in, too?" Fred asked.

"Yeah, I was the one who found her and took her to the hospital," he said, uncomfortable in the knowledge this boy likely thought he'd hurt Kara.

His eyes widened when Fred said, "I told them you'd be the last person on earth to hurt her. I've seen you around her. You treat her like she's a piece of crystal. I guess they have to cover their bases, though. Let's get this over with." Fred reached over and slapped Nate on the back in a gesture of solidarity.

The questioning lasted fifteen minutes. Many questions *were* about Josh. The police knew more about him than Nate guessed. He was relieved Josh was in hiding. Luckily, they believed the story he'd kicked Josh out after their altercation.

"Leave directions to the cabin, so we can check if he came back without you knowing it," the officers insisted. Nate gave them detailed directions, knowing it meant he'd have to relocate. He couldn't afford to have the police show up at an inopportune moment.

As they left the jail, Fred offered Nate a ride to the hospital. More than an offer for a ride—it was a gesture of friendship. Fred talked about his date with Kara. He listed Kara's questions while watching Nate's face intently. "I figure it's only fair for you to know what questions she has. She's a real special girl and neither of us want her hurt."

"You're right about that. Thanks for telling me. She told me she wanted space while she figured things out. I guess she used you as a sounding board. I'll have to address her questions when she's ready." Nate sighed. "I want to be the man she wants me to be, but I don't know if I can. I'll let her go before I hurt her more than she's been hurt. I couldn't stand that." Fred nodded in silent understanding.

Word spread via the small town grapevine Kara was in the hospital. Her room was filled with visitors when a nurse bustled in.

Arms akimbo, she said, "No more than two visitors in the room. The rest of you have to wait until her parents leave. Remember, two at a time. Don't stay more than fifteen minutes. Kara's parents can stay as long as they wish."

With disgruntled expressions, the crowd of visitors filed out to the waiting room. In the spirit of cooperation, the group decided they'd go in the order in which they'd arrived. Lois and Linda arrived at the same time as Bob and Joyce. The twins won a coin toss, so they carried in the bouquet of flowers from the group. Their usual vivacious selves, they cheered Kara up in spite of her pain.

One-half of the second group was not as welcome. Bob and Joyce entered next. Bob was welcome.

"Wow, Kara, you don't look so hot. Are you sure you're up to this?" Bob asked, uncertain about staying the time limit.

"I'm okay. I'll take a nap after everyone leaves anyway. It is good to see you."

"Gee, Kara, your boyfriend really did a job on you, didn't he?" Joyce smirked, but before she could respond, Bob had Joyce by the elbow shoving her out the door.

"Sorry, Kara, get well soon," he said over his shoulder as he pushed the struggling girl from the room. Kara heard his angry voice, "What the heck is the matter with you? Can't you be polite—just plain decent?"

"The police questioned him, so they must think he did it."

"Yeah, well they questioned Fred, too. Maybe they think both ..." Bob's angry voice faded away as they walked down the hall.

She sighed, her eyes closed against her pounding head. Apparently, Joyce *didn't* know how to act decent. She was thankful Bob came to her defense so rapidly. Hearing the sound of movement, she opened her eyes. Fred and Nate stood at the foot of the bed.

"Do you want to sleep?" Fred asked. "We can come back this evening." Both looked mildly annoyed; probably at Joyce.

She smiled and reached her hands out to them. "You're the two I want to see."

I'm sorry, Kara. I should have made sure you were safe inside. This is all my fault," Fred moaned.

"Don't be silly. I wanted to stay out and look at the stars."

"You got your wish, but I doubt they were the stars you meant!" Fred's silly joke made her smile, even if the memory hurt. He tried to make her feel better. She squeezed his hand in acknowledgement.

"Look, I'm going to leave you and this big galoot alone. Get better soon." Fred bent to place a kiss on her bruised forehead, then slapped Nate on the shoulder. As he left the room, he closed the door behind him.

"He's a decent guy. I like him." Nate stared at the closed door and turned to face her. He reached out and gently caressed her bruised jaw. "Josh is gone. He won't be back unless I let him. You don't have to worry about him hurting you again. It never should have happened in the first place. I am so sorry."

"I know what it must have cost to force your brother away. I'm sorry."

He frowned and toed the floor. "Fred told me you had questions for me. If it's okay with you, I'd like to hold them until tonight—after everyone is gone. You look like you should sleep anyway." He saw the tears pool in her eyes so he bent to kiss her. He kissed each tear-filled eye then the tip of her nose.

"Please don't cry, Kara," he whispered. "No matter what, things will be all right." His lips brushed her mouth with a tender kiss. He sighed as he straightened. "We'll talk after everyone is gone," he repeated. "Oh, Kara, I may bring a surprise guest." Nate gave a sly smile and a wink, and then turned to leave the room. She heard him tell a passing nurse she wished to sleep and hoped no one would disturb her.

Chapter 8

After he left the hospital, Nate wandered aimlessly. He didn't want to go to the cabin and take the chance of running into the police as they searched for Josh. No one was home at the Carson's house. He didn't know what he could say to Pete and Joann, anyway.

He wandered up to his fishing hole, not to fish, but to sit and think. Fred told him Kara's questions. She'd kept her promise not to tell what he was. So she must have questions she didn't ask Fred—questions about being a vampire.

She wanted him to attend church with her. He knew that, but why couldn't she understand? God hated him. God would never want him to defile his holy place. She was right when she called him a murderer. Nothing could change that fact. God would never forgive him for all the deaths, especially the deaths of the innocents, Grace, her mother, and the precious baby—all the children in the Hooverville. Why would God forgive him when he couldn't forgive himself? He thought about the family and the tiny baby on lonely nights and how young the girl was. The baby who reached out only wanting to be held. It caused him endless grief. He lay all day on the bank of the pond, stared into the slowly darkening sky. It held no answers.

Realizing his need to hunt, he trailed a coyote through the brush. Yes, he'd killed in the past, but he could stop killing humans today. It wouldn't make up for the past, but it was something. He could easily keep a promise to drink only animal blood. He'd done it in the past. He could do it again. He'd do it for Kara.

He waited until the hospital night shift came on duty before he made his way to the Carson's house. "Fosdick?" he whispered. He heard

76

a thud and a meow by a nearby tree. A pair of golden eyes looked up at him.

"Do you want to go see Kara?" The cat let out a soft yowl and walked directly to him. He bent and picked up the cat.

"You're quite the kitty, aren't you? I swear you know exactly what I say. I'll bet that's why Kara loves you so much. I've heard her talk to you. You listen, don't you?" He whispered to the cat all the way to the hospital. "Remember, we have to be quiet here so they don't throw us out."

He ghosted down the empty hallway to Kara's room, opened the door enough to slip inside with the cat cradled in his arms. He didn't say a word. On silent feet he moved to the bed and set the cat on it. Fosdick padded his way to the pillow next to Kara's head. Kneading the pillow, he began to purr. Kara's eyes blinked, opened wide as she whispered, "Fosdick, how on earth did you get here?" She hugged the cat close.

"I told you I might bring a surprise guest." Nate grinned down at her joy at the sight of her beloved feline friend. "I thought you might want him here. He might make tonight a little easier—for both of us."

"Thank you, thank you so much." She reached for his hand and squeezed it. How sweet to bring Fosdick, who brought her such comfort.

"We might as well get the questions out in the open." He pulled a chair close to the bed so their voices wouldn't be heard in the hallway. "Fire away."

"You told me you wanted me with you forever. How does it happen? I mean, you ... said you were s ... sort of de ... dead." She stumbled over the words. "Wouldn't it mean I'd have to be dead too?"

Nate's head snapped to attention like he'd been slapped. "I guess it would. I, uh, I just never thought about that part."

"Isn't it kind of important ... my being dead? Did you think what it might do to my parents?"

"Umm, I ... a ... no, I didn't. I didn't think about them at all. All I thought was I wanted you with me." He ran his hands through his hair. "I guess it's selfish on my part. I need to think more about this."

She stared at him wordlessly for a moment. With a hesitant sigh, she continued. "Okay, what about church? Why won't you go with me?'

"I thought it would be obvious once you knew what I am. You *know* I am selfish. You *know* I am a murderer. God wants me to burn in hell. He doesn't want me to defile a holy place like your church. If he had any love for me, he would have let me drown in the flood when my parents died. He didn't. I've ended up distancing myself from all that is holy by my very existence, Kara." He bowed his head in misery.

"No, Nate. You're wrong. God loves us all. Yes, you're a sinner, but so am I. So is every other person on this earth. It's not about the sin—it's about God's forgiveness. He's waiting for you to ask for forgiveness. His arms are open; waiting. But it's up to us. He'd never force us. He offers it as a gift."

"I don't know, Kara; it sounds too easy. I mean, it's one thing to forgive a little lie, or something small, but multiple murders? I don't believe it's possible. Do you have more questions? I need more time to process this." He began to pace the room. He repeated, "Any more questions?"

"No, those were my main questions. Remember you're a sentient being, even if you are a vampire. God would forgive you if you asked him." She patted the bed next to her. "Come up here with Fosdick and me." She opened her arms to comfort him. They lay side by side without speaking. Neither of them had words left to say. Fosdick moved between them. His purr soothed them both.

Nate and Fosdick were forced to hide every time the night nurse came to check on Kara. They crawled in bed beside her afterwards. Kara fell into an uneasy sleep. Nate couldn't bring himself to leave her side until the sky began to lighten.

"Come on, old son. Let's get out of here and get you home." Fosdick reached one paw up, placed it on Nate's cheek. "Thanks, buddy, I like you too. I'll bring you back tonight. Remember to stay outside."

When Nate picked up the cat, he curled into Nate's neck. Nate smiled at the big orange feline. "I'm glad we're friends. I never had a cat for a friend before. In fact, you and Don José are the only animals who let me pet them since I was changed." They ghosted outside into the brightening day.

Nate loved this time of day. The stars and moon were visible, but the edge of the sky showed a rosy glow, announcing the sun's arrival. It's peace and beauty calmed his anxiety.

⁓○

Kara awoke to a tender, but no longer painful head. She hadn't lost the overwhelming desire to shut her eyes to sound and light, though. As she stretched out to check her other injuries, she noticed a clump of cat fur on the bed. It wasn't a dream; Nate had brought Fosdick. They had discussed her questions. She grinned thinking how Nate sneaked Fosdick in to the hospital. It was a good idea.

He was thoughtful, but it didn't change the fact she had to make serious decisions about their relationship. The thought of her choices brought tears to her eyes. *Who would she hurt when she chose? Her parents would be devastated if she disappeared. Nate? She didn't want to think about his pain either.*

The wheels of the food trolley squeaked up the hallway. Curious, she wondered if they'd bring Jell-O and broth again or a tasteless bowl of farina. She didn't care; she was hungry. She needed food to think... to make those difficult decisions.

She guessed right about the farina. This morning it came with tea and toast. After she'd eaten the nurse returned to remove the tray and chart the food consumed. Kara asked, "Can I take a shower this morning?"

"Sure honey. Lean on me until I help you in the shower. There's a seat, so use it. I don't want you to fall if you have a dizzy spell. Push this button when you're finished or if you need me." She pointed to an emergency call button. She left her to shower on her own.

The hot water felt good on her stiff body. It soaked away the soreness from the bruises and helped clear her foggy brain. Glad of the seat since her legs were shaky. She'd need help to get back to the room. The nurse returned when she was barely dry, with a towel wrapped around her hair. The nurse helped into a clean gown and took her back to bed. A second dry towel was brought to help dry her hair.

As the nurse turned to leave, Kara asked, "Is there some way you can restrict visitors for the morning?"

"Why sure, honey. Too many yesterday?" Without waiting for a response, she asked, "Who do you want on the list?"

"Just my mom and dad. I want to rest this morning." She laid her head on the pillow, surprised how good it felt to lie down.

"Done and done," the nursed said with a conspiratorial grin. "Just let someone try to get past me." Kara smiled as she thought of the staff personnel Nate had sneaked past last night, unseen, while he carried her cat.

She called home to ask, "Mom, could you look in my top right-hand dresser drawer? See if my New Testament is there." The small copy she'd received from the Gideon's a few years ago could easily fit into a pocket. "Would you bring it when you come this morning? There are a few passages I want to read."

"Sure, Kara. I think your dad has plans to sneak some goodies to you."

"Thanks, Mom. I'm starving. The food here is awful, very bland. I miss your cooking."

"We'll be there in a few minutes, so try to hang on for that long," she snickered.

"I'll try. Oh, and Mom, would you bring a pen and paper, too? Just in case I'm inspired to write down any brilliant thoughts I have while I'm doped up," she giggled at her joke.

True to their word, her parents walked through the door ten minutes later. Pen, paper, and New Testament in her mom's hand. A box of donuts tucked under her dad's arm.

"I thought you could force down a couple of these," Dad chuckled jovially.

She smiled and opened the box. At the top lay jelly donuts. Her heart lurched as she remembered the last time she'd eaten them. Was it only two days ago when Nate licked the jelly from her chin? The horrible day he'd revealed himself as a vampire in order to save her life.

Confused by her expression, her dad asked, "Those are your favorites, aren't they?"

"Yeah Dad, they are. Thanks. She grabbed one from the box and took a bite hoping she wouldn't choke. "Have some," she mumbled, her mouth full. She held out the box.

"Don't mind if I do," her dad said. He reached for one.

"Pete, don't forget who those are for," her mom admonished. "I'll bring clothes for your release tomorrow, Kara, so you can dress. I don't expect you'll want to leave in a hospital gown—have it flap in the breeze as you get into the car."

"Agghh! What a pretty picture," she threw her hands in the air, horror written on her face. Her parents stayed a few minutes before they left for work. She set the box of donuts on the bedside table. She couldn't stand to see another jelly donut. The memory conjured too much pain.

In contemplation, she picked up the New Testament and marked a few verses for Nate. She wrote a note for him, listing the specific verses she marked for him to read. The verses were important to understand the concept of forgiveness. She accepted it was highly unlikely she'd be the one to help him understand the message. She folded the paper to fit inside the small book and set it on the table next to the donuts.

Grabbing another sheet of paper, she tried to compile her thoughts. She wanted them in a logical order. It was hard. Not only was she going to break off their relationship, she would break both their hearts. She wanted to be clear, firm and kind. If she had to hurt him, she didn't want to prolong the pain.

Setting the pen aside at another thought, she wondered if she could follow through with it. The longer she thought about it, the more she intended to follow through. Her intentions was wrong, but she didn't care. There were bound to be consequences for her actions. Whatever they were, she'd face them head-on. Besides, who would it hurt other than her? No one else would ever find out. She determined to do it.

By the time she finished, the lunch trolley was rolling down the hall. She longed for real food. An orderly brought in the tray and removed the lid. A hamburger lay on the plate along with tiny tubes of mayonnaise and ketchup. A wilted leaf of lettuce and a pickle wedge laid next to the burger. It was food! The side dishes included mystery vegetable—a green mush of something—and orange Jell-O. The hospital must have gotten a bargain on orange Jell-O since it accompanied everything but breakfast.

After she finished lunch, she read over what she planned to say to Nate. She tried to come up with additional verses to add to the other list, but came up empty. She was too focused on her plan. She prayed God would forgive her—though she'd never be sorry.

Trying to catch a nap before the influx of visitors, she laid her head on the pillow. Yet every time she closed her eyes, she'd see Nate; his sideways glance as he looked from under the sweep of lashes with his half grin. She'd watch his beautiful face change to one of deep sadness. She tossed restlessly before falling into an uneasy sleep.

She and Nate and lay in the grass by a mountain stream, her head resting on his shoulder. Though sunlight sparkled the water, black storm cloud rolled over the horizon, coming ever nearer. The high winds of the approaching storm frightened her, whipping her hair in every direction. She turned to bury her face in Nate's chest; seeking solace in his arms. When she turned there was nothing in her arms but his empty jacket. Nate was gone and she was alone as the storm raged. With a cry, she woke up.

All of her friends—with two exceptions, Nate and Joyce—showed up during visiting hours. Of course, Joyce wasn't a friend. It was a relief not to have her there. She didn't feel up to fielding her snippy remarks. *Where was Nate?*

When Bob and Geoff came in they fell on the donuts like starved dogs. Lois and Linda each accepted one donut and daintily shared it, while the two boys tried to stuff whole donuts into their mouths in a bizarre eating contest. It must be a guy thing.

Fred trailed in after the others. He brought flowers and a box of chocolates. With a warm smile, he handed the gifts to her.

"Chocolates!" came a dual shout from Bob and Geoff.

"These are for Kara. Keep your big mitts off them!" Forming a cross with his index fingers, he ordered the boys away from the chocolate, grimacing in a threatening manner.

"Ooo...we're scared," Geoff said mockingly.

"Bring it on." Bob squared off, hands raised like a boxer.

A nurse walked through the door scowling. "May I remind you patients are trying to rest? I suggest you settle down or leave." She crossed her arms waiting for a response.

"Sorry, we'll behave," Bob and Geoff said in unison.

"See that you do," she said firmly as she turned and marched out the door.

They grinned at her retreating back. Bob gave a mock salute, but they settled down.

By the time the group left, she was exhausted. The visit took a lot out of her. She closed her eyes and napped until the dinner tray arrived. This time she wasn't hungry. The chicken and potatoes weren't like her moms. The corn was a soupy mess. She couldn't face the thought of orange Jell-O again. She took a few bites of the chicken and pushed the tray away.

Why hadn't Nate come? Was he so upset over her questions he wouldn't face her? Maybe he was mad and she'd never see him again. It was stupid to worry she might not get her good-bye. It didn't make sense to feel that way. She planned to tell him to leave anyway. But she knew why she wanted him to come. She wanted him to know much she loved him, in spite of the fact they couldn't be together. She prayed her action would give them closure.

Her parents popped in for a minute—to drop off the clothes she'd wear home. Exhausted from lack of sleep and worry, they were behind in chores.

"I wish I could have spared you all the worry."

Mom waved the words away. "You'll be home tomorrow. What are you hungry for? I'll fix something special for dinner," she promised. "Do you want to invite Nate for dinner?"

"I'm not sure he can make it. I'll let you know later if he can come." Her face a mask, she ached at the question and her inability to give an answer.

Dad pinched her toe as he quipped, "Okay, sweetheart. Good night, sleep tight, and don't let the bedbugs bite." Her face frozen, she forced a smile at the familiar joke he'd used since she was child.

As soon as they were out the door, she released the tears. She didn't sob; they poured silently down her face. Was possible to become dehydrated from crying? If so, she was heading that way. The tears continued until she'd cried herself to sleep.

"Kara," a voice whispered. "Kara, wake up." Nate had come with Fosdick along. Before she could speak, his fingers touched her mouth.

"Please let me talk first. I don't know if I can get through this otherwise." She nodded. "Your questions made me think," he began, pacing back and forth next to the bed. Both hands combed through his hair.

"They made me question my own motives. See, I decided the other day I didn't want you to think of me as a murderer, even if I'd been one in the past. I decided I'd never kill another human. I can easily exist on animal blood. I did it before, so it wouldn't be a major problem. It wouldn't change the past, but you'd know I'm trying to become a better man. Then you asked if I'd have to kill you to change you. I never thought of it like that. I thought of it as a gift, not as taking you from people who love you. Suddenly it seemed so wrong, so selfish." He gestured wildly in frustration.

"I don't want to hurt Pete and Joann. They've been nothing but kind to me. They made me feel part of a real family." The pain of this epiphany lined his face. He sighed.

"So, Kara, I've made up my mind. I'm leaving tonight. I have to leave for your sake and for your parents' sake. It would be wrong to take you away from them. I only wanted to see you to explain. I have to leave because I love you so much."

"Nate," she whispered. "Come here." Sliding out of bed she reached for the buttons on his shirt. His eyes widened as she pulled him to her. "You're right, Nate," she whispered, her mouth on his. "We have to say good-bye before we hurt my family or each other even more. Before we do, I want you to understand how much I love you and how hard it is to say good-bye." She pulled him to the bed as she slipped her shoulders free of the loose gown. It fell to the floor.

Nate choked and tried to step back. "No, Kara. Are you sure? Are you positive you want to do this?"

"I want to make love to you. Since we can't stay together, I want every possible memory of us—together. I don't care if it's right or wrong." She whispered, as she stroked the smooth skin of his bare chest.

"You can change your mind." He tried to pull away. Her answer was to reach and pull him closer.

His only response was a slight moan as they came together.

Afterward they lay together, not talking. Wrapped in a tangle of arms and legs, he watched over Kara as she slept. He brushed her face with his fingertips; traced the outline of her eyes, her lips. He stroked her silken hair; memorized her every feature.

He had to leave now, while he had the courage. It killed him to say good-bye. It was harder after making love. He couldn't believe she gave herself so willingly, twice, knowing what he was. Her trust touched him deep in his heart. She'd always be a part of him, because he traded a piece of Kara's heart for the one he'd leave with her. He felt an invisible bond that tied him to her. He knew without a doubt he would love her throughout eternity.

Taking care not to jostle the bed, he untangled himself from Kara and stood to dress. As he did, he knocked a small book off the stand. A note addressed to him tumbled out. Apparently, it was something Kara wanted him to have. He didn't take time to read the note or the book title. Whatever it was, it was from her. He shoved the book in his pocket. He'd read it when he had more time. Fosdick padded over and jumped nimbly to the bed. "Do you want to stay with her the rest of the night, old son? Okay. The staff is going to wonder how you got here come morning."

Nate smiled sadly and scratched the cat's head while Fosdick began his deepest purr. Nate drew a deep breath and put a hand over his eyes. The cat gave a quiet meow. "I know, buddy. I'll be okay. Take care of Kara," he spoke huskily. "See ya." He paused. "Sweet dreams, Kara." Nate blew a kiss, turned and slipped out the door.

Chapter 9

Shortly after dawn, she stirred, and woke with a smile. She reached for Nate, but only felt the warm fur of her cat. Her eyes flew open and darted around the room. True to his word, Nate was gone. Her world shattered. They'd made the right decision for everyone's sake, but the reality left her in agony.

Her chin trembled, as she forced herself out of bed. Blinded by tears, she grabbed the clothes she'd wear home and stumbled to the shower. Fosdick lay curled on the bed his eyes peeking from under the blanket. "You stay here until I get back," she whispered.

She trusted the shower would wash away all signs pain and their love. She'd live with their decision; be as courageous as Nate who left for her protection. Whatever the future brought she'd face it, her head held high.

The food trolley arrived seconds after she returned to her room. Fosdick remained in hiding, buried beneath the blanket, when her tray was delivered. She sat in the chair and pulled the tray table close. The New Testament and note were missing from the table. Though she'd forgotten them, Nate found and took them. She offered a prayer in the hope he would understand forgiveness without her help.

Not hungry, she broke the bacon into bite-sized pieces and fed them to Fosdick. Bacon was his favorite treat. He rewarded her by head butting her hand, then meowed his thanks before attending to his morning ablutions.

Arriving on the run to pick her up, her parents looked harried. After a quick hug, her dad rushed to the business office to pay the deductible on the insurance. As her mom gathered her things, she gave a sudden start. "How in the name of all that's holy, did Fosdick get here?"

"Gee, Mom, I don't know. He was asleep on the bed when I woke," she said guilelessly. "You don't suppose he tracked me here, do you?"

Her mother looked suspicious, "Kara Marie Carson, are you sure you didn't ask one of your friends to bring him here? It's against hospital regulations."

"Honest, Mom, I didn't ask anyone to bring him." It was true. She hadn't asked Nate. He brought the cat knowing Fosdick would be a calming influence. Nate knew what she needed—well almost always. She blushed, picturing his shocked face last night when she pulled him to her bed. She turned away from her mother under the guise of searching for something.

"Can we hide him when we leave?" Without warning, Kara giggled. Her giggle bordered on hysteria, which she barely managed to control. Her mom assumed she giggled over the cat.

"Maybe you can pretend he's a stuffed toy. Can you keep him still enough?" Her mother's face threatened to break into a grin.

The door slammed open as her dad raced into the room. "You're free to go as soon as the nurse brings a wheelchair."

"I don't need a wheelchair. I'm not an invalid," she protested. "Let's go!"

"No, you're not an invalid," Dad agreed. "But it's hospital regulations."

She spotted the paper bag which held the clothes she'd worn when Nate brought her here. She grabbed a dirty shirt and swaddled Fosdick like a baby. Her dad's mouth dropped open when he saw the cat. He sputtered as the nurse backed into the room with the wheelchair. His jaw snapped shut as he stared at his wife and daughter, both in on the deception.

"Thanks for everything," Kara said as she got into the wheelchair. The nurse smiled as she pushed her toward the lobby. If she noticed the cat, she didn't mention it.

Safely escaping detection, her mom said, "I hope you don't mind if we leave after getting you settled." Not waiting for a response, she continued, "We're running behind at work and I want to shop for a special dinner. Which reminds me, is Nate coming for dinner?"

She turned away. "No, Mom, we broke up. I won't see him anymore." She choked the words out. "Before you ask anything, I don't want to talk about it. I'll probably sleep this afternoon, so it's okay if you're not home."

Her parents stared at her, then at each other. "Whatever you say, sweetie." This was dangerous territory to explore.

Once inside, she fed Fosdick. All he'd eaten was the bacon from the tray at the hospital. While the cat ate she played with Don José. Donnie was supposed to be her mother's dog, but he plainly favored dad. What made it funny was Dad claimed to dislike little dogs. He never noticed Don José's small stature. She guessed he thought of him as a large dog trapped in a small dog's body.

When she tired of playing with the dog she wandered into her bedroom. No, nothing changed there; nothing changed anywhere she looked. If everything was the same, why did her world feel destroyed? Tears trickled down as the phone range. She snuffled a "hello" and heard Fred's cheerful voice.

"Hey Kara, do you feel like company? I thought if you did, I'd bring lunch. Would it be okay?"

"Thanks, Fred, I could use a little cheering up."

"Are you hungry for anything special? Burger, pizza, steak tartar?"

She chuckled at his joke. "Surprise me—but not with steak tartar."

Fred was the one person she was willing to see. He always sensed when to talk and when to be silent. He was comfortable. It was one thing Nate never was—truly comfortable. Nate was ... well, Nate. She wanted to impress him. Fred was a pair of comfy old slippers. She didn't have to be perfect for him. She wondered if he'd be insulted at the analogy. Probably, but she liked it.

He brought hamburgers, onion rings, and milkshakes. Hungry, they ate immediately. Besides burgers, he brought news of his induction date. He'd leave for basic training in two weeks. Two weeks after he left, she'd leave for Flagstaff.

"I'll miss you," she said robotically, and then realized she *would* miss Fred. She'd miss him because he *did* make her comfortable. He made her feel good. He was her very best friend, especially since Brig was in Phoenix and was a terrible letter writer. She'd only written once this summer.

"I'll send you my address as soon as I can. That way you can tell me all about college life and I can complain about my lack of sleep!" He grinned at her.

She reached over and hugged Fred. "I really will miss you," she said, "You're probably my best friend now."

He looked at his lap. "Thanks Kara; it means a lot. Right now things are awkward at home. I need a friend I can talk to. The guys don't want to hear my problems, so I guess you're elected."

She pulled herself out of self-pity to stare directly at him. "What's going on?"

"Isn't that supposed to be my line?" was his self-mocking reply.

She paused and then said, "Maybe we can share our problems since we both have them."

"Okay. Here's the deal, Mom's dating a loser. The guy drinks too much, eats all our food, and orders Mom around while he sits on his backside. I don't think he works. The worst of it is she's talking about moving in with him. Is she desperate for a man? He sure as heck isn't going to take care of her. She'll end up supporting him. It's disgusting."

Since she had no idea what to say, she squeezed his hand in sympathy and agreed the situation made it hard for him to leave his mom.

"Now it's your turn. What's going on?" He took her hand and gazed steadily into her eyes. He waited in silence.

Her mouth opened then closed. After a couple of minutes, she worked up her courage and took a deep breath. "Nate's gone. We broke up. It was a mutual decision and now he's left town for good." She sobbed out the last few words. Fred didn't say a word; he put his arm around her, held her while she cried. "I don't know why I'm crying. I'm the one who started it all. Even though we're so mismatched, I love him. Isn't that stupid?"

"No, it's not. You don't just stop loving someone, Kara. It's not a switch you flip on and off. I promise, things will get better. Give yourself time to heal." He turned her to face him, her cheeks between his hands. He gazed deeply into her eyes. "You're going to love and be loved again. Whoever the lucky guy is, he'll be the perfect match for you."

They sat in companionable silence for a while when she leapt to her feet. "Can you stay for dinner? Mom said I could ask someone." She spoke in such a rush of words they were hard to understand.

When he understood, he said, "Yeah, thanks. It would be great for several reasons. First, I get to spend more time with you. Then, my mom is not the best cook in the world, so I won't have to eat her crappy cooking and pretend I like it. Last, I won't have to see the major loser tonight. Can't get better than that."

Yeah, and I won't have to think about Nate or to talk to my parents about why we broke up. Can't get better than that.

If her parents were curious over Nate's absence—why they'd broken up, they didn't ask. They must have wondered why Fred was there. She saw their surreptitious glances, but they were polite enough not to mention it—at least in front of Fred.

Throughout dinner and during the cleanup Fred kept up a steady line of chatter. He praised mom's cooking—which was good. He questioned Dad about the hardware store and asked how it was doing. He threw enough comments her way to make it seem she was a part of the conversation, though it was difficult to keep her mind on what was said.

The last dish dried, he turned her way. "Wow, Kara, you look tired. I've probably overstayed my welcome. He turned to her parents. "Thanks so much for having me over. I've enjoyed visiting with you all. Kara, walk me to the door?"

"Bless you for being a saint," she whispered. "You did a perfect job of keeping them busy."

"That's me, Saint Fred." He snorted. "When I leave, call out you're really tired. Go straight to bed." He spoke in an undertone so Mom and Dad wouldn't hear him.

She gave him a bear hug. "What a great idea. You've thought of everything. See you soon, Fred!"

As soon as the door closed she called, "I'm really tired. I think I'll go straight to bed." She yawned loudly and hoped they wouldn't follow. She'd talk to Fosdick—tell him it hurt to separate from Nate, even though he'd borne witness to both their conversation and love. She'd tell Fosdick how much she appreciated Fred's support today. She'd ask the cat how she was going to make it through the coming days.

After that Fred came over daily. Some days he came for a few minutes, others he stayed hours. Always solicitous, he'd ask if he could bring anything. One night he brought pizza for dinner.

While her mom made the salad, she and Fred sat together on the couch. "I leave for boot camp in two days. I'm not sure if I'll have time to see you tomorrow, so I wanted to say good-bye tonight."

She immediately felt guilty. Focused on her own problems she forgot he'd leave so soon. "Oh, Fred," she moaned, "I'm going to miss you so much. What am I going to do without Saint Fred?"

"I am no saint, Kara." His voice was low and husky. He grabbed her and gave her a hard kiss. He pulled away, looking as shocked as she felt. "I'm sorry, Kara. I don't know what got in to me." He gasped and stood. "Look, I'll send my mailing address as soon as I can. I hope you're willing to write."

"Of course I'll write," she whispered blinking back tears, not knowing what to think. "I won't forget. You're too important to me."

He smiled wryly. "I wish that was true." Fred turned and walked out the door without looking back and without eating any of the pizza.

After he left, all she could think about was Fred. He was nice-looking, but not amazingly handsome like Nate. He was almost as tall but skinny as a rail. He did have nice eyes. They were a kind of medium brown with dark lashes as long as Nate's. All in all, a very nice-looking guy. If she'd met him first, and if he wasn't playing the fool, he could have easily become her boyfriend.

As it was, in the brief time they'd been together, she liked him a lot—much more than she expected. She'd looked forward to his letter.

The next two weeks were filled with work and making lists of what she absolutely had to take to college. As soon as she finished one list, she'd scratch off items and add others. Finally, she settled into packing the bare essentials. As the last day approached, Mom came into the bedroom, mail in her hands. "Looks like you got a letter today."

Snatching it from her hands, Kara tore it open. Even knowing it was from Fred, a small part of her hoped it was from Nate. But Fred's letter was sweet.

> *Dear Kara,*
>
> *This will have to be short because the sergeant just announced another march with full gear in fifteen minutes. I used to think I was in good shape, but, man, am I worn out!*
>
> *We're up before dawn and on the go until eight at night with lights out at nine. It was hard to sleep the first couple of days in the barracks, but now I think can sleep on my feet.*
>
> *Use the return address on the envelope—and write soon. Do you have a picture you could send me?*
>
> *Your friend,*
Fred

She immediately dashed off a note to send back:

> *Dear Fred,*
>
> *Your letter came the day before I leave for college, so I'm also dropping a very short note. I promise a longer one after I arrive on campus.*
>
> *I'll try to give you a description of my room and the campus. If I can find a picture postcard of my dorm, I'll*

send it. I'll look for a picture of myself to send, too. How about one of you? I'd really like one of you, too.

I hate packing! I hate trying to make decisions. I'll be glad to be done with it.

My bruises have faded, so they're barely visible. My head is back to normal—whatever normal is. Ha, ha.

Get as much rest as you can!

Love ya,
Kara

"Mom, can we run this to the Post Office before the final pick up? Don't want Fred to think I forgot him."

"Sure honey. Speaking of Fred, I heard his mother quit her job. She's leaving town with a man she met recently."

"Oh no! Fred was afraid of that. Did you ever meet her? He never said as much, but she sounds unstable from what he did say. He's afraid the guy is a loser and is only interested in having his mom support him. I feel bad for Fred."

"It's probably best to avoid gossip about someone I barely know." When mom hedged her answer in a particular way, it gave a good clue about Mrs. Jacobs.

Chapter 10

The next morning, she hugged Fosdick, and whispered she'd miss him—miss his purred lullaby. Anxious, he danced at her feet, understanding something odd was happening and it concerned her. The cat continued to wend between her ankles while she packed last-minute items.

Joann had breakfast on the table when she went into the kitchen. Her voice was super cheery and dad's was falsely hearty. An indication they would miss her. She fed Fosdick and Don José giving them extra pats and hugs before eating.

Her parents kept up a steady stream of conversation—how much fun college would be and what a great experience it was. She knew that and she *was* excited. But, she'd never been away from home longer than the week she'd gone to camp. Sure, she stayed overnight with friends on occasional weekends. Twice, she stayed an entire week with long-time friends who invited her to their cabin in Lakeside. But she'd never *moved* away. Her eyes and nose got all prickly as she explored her feelings. She decided to stop that particular exploration before she cried. As for Nate, she blocked all thought of him.

After breakfast, they shoved the dirty dishes in the dishwasher. While Dad loaded her suitcases, footlocker, and boxes into the trunk, she said her final good-byes to her cat and dog. Both wound between her feet. She picked them up, one at a time, hugged them. Don José licked her cheek, while Fosdick voiced anxious mews. Donnie-boy would be okay. He'd miss her, but he had Dad. Fosdick depended on her as much as she depended on him. It would be hard for him while she was gone. She gave him one last hug. "Take care of yourself until I come back," she whispered.

❧

The drive to Strawberry was as familiar as it was beautiful. She'd been this route many times with Nate, but the road beyond was unfamiliar territory. In passing, she'd heard the terrors of driving to the top of this eight thousand foot escarpment. Her cousin, Geoff, agreed with this assessment. It was scary. The climb began as soon as they left the tiny town. The narrow dirt road made numerous switchbacks as it made a constant climb.

She gasped as vehicles came around S-curves dangerously close avoiding the cliff-side of the road. When the first logging truck passed them on its downward run, she held her breath expecting to be side-swiped. The rumble, as it ground into a lower gear as the grade steepened, was the sound of nightmares. She let out a ragged breath when it passed them.

Time seemed to stand still while the car inched it way up. But while their speed was slower than on the pavement, they made good time.

"We're almost to Happy Jack," Dad called over his shoulder.

She straightened in her seat to see what a "happy jack" was. The spot in the road wasn't a town or even a village. What was a couple of buildings at a bit of a crossroad? Was hamlet was the word she searched for? Whatever, the best part was a beautiful meadow where a herd of elks grazed. She'd never seen a live elk, but eyes wide she recognized them. Much larger than deer these stately animals moved away with quiet dignity from staring eyes into the shadowed tree line. "Wow, Dad," Kara breathed, "those were elk weren't they?" Her mouth hung open at the sight of the elk

"Yes, indeed. What did you think of them?" His eyes crinkled in the rearview mirror.

"Wow!" She was speechless. Overwhelmed by this magnificent herd; she failed to notice a left turn at the crossroad that returned the road to pavement; the worst was over. Little of the remaining trip registered until she saw the "Welcome to Flagstaff" sign. They'd arrived at her new home—for the school year.

A packet, which arrived three weeks earlier, gave dorm information and a freshman week schedule. Her parents knew exactly where to go. They helped unload her stuff and carried it to her room—a single—which was shockingly small if adequate. They hung clothes and put folded items in a small chest of drawers. Since it was required she attend an assembly, her parents hugged her and left her on the steps of the dorm.

She didn't have time to do anything except find the building where the auditorium was located. The assembly was for freshman and transfer students, so it was at full capacity. It turned out to be fun as well as informational. They sang a silly indoctrination song—totally ridiculous and a great icebreaker. She received her freshman beanie and a houseplant as a gift from one of the organizations.

When she got back to the dorm, announcements were posted stating the location where students could pick up bed sheets and meal tickets. It was in the main lobby. After nine there'd be an all-dorm meeting to discuss specific rules they'd need to follow.

She carried her sheets back to the room and made the bed. The room was marginally homey with the addition of the electric blanket and pretty blue bedspread. But it wasn't home.

A girl with an infectious laugh, her next-door neighbor, introduced herself as Jillian. She stuck her head in the door. "A bunch of us are going downtown to find things to personalize our rooms," she announced. "Wouldn't it be nice if we can make them look more like dorm rooms and less like a prison? Would you like to come, too?"

Glad to go if for no other reason than to get acquainted with her dorm-mates, she eagerly agreed. She bought a brightly colored rug—striped in shades of blue and a bright blue ceramic planter for her new plant. Both would complement the bedspread and would add a tiny bit of personality to the drab little room. She'd pick up more stuff as there was time.

By the time they returned to the dorm and put their packages away, it was time for dinner. The dining hall was across the street from the dorm, so they didn't have to consult the map.

The cacophony of sound and the size of the cafeteria overwhelmed her. Food was abundantly displayed and offered unnecessary choices. The desserts alone, offered temptation beyond her resistance. With an instinctual perception she understood the expression "the freshman fifteen". After stuffing herself she knew she headed toward the extra fifteen pounds. She'd have to be careful.

The girls at her end of the hall were an affable bunch; they knit together as a team from the beginning. They established an open-door policy—if a door was open, any one of them could walk in. If the door was closed, they'd knock and wait for admittance.

When time came for the dorm meeting, the six girls trooped down in joyous abandon. They learned the dorm rules: specifically those about men in the hall. Campbell Hall was, of course, an all-girls dorm. A man with permission to help with a heavy load announced his presence by calling out, "Man in the Hall." If one had a date, the young man presented himself to the front desk and the girl on duty would call their date.

The doors were locked promptly at ten p.m. during the week and midnight on weekends. They were required to be within those locked doors on time or face being "campused," the euphemism for being grounded. After the meeting concluded, they giggled a path back to Lower Morton Hall, their wing of Campbell Hall.

Scheduled for a seven-thirty biology class, she said goodnight to her new friends and went to her room. She put on her pajamas and brushed her teeth in the tiny sink in the room. As she crawled between the sheets, she remembered her promised letter for Fred. Too late to write much, but she began a letter and would finish it between classes tomorrow.

Dear Fred,

The drive over the Rim was terrifying. I'm glad I don't have to go over it often. I did see a herd of elk, though, and they were amazing, so dignified and graceful.

The campus is beautiful. I live in one of the oldest building here—Campbell Hall (my room is in Morton Hall; a wing of Campbell). It is made of a beautiful red stone. I've heard rumors it used to be a mental hospital. There is supposed to be a cell in the basement, but I haven't seen it yet.

We had a busy day today and I just finished a dorm meeting. I was getting ready for bed when I remembered I promised to write today.

I have a 7:30 class, so I have to be up and out early. I'll finish this tomorrow. Sorry. I am just so tired. I feel badly even complaining to you. My tired is nothing compared to yours. Anyway, more tomorrow!

She turned out the light and crawled into bed, but her restless eyes stare into the darkness. The two-inch gap under the door cast light across the floor and sound invaded the room. The hall lights—at least some of them—stay on all night. The whispered voices and laughter coming from other rooms emphasized the cave-like solitude of her room. She smothered in loneliness. As she tossed in the strangeness of the bed, she listened for the comforting whispers of her parents, but the voices were not theirs. Where was the warmth of Fosdick's body, cuddling next to her, lulling her to sleep with his soothing purr? Most of all she missed Na— No, she rebuffed all thoughts of him. He was the past. She'd focus her thoughts on today and tomorrow. After a restless hour, she shivered over to set the alarm, deliberately set across the room to force her from the womb-like comfort of bed. Slipping between the cooling sheets, she fell into an agitated sleep.

The jangle of the alarm jerked her from the bed as the shock of the cold floor jarred her awake. Grumpily grabbing a towel and a bar of soap, she slumped down the hall toward the showers. Most people were still asleep in this early morning half-light.

After a quick shower, she dressed, found her biology book, and ran across the street. None of her new friends had early classes so she entered the cavernous dining hall alone. She left her book on a nearby table, picked up a tray, and selected a glass of orange juice and milk. Deciding on bacon, eggs and a muffin, she made her way to the table.

"Hey, pretty lady, is this seat taken?"

Perplexed, she stared at the guy talking. The rest of the table was noticeably empty except for the boy halfway down the table. From the enormous size of his biceps and the girth of his torso she guessed the guy before her was a jock—maybe a guard.

"Ah ... no; it's available." The rest of the table was noticeably empty except for a boy halfway down studiously studying his bowl of oatmeal. A choking sound came from the oatmeal guy as he tried and failed not to laugh at her dismay.

The egotistical jock flexed. "I just hate to see a pretty little lady by herself, so I figured you'd like some company."

Barf. He needs a better pick-up line. His arrogant attitude turned her stomach. *God's gift to women, no doubt.*

"Thoughtful. But I'd like a little quiet right now." She tried to blow him off as politely as possible.

"Well, sure, honey. How about I meet you later and we can have a little fun."

Honey? He called me Honey? What kind of a narcissistic jerk would call a strange girl 'honey'?

Bile rose in her throat, as she answered, "Find a mirror. You'd be happier with your own image. I need to go to class." Unable to swallow the half-eaten food, she dumped it in the garbage. He gave a one-fingered salute as she walked past.

Halfway to her class someone yelled, "Hey, you dropped this, funny girl." Behind her trotted the oatmeal guy. He grinned impishly and handed her notebook to her. "I loved it when you took the wind out of the testosterone-loaded jock's sails. Good for you. I'm Jerry."

She smiled back at him. "Thanks for bringing my notebook, Jerry. Where are you off to?"

"Can you believe I got stuck with an early biology class? I'll find out where it's located, but I don't plan on being up this early often." He shrugged his shoulders. "I have to make the old man happy by going some of the time, anyway."

"I got stuck with early biology, too," she grinned. "Maybe we can poke each other to stay awake. My name is Kara."

"Hey, Kara. Your name reminds me of my girl back home. Her name is Carla. Dad wants to separate us. He says he wants me to make something of myself. Funny, I thought I was something," he offered wryly.

"Well, if it means anything, I think you're something, too. I'm not quite sure what it is ...," she joked. She liked this guy's self-deprecating humor.

They found the huge classroom. Her largest class in high school held thirty-two students. This held space for well over a hundred. Jerry and she continued to talk as they found seats together about halfway back. As the seats filled, they shared the Reader's Digest Condensed version of their lives. She described the girls at the dorm. He told her how his dad pushed him to go to college, when all he wanted was be a mechanic and marry Carla. She told him bits about her breakup and how she didn't plan to date anyone seriously.

He offered to bring over a few guys from his dorm before dinner. Everyone could get acquainted. "If anyone wants, we can get a group to go out for coffee or cokes after dinner." This was too good to be true. She told him she'd loved the idea. A few friends of both sexes getting together to have fun—nothing serious.

She had an hours break between classes, so she raced back to the dorm. Two of her hall mates were there: the laughing Jillian, and the quieter April. Both girls liked the idea of meeting the boys later—especially since it would be casual, with no strings attached.

With her remaining few minutes, she added lines to Fred's note. She wanted to mail it today.

Back again! I made it to my early biology class this morning. I made a friend. His name is Jerry and he doesn't want to be here at all. He wants to marry his girl back home—her name is Carla—and be a mechanic. His dad wants him to "be something." I liked what he said then. He said, "I thought I was something."

I made friends with several girls in my hall. First, in the room on the right is Jillian. She is tall and sort of skinny, and has a cloud of blond curly hair. She's fun and always laughing.

Across the hall is Suzy. She is very warm and friendly. She is also a very pretty blond. Next to her is Mary, also warm and friendly.

Across the hall from Mary is Betty, who is more studious than the rest of us—of course, it's early in the year. Last, is April in the room on the left. She is very quiet, thoughtful, dark-haired and pretty. I think she is a lot like you. I can talk without her judging or gossiping behind my back.

I miss talking to you. I'll write more soon.

Love ya,
Kara

She folded the letter and put it in an envelope, then walked over to the student center to buy a stamp and look for postcards of campus. She found one of Campbell Hall taken at an angle, so there was a little bit of Morton, too. She took a pen and drew an arrow at the Morton entrance and wrote, "This is where to find me" on the back. She stuffed it in the envelope and dropped it in the mail slot. It made the pick-up time, which was in less than an hour.

The day raced by with her huffing across campus, the seven thousand foot elevation was killer when she was used to lower elevations. Especially when she was forced to trudge across campus, with every class was on the opposite side of campus from the last. *That may be a hallucination caused by lack of oxygen,* she thought as she hurried across campus.

One classroom offered an excellent view of a prairie dog village. Of course, the windows were placed so high you had to stand to see it. The prairie dogs were such funny little creatures. One would stand tall, to keep watch as the others search for food. It would bark out a warning at any perceived danger. The others scurried into their holes, and then popped out moments later to see if the threat was gone. She'd have to tell Fred about them. He'd enjoy hearing about their funny antics.

She began another note to him that very day—she would make it a friendly journal. She expected to hear back from him soon. She missed him as much as she missed Nate, but in a very different way.

Good to his word, Jerry showed up in front of Morton promptly at four-thirty with a half dozen of his friends. Her friends joined them. They sat on the steps of Morton or under a nearby tree as they got acquainted. It was plain simple fun. The boys agreed to come back to the dorm at seven to walk together to a nearby coffee shop—no strings attached.

When they reached the coffee shop, they ordered a huge basket of fries, another of onion rings to share, and cold drinks or coffee. Everyone laughed and joked until it was time to leave. As she slid out of the booth, she heard dates made. Jerry came up behind her and whispered, "Hold my hand while we back to the dorm; it will discourage the wolves from attacking." He chuckled down at her. She took his proffered hand, knowing it would keep girls away from him as well.

The weeks that followed were more of the same light-hearted activities, the group attended football games and the after-game dances. The only difference was Jerry usually smelled of alcohol and seldom made it to biology class. The first week he made two of the four.

During the following weeks, the group settled into couples. Jerry continued to sit with her. He made less than half of his classes. When he came to biology, he was hung over, if not out and out drunk. She worried about him.

"Don't worry about me, Kara; I'm having a good time," he mumbled one morning in class.

"Oh, yeah? You look like you're having a dandy time. Red eyes you can't focus. You can barely stand. How much did you drink last night?" She scolded gently. "Tell me what's wrong."

"I don't belong here, Kara. I don't know where I belong. Not here. Not at home where my dad thinks I'm a loser." He slouched away after class and virtually out of her life. She heard he was put on academic suspension, so he left campus. His drunkenness had become the stuff of legend around campus.

She hoped he'd go home, marry his girlfriend and have a happy life. But she was sad she didn't get to say good-bye. Her sadness was short-lived. It lasted until she checked for mail. There was another letter from Fred.

> *Dear Kara,*
>
> *Thanks for the letter. I know what you mean about the drive over the Rim. I'm not too wild about it either. I hope you like the drawing I enclosed. I remember the first time I saw an elk. You're right—they're amazing creatures.*
>
> *Two more weeks of boot camp then I get to come home on leave! I may risk life and limb and come over the rim to see you,*
>
> *I don't know if you heard, but my mom took off with the loser. The house was paid for with my dad's insurance and both our names were on the deed. She signed her half over to me. I guess I'll rent it out until I finish my tour of duty. I'll have to pack up personal things before I come to see you, but I'll be there.*
>
> *I haven't been assigned anywhere yet. The Army could send me for specialized training or just send me somewhere in Asia. I hope I get to stay stateside a little longer.*
>
> *You'll be surprised to see me. I am about twenty pounds heavier than I used to be. I have actual muscles now. It is all those darn pushups, chin-ups and running the obstacle course. Speaking of those muscles—every one of them aches right now.*
>
> *Love ya back,*
> *Fred*

She unfolded the second sheet of paper—part of a paper sack. It was a pencil sketch of a bull elk, head held high. It looked out from the paper straight at her. It was beautiful. Surprised Fred was an accomplished artist, she rushed from the room, trotted to the bookstore to look for art supplies. After a search she bought a couple of sketchpads and artist's pencils; exactly what she wanted. Her folded journal pages were tucked inside along with a scrawled note of thanks. The package was a hint for future correspondence. Wrapped in brown paper and addressed, she carried it to mail at the student center.

Chapter 11

A wave of dizziness hit her as she got out of bed for class. Barely reaching the sink, she vomited. A cold sweat covered her face as she sank to the floor. *Oh no, this is not a good day to come down with the flu. I have a quiz this morning.* She pulled herself to her feet, dampened a washcloth and staggered back to bed.

After a few minutes, she managed to get up and dress in the wrinkled clothes she'd worn the day before. All she needed for the quiz was paper and pencil. She clutched them and made her way to the cafeteria. A piece of dry toast scraped it way down her throat and lodged in her stomach. A hot cup of tea warmed her stomach and eased the desire to vomit. *Too many greasy French fries last night,* she told herself.

When she arrived class, the proctor was passing out the quiz. He stopped briefly at her desk. "Are you feeling all right, Miss Carson? You look a bit peaky."

"I was queasy this morning, but I'm better now." She gave a wan smile.

"Good. Perhaps no more late nights before a quiz, then?" Usually, his cute British accent charmed her, but not today. In response she nodded, knowing she hadn't been out late.

The next two mornings were repeat performances. The dizziness, the vomiting, and cold sweats came again. Kara complained how she felt to April Canfield, her most trusted friend on campus. April gazed in concern, leaned close, and whispered, "Kara, could you be pregnant?"

April's question sent her into another round of dizziness. But she didn't vomit. Instead, her mouth fell open. Arms across her face, she moaned, "No, I can't be, I just can't be. It was only once. You can't get pregnant the first time, can you?"

April offered a sorrowful look. "Yes, you can. My sister did. It broke her heart when she dropped out of school. She went to live with my aunt and uncle until the baby came. My Aunt and Uncle adopted the baby. But there's no point in worrying until you see a doctor. It might be the flu or something else. I'll go to the doctor with you if you want." She wanted her support very much.

She was able to see the doctor right away. April sat in the waiting room while the doctor examined her. Humiliated, she closed her eyes for the final portion of the exam. It seemed a personal violation, though necessary.

"Miss Carson, you're about eight or nine weeks along in your pregnancy. I'll write a prescription for prenatal vitamins. Here's information on adoption, unless, of course, you plan to marry." He spoke in the kindest way possible, but all she felt was pure, unadulterated panic.

If it was Nate's baby and, it had to be, since he was the only one she'd *ever* been with, she couldn't possibly give it up. The baby was a part of what they'd shared—a part of him. But how? How could a vampire father a child? He said he was sort of dead. She was confused.

Thinking back to the day she ... seduced him; there was no other word for what happened, she knew there'd be consequences. A *baby* was a consequence she never considered. Nate was a vampire. She never thought it was possible for him to father a child. They'd made love only the one night. It wasn't fair.

Mechanically, she dressed, entered the waiting room, and fell into April's waiting arms. "What am I going to do now?" she wailed.

She shushed her, gently rocking her. "Let me think. What about the boy you've been writing—the artist? Maybe you could write him. From what you've said, he's a sensible guy. Maybe he could help you make decisions."

Yes, she'd write Fred. He'd help her think this through—see options she hadn't considered. How could she tell her parents? They'd be crushed. What about school—she didn't want to drop out of school when she'd barely begun. Her parents would want her to give up the baby. While she didn't want to be pregnant, she wouldn't give Nate's baby to strangers.

"You're right, April. Fred's the one person, other than you, I'd trust for advice. He helped me out in other difficult situations—saved my sanity, so to speak. I'll write him right away. You need to understand, he may not want to help. He's not the baby's father." If April was surprised, she didn't show it. She just nodded and helped her back to the dorm.

She locked the door to her room and wrote the hardest letter she ever written.

> *Dear Fred,*
>
> *I need your wise counsel. I find myself in a situation where I literally don't know what to do. You are the only person I trust to help make decisions—decisions which will affect my whole future.*
>
> *Darn it, Fred, there's no point in beating around the bush. I'm pregnant. It's Nate's baby. I don't want to give up my baby, but I don't have a clue what to do. How am I going to tell my parents? What am I going to do about school? I am so scared. Please think about your wayward friend and see if you can offer any advice.*
>
> *I know I have no business to ask for help under these circumstances, but I hope you will.*
>
> *I'm sorry to be such a huge disappointment to you and my parents. I've let everyone down.*
>
> *Kara*

She tapped on the shared wall between their rooms and April came to take the letter to mail. "I'll bring back something to eat," she promised. "You won't have to talk to anyone until you're ready."

Later, she returned with a burger and a milkshake and sat with Kara while she ate. She didn't offer advice, but instead chatted on about her classes. When April left, someone asked her where Kara was. Pressing an ear to the door, she listened to April's response.

"Kara has the flu, so she's going to stay in her room tonight." She knew she could trust April to keep her secret.

Six days later a voice called from the hallway: "Phone call for Kara Carson." She ran down the hall to the phone booth.

"Hello?" She gasped, breathless.

"Kara? It's Fred. I got your letter. I want you to know I have options in mind. I'll come straight to Flagstaff as soon as I get leave." Fred rushed his words.

"I'm sorry to drag you into my mess."

"Don't apologize. Look, I don't have time to talk now, but don't worry. I may I have it all figured out. I've got to go. I'll see you soon. Bye, Kara."

"Bye, Fred."

Who could ask for a better friend than Fred? He's changed his plans to help her out. She didn't deserve him as a friend. Hopefully, he'd have the time to pack up things he wanted from his house and find a renter before leave was up. She tapped on April's door on the way back to her room told her about his call.

"It looks like he wants to be more than friends, if you ask me." She smiled, one eyebrow raised.

It hadn't taken Nate long to pick up Josh's trail. It was well hidden, but he knew Josh like the back of his hand. He knew to watch for occasional rock cairns on the trail. He tracked him for fifty odd miles before he found the small cave where Josh hid.

Josh flung himself at Nate babbling, "Man, I am so glad to see you. I am *so* sorry. All I've done is worry about how I messed things up for you. Is Kara okay? Is she still mad at me?"

Nate rubbed his forehead, sighed. "Sit down, Josh. I'll answer all your questions. First, Kara's fine. She's not mad, but she is terrified you'll come back and attack her again. I'm glad you're sorry—you should be. But so am I; sorry I got involved with Kara at all. You were right; I should have stayed away from her for her own protection. She and I talked it over. We agreed we couldn't see each other anymore." His voice shook. "I promised her I wouldn't go back."

"What?" Josh choked, "but you love her, man. I messed things up for you, didn't I?"

"Not really, it was going to end, sooner or later. I realized I couldn't change her. I'd have to kill her to change her, but I couldn't hurt her or her parents in like that. See, Josh, I made a promise to her and myself .... I'm done killing humans. Never again." Nate sighed heavily. "Now I have to live up to the promise."

Josh sat stunned at Nate's pronouncement. "I don't know what to say, man, but I'll try to help any way I can."

"Thanks. Right now, I need to stay on the move, get far away from here. Maybe distance and a change of scenery will help." Nate's shoulders slumped as he stared at his feet. It broke his brother's heart.

"Let's take off in the morning. We can hunt tonight; there's plenty of game around. Rest up tonight and be fresh tomorrow."

Josh tried to shoulder the decision-making. If his brother was going to refuse humans blood, he would too. If it helped Nate, it would be worth it.

Nate nodded. He wasn't hungry, but he'd have to feed before he left on a long journey. His feet dragged as he left the cave. *Why can't I just die?*

They traveled to the Four Corners area the next day. It was ruggedly beautiful country. The red rocks caught the light and shadowed the land. Nate couldn't get Kara off his mind; he wondered how far he'd have to travel to forget her. Could he ever forget her? Every time he closed his eyes, he saw her face. He hoped she'd be happy. She had so much ahead of her. College. Marriage. The thought of her married was a stab of pain. He wished she'd find a nice guy. Someone like Fred. He knew he was obsessing. He had to find a distraction from the bond that pulled him to her. Why was the pull so powerful? He'd had sex with other women, many who he didn't kill. His reaction was different with

Kara. Could love be the answer? She was the only girl he ever loved. It was more than that, though. I had to be the combination of love and making love, because what they did was an act of love. He was bound to her as surely as if chained.

⤳

They reached a small village in late morning. Men swarmed everywhere; it was a beehive of activity. Reminding Josh of the no-humans-as-food rule as the boys entered the village. "What's going on?" he asked a man, noticing a camp set up.

"We're here to help build a medical clinic for this rural region. Once the clinic's complete, doctors will volunteer time to help area people with medical needs."

Nate asked, "Do you want a couple extra volunteers? My brother and I don't know much about building, but a couple of strong backs might be useful." They were directed to the project coordinator who was studying a blueprint.

"Can I help you?" The man looked up with a smile.

Nate repeated his offer to volunteer.

"Welcome. I'm Mick. We can use all the help we can get. This project is completely built by volunteers. A few of them are licensed contractors, so it can be a 'learn as you go' project for you. We're going to pour concrete today and we have to get the rebar in place before its poured. If you can help get it moved, it would help." Mick noted their perplexed expressions. He pointed to a spot where building supplies were to be unloaded. "Come on, I'll show you what I mean."

Nate and Josh spent the summer working with the men in the camp. By summers end, they'd learned a lot about construction from the ground up. The best of all, they made many human friends.

When those friend were trapped by a raging forest fire Nate faced his greatest fear, death by fire, to save the lives of the men. They'd been forced to leave because news of the impossible rescue reached the media. There was bound to be questions they couldn't answer and they couldn't face exposure.

Chapter 12

"Hey, Kara, you've got a guest in the lobby, and is he ever built!" The comment came as a surprise because it came from Betty. Betty usually had her nose in her books and never gave a second look to the guys they hung out with. She didn't take the time to question her, though. There was only one person she expected to see. It must be Fred.

She flew to the end of the hall and ran down the stairs. She paused at the landing to walk sedately the last few steps to the bottom, so the dorm mother wouldn't reprimand her. As she took those last steps, she scanned the room. A man in uniform stood with his back to her, staring into the flickering fireplace. Her eyes widened as she walked up behind him. He was indeed "built" now. His once skinny frame had filled out. He *had* developed muscles at boot camp.

"Fred?" she asked quietly. He spun around, a smile breaking over his face. Taking the final steps, she hugged him.

He enveloped her in his arms and whispered into her hair, "Kara, it's good to see you. I've missed you. Is there somewhere we can talk privately?"

She nodded, but remembered it was a weekday. "Yes, but I have to be back in the dorm before ten o'clock." Arm in arm they strolled out the door. Her friends clustered at the base of the stairs gawking. Apparently, Betty was quick to notify them of her "built" date.

She wondered if Betty mentioned he was handsome. Fred was undeniably handsome now. He'd matured physically in a way which enhanced his looks. He'd been cute in a skinny, boyish way. No one would call him cute now. Handsome, good looking, even Betty's term "built" worked. But, no one would call him cute.

They got into his car and she directed him to a nearby hill that over-looked the main part of the campus. They wouldn't be bothered, though several cars shared the hill with them. While the view was beautiful, the people who came here weren't interested in the view or who shared the hill with them.

Fred turned to face her, his brown eyes boring into hers. "I've thought about this a lot, Kara. In fact, I've thought of nothing else since I got your letter. I asked the chaplain's opinion, too. The best thing we can do is to get married."

Her mouth drop open. Before she could say a word, he held up his hand and continued. "We don't have much time for you to decide. I know you don't love me. I hope over time, you'll learn to. But the longer we wait, the less time we have to get you set up in an apartment. Also, the longer we wait, the harder it will be to hide your pregnancy. If you agree, we could drive to Las Vegas over the weekend and get married. Geoff could be my best man, and you could ask one of your friends to act as bridesmaid. Will you do me the honor of marrying me, Kara Carson?"

A million thoughts raced through her brain, but her main concern was for Fred. It wasn't fair to him. She'd screwed up her life. She didn't want to screw up his, too. "Why would you marry a pregnant girl who is carrying someone else's baby? Don't throw your life away, Fred."

"I won't be throwing away my life. *You'd* be giving me a gift, Kara. See, I've loved you since the first time we danced together at the Lawrence's barbeque. You were dating Nate. I never felt I had a chance until he left. The time I spent with you then made me love you more. Now, maybe you'll give me a chance."

"Before I answer, there's more you need to know. If you want to change your mind, I'll understand. You might think Nate took advan-tage of me at some point. He didn't." She stared at her lap as tears trick-led down. "I seduced him. The last night in the hospital—I literally pulled him into bed. You see, this is my entire fault." She covered her face, unable to see his look of disappointment.

He put his arms around her and pulled her against his chest, strok-ing her hair. "Kara, Kara, it doesn't matter. Like I said, I love you. I know how you feel about Nate, but he's gone. It's in the past. We can wipe the slate clean. If you agree to marry me and you're my wife, your baby will be *my* baby, too. Maybe someday you will love me as much as I love you. Please say yes."

Unable to speak, she nodded. He kissed her firmly on the mouth. His thumbs wiped the tears from her eyes. He smiled joyously. "Let's tell Geoff not to make other plans for the weekend!"

They returned to the dorm seconds before curfew. She danced up the stairs to her room. Noticing April's door ajar, she tiptoed over and whispered, "Can I come in." April leaped up from her chair, grabbed her by the hand, jerked her through the door and slammed it behind her. Her eye wide, she asked, "Well?"

"Do you have plans this weekend? I want you to be my maid-of-honor. We're going to Las Vegas to get married." The remark didn't come off as casually as she hoped.

April let out a whoop, grabbed Kara, and spun her in a circle. "I *knew* he wanted to be more than friends. Yes, yes, yes, I'll go with you!" She hugged her, spun her around again. Kara was dizzy and laughing. April stopped, suddenly serious. "Tell me Kara, do you have any feeling for him?"

"You've read parts of our letters. Fred is the kindest, most loyal person I know. Honestly, I'm not sure if I love him, but given time for the shock to wear off, I could." April understood what Kara struggled to say.

They packed their bags Friday, so they could leave either that night or the early Saturday morning. She and April selected dressy outfits for the ceremony from their limited wardrobes, giggling like excited schoolgirls.

Between classes on Friday, Fred accompanied her to meet the Dean of Women. They wanted to check on appropriate housing for her. Since Fred would be returning to the Army, Kara wasn't sure if she'd be allowed in married housing. Nor did she know if any of the couples' apartments were available. The dean was sympathetic. "There'll be a unit available the beginning of second semester. Since you're not showing yet, there's no reason you can't stay in the dorm until then."

They filled out the necessary paperwork. "Come to the office before second semester starts. You can pick up the keys and get your personal things moved into the apartment. The units are furnished. You'll need sheets and blankets for a double bed and cooking utensils.

"That's one thing done." Fred sighed. "I wish I could stay to help you move, but Geoff will help. At least I know you'll be someplace safe. Now that's taken care of, let's gather the troops to decide when to leave." He put his arm around her in a casual way and led her back to his car. They picked up Geoff and then picked up April. They went to a pizza parlor to plan the trip.

The decision was made to leave at the crack of dawn Saturday morning—at o'dark-thirty, according to Geoff, and arrive in Las Vegas late morning or early afternoon. Fred reserved two single rooms—one each for Geoff and April—and a double for them. They'd check into the rooms, find a wedding chapel, and get married Saturday. Otherwise, she'd sleep with April.

They'd return to Flagstaff Sunday afternoon; ready for Monday classes. Kara signed out of the dorm for a full week. Fred reserved a motel room close to the campus, so they'd stay at the motel until the following weekend when they'd drive over the Rim to Payson. She dreaded telling her parents they were married. It all sounded easy, but she doubted it would be that easy. Though her parents liked Fred, they weren't going to be happy.

The drive to Las Vegas was less than scenic; it was barren country. The group was excited by the drive over Hoover Dam. It was huge! The dam was built during the depression, less than forty miles from Las Vegas. Built when temperatures sometimes reached 120°, the work was difficult. At 726 feet in height and 1,224 feet long it was the world's largest man-made structure at the time it was built. They parked the car to study the awe inspiring structure before resuming the journey.

When Fred pulled into the parking lot of the Stardust Hotel she was shocked, expecting a small motel—not this big, beautiful hotel. Fred must have paid a small fortune for the weekend. They arrived too early to check into the rooms.

The concierge directed them to an all-you-can-eat buffet inside the hotel. Kara held an available table near the ladies room while the boys and April filled their plates. When they returned to the table, she grabbed her plate. Assaulted by the smell of food; she took tiny portions. While the boys ate as if it were their last meal, April and she nibbled at their selections. When Geoff came back with seconds, she excused herself and charged for the ladies room. When she returned to the table, Fred was watching in anxiety. April had the foresight to bring her soda crackers and a cup of tea.

"I'm fine, Fred, don't worry. April, thanks for the crackers." Getting sick at the drop of a hat wasn't her idea of fun, but she was used to it.

While she nibbled on crackers, Fred and Geoff left to pick up their room keys. The suitcases were in the lobby by the time April and she joined them. A bellhop took charge of the luggage. With the help of a cart, he took the bags to their respective rooms. Fred asked the desk clerk where they could find the nearest wedding chapel. The clerk presented him with a map to all the local chapels.

The girls went to dress for the big event. Her eyes widened as she came out of the bathroom where Fred waited in his dress uniform. "Fred, you look wonderful." She added flirtatiously, "I love a man in uniform."

"Not just any man in uniform, I hope. I'll have to watch you around the bellboy," he quipped. "Speaking of looking wonderful, you take my breath away." They smiled shyly at each other. He took both of her hands in his as he gazed in her eyes. "Last chance for you to back out," he said, cocking his head, a flash of fear in his eyes.

"Not on your life, buster. You're stuck with me—or will be in a while." She smiled nervously and watched his fear dissipate.

She and April were dressed in cocktail dresses they'd worn to semi-formal dances. Hers was a beige silk sheath and April's, an ice blue taffeta sheath. She and Fred looked good together. Her dress complemented Fred's uniform, so they looked like a couple.

When they met Geoff and April in the lobby, a complete stranger walked up to Fred. "I want to thank you, son, for serving our country.

I served in the Big One. It does my heart good to see someone who proudly wears the uniform."

"Thank you, sir. I appreciate it." A pleased smile passed over Fred's face at the old fellow's comment.

"I don't want to hold you up; it looks as if the four you have big plans for today." As the stranger looked them over, their faces broke into grins. Kara blushed.

"Yes sir. Kara and I are getting married." Fred pulled her closer and smiled proudly down at her.

"Well, that's great news! You have my best wishes for a long and happy marriage. Get on your way and tie that knot." He slapped Fred on the back, turned and walked toward the front desk.

"That was nice of him, wasn't it?" She said as they walked to the car. Fred nodded, but he was focused the map from the desk clerk.

"There are several chapels down this direction. Shall we take a look?" He pulled out on to the main road. The first one was two blocks away and looked shabby. The second, however, was a little dollhouse surrounded by a white picket fence, so they stopped at it.

A bell echoed somewhere in the back of the chapel as they walked through the entrance. A plump woman in a flowered dress hurried out of a back room. "Ah, it looks like we have a happy couple ready to engage in holy matrimony." She clapped her hands in delight.

Kara struggled to control her giggle at the formality of the woman's words.

"Yes, ma'am," Fred replied. "I was told you'd have the necessary paperwork." It was as much a question as a statement.

"Indeed, I do. Indeed, I do. If you'll follow me to the back room, we'll take care of the formalities now. Are these your witnesses?" She nodded toward April and Geoff.

"Yes, ma'am, they are." Fred held his military bearing. He looked so handsome in his uniform, she couldn't take her eyes off him. It was good to focus on him because she was on an emotional roller coaster. Probably hormones. She couldn't decide to laugh or cry. She anchored her eyes on him and took several calming breaths.

"Oh good; they can go ahead and sign the papers right now, too. No need to wait, no need to wait. Follow me." She bustled into a small office and pushed an intercom button. "You need to prepare for a ceremony, Leroy," she exclaimed with false excitement.

She shoved documents toward them and pointed where they needed to sign. Low music began to play in the chapel. "All right, you gentlemen wait at the front of the chapel. Ladies, follow me." She took Kara and April by the arms through another door into a smaller room piled with artificial flowers. "Go ahead, pick a bridal bouquet, dearie, and then go through that door." She pointed to a second door at the end of the room which led to the back of the chapel.

As soon as April and she walked through the last door, Mendelsohn's "Wedding March" began to play. April walked forward, and turned to the right of a balding, chubby little man who was dwarfed by Fred and Geoff. As April reached the front, Fred grabbed her hand briefly. Kara didn't have time to wonder why. She was waved forward by the woman in the flowered dress.

Fred's eyes made her heart wrench—they held such a mix of hope and desire. She prayed she wouldn't let him down. She glided forward to take his hands. The minister, or whatever he was, repeated the age-old words of the ceremony. When he said her name and asked her to repeat those sacred vows, she whispered them, as tears trickled down her face. Was it any wonder she cried when she had doubts about disappointing Fred? She whispered a pray she'd make him happy.

The minister asked if they had rings. She gasped. Rings? She hadn't thought about a ring. April nudged her and slipped a ring in her hand.

Fred's voice filtered through a growing haze: "With this ring I thee wed and all my worldly goods to thee endow." He placed the ring on her finger.

Taking a deep breath to clear her head, she repeated the words back as she gazed into his eyes. She placed the ring on his finger. Fred made good on the final words of the ceremony: "You may kiss the bride." His kiss left her breathless and blushing. Geoff and April laugh.

"Okay. Enough, already." Geoff joked. "Get a room. Oh, that's right you have one." He laughed harder.

The lady in the flowered dress handed the papers to the minister to sign. He placed them in an envelope before he handed them to Fred. It was official: they were man and wife. The lady threw a handful of rice and yelled, "Congratulations. Congratulations!" They ran for the car.

As they drove away, Geoff asked, "Does anyone else feel like we've been run through a cattle chute?" Kara broke out in a paroxysm of nervous giggles. That was what it felt like, until they got to the vows. Those were precious and beautiful words.

When they returned to the hotel, they agreed to meet for dinner. The girls wanted to change clothes and April and Geoff thought she and Fred deserved some space. Both were nervous. She didn't know what to expect and neither did Fred. She had little experience and Fred had none.

It might have been purely hormonal on her part, but she was surprised by her desire. Fred locked her in his embrace as he fumbled for the door key. Barely in the room; he struggled with the zipper on her dress. As the dress slipped to the floor, he picked her up and carried her to the bed. He hesitated. "Kara, I don't want to rush you. You may not be ready yet."

"Of course, I'm ready. Fred, I owe you so much ..."

"Don't agree to have sex because of some misguided idea you owe me something. I'd rather wait forever. You don't *owe* me a thing," he snapped angrily.

"No, no, you don't understand. I'm not saying it right. Please listen to what I'm *trying* to say."

Fred nodded, but recalcitrant, turned his face away. She sat on the bed, legs tucked under, and reached for his face. She turned his head her direction, but his eyes refused to meet hers.

"I do owe you a lot, but it isn't why I want you now. When Nate left, it was by mutual decision. I thought I loved him and in a way I did. We shared a strong physical attraction. But there were too many ways we were different. There was no real future for a relationship. We had nothing to build on. When I made the decision to break up, I listed the characteristics I wanted in a husband. The day you asked me to marry you, April asked if I cared about you. I thought about the list I'd made.

The list described *you*. You are exactly the kind of man I want in my life." She ticked off the reasons on her fingers. "First, you're a friend. Then, you're a person who shares my beliefs. I know I can trust you. You're the man I can be happy with the rest of my life.

"It's true I'll never forget Nate. No woman forgets her first love." She rested both hands on her abdomen, "Now I have second reason I'll never forget him. But *you* are the one who can make me happy over the long haul." She rose on her knees, put her arms around him, and slowly kissed him. He'd listened and understood what she struggled to say.

They managed to make it down to dinner and tried to ignore the ribald comments Geoff made throughout the evening. The four of them spent time wandering around the casino, fascinated by the flashing lights. But the cacophony of sound; the loud voices, and the clatter of coins were overwhelming. Although they worried they'd be kicked out of the over-twenty-one area, no one questioned them. She tried to make sense of the craps table. A lot of money flew around while people yelled "7 come 11" and "snake eyes." The chips were laid on different places on the table, but it made no sense to her. The cloud of smoke over the area gave her a headache, so they drifted to a lounge show.

There were a few smokers so the veil of smoke was not as heavy as in the gaming areas. The music was pleasant and allowed conversation. They made plans for the following day, agreeing to meet in the lobby for a late breakfast. They left April and Geoff sitting, heads together, in the lounge as they strolled back to their room.

Fred signed their room number to the check for dinner and the drinks in the lounge. She worried he'd run short of cash. Surreptitiously, she checked to see how much she had in her wallet, in case he needed it.

When they got back to the room, a huge basket filled with cheese and crackers, caviar, cookies, candy, a bottle of Champagne with two flutes waited. A note simply read, "Congratulations to the happy couple. Best wishes for a long and happy marriage!" There was no signature, but they could guess who sent it—the man from the lobby. Those were the very words he'd said.

Deeply touched by his generosity, Fred opened the bottle so they could toast the unnamed man. Though they weren't hungry, they decided to try the caviar. She put a small amount on a cracker. As soon as it hit her lips, she dashed to the bathroom. It was disgusting! Caviar must be an acquired taste. It shouldn't surprise her; they were fish eggs. After she washed her face, brushed her teeth and rinsed her mouth, She went back to sip more Champagne and nibble on crackers—with cheese. Nothing came back up, so they finished the bottle.

She woke the following morning with a splitting headache, which she blamed on the Champagne since she wasn't used to alcohol in any form. Holding her head between her hands, she crept out of bed. She didn't want to disturb Fred. There was plenty of time before they had to dress for breakfast. She got in the shower praying the hot water would help her head.

As water hit her body and steam rose around her, the shower curtain slid aside. Fred stepped into the shower behind her.

"This is an arid region, we should conserve on the water," he whispered seriously. A smile tugged at his lips as he gazed down at her. He grabbed the bar of soap and gently began to wash her back. He placed a row of kisses down the side of her neck. She would have blushed, but her head hurt so bad she couldn't think. It was quite possible they were going to be late for breakfast.

April and Geoff were lost in conversation when they made it to the lobby, only fifteen minutes late. "Well, you are among the living. We were ready to send a search party!" Geoff joked.

"I'd say I'm sorry, but I'm not." Fred grinned. She couldn't keep the smile or the blush from her face either, "We had something important to do."

"Yeah, I'll bet you did." He raised his eyebrows and smirked. Geoff jumped up and grabbed April's hand, and pulled her to her feet. "I'm hungry; let's eat!" Something about the exchanged glance made Kara wonder if something was going on between them. She had to find a way to get April alone.

Her head felt better, so she decided she was hungry. They filled their plates at the breakfast bar. She ate more food than she'd eaten in weeks. It was as if someone threw a switch in her. She ate almost as much as the boys. Geoff asked if it was a contest. Happily, she didn't feel sick after devouring the food. Anxiety may have caused some of the morning sickness. She hoped it was thing of the past.

When April rose and excused herself to go to the ladies room, Kara jumped up to follow. With an anxious frown Fred watched her, but she shook her head to let him know she was fine and trotted after April. The door barely closed when she asked with cloying sweetness, "Is there something you wanted to tell me?" She dragged out the words, "Maybe about Geoff?" April's face turned crimson.

"Um, I, um, think I may like him ... a lot. Also, I think he likes me." She smiled shyly as Kara grabbed her in a bear hug.

"I'm so pleased, I mean, you two are my favorite people. This is great. Maybe you can be my cousin-in-law if there is such a thing." She couldn't contain her excitement over the possibility.

"Whoa, Kara, don't rush things. Let's give it time. I have to admit, though, it's easy to think that way. He's nice, and funny, and so cute." Her eyes had gone all dreamy.

"If I must, I must, but I would love to have you two ... well you know. I won't repeat myself, but I am going to think positive thoughts!" Laughing, they hurried to rejoin their two men.

By the time they finished eating, they were eager to get on the road for the return trip. Bags mostly packed, they returned to the room to throw in last minute items, including the leftover treats to snack on in the car.

Fred carried the bags to the car while she watched for Geoff and April. Fred returned before they showed up. She followed him to the front desk to pay their charges—in case he needed more money.

When Fred gave the man the room key, he told the concierge he'd pay for Geoff's and April's charges as well.

The concierge looked up with a smile and said, "All the charges have been paid for you and your entire wedding party."

Fred frowned in confusion. "I don't understand. What do you mean?" Their heads swiveled to each other then back to the clerk, trying to make sense of it.

"Apparently, you made a good impression on one of our regular guests. He left orders that any and all of your charges were to be billed to him." The man nodded, as if confirming it was true.

"What's his name? We want to thank him for his kindness. It's such a lot of money to give to strangers." Fred was thunderstruck.

"He wishes to remain anonymous. I think it is safe to say, for him, money is no object. If you wish to leave a note, I'll see he gets it." The concierge, ever courteous refused to answer more questions. He provided them with pen and paper for a note.

Dear Sir,

We don't know how to thank you for the extraordinary kindness you have shown. We feel blessed by your generosity. Perhaps someday we'll have the ability to bless someone else's life in a similar manner as well. Thank you.
Sincerely,
Fred and Kara Jacobs

He folded the note and returned it to the concierge as Geoff and April made their appearance. Fred carried April's bag to the car. He told them of the astonishing happenings. They were silent as they got into the car. Fred shook his head in wonderment and said, "I'll pray for God to bless the man, every day for the rest of my life." Her sentiments exactly.

The return trip was uneventful, so they took turns sleeping or driving. Exhausted from the rushed activity of the past few days and the late nights, no one felt like talking. When they pulled in front of Morton Hall, Geoff jumped out to help April with her bag. As the couple walked away, Kara was sure she heard Geoff mention something about meeting her later. She smiled smugly.

As soon as they dropped Geoff off, they drove to the motel; their home for the next few days. It was small and tidy, complete with a tiny kitchenette. They planned to eat their meals in the room. She recalled the playhouse she had as a child. Only she was no longer a child, nor was this playing.

The honeymoon was over, so to speak. Time to sit down and seriously figure out their future—including how to tell her parents they'd eloped. News about the coming baby could wait. Her parents were bound to be suspicious over the hasty wedding, but they'd be upset enough for now. She'd take things one step at a time.

Chapter 13

Fred waited in the packed car while she finished her last class Friday. The time had come to face her parents with the news of their unexpected marriage. Neither Kara nor Fred looked forward to their reaction, but they had to be told—the sooner, the better.

"I don't want to lie, but is it a lie to withhold part of the truth?" She trusted Fred for an honest answer.

"In this case withholding the truth is best, Kara. We want your parents to think I'm the baby's father when you can't hide your pregnancy any longer. It would hurt more if they knew the full truth." Fred wrestled with the question from the time he received Kara's letter. He wasn't sure what was right, either. Was there an absolute right way? If there was, he didn't know what it was.

"They're going to be upset by the pregnancy, no matter what. My biggest fear is they'll be upset with you. Will they forgive you when they don't understand you've helped me? You don't deserve their anger. I do."

"I could be the baby's father with all the time I spent alone with you after the break-up with Nate. I'd rather they be mad at me than at you," he said with a wry smile. "You're their only daughter. I hate the thought of them angry with you. Besides, I'm going to leave. You're the one who'll need to need their help. I'll bet by the time the baby comes, they'll be willing to forgive me."

"I hope you're right. Are you okay if I nap in the car? I am tired all the time now." She hated to complain, but it was the truth.

Fred patted his leg. "Lay your head right there, sleepyhead. I'll wake you when we're almost there." He stroked her hair as she sighed and nestled her head on his lap.

It seemed mere moments when she felt a gentle touch and heard him whisper. "Wake up, Kara. We're past Pine and almost to Payson. Shall we face your parents now or wait until morning? We can sleep at my house."

"We'd better see them tonight and get it out of the way. Tomorrow won't be any easier. If things get too bad, we can leave and sleep at your house."

His face brightening he said, "I remembered something. It's not my house—it's *our* house. You're right, though. We'd better get it over with ... and like you said, if we need to, we can escape to *our* house." His emphasis made her grin.

"Shall we eat first? They're probably eating dinner about now." As well as being sleepy, she was always hungry. But, if one more friend said she was eating for two, she was going to explode.

As they drove to the Burger Hut, the memory of Nate caused a momentary stab of pain. She mentally shook herself, resolved. Fred was the right man for her. She loved him, but a part of her would always love Nate, too. She shoved the thought away.

After they finished the burgers there was no more reason to delay. They had to face her parents. Fred drove straight to the house. She tapped on the door, threw it open at the same time, and yelled, "Surprise!"

Her mom and dad came out of the kitchen. Mom held a dishtowel. They'd just finished dinner. Don José raced in, barking at the top of his little lungs. He leaped around like a demented grasshopper. Fosdick twined between her ankles, mewing in pleasure.

"Kara! What a surprise ... and Fred?" His name came out as a question. "Are you home on leave?" Both her parents hugged her, but she saw their concern; wondering why they showed up unexpectedly and why they were together.

"Yes, ma'am, I am home on leave." Kara grabbed Fred's hand interrupting him. "Mom, Dad. Fred and I have a surprise. We got married last weekend."

Her dad, slack-jawed, stared at them. Without a word; he turned on his heels and marched back into the kitchen. Mom babbled, "Huh? You did what?"

Dad came back with a glass in one hand and a bottle of Wild Turkey in the other. His first words were, "Sit down." He wasn't smiling. "What in the name of all that's holy possessed the two of you to run off and get married?" He took a large swallow of the drink he'd poured, and glared waiting for an answer.

"Dad, you know Fred is being sent away as soon he returns to camp. We didn't want to wait until he finished his tour of duty." She thought the argument was reasonable.

"But, Kara," Mom asked, "what about your education?"

Fred jumped in. "We've thought about that. Kara will work part-time while I'm gone. She'll stay in school, live in the dorm until semester break, and after that, she'll move into married couples' housing. I'll send her money every month, so she should get along fine." Fred appeared confident. "Of course, I'll see her when I'm on leave." She prayed double-teaming her parents would distract them.

Dad finished his first drink and poured a second. He *never* drank more than one drink—two small drinks if they entertained. This was not a good sign.

"You're both too young to think of getting married! Did you stop to think marriage is permanent? You aren't going to be able to support my daughter on your pay," Dad growled as he punched a finger at Fred.

She jumped back into the fray. "Like Fred said, I'll work part-time to help supplement our income. If I need to, I'll work full-time in the summer, but I hope to take summer classes so I can finish early. By the time Fred finishes his tour of duty, I can apply for a teaching job while he goes to school."

Dad downed his second drink, poured a third, his speech slurred. "I thought you had more sense, Kara."

Mom was shell-shocked, but a pragmatist. She said, "It's too late to worry if it was the best idea or not. What's done is done."

Kara didn't let go of Fred's hand the entire time, nor did he try to pull away. She was glad to have him by her side for moral support. Most likely he felt the same way.

Still practical, Mom asked if they'd eaten. When they said they had, she offered dessert—a chocolate cake. As they strolled into the kitchen, Dad stopped and poked Fred in the chest with his finger. "You'd better take care of her or you're going to be damn sorry!" He stood six foot two, when he was upset he appeared to grow in height and breadth, like the new comic book character, *The Hulk.*

Fred squared his shoulders and looked in her dad's eyes. "You can count on it, sir. As far as I'm concerned, your daughter is a gift from God. I don't take her love lightly. I plan on taking very good care of her."

They sat around the table; all uncomfortable. She ate a slice of the cake. While it was delicious, she struggled to swallow it. She was too tense.

Her dad shoved his half eaten cake away and said, "I think I'll go to bed." It was a good idea since he wasn't too steady on his feet after all the Wild Turkey. Don José, who'd kept his distance, trotted after him. The poor little animals weren't used to raised voices.

"Mom, should we sleep here or at Fred's house."

Shocked, her mom said, "Here, of course. You're going to have to put clean sheets on the bed. I didn't make the bed in case spiders got in it."

While Kara didn't understand her reasoning, she didn't care. Emotionally exhausted, she grabbed the sheets out of the linen closet and hurried to the bedroom, Fred and Fosdick hot on her heels.

"I hope you don't mind sharing with Fosdick—he always sleeps with me." Fred stared at the cat then back at her, in a quandary.

"I'm not crazy about sharing you with anyone, but I guess the cat can stay. I suppose I need his approval, too." He grinned as she nodded. Fosdick gave Fred his seal of approval. He chose to sleep above her head instead of between them. Fred gave Fosdick his full approval after that.

Morning came sooner than she'd have liked. She squeezed her eyes closed, hoping it wasn't time to face another uncomfortable day. Both Fosdick and Fred noticed her faking sleep. Fosdick head-butted her, purring. Fred whispered, "You're kind of cute when you scrunch up your face like that." She giggled, grabbed Fosdick in a hug, and then reached for Fred. As she kissed him, his lips curled into a smile.

"Shall we pull the blanket over our heads and refuse to get up or shall we get up and pretend we're not scared witless."

"I vote for refusing to get up," she giggled, pulling the blanket over their heads. She froze at the quiet tap on the door.

"Kara, Fred, are you awake? Breakfast is almost ready. We have a lot to do today." Whatever did she mean? Did she mean her and Dad, or did she mean all of them?

Trying to sound sleepy, she yawned. "Yeah, we're awake. We'll be out in a minute." Fred made another grab for her, kissing her soundly before he let go. They pulled their clothes on and then ran to the bathroom. Dad had a firm, fast rule. No one came to the table without washing their face and combing their hair. When she told Fred, he was quick to comply, hoping to start the day on the right foot.

Mom made a special effort with breakfast. There were hot biscuits and sausage gravy as well as eggs. It was Kara's favorite breakfast; saved for special occasions. Mom was trying to make the best of things. Dad was quiet, very subdued. Hung over no doubt. She knew he wasn't happy about their hasty marriage, but he made an effort to be agreeable. It must have cost him a great deal of effort. He had so many plans for her. Now he must wonder if those long-made plans would ever come to fruition.

As they sat down, making the usual pleasantries over the food in a false expression of normalcy, Mom spoke up. "There must be a lot of things you'll need to set up a household. I thought we'd make a list and go shopping."

"Mrs. Carson? I plan to rent out my house. We can take what we need from the house beforehand. A list is a great idea, but we should check my place before we buy anything I might have."

"Good idea, Fred, but you should have a *few* new things as wedding gifts." Mom was insistent.

"Thanks, Mom and Dad ... Thanks Mr. and Mrs. Carson." Fred and she spoke in unison.

Dad growled, "You'd better start calling us Pete and Joann given the circumstances." He faced Fred. "I know you're a fine young man, Fred, even if I wished you and Kara had waited, but ... I couldn't have asked for a better man to join the family." He stuck out his hand, his eyes glistening.

"Thanks, sir, I mean Pete. It means a lot to me." Fred's sincerity touched her heart. Apparently, it touched her parents as well. Mom reached out and patted his arm and Dad managed a weak, but sincere, smile.

After they cleaned the kitchen, Mom grabbed notebook paper and began scribbling headings on different sheets. Obviously, bedding was one item on the list.

"Mom, we have bedding—sheets and blankets."

"Yes, but you need one new set as a wedding gift." The lists included everything from towels to kitchen utensils. They included dishes, pots and pans, and spices—things Kara hadn't considered.

"We won't need most of these things until I move into married housing. We can check what Fred has before we shop. We'll store boxes until it's time to make the move."

The rest of the day was a flurry of activity selecting what they wanted from Fred's—*their*—house and packing it up.

"What do you plan to do with everything else, Fred?"

"I'm coming back to pack up personal items for storage. The rest I'll donate to charity, sell, or leave for the renters."

They hauled the labeled boxes back to store at mom and dad's. They tried to organize them with most important items at the front with the least important in back. It was a daunting task.

Her mom said, "Why don't we save the shopping for later? We can shop tomorrow. The gift items I'll find in Phoenix. There's a better selection there and since we have time yet ..."

"Good idea Joann. Let's cleaned up and I'll take you all out for dinner," Dad said.

It was a great idea. Drained of energy, she dreaded the thought of cooking dinner and cleaning up. Eating and going directly to bed was much more desirable. Would her parents notice her lack of energy and begin to question why?

They went to dinner at the Elks Club, where Pete had been a member since he moved to Payson. The steak dinners they ordered were excellent, but she was too drowsy to fully enjoy it. Fred did though. He finished the rest of her steak. She wasn't much of a cook. She should find simple recipes to feed Fred something other than burgers and pizza when he returned home.

She and Fred chose to go to church Sunday morning hoping to see any friends who were there. She told her parents they'd shop after church. They had to leave by mid-afternoon for the drive back to Flagstaff. Her parents wanted to have the day with them, but weren't upset by the decision. She and Fred upset any plans her parents might have had. The extra time allowed them to catch up on things they wanted to do.

⁓◯

"Who do you suppose will be at church?"

"Geoff said he'd be there, so we'll see him."

"I'll bet he promised to give April a rundown on how it went with my parents."

"You can bank on it, Kara. Those two were as worried as we were about their reaction to our hasty marriage."

Geoff leaned against the fender of his car. He'd been watching for them. "So how did it go? Did Aunt Joann and Uncle Pete have a fit?"

Fred grimaced. "Let's just say Friday night was not pleasant. Yesterday was okay though. They've decided to make the best of it."

She interrupted. "A bottle of Wild Turkey sacrificed its life, though."

Geoff guffawed. "I'm glad to hear it went well. I've seen Uncle Pete mad and Aunt Joann is no one to mess with either. At least the Wild Turkey and Uncle Pete's head were the only casualties." Geoff sighed in relief. "Are you driving back today?"

"Yeah. We're going to leave a two or three hours after church. You, too?"

"I've got my car packed, so I'm ready to roll following church. I miss April." His eyebrows rose suggestively.

"Tell April I'll be back in the dorm tonight. Fred is coming back here to clear out more of his house." She'd miss him, even knowing he'd be back for the weekend—their last until who knows when. After that, he'd to head back to camp. The base chaplain arranged those extra few days for them to be together, but the time had flown. "Who else is here?" she asked.

"Besides me, the twins are here and, you're gonna love this—Joyce." Geoff tried to stifle a laugh, but his lips twitched in amusement. She groaned.

Fred put an arm around her and turned toward the entrance. The first hymn was playing, so she wouldn't have to talk to Joyce, but it didn't stop her from hearing part of her comment to the twins, "She's probably knocked up—"

Kara face redden and she sucked in an angry hiss. Fred bent down and whispered, "Let it go, Kara. She is blind jealous of you and has been since she first met you. You're prettier and kinder. She's not worth getting upset over."

He went on to call her a name she longed to use, but it wasn't exactly appropriate for church. She grinned up at him and struggled not to laugh, biting her lip to control the impulse.

When they returned to her parents' house, Mom had worked overtime on preparing Sunday dinner. She fried chicken, and had mashed potatoes, green peas, dinner rolls, and ice cream for dessert. The home-cooked meal tasted better than the steak the night before.

After they ate and cleaned up the dishes, they only has an hour to shop. Mom suggested they stock up on spices and cleaning supplies— another thing Kara hadn't thought about. Who wants to think about cleaning toilets when they're first married?

Admittedly, she wouldn't want to go too long without cleaning them. Her parents paid almost a hundred dollars for just the basics. That much money would take a healthy chunk out of the salary of middle income people. There were so many things she needed to learn; shopping, budgeting, cooking, cleaning ...

She knew the basics in cooking and cleaning. She could cook breakfast, bake a potato and make salad. She could dust, run a vacuum, and do laundry, but it was the extent of her talents. She was glad she'd acquired those meager skills.

When they were ready to leave, she found Fosdick and gave him a hug. She promised to see him soon. She hugged her parents and Fred followed suit, except he shook her dad's hand. The drive over the Rim was almost as horrific as the first time. It was a relief to know they wouldn't run into logging trucks. Logging was at a temporary standstill.

She managed to stay awake until they reached Happy Jack. Her head lolled onto Fred's shoulder and stayed there until they reached Flagstaff.

Fred whispered, "Sweetheart, we're almost there. You need to wake up."

She didn't want to wake up. If she did, he'd leave her. She wanted to stay with him. It was irrational, but her stomach roiled at the thought of returning to the dorm. Tears threatened to spill over.

Fred lifted her chin and said, "I'll be back by the time you get out of class on Friday, so we'll have the entire weekend together. I reserved our room at the motel before we left to make sure we'd have it for next weekend." He kissed her and pulled her to his chest. "I'll carry your bags inside, Kara. You should get some rest. This weekend took an emotional toll and you'll want to be ready for classes tomorrow."

He carried the bags inside, calling out "man in the hall" as was required. She accompanied him back to the steps of Morton. He gave her a quick kiss and turned away, but not before she saw his face twist in pain. He gave a final wave as he drove away. He didn't look back. He didn't want her to see him grieve.

Kara sank down on the worn steps of the dorm. She couldn't walk the few steps to her room. His grief was the proverbial last straw. It broke down her unstable emotional strength.

With quiet grace, April sank down next to her. Taking her hand, she sat in silence until Kara turned her head. "Are you ready to go inside now, Kara?" As Kara's nod, April stood and pulled her to her feet. Side-by-side they walked into the dorm.

All her friends helped get her through the long week until Fred returned. Though the days were endless, Friday came and with it came Fred.

They spent the weekend evenings in seclusion in the motel. They made small talk while locked in each other's arms. The time they spent together was as precious as it was private. On Saturday morning, bundled in coats and gloves they walked the nearby forest trails, and picnicked by Lake Mary. In the afternoon, they drove to Sunset Crater to explore its strange beauty. Fred took his sketchbook to put his memories on paper. She wished he would draw himself, but he never did. She wished she had a camera to take a photograph of him, but didn't have one. She tried to memorize his face as she memorized Nate's those few months ago.

Sunday they opted for complete privacy; they stayed in the room and prayed for the strength to live through the lonely weeks and months ahead.

Fred said, "I should get my assignment when I return to base. Either they'll decide to send me for advanced training, or they might send me directly to Vietnam. As soon as I know, I'll call you."

Why do some days drag; each day like a week? Yet when you want time to slow, it races past in a blur that leaves your head spinning. That was how the last weekend felt. Fred arrived and then it was time for him to go. Logically, I could put together a timeline of how we spent each hour. Emotionally, I'm drained by the speed of the weekend's conclusion. She felt a sense of déjà vu as she returned to the steps of Morton Hall, but this time not knowing when—or if—she'd see Fred again.

Fred held her in his arms and whispered, "Don't worry, honey. I'll be fine. We'll get through all this. I'll come home to play with our baby and to love you forever. Please, don't cry, Kara; you're breaking my heart," he begged, gazing down at her tear-streaked face.

"I ... I'm fine," she choked through her tears. "I'm sorry, Fred. I want to be brave like you. I promise I'll try not to cry. Don't worry about me, but call as soon as you're given your new assignment, will you, please?" He nodded, pulled her into a tight embrace and whispered his final good-bye.

As before, he turned quickly away, ran down the steps, and waved from the car as he drove away. Again, she got a glimpse of his tortured face. Again, April came to sit with her, to wait until she had the strength to move—the strength to breathe and the strength to live with the knowledge she could lose Fred when she barely had him.

She wasn't sure where Vietnam was. Never much of a news buff, so anything that didn't have a direct impact on her life was of little import.

Vaguely she remembered a history class in high school where they brought in international news items to share every Friday. One article she'd taken was on Indochina, which was part of the world Fred might be sent.

She wasn't sure where it was when she taken the item to class. She parroted the article, having no real indication what it concerned. Then she let the information filter out of her long-term memory. It was boring. Now she wished she'd paid attention because *now* it could have a major impact on her life.

Once Fred said he might be sent to Vietnam, she became obsessed with the news. She didn't like what she saw on the television or read in newspapers. They called it a military action—a fancy way of saying an undeclared war. Men were killed every day in that *military action*. She was sick with anxiety over the possibility Fred could go to the war-torn land. She prayed hard he could serve out his duty tour stateside, but she knew the chances were slim to nil it would happen.

November sixth, she got the call. The news was not what she'd hoped. His battalion was headed to Vietnam. He called from somewhere in Washington State. She thought it was Fort Lewis, but her mind was in a fog. The fort was the leaping-off point to *Nam*, as he called it. "I've got to cut this short, sweetheart. The other guys in the platoon are queued up waiting to call their families, too. Write to me at the same mailing address, Kara. The military will forward it on. Gotta go, the guys are waiting. I love you."

She focused hard on his words, especially the part where he said he loved her. She mumbled she loved him, too and tried to say she wouldn't worry, but she choked on the words. She memorized Fred's last words, "Gotta go. The guys are waiting. I love you." The line went dead as she sat holding the receiver. She stared blankly at the wall.

Chapter 14

When her legs allowed she stood and replaced the receiver. Filled with new resolve, she was determined to move forward with her life. Resolved to succeed in her classes and become the person Fred thought she could be. She'd make him proud.

Kara tore into her assignments as if they were life-and-death missions. In a strange way, they were. It was essential she finish classes and graduate before Fred got out of the Army. If she found a job by the time he returned, she could help with expenses. Though he'd have his veteran's money for school, they'd have plenty of other expenses, especially with the baby.

They'd discussed this while he was here, but she never absorbed depth of its importance. Now it was real, not just a vague plan they'd made in the surreal days after they'd married. She reached a point where she was no longer a victim. She didn't need to be rescued. She was going to fight her own battle on the home front. She'd embraced the challenge.

Sixteen days later, she bounced into the hall at Morton, excited over an aced biology exam.

Loud voices came from down the hall—someone laughing or possibly crying. Confused, she hurried to the open door of Mary's room. Her friends gathered around Mary, who lay screaming on the bed. Jillian leaned over to grab her. Still puzzled, she wondered, *"Is it a game?"*

"What's going on?" She asked tentatively.

"President Kennedy has been shot!"

"Yeah right. That joke's in poor taste isn't it. I don't care what your political leanings are. What's really going on?" Personally, she had supported the Arizona candidate, Barry Goldwater—like it mattered now.

Jillian stared at her, horrified. "Listen to the radio, Kara," she hissed. "They don't think he's going to live."

Her heart dropped to the pit of her stomach. *The President shot?* The thought was outrageous. Such things didn't happen in the USA. In the blink of an eye her world changed.

None of them could face more classes that day. Although Thanksgiving break didn't begin until the weekend, she didn't care. She wanted to go home to see her parents. Go where she felt safe—where people didn't assassinate the President.

The girls left the dorm en masse headed to the student center for more information. Geoff stood waiting outside the dorm with other boys they knew. The entire group decided go to the nearest church to pray for the President, Mrs. Kennedy, and Gov. and Mrs. Connally of Texas.

Mrs. Kennedy hadn't been shot, but reports said the President's brains splattered over her clothes and on her hands. Kara couldn't get the horrible image from her head. Gov. Connally was critically injured—shot in the back. His wife, like Mrs. Kennedy, was not physically harmed, but was frantic. Both women were seated next to their husbands when a madman gunned them down. She couldn't imagine the shock and horror those women must feel.

The nearest church was Our Lady of Guadalupe Catholic Church. The group filed into pews near the back. An eclectic group made up of Protestants from differing denominations, agnostics, Mormons, Catholics and Jews. They'd come together to pray for their country and to reach a measure of understanding. In that hour of solidarity, her faith was built. The country would make it through the upheaval with the combined strength of it's people. But she still wanted to go home.

When they returned to campus, the dean announced students should to return to classes. Ha! There was no way on God's green earth she could sit through class and get anything out of it. She turned to Geoff and asked, "What will you do?"

"I'm leaving as soon as I can throw clothes in the car. Do you want to go with me?" Determined, he gestured broadly. "Let the dean do what he can. He can't kick all of us out, can he?"

She turned and saw cars queuing up on both sides of the street loading for departure. There was going to be a mass exodus from campus and she was going with them. Geoff was right. The dean couldn't kick them all out. She didn't hesitate, she shouted over her shoulder as she ran toward the dorm, "I'll be ready and waiting!"

Geoff must have asked April what she planned to do. She had no transportation home. She came into Kara's room as she hastily threw clothes in a suitcase.

"Kara, I can come home with you? I have no way to get home. I don't want to stay here alone."

"Of course you can. My parents won't mind." Her parents would welcome April. They'd understand the girls wanted to be together during this time of crisis.

The radio worked intermittently as they crossed the Rim. From what they picked up, the shots were fired from the Texas Book Depository. By the time they reached Payson the station reported the police had arrested a man named Lee Harvey Oswald. He'd been arrested and charged with the murder of President Kennedy and a Dallas police officer.

She shook her head in disbelief. She recalled the famous radio drama *War of the Worlds*, in which people believed a space invasion to be real. An actual panic had ensued despite repeated announcements the show was a drama. Could this be some elaborate hoax? The grim truth was revealed as television played out the horrific scene ad nauseam.

Mom and Dad's closest friends came over that night to mourn the President's death with them. They, like her friends on campus, wanted comfort of family and friends as they faced this national tragedy. They watched the news the in morbid fascination for hours on end. The news was rife with speculation. Was there another shooter? Reports came of shots fired from a grassy knoll near the assassination. Was it a conspiracy? Had Oswald been in league with the Russians? These were among the many assertions on which the media speculated hour after hour. Kara was ready to scream in frustration.

On November twenty-fourth, the announcement came Oswald would be transferred from the Dallas Police headquarters to the Dallas county jail. The live broadcast was on the screen when a man pushed his way through the officers surrounding Oswald and shot him, point blank.

Except for the repeated broadcasts of Kennedy's assassination, she'd never seen anyone murdered. She'd watched numerous war movies with John Wayne and Audie Murphy. But they didn't count—that was acting. There was never any blood at all. Death was neat and tidy. Bang—fall down—that was it.

So she was horrified by her reaction of Oswald's murder—she laughed. She jumped up and down and laughed as she watched the assassin get blown away. It served him right for killing a man who taught them to ask what they could do for their country. Was it wrong to rejoice in yet another murder? He was going to be executed anyway. Was it different? Of course, an execution is the consequence of his actions. Murder is ... well, murder. But then dead is dead.

She wished Fred was with her. So logical and sensible, he'd help her understand the right and the wrong of her reaction to Oswald's death. Shaking herself, she recollected her resolve to be strong. She thought, *I'm an adult. I'll use my head and not let emotions rule my life. I won't let this throw me off track to reach my goals.* She wished, however, she'd find a letter from Fred when she returned to campus.

When April and she went to bed, they whispered for a couple more hours instead of going to sleep. Fosdick came along with his own brand of comfort.

"Geoff and I are getting awfully close. I'm concerned we're getting too close. Do you think if I ask him to cool things down, I'll lose him?"

She thoughtfully considered April's question. "I can't say for sure, but I know Geoff pretty well. If he likes you as much as I think he does, I don't think you'd lose him. He'll respect your decision. Believe me, I understand how fast things can get out of hand. You'll have my full support."

"Thanks, Kara. I do care about him, but we've known each other for such a short time. I want to be certain how we both feel before we do anything we might regret, especially since we have three more years of school ahead."

April hesitated. "You told me Fred isn't the father of your baby. If you ever want to talk about what happened, you can, but if you would rather not ..." She let her sentence hang, allowing Kara to decide what, if anything, to share.

After pausing to evaluate what was safe to share without betraying her promise to Nate, she whispered, "His name is Nathan—Nate. I met him the first day I moved here and I fell head over heels in love with him. It was obvious to everyone he loved me too. Hands down, he was the most handsome guy I've ever seen. As time passed, though, glaring issues came between us. One was the lack of shared faith. Nate wasn't a believer. He wouldn't even consider going to church. That was a major issue; there were other issues where we couldn't come to terms, too. I was afraid we'd never have a lasting relationship.

"One night Fred and I talked. I asked his honest opinion of Nate. Fred is the fairest person I know. He'll tell the truth even if it hurts him. His opinions were identical to mine. He even said that it was obvious Nate loved me. Anyway, Nate and I discussed our issues. He asked if he could think them over before we made any decisions. I agreed. In the meantime, I made a decision of my own."

"When Nate returned, he said he couldn't change who he was, nor did he want me to change. He decided to leave before he'd hurt me anymore. I'd come to the same conclusion ... to break up.

"My other decision was to go to bed with him before he left. I seduced him. Ever the gentleman, he offered me an out, but I refused. I knew there'd be consequences, but I never expected to get pregnant. Not the first time. I was so naive." She gave a wry chuckle. "Fred became my support after Nate left. I never told him what I'd done. When I followed your suggestion to write Fred, I hoped for advice. So when he offered to marry me, I was stunned.

"Of course, I had to tell him what happened was entirely my fault. He didn't care. He said he'd loved me from the first time we met. He's such a decent guy. I don't deserve him, but I'm glad he wanted me. He's exactly the kind of man I want in my life."

April reached across Fosdick and hugged her. "I knew you must have loved the father. You're not the kind of girl who sleeps around. So ... you're not sorry you broke up with him?"

"No, I'm not. I'll always have a special place in my heart for him, though. First love and all that." She smiled wanly in the dark. "The baby, of course, is a constant reminder—another reason I'll never forget him. Fred knows and understands that, too. In fact, Fred and I prayed for Nate and his brother Josh. But I hope I never see them again. If he shows back up, I've asked my parents not to tell him anything about me. It would be too hard to explain about the baby. What would I do if he wanted to keep in contact because of the baby? It would be a raw wound for all of us."

⌐◦

The day before Thanksgiving was a busy one. They tried to get as much done as possible. It was controlled chaos. The turkey would go in the oven early in the morning. They'd eat mid-afternoon. Tomorrow Mom would be busy no matter how much they did today.

Geoff and Aunt Frieda were coming for dinner, as would Enid, a widowed friend of her mom's. After breakfast she and April put the extra leaves in the table and set it with the good dishes. Breakfast was simple and light, but a feast would follow! She could hardly wait.

They agreed for Thanksgiving Day there'd be no television. It was a day to celebrate. They didn't need reminders of the assassination. Nor did she want any war news. She stopped, mid-step, and wondered what Fred and his fellow soldiers would eat. She closed her eyes and prayed they'd have a hot and festive meal, not their usual C-rations.

⌐◦

After everyone stuffed themselves in a personal salute to gluttony, April and Geoff went for a walk. They invited Kara along, but she begged off, hoping to give them privacy so April could address her concerns. Surely, Geoff was the man she thought he was and would not take offense. But she couldn't ask April until after they went to bed. When Geoff and April returned from their walk, however, Geoff had his arm around her and both looked relaxed and happy.

That night they snacked on turkey sandwich and a second piece of pumpkin pie, before they went to bed. The kitchen was spotless. Fosdick and Don José had joined in the festivities of the day with a dish of minced turkey for dinner. She laughed at their self-satisfied expressions as they trotted to bed.

As they put on pajamas, April told her about the conversation with Geoff. "It was funny, Kara. It turned out he felt pressured, too. He assumed I wanted more and wasn't sure *he* was ready. He was relieved. I am glad you suggested I talk to him. Now we can date without pressure."

Did she suggest they talk? She didn't remember, but it didn't matter since it turned out well. Exhausted by the day's events, they were ready for sleep.

As she closed her eyes, her thoughts turned to Fred, far from the comforts of home and family. She hugged Fosdick and let the tears come. As they fell, Fosdick's purr grew louder. He nestled close and nuzzled her face. She whispered her worries about Fred. The cat's rough tongue licked the tears from her face until she giggled. His sandpaper tongue hurt, but it was a good hurt. She prayed for Fred's safety. With a sigh she prayed Nate and Josh were happy wherever they were.

Chapter 15

Nate and Josh spent months in the wilds, far from human habitation. Hiding out since questions arose on how Nate had been able to rescue his friends from the fire. The tabloids had a field day loaded with speculation. No human could possibly have done what he did. Was he an angel come to save them? Perhaps the rescuer was an extra-terrestrial. The ridiculous speculations came to an end so they felt it was safe to return to a city. They traveled south-west to the City of Angels—Los Angeles and applied for jobs at a mission. It was close to their temporary refuge.

The mission manager, a man named Dale, gladly answered employment questions. "You can pick up odd jobs if you wait on the corner, but you have to be there early—by seven in the morning. Men stop looking to hire minimum wage laborers. If you're hired, they'll drop you back here in the evening. Do either of you do handyman work?"

"Yes sir. We spent time on building projects. Both Josh and I can do minor electrical and plumbing. We learned to hang doors and windows."

"Great. We need a good handyman right here. Also, we need reliable help in the kitchen. That job starts out as dishwasher, but you'd learn basic cooking skills if you pan out. If you're interested, both pay minimum wage plus meals."

"If you're willing to give us a try, I'll be your handyman."

I'd like to work in the kitchen." The kitchen work was hot, but heat never bother Josh, who'd opted for that position. Careful to pace himself, he worked fast enough so Amos, the chef, asked him to help prep and serve meals.

The kitchen was hot and noisy, but the men who worked in it were a nice enough bunch. Most had trouble staying away from the bottle or drugs. They'd lost their families and their self-respect along the way. Though they'd lived rough lives, it was obvious they were trying to begin again.

AA meetings were a regular activity at the mission. Most of the men attended the daily meetings, relying on a higher power to guide their lives. Men who refused to attend were served a hot meal and sent on their way. Those who listened were offered counseling, bed, and board.

The chef was a huge black man named Amos. His muscles made his sleeves bulge. Amos could handle a chef's knife in a way that mesmerized Josh. He sliced and diced so fast his hands were a blur. He finished a huge pile of carrots, onions, cabbage, and celery while another man chopped potatoes for vegetable soup. Amos helped finish the potatoes and dropped all the vegetables into a huge vat of simmering broth.

"Man, I have never seen anything like that. Could you teach me how to do it?"

"Why sure, son. Come on over here and I show you how it's done on these here rutabagas." Amos grinned a snaggled-toothed smile at Josh.

"What's a rutabaga?" Skeptical, Josh wondered if Amos was pulling his leg.

"You ain't never had no rutabagas before? They kinda like a turnip, but sweeter. Real good in stews and soups. Now here, grab on to this here knife like this, then grab on the rutabaga like this, be sure you keep your fingers out of the way, but sorta push it right along under the knife."

Amos stood to the side to let Josh try his luck. Josh did his best, but he was nowhere as good as Amos. He wondered if Amos was a vampire—one with special knife skills.

Amos slapped him on the back and said, "That was real good for a first try. It takes a lot of practice to get as good as me." He laughed deep in his chest. "You gonna get plenty of practice here, boy! I'm gonna see to that." Josh smiled up at the big man, knowing he'd received a major compliment.

Fragrant soup simmered on the commercial-sized range and the yeasty smell of bread came from the huge ovens. Josh helped a guy named Mick set the tables for the lunch crowd when Amos called Josh back to the kitchen.

"We gonna have spaghetti for dinner tonight, so I'm gonna need me some onions and garlic chopped up. You ready for more practice?"

"I sure am." Maybe it was stupid to be excited about chopping up vegetables, but Amos made it an art form, poetry in motion. Josh determined to get as good as possible.

Nate with toolbox in hand, repaired a door torn from its hinges by an angry visitor the night before. As he worked, he contemplated what Dale said. "The man was coming down off of drugs. He decided staying clean wasn't an option, so when a staff member tried to calm him, he flew into a rage. With amazing strength, knocked him aside as if he was a toy. He ripped the door from its hinges, and threw the door at a resident—broke the guy's arm. It's hard to understand a distorted mind, but occasionally we pull one back from the brink."

"I don't understand why you'd want to try. Why put yourself in harm's way for someone like that?" Before Kara, he'd have made short work of them, either ripping out their throat or snapping their neck.

Dale stared at him in silence. With a slow smile he continued, "Because of the success stories. Imagine one of these men lying out on the street dead drunk or strung out on drugs, filthy dirty and smelly. Then imagine that same man a year or two in the future. Clean-shaven and in clean clothes, back with his family. Holding down a steady job. Isn't it worth it—to save those we can? I think it is." Dale's compassion made Nate ashamed.

"I guess you're right, but it would be nice if the odds were better."

Dale nodded with a smile. "Yes it would, but our Lord shared a parable about a shepherd who searched for one lost lamb. He didn't think those were bad odds. Saving one lost sheep was a cause to rejoice. I think it still is." When he walked away, he left Nate deep in thought.

What was it with these believers? Where do they get that kind of faith? Mick and the men they'd volunteered with in Colorado had that

146

same kind of faith. They didn't know him or Josh, yet trusted them. Was Kara right about her God after all?

It took the rest of the morning to get the door properly hung, but it opened and closed with ease when he finished. Close to lunchtime, he washed hands and went to the cafeteria.

A loud commotion came from the kitchen. One man roared obscenities while another tried to calm him. "I'm gonna rip your guts out, you old s.o.b." A knife-wielding man faced a mountain of a man in there.

"Now why you wanna go and do something like that?" The big man soothed, saying, "You gonna ruin everybody's appetite, you screamin' like that. I don't wanna hurt you, son, so you just lay that knife down on that counter."

Instead, the man lunged, knife slashing. Before he'd taken two steps, he was on the ground with his arms pinned behind his back. The knife lay harmlessly on the floor. He screamed like a banshee. Josh had come out of nowhere to take down the knife-wielding maniac.

The big man came over to help Josh hold him. "Somebody call the po-lice!" Alerted to the incident, Dale dialed for help before Amos yelled.

Nate knew his brother wouldn't have been hurt, even if he'd been cut, unless he'd been stabbed in the heart, one of the ways to kill a vampire. It was a shock, though, to see him attack someone that crazy without killing the man on the spot. He wasn't sure which surprised him the most. Josh must have learned self-restraint. Nate held back a laugh. Kara would be surprised. At least she would have been if could tell her. Nate sighed and shook his head.

The practical reason he was glad that Josh hadn't been hurt was he healed so quickly. Questions would've begun and they'd have to move on. *Maybe leaving wouldn't be bad.* They could travel through Payson and get news about Kara. As quick as he had the though, he shook it off. He promised to stay away from her. He'd keep his promise, no matter how it hurt.

Squatting next to his struggling brother, he said, "Nice take-down, Josh. You did good."

"Thanks," Josh grunted with effort. "Got any duct tape ... in that toolbox of yours? This dude's ... hard to keep down." He nodded his head down at the crazed man who bucked like the meanest bull on the rodeo circuit. "This big guy helping me ... is Amos Maxwell, the head chef, so ... if you want any lunch ...you need to help us with ... Mr. Charm here." He gritted his teeth with the effort.

Nate laughed and got the duct tape. He taped the man's legs together and then his wrists halfway up his arms. Since the man continued to pour out a string of vile obscenities, Nate slapped a long piece of the tape over his mouth. The man's eyes bugged out, but all he could do was flop like a fish, helpless in his rage.

When Josh and Amos were free to stand, Nate gave his brother a quick one-arm hug. He turned his attention to Amos. "Hi, Amos. I'm Nate—Josh's older brother." The two men shook hands. "Now that we have this guy trussed up like a Christmas goose, are we going to eat? Something sure smells good."

"That's some of the finest vegetable soup you will ever have. Your brother is on his way to being a fine cook hisself. Pretty soon he'll be choppin' those vegetables about as fast as me—that's saying something." Amos smiled in approval in Josh's direction.

Amos directed the kitchen crew to load up the serving table, while he pulled the dinner rolls from the oven. Amos told them that he never made their bread. It was all donated, but the rolls went well with so many things that he usually made a batch three times a week.

Nate and Josh waited to eat until the police came to haul the troublemaker off to jail. The arresting officers made no attempt to hide their laughter when they saw the duct-taped addict lying on the floor. "I'd say you did a good job restraining him. We'll take him to headquarters like that, that is, if a couple of you fellas will help carry him to the car.

Nate and Josh volunteered. One under each arms, while one officer grabbed his feet, and the other supported his knees. They set the man on his feet when they reached the police car long enough to get door open. As he kicked his taped legs for all he was worth, but they forced him into the patrol car.

"I can't wait to get to the station." The cops chortled. "I wonder who we can get to help get him inside to book him. You two don't want to come and help, do you?" Josh and Nate begged off, chuckling at the friendly joshing.

Many residents of the mission stayed out of sight or well out of the way while the police were there. They weren't on the best of terms with the police themselves. Now they rushed to line up for lunch as Nate and Josh returned.

Amos hollered over to them. "You go ahead and get in front of the line to eat. You done earned that today. He smiled his big snaggled-toothed grin in their direction. The men in line stood back to give them room.

Amos was right to brag about his vegetable soup and the rolls. They were excellent. The rolls were soft and yeasty, and worked great to sop up the soup as they neared the bottom of the bowls. The soup couldn't have been any better. The vegetables were tender, but not mushy, and the flavors melded into—well, perfection.

Nate went in to the kitchen to give Amos his verdict on the lunch when he noticed two cabinet doors hanging off-kilter. "Would you like me to fix those for you? It shouldn't take long, and I'll keep out of your way."

"That would be nice. The best the last guy did was keep 'em on, but they won't stay closed like they's supposed to." Like Josh, Nate worked slower than he could, knowing Amos watched as he worked.

"You two boys are a wonder," Amos remarked. "Your daddy must of taught you real good how to work. He'd be mighty proud to see how you're doing."

They shared their usual story of being orphaned. "Now ain't that too bad. Family's important. It's good you two stay close to each other. I ain't seen none of my family for nigh on to twenty years. See, I was a Navy cook, but the bottle took me over those long days and nights at sea. They kicked me out of the Navy right as the war ended. I never went home again. I shamed my family 'cause I couldn't seem to stop drinkin'. Well, I finally ended up here, got cleaned up and started going to AA.

I've been dry for six years now, but I still can't face my family." The big man shook his head sadly.

Nate wondered how to help the big man make peace with his family. He agreed: family *was* important. He'd ask Dale if Amos had family living, surely they'd want to know.

"Hey, Dale, is there anything else I can repair today?"

"There's a toilet running on the second floor and a leaky sink on the main level. Neither should take much time"

Nate asked his question. "What do you know about Amos's family?"

"Why do you ask?" Dale's reply was terse. He listened, eyebrows raised.

"I'm not being nosy; well, I guess I am, but it's with good intentions. See, we talked about the importance of family. Amos told me he hadn't talked to his family in almost twenty years. He said he shamed them and couldn't face them. It appears to me he's a good man—at least he is now. I got to thinking; shouldn't his family have a choice in the matter?"

"Hmmm. I suppose they should, but I don't want Amos upset by you asking a bunch of questions. Nor would I want to raise his hopes up needlessly." Dale scratched his chin and stared at Nate.

"Neither would I. I guess that was why I wondered what you might know. Is there a way to track them down without Amos's knowledge? If they wanted to contact him they could, but he wouldn't have to know until then."

"You may be on to something. I don't have the time to search for someone who may have died or moved from their last known address. Tell you what: I'll let you read his contact information if you swear never to tell Amos what you're up to." Dale reached into a drawer. After a brief search, he pulled out a file. "I hope you realize how important confidentially is here, I trust you'll not to share any information in that file."

"I won't. My only interest is to help Amos reunite with his family. But if you don't mind, sir, I'd like to tell my brother. I guarantee you can trust Josh. He knows I'd kick his butt if he told anyone."

Dale chuckled and gave his approval. "Restrict your search to after hours or on your days off."

Nate agreed, then considered the best way to search. Public libraries kept phone books from other states, so he decided to begin there. He and Josh would load their pockets with coins to make as many long-distance phone calls as necessary.

When they left the shelter for the abandoned building where they lived, Josh said a room was available at the mission. "It has bunk beds and there's a bathroom across the hall. What do you think?"

"Is there a specific time we'd have to be inside? Maybe we should find a rental instead. We need to hunt. No matter how good the vegetable soup, we'll need blood. In fact, I need to hunt now."

"I didn't think to ask, but I'll find out tomorrow. I wouldn't mind hunting myself. I hope we can find something other than rats, though. I hate rats." Josh shook his head in disgust.

"Most cities have coyotes in them and I'm sure there's an abundance of other feral animals. We'll hunt for them. I've got a couple of things to talk to you about. What would you think about trying to track down Amos's family—see if they're interested in reconnecting with the big guy? With all his talk about family, I'm positive he misses them."

"That's a great idea. What if we find them and they don't want to see him?"

"Exactly why we're not going to say one word to him or anyone else. Dale knows, but none of us wants to see the big guy hurt."

"Got ya. What else did you want to talk about?"

"I wondered why you didn't kill that maniac in the kitchen today. I don't mean drink his blood or anything like that, not in front of everyone, but why didn't you snap his neck?

Josh came to a complete stop, forcing Nate to turn to look at him. "You have to ask? Nate, I promised you I'd never kill another human. I know you made the promise for yourself, but I'd messed up your life so bad, I swore I'd help in any way I could—even if it meant no more human victims. I intend to keep that vow."

Josh's wide-eyed explanation brought Nate up short. He remembered those words, but Josh was so thoughtless he never expected he'd keep his vow.

He bowed his head. "I am sorry, Josh. I never believed you'd follow through. I assumed you spoke out of the emotion of the moment." An overwhelming surge of love washed over him.

"No, man. I meant every single word of it. It's like Amos said, 'family is important.' I never want to hurt or disappoint you again." Josh's voice was husky. He hugged his brother.

After they slugged each other's arm, they hunted in earnest. They made it a game, to see who could come up with the first kill. Josh ran across the street. He listened down the opposite alley. He made the first kill, when he found a large raccoon raiding a garbage can. Nate was moments behind as he found a mangy coyote. He'd was right; coyotes lived in the city.

When they were satiated, they searched for the nearest library. A branch location was open. They walked in and searched for a desk clerk. Eventually, a pretty, petite young woman walked up to the desk pushing a cart. "Can I help you find something?"

"Yes, Miss. Does this branch carry telephone books from other states?" Nate figured he would cut to the chase and not waste time searching for something not there.

"We have a few. Is there a particular state you are interested in?" Nate told her the name of the state and the city that Amos had come from. He hoped they'd be lucky first time out.

"Oh, I'm sorry, but we don't carry that one here. Your best bet would be to go to the main library. Let me write down the address for you." They followed her to an office where she wrote it down.

"Thank you, Miss; you've been a great help." Nate turned toward Josh who stared at the young woman. She was pretty thing with soft blond hair and bright china blue eyes. Obviously, Josh had taken in every aspect of her looks. Nate nudged him to get his attention. Josh glanced at him then turned toward the young woman. "Uh, Josh. Think about what you're doing. You know it didn't turn out so well for me." He kept his voice low so the girl couldn't hear him.

"Umm, I know, all I want is to see if she'll go for a cup of coffee after she gets off work. That's all. I'll behave, Nate." Josh was completely distracted.

"I'm not worried you'll behave; I'm worried you'll get hurt."

"I know, I know. She might refuse to go out. I'm just going to see. Wait for me while I ask her." Against his better judgment, Nate agreed.

The young woman's eyebrows raised as Josh returned to the desk. "Can I help you with something else?"

"I wondered if you ...ah ... would like to get a cup of coffee after you ...ah ... get off work." He gave his most ingratiating smile to the girl.

"Thank you, but I never go out with strangers." She smiled sweetly back at Josh, her eyes dancing.

"I'm Josh and you met my older brother—Nate—over there. It's just for coffee or whatever you want. We're new here in town, so it would be nice to make a friend."

She gave him an appraising look. After a pause, she nodded her head. "I may be sorry, but okay." Her lips lifted into a smile. "I get off at nine. There's a twenty-four hour coffee shop around the corner. Turn right when you go out the main door. I'll meet you there."

"Great! Oh, what's your name?"

"It's Elizabeth, but everyone calls me Liz.

Saturday morning Nat and Josh traveled unfamiliar streets to the main library. Nate made a beeline to the main desk for information. "Walk down this aisle to the fourth center shelf. You'll find note paper and pencils available if you need them."

"Thank you, Ma'am." Nate found the phone book for the last known city for Amos's family. Josh reached for one nearby as they began their search. To begin, they searched for Amos's father. The search broadened for anyone with the same last name. Each wrote down possible names and phone numbers. After exhausting the names available in the state, they put the phone books away. It was time to make calls.

The monologue was always the same. "Hello, I'm looking for any surviving relatives of Amos Maxwell. Mr. Maxwell served as a Navy cook during World War II. Are you by chance a relative?"

People's responses differed. Some apologized, saying they weren't related. A few were angry at being bothered. Others tried to be helpful. When they began to get discouraged, they hit pay dirt.

The young man who answered the phone asked, "Did you say Amos Maxwell? That could be my daddy's brother. Can I get you to call back in an hour? He ought to be home by then. It'll give me a chance to prepare him. Is it bad news?"

"Not at all. I'd say it could be good news." Nate brightened and began to smile.

"Good. He doesn't need more bad news. My granddaddy passed last month, so he could use all the good news he can get."

"Okay, son. I'll call back in an hour." Nate shook his head with a frown as he related the death of Amos's father.

"I'm sorry his daddy died, but he has a brother and a nephew. He may have other relatives living, too."

"You're right. I should be happy." Each minute was agony, but the hour passed. Nate re-dialed the number. Snatched up on the first ring, an anxious voice shouted, "Hello? Are you calling about Amos, my brother?"

"Yes sir, I am if he is the Amos Maxwell that served at sea on a Navy vessel during the war."

"Did that Amos become an alcoholic?"

"Yes sir, he did. But he's has been clean and sober for many years now." Nate wanted to get that news in fast, in case the man wanted to avoid his alcoholic brother. Instead, he heard a sob from the line.

"God be praised. Thank you, Jesus. We thought he was dead. The letters we sent all came back marked unknown. You're telling me he's alive?"

"Yes sir, he is. He told us he'd let his family down—shamed them. That's why you haven't heard from him. My brother and I work with him. He speaks so lovingly about his family—his shame for becoming an alcoholic. We figured you should have a chance to choose for yourself. Amos doesn't know we're trying to find you. We didn't want him hurt, but if you want to see him ..."

The man bellowed, "Want to see him? Of course, we want to see him!" "He's family. He should have come home years ago."

"Let me give you the information where we work. Understand, I won't tell Amos we contacted you. Come when you're ready." Nate smiled broadly. He gave the man the address of the mission. "Josh and I look forward to meeting you."

Chapter 16

As they sauntered down the street the men speculated how Amos would react when saw his brother. Josh paused when he spotted a clock above a jewelry store. It reminded him of his date with Liz. He slapped Nate on the shoulder and raced off in search of a good pizza parlor.

When Josh forced himself to leave Liz's side that night, he thought, *Dear God in heaven, was that what Nate went through every time he saw Kara?* He never understood how hard it was to want someone, and you know you might not be the best partner for them. Now he did. His dead heart ached, but how could a dead heart ache? He had to talk to Nate. Now.

Nate's shoulders bowed and his head hung at Josh's query. He understood the pain all too well. But there were no easy answers in this world. All they could do was make the best possible choices and hope things worked out. The bigger question was best for whom? His decision was best for Kara and her family, but what about him? Was it best for him?

He sat through the night pondering how his life had changed. The things he'd learned, the friends he'd made along the way, and the way Josh had changed. Dawn peeked over the horizon when he concluded it was for his best too. He understood the ache in Josh's dead heart. His ached. Every single day he felt the pain of separation from Kara. He wanted her companionship and he wanted her physically, but it was not to be. Did love and growth always mean pain? He sighed as he watched the sky lighten and the stars fade. He stood and he roused his brother from sleep.

The young men arrived at the mission in time for Sunday chapel. All were expected to participate, even Nate and Josh. Josh was excited, but Nate remained reluctant. His reticence was based purely on fear. He couldn't face this God who hated him for all his murders.

During the sermon about the stoning of Stephen, Nate's mind wandered. He knew about Jesus. His mama told him stories about Jesus when he was a boy. She told him she named after someone in the Bible, too—a prophet, maybe. He hadn't thought about Mama in a long time. He tried to picture her face, things she'd said, but his memory was fuzzy. One thing he recollected was the comfort of her arms as she held him when he was frightened.

Suddenly aware of his surroundings he heard Dale speaking about some guy named Paul. He wondered what happened to the story of Stephen when the Dale's next words amplified, "... And in spite of his participation in Stephen's death, God chose him as his own. He chose Paul to preach the good news to all."

Nate's hands shook. Was it possible? He'd have to read the words himself. Josh borrowed the Bible Kara gave him and read it daily. He'd get it back so he could read this passage—maybe more. Kara had left a list of verses for him, but he'd never read them. If Dale was right, there was a chance he *could* be forgiven. Lightning hadn't struck, nor did the roof fall in—two events he'd joked about, but thought might happen if he entered a church.

He went through the day in a haze of confusion. He talked to the men, did necessary repair work. Sundays, Dale only wanted him to do what absolutely must be done. When he sat with the rest of the men for supper, Nate noticed Josh watching him. His brother knew something was bothering him. He'd be questioned as soon as they could talk in private.

They no sooner left the mission when Josh turned to his brother. "What's with you today? You've had a weird look on your face most of the day. Like you were there in body only. It was kind of creepy."

Nate threw back his head and laughed. "I didn't think I acted weird. Did I?"

"Yeah, you did. Maybe not everyone noticed, but I know you and you were definitely weird. So what gives?"

Nate ran his hands through his hair. "Did you hear what that Dale said about that Saul guy—the one who became Paul?"

A slow smile spread over Josh's face as he nodded his head. "You mean the part about how God chose him even though he participated in a murder? Yeah, I did."

"If it's true, could God forgive me, too?" An echo of forgotten hope rang in Nate's voice.

"I think you've got the idea, big brother. God forgave me back at that camp where we worked. Mick helped me understand." His grin was huge, like the Cheshire cat's. "I'm glad you finally got it. I wasn't sure how to talk to you, but those guys made it clear. The Bible Kara gave you helped too. You need to read it, too ... maybe talk to Dale."

Nate nodded; surprised Josh accepted this. "Why didn't you say anything? Make me understand."

"It's a gift, Nate. You don't shove it down someone's throat—you offer it. It's up to them to take it or refuse it." Josh shrugged his shoulders.

Where had he heard that before? It was Kara, she'd said it to him.

The rest of the week continued with a day-to-day routine. Part of Nate's new routine meant time in the Bible. He questioned Dale about God and what the Bible said. He asked what Josh meant by forgiveness being a gift.

The two boys anxiously awaited word from Amos's brother. Was he coming soon? Was he going to write first or just show up? They prayed for a happy ending for the big guy, since he'd given so much of himself to the men of the mission.

The problem was no one else was qualified to cook for such a large crowd. While Josh learned more every day, he wasn't ready to tackle a job this size. Chances were strong Josh couldn't stay long enough to develop the necessary skills. Then there was a chance Amos might want to stay within the safe walls of the mission.

After dinner on Friday evening, the doors burst open. A large man in a three-piece suit walked in. He asked for Nate, Josh, or Dale. Nate, who was waiting for Josh, realized immediately who the man was. He was a smaller, dapper version of Amos. Nate took him in tow and escorted him into Dale's office.

Dale looked up in surprise, since the men usually knocked, but he, too, recognized the man. He jumped up from his desk, came around and introduced himself to Mr. Arthur Jackson. "Nate, get Josh and Amos. Have them come here, so they can meet in private."

Nate held himself in check as he went to get his brother and Amos. His instinct was to blur there and back—anxious to see Amos's face when he saw his brother. Casually, he mentioned Dale wanted to see them in his office. His too bland expression betrayed him to Josh.

Amos, grumbled. "I'm tryin' to get this here cherry crumble made for dessert for tomorrow. What's he wantin'?" Nate, his face innocent, shrugged his shoulders.

They walked across to the office. Nate opened the door, stood aside for the others, then walked in behind them. Amos looked straight at Dale as he walked in, but he realized someone else was in the room. He glanced around and staggered back a step. Nate and Josh steadied him.

He whispered, "Arthur? Are you my little brother Arthur? You was jus' a skinny little kid of fifteen the last time I saw you. Now look at you. You're all growed up and lookin' fine." Amos's smile was as broad as could be, denying the tears welling up.

Arthur stepped forward and embraced his brother. "Amos, we all thought you were dead. The letters we sent through the years were returned. We just didn't know where to look anymore. These young men called my son—your nephew—to let us know you were alive. We want you to come home. Sissy is waiting at the hotel and so are my wife and children. I want you to come meet them tonight."

"I gotta finish makin' my dessert." Amos searched around, perplexed. "Where's daddy?"

Josh spoke quickly. "Amos, I'll finish the dessert. The recipe is on the counter. Go with your brother. See your family and get caught up on the news."

Amos nodded his head, overwhelmed. Arthur put an arm around him. With furrowed brows he said, "I've got some bad news, Amos. Daddy passed two months back."

Amos reached in his back pocket and pulled out a stained hand-kerchief to wipe his eyes. "I guess I'm none too surprised. I jus' wish I could of seen him one last time. You know, jus' to let him know I'm okay. I'm good with the Lord now, too."

"Daddy was at peace the last few months of his life. I think he knew that." Arthur's reassurance calmed Amos as they walked out the door.

Nate and Josh ambled over to the kitchen where Josh finished the last few touches on the cherry crumble and put it in to bake. The boys were excited about Amos meeting his brother. As they speculated who would take Amos's place if the big man decided to go home with his family, Nate said, "We'll have to leave it in God's hands."

Josh wheeled around to stare at his brother. "Is there something you neglected to tell me, man?"

"You were right. If the Lord can love other murderers and forgive them, he can forgive me. I don't understand it, but Dale told me other stories about men God loved that were murderers—Moses, David, a guy named John Newton. He's the guy who wrote the song *Amazing Grace*. He was a slaver. If God could forgive them, He can forgive me, too." Nate's eyes lit with confusion and joy.

Josh grabbed his brother's arms and shook him slightly. "It's about time. Nate nodded in agreement.

When they returned to work the next morning, Amos was hard at it, fixing the morning meal. He grinned his big smile as they entered the kitchen. "I gotta thank you boys for what you done. It was mighty nice. I saw my sister, met my sister-in-law, my niece and nephews last night. Being surrounded by family was pure heaven."

"So what are you going to do now?" Josh didn't mince words. "I assume you're going to go home. You should be with family."

"You right about that, but it ain't that easy. These men here are like family to me, too. I jus' can't up and leave 'em. No. Arthur, Sissy, and I talked about it last night. I am gonna go home, but not 'til I find me a replacement cook. I need somebody who will feed these men—body and soul. That ain't gonna be easy to find."

"I guess we all need to pray about it, don't we Amos?" Nate said softly.

"Yes sir, you got that right. The only way I can go back home is when the good Lord sends somebody."

⌒○

Three days later, a tall, skinny man walked into the mission. He asked if there were any jobs. Nate took him to Dale's office and knocked. He opened the door at Dale's bidding. After he told Dale the man was in search of work, Nate backed out the door. He speculated what kind of work the guy wanted. Not only was he extremely skinny, he wore a hopeless look about him.

His questions were answered a few minutes later when Dale, the skinny guy in tow, headed for the kitchen. Dale yelled over to Nate to follow along.

When they got into the kitchen, Dale introduced the stranger. "This is Maxwell Halter. He goes by Max. Amos, Max cooked for a cruise line, but he fell on hard times. I said we'd give him a chance. He'll work under your direction for a couple of weeks. Keep a close watch on him and report any problems to me. Do any of you have questions? If not, I'll head back to my office." He stopped to shake Max's hand. "Good luck, Max. I'll talk to you soon."

Nate went upstairs to take care of yet another backed-up toilet, knowing he'd get a full report from Josh. Curious about Max, he wondered what made this dour man tick. Right now, he didn't look like much, but looks could be deceiving.

It wasn't until after lunch break that Nate and Josh had a chance to talk. "The guy knows his way around the kitchen—that's for sure. He's as good with a chef's knife as Amos. We finished dinner prep before lunch. The guy is awfully quiet. All he's said was 'yes, sir' or 'no, sir' to everything Amos asked. It was kind of weird. Everyone skirted around him since no one knew what to say."

"Does he have a family?"

"Well, no. That was one of the questions Amos asked him and all he got was a 'no, sir' answer." Josh frowned in frustration.

"I suppose we'll have to wait for him to settle in to get any real answers." Nate ran his hands through his hair. Could this man be the answer to their prayers— let Amos move back to his family?

Several days passed before more was learned about the mysterious Max. He opened up after he heard Amos talk about his family. "You're real lucky to have family. I had a family. My wife, Gladys, and two boys, Charlie and Leonard, lived with my parents in our family home. When I was out on a cruise the house caught fire. It was an old place." He paused, drew a deep breath and continued. "They didn't wake up in time. The firemen said they were dead before the place finished burning. Not one of them made it out alive."

He stared off into space. "The report said the old wiring caught fire. I couldn't cope with the loss of my entire family. I couldn't eat; couldn't sleep. I tried sleeping pills and alcohol. Everything I tried made things worse. The cruise line had to let me go. I don't blame them. I couldn't do my job. The loss of my job forced me into rehab. It was tough, but I made it through. Like they said, 'Take one day at a time.' But it's not an easy thing to do when you've lost everything. Some days a single hour is a struggle."

Laying a hand on his arm, Josh told their tale. "Nate and I lost our parents in a flood. A few years later, we lost our foster family in a fire. We were the only two who survived. We'd gone hunting. When we came back, the house was a blazing inferno. We heard their screaming, but we couldn't get to them. It was hard to take." It was quiet for a moment as Josh sighed.

"How did you deal with it?" Max wondered.

"I hated the world and everyone in it for a long time. I finally found peace in my heart. Now I'm a happy guy. I hope you find that peace. Talk to Dale. He might be the one to help you." Josh empathized with the man and hoped Max could find the same peace he and Nate found.

Chapter 17

When she returned to campus, Kara was delighted to receive long-awaited letters from Fred. The military didn't hold to a regular mail delivery schedule. But she wasn't going to complain since she had letters in hand. Anxious to read them in private, she returned to her room.

Dear Kara,

I miss you so much. I hope you and the baby are doing fine. I'll bet you are beginning to show by now. Don't forget to ask Geoff to help when the time comes for you to move into the apartment.

Vietnam is like stepping into another world. I can't imagine any place being so different from the beautiful high desert and the mountains of Arizona.

When we got off the plane, it was like stepping into a steam bath fully clothed. The sweat pours off of me in this place. I don't know if I can adequately describe it to you. Saigon is like a swarming anthill. It's a combination of all the military forces there—with men on foot, various types of ground vehicles trying to blend with all the locals. Locals who push items into our faces in an effort to sell us anything and everything. I mean that quite literally. You'd be shocked at what goes on here. The commander warned us not to trust anyone—not even old people or little kids. It's strange not to be able to trust the people around you.

We get our orders tomorrow as to where we'll be sent.
I wish it was home. I'll send you some drawings soon, too.
I miss you a bunch.

Love,
Fred

It was easy to tell Fred was homesick from the letter. She tried to compare his feelings with how she felt when she'd come to this campus, but there was no comparison. No sense of the familiar, only a strange climate filled with unfamiliar people. She rubbed the moisture from her eyes. She missed Fred terribly, but she had to keep her letters upbeat. It wouldn't help him if she whined.

She checked the postmarks on the letters and tore open the next one.

Dear Kara,

I haven't heard a word from you yet, but from what the old-timers say, that's to be expected. Did you get my other letter? I hope you don't worry.

Lately, we have been slogging through rice paddies on a regular basis. I came face-to-face with a little kid riding on the back of a water buffalo. They look scary, but actually, they're gentle creatures. I'm enclosing a picture for you. So you'll get a general idea of the area and the people.

Some days I swear I'll never be dry again. It rains a lot. We try to keep our feet dry, so we change our socks often so we don't get foot rot.

I have to close because they're going to pick up the mail soon. I want you to know that in spite of my complaints, I'm fine. I love you a bunch!

Fred

The folded picture he'd enclosed was a drawing of a small boy on the back of a huge beast she could only compare to a Texas longhorn.

The rice paddies had small dikes surrounding them. They reminded her of her grandparents' yard in Phoenix. They watered by irrigation, flooding the yard. It slowly soaked into the arid desert soil. She reached for the last letter.

Dear Kara,

We went into to town (Saigon) for a couple of nights. All the guys want to go to bars. Frankly, there's not much else to do except sit around base. The bars are nothing like I've seen before. They are full of bar girls hanging around trying to get us to dance or buy drinks. At least they play familiar music. You know I like to dance, but the girls want you to buy their drinks or other services they provide.

I've seen the only movie playing at the base and read a lot at the base library, so I went out with the guys for a change of pace.

All I could think about was dancing with you. Holding you in my arms and from there ... Well, you get the picture. I miss you so much. I miss the way you smell, the touch of your bare skin next to mine, the way you laugh. I miss every single thing about you, Kara. I love you so much. It's hard to be so far away.

We just got news that the President was assassinated. The whole camp is in an uproar. I expect we'll get more details soon.

Love,
Fred

Her tears a flooded. She missed him in the same way he missed her. She felt his arms around her in bed at night. Listened to the beat of his heart. His unfailing good humor, which was being sorely tested. She tried to focus on the good things she had and the time he'd return to her. She answered his letters immediately.

Dear Fred,

I got three letters from you today! It made me so happy. I assume you have gotten mine, too, including the one about poor President Kennedy. It's funny, now that we're back on campus, I don't think about him so much. I have too much else on my mind.

Yes, I am fine. The OB says the baby is growing at a normal rate. My clothes are getting tight, especially around the waist. I had to set aside two outfits and all my jeans, too. Elastic waistbands are my new style. I'll probably have to tell Mom and Dad soon.

Classes are going well. I'm keeping my grades up. I should have a good GPA by the end of the semester. I may even make the Dean's list. Keep your fingers crossed for me.

Geoff and April plan to help me with the move, so don't worry, it's all handled.

Speaking of worry, what is this about bar girls? Tell them to keep their hands off my man! Sorry, but I have to tease you a little. Go ahead and dance, but think of me when you do.

By the way, I love the picture of the little boy on the back of the water buffalo. I am going to find a frame for it.

I miss you too, Fred, so much it hurts. I dream about you. I wake when I've reached for you and realize you're not next to me. Please take good care of yourself—and don't forget to have plenty of dry socks on hand. You can't dance if you rot off your feet!

Geoff and April ask about you all the time. I'll share parts of your letters. I love you very much and look forward to the day when you return to me. You're always in my heart.

Lots of love,
Kara

She re-read the letter to make sure it said what she wanted it to say. She wanted to get it in the mail before pick-up time. She found an envelope, addressed and stamped it, and then put the folded letter inside. Grabbing her books for afternoon classes, she picked up the letter and headed out the door.

A month after Max revealed his past to the staff at the mission; the word came down from Dale. Amos planned to leave in two weeks. Max would take over as head chef at that time. Everyone who worked with Max reported a slow, but steady improvement in his attitude. He smiled more often and began to reach out to other men in friendship. In a little more time, he'd have the routine down pat. He learned Amos' recipes of the men's favorite dishes. Food at the mission was basic, low-cost food. It had to feed all who came. But that didn't mean it couldn't be tasty.

As the time got close, Amos danced with excitement. "My brother is gonna set me up in my own place. I'm gonna be cookin' simple meals, but I'm gonna throw in Cajun cookin' too. Fried okra, red beans and rice, shrimp, jambalaya, crawfish, greens. Um ... mum ... You boys will have to come visit and try out some of my good cookin' there."

Nate and Josh laughed. "You can bet on it. We'll pop in and surprise you! You'll see two hungry people when we do."

"When you come, I'll throw in sweet potato pie! You gonna love that." Amos grinned at them and chuckled. "My brother is gonna get me some new teeth, too. I'll be so handsome you may not recognize me." He threw back his head and laughed.

Everyone at the mission would miss the big man—not only his cooking, but his unfailing good humor. But not one person begrudged the fact that he was going home. The men planned a surprise party for him before his brother came to take him home.

Dale had them all come into his office individually during the week to take pictures of them. He put all their names on the back of the pictures. Put the pictures in a photo album for the big guy to take with him.

He'd never forget the men from the mission. Max planned to make a sheet cake. Josh would make punch and coffee for a going-away party. There was lots of laughter and a few tears disguised as something in his eye before he went to start his packing. He would be missed.

Nate gave the appearance of being happy, but Josh noticed an increasing restlessness in him. He wasn't sure if he should bring it up or wait for Nate to talk about it. He decided to give him more time, because he was eager to see Liz.

That evening, he paced back and forth in front of the coffee shop, waiting for Liz to show up. He wished he'd talked to Nate, because he planned to reveal what he was to Liz tonight. He took a deep breath, although he didn't need the oxygen, the act helped him relax—a little. He checked the time. She said she might be late, but how late? He strode toward the library to check. He couldn't stand to wait any longer. He was anxious to talk to her.

As he rounded the corner, he heard a scream. Down the block Liz grappled with a man. Josh blurred into motion and reached her a second after he saw the flash of a knife. He grabbed her attacker and launched him into the street. The man landed in a crumpled heap and stayed down, seriously injured or dead.

Liz lay in a growing pool of blood. Kneeling by her side, he lifted her head. Her eyes fluttered open. Her lips moved, but without sound—only a gurgle of blood. He bent close and saw she was trying to say something. Liz mouthed "I love you".

He had no choice. He heard in the past vampire blood could heal, but if the person died, they automatically became a vampire. He didn't know if it was true. He'd never had a reason to try it—but, please God, let it work. He bit open his wrist, shoved it to her lips. Could she ingest enough blood for it to work—assuming it worked at all?

"Liz, I want you to know, I'm a good vampire. So is Nate. We gave up human blood. I want you by my side for eternity. 'Please God, let this work. Maybe I'm selfish, but I need her.'" He tried to hold back a sob as he held her close to him. He rocked her back and forth in his arms as gurgling stop. He was afraid to look at her.

He held her limp form until her body stiffened, then relaxed. She gasped, "Wha-what happened? I feel so strange."

The blood worked. He picked her up and carried her to her apartment and got her cleaned up. "I'm hungry," she said.

Josh thought he knew the reason for her sudden hunger. He hoped and prayed he was right. He leaned forward and laid his head on her chest. There was no heartbeat. He drew in a stuttering breath. "Liz, I hope you're gonna be happy about this. You're a vampire like me."

She smiled questioningly at him. "Am I a good vampire?"

"Probably not yet, but I'll teach you to be good. He took her hunting and showed her how to kill without making a mess.

When they finished hunting, they met with Nate to bring him up-to-date on what occurred that evening. "I think it might be a good idea if you took her to the mountains. Keep her away from people for a while—at least until she gets used to her new diet and life. It would be safer for all concerned. Think of it as an extended honeymoon."

Both Josh and Liz smiled at that. "What about work? I can't leave the mission in the lurch." Josh worried who'd cover for him with Amos leaving.

"Tell you what: You go in tomorrow morning while I stay with Liz. Tell them I'm sick. At the same time, ask for a leave of absence. Heck, tell them you're getting married and you'll be gone for a month-long honeymoon. You can say good-bye to Amos. I'll take Liz to the library. She can ask for a leave, too."

"What about my apartment? The rent is coming due and I won't have the money if I don't work," Liz asked

"Don't worry about that, sweetheart. I've got money saved, so we can pay the rent ahead. We'll need a place of our own anyway. I'll move in with you when we get back." Josh threw a possessive arm around Liz. She smiled as he bent to kiss her.

When he looked up, there was pain on Nate's face. He hadn't thought his attachment to Liz might hurt Nate. They'd never lived apart since they'd become vampire brothers. Now Nate would be alone.

Chapter 18

After the couple left on their trip, Nate moped around the mission. Amos was ready to leave and he'd miss the big man. Dale noticed his depression, called him in to his office. "Nate, what is going on? I'm worried about the way you've be acting. Do you want to talk? Remember, I'm here to help, son."

Nate slumped into a chair, face in his hands. "I'm not sure what to say. It's all mixed up. I'm happy about Josh and Liz going on their honeymoon."

Hands shoved in his pockets, he stood and paced the room. "Really. I am happy for him, but I lost the love of my life several months ago. Now I'm losing my brother. What do I do about that? I don't want to pull him down when he's happy. But I'm lonely ... and jealous, too. I thought I was going to get the 'happily ever after' he got. It didn't turn out that way for me. I don't know what to do."

"If you could choose to do anything right now—right at this moment—what would you do?"

Nate stopped pacing, his brows drawn. "I'd find Kara. Tell her how I've changed. I'd hope she'd reconsider and take me back. She has a great family and I don't want any of them upset."

"What if she wants nothing to do with you? Will you be okay with that?" Dale studied Nate's face.

"No, I'll never be okay with that ... but if that's the way it is, I'll have to accept it and learn how to live without her. I'll always love her."

"Would you like the time to go talk to her?" Dale asked.

"Yeah, but I promised I'd leave her alone. Would it be going back on a promise?" Nate's eyes squeezed shut recalling the night he left Kara.

"How long has it's been since you broke up?"

"Almost a year."

Dale sat his hands folded, his head bowed. "That's a reasonable amount of time to check back. The reality is, Nate, during the past year she may have moved on. She may prefer you to stay away. Be ready to face the possibility. If you want the time off, you can have it. We'll get by short-handed for a couple of weeks."

"I'd like that, but I'll wait until Amos leaves. An extra few days may help me prepare for whatever happens. Thanks Dale."

"You're welcome, son. You know all our men have problems; if a little time off will help you with yours ... I'm happy to give it to you. I am glad you'll wait until Amos leaves, though. He's come to consider you and Josh good friends. I'm sure he'll appreciate it."

Following dinner that night, Nate and Amos, who was all smiles, talked. "You never gonna guess. My brother leased a spot for my café already. When I get there we're gonna sit down and list all the supplies I'm gonna need. Decide on a menu. You remember us talkin' about some of the dishes I want to fix—sweet potato pie for dessert. Mmm-mmm. How does that sound?"

Nate grinned at his friend. He enjoyed his excitement. "You make my mouth water talking about it."

"I been thinkin' about servin' up breakfast, too. Ham and red-eye gravy, grits, hot biscuits, and eggs. I may throw in a few other things, but I'm gonna stick with the basics to start with. I'm hopin' I can open within the next month, but there's a lot of little details to plan."

"I promise I'll come try some of that food as soon as possible. I'm sure Josh and his wife will too. Did Dale tell you I'm leaving on a short trip?"

"No, son, he didn't. What's up?" The big man watched Nate's face.

"I'm going to see if I can win my girl back again. It's been almost a year. I'm praying she's forgiven me." Unable to meet Amos's eyes, he rubbed his forehead.

Amos's huge paw gripped his shoulder. "I can tell by lookin' at you that you love this girl. I hope and pray it works out for you. But you might have a tough row to hoe, son. Whatever happens, there's a lot of people who care about you. You're not alone."

Nate bit down on his lip. "Thanks, Amos. It means a lot to have friends like you."

"You let me know what happens so I can be praying for you, son, okay?"

Nate nodded "I guess I better get busy. Finish my repairs. I don't want leave work undone when I go."

Arthur came the next day, accompanied by his oldest son. Amos' few things were packed and waiting in Dale's office. As Amos went to retrieve his suitcase, he ran the gauntlet to get through the room. Every man present wanted to shake his hand, and wish him well.

Amos smiled through his tears as greeted his brother and nephew. Dale raised a hand in blessing. He prayed for a safe trip and a happy life. Nate hugged his big friend, shook Arthur's hand and walked them through the crowd to the door. "Adios, my friend. Vaya con Dios—Go with God. Don't forget, I get free sweet potato pie when I come!" Amos bellowed a laugh.

Nate spent the remainder of the weekend repairing everything that hinted at a problem. "Dale, I'll leave Monday. If my brother gets back before I do, don't tell him where I went. Just let him know when I'll be back." At Dale's questioning frown he added, "Josh felt partly responsible for the breakup. I don't want him upset."

"I understand. I'll remember you in my prayers, Nate. Have a safe trip. Remember the *one* who has your best in mind." As Nate walked away, Dale bowed his head in prayer for the young man's peace of mind and protection from evil.

Her friends from the dorm took turns staying nights at the apartment as time for the baby drew near. She hoped one of them, preferably April, would be with her when she went into labor.

Fred and she discussed names via the mail, but they hadn't made a definite decision—at least for a boy. If it was a boy, she wanted to name it after Fred. Fred fussed. He didn't want a son called "Freddy." He hated his nick-name. As for Fred, Jr.—he hated that, too. His suggestion was

Peter after her father, or Nathan. She hadn't heard back with a response on her latest suggestion of Fredrick Nathan. They could decide on nicknames later. But, it wouldn't be Freddy. Rick? Possibly.

Girls' names were no easier. She didn't want a "little Kara." Fred was vehement against using his mother's name; angry at her behavior. He thought it showed a distinct lack of morals. His baby girl wouldn't suffer from the association.

Personally, she thought his wounds were too raw and hoped he'd forgive his mother in time.

Both of them liked the name Joann, but she didn't want it as a first name either. Again, there was the chance of a cutesy nickname.

Fred came back with Natalie Joann. It didn't matter to him if the baby was boy or girl; he wished to honor Nate through the naming of his child. Natalie was the closest girl's name to Nathan. She liked the name. Secretly, she hoped it would be a little boy for Fred; although he clearly stated he didn't care either way. All he wanted was a healthy baby and an easy birth for her.

Mom's friends threw her a baby shower. Though no one said so, they obviously suspected Fred and she had put the cart before the horse—all counting on their fingers from the day they married to the date of expected birth. The obvious fact was delivery would be "early." Fortunately, none of them—especially her parents—knew the real truth. They were upset enough about the timing.

Her friends threw a second shower after they saw the gifts she'd received. This baby was coming into this world with plenty of clothes, blankets, and even a crib and stroller. She was touched when Jillian crocheted a soft multi-colored pastel baby blanket and Mary sewed a bunting out of a darling pale green flannel material. It would be plenty cold for a while, so the bunting would get plenty of use.

She thought of the old rhyme, "Bye, baby bunting, daddy's gone a-hunting ..." Her daddy had gone a-hunting, but what he was hunting was hunting him back. She frowned, worried about Fred. It was harder and harder to watch the evening news.

April stayed over after the shower. They washed and put away all the tiny things. They ooo-ed and ahh-ed over each item a second time as they put them away. The crib was made with new sheets and blankets. She was ready for the big day.

Fred mailed a series of baby animal prints he'd drawn to frame and hang in the baby's room. He'd drawn a puppy, a kitten, a fawn, a bear cub, and even a gangly elk calf. The pictures were bright and cute. Everyone commented on them when they visited. People who'd never seen his drawings were amazed at his talent.

Mom and Dad purchased the crib for the baby and as an extra surprise, a rocking chair. Mom swore it would come in handy. She could rock the little one to sleep or sooth it when it was upset. Kara loved it. It was relaxing now—even if she struggled getting out of it. Then again, she had trouble getting out of anything. She didn't bend any more. She used folding chairs in classes. The desks provided didn't accommodate her ever-expanding belly.

April and Geoff planned to spend the weekend with her. They were bringing tonight's dinner. The baby dropped by her last doctor's appointment and the doctor said it could come any time. As far as she was concerned, *now* was a good time. She was scared to go into labor without Fred. However, it's wasn't like they had a choice in the matter.

She counted herself lucky to have supportive friends. Her friends organized a schedule to watch the baby when she returned to class. Each them had an hour or so during the day to baby sit. That was another thing: She was sick of calling it "the baby" or "it." She wanted to hold little Fredrick Nathan or Natalie Joann in her arms and call *it* by name.

April and Geoff were always cheerful company. After dinner, they played cribbage well into the night. April would sleep with her, while Geoff threw his sleeping bag on the floor in the baby's room. It was late when they said their goodnights. Weary, she crawled into bed.

In the wee morning hours, she awoke with a sense of uneasiness. It was time for her nightly trip to the bathroom—another irritating pregnancy issue. As she sat on the commode, she had the feeling again. As she stood, a severe abdominal cramp bent her over. It subsided rapidly, so she hurried back to the warmth of the bed.

As she dozed off, another cramp gripped her. She crept into the living room to watch the clock. She suspected she was in early labor. Seven minutes later, another cramp hit. *Shouldn't pains should be farther apart when you start labor?* Her doctor suggested she call when they were ten minutes apart. It was barely six minutes later when she doubled over with the next cramp. She no longer had the luxury of waiting.

"Umm, April, Geoff, get up. It's time." Her voice was urgent. They leaped out of bed.

The doctor's phone number was posted next to the phone. Geoff jerked on his clothes and dialed the doctor. April rushed out with the bag they'd packed for the hospital. Geoff ran to warm up the car while April brought her robe and slippers.

The trip to the hospital was a blur of pain and more pain. The tension in the set of Geoff's shoulders and the anxiety in April's eyes was proof of their concern. She bet they hoped and prayed she wouldn't deliver in the backseat of Geoff's car. She'd laugh at the thought if another contraction hadn't hit. At that moment, she didn't care where or who delivered the baby; she wanted this over.

Geoff and April helped her inside the hospital. The night nurse grabbed a wheelchair and rushed her into another room, to help her into a hospital gown. As they finished; she leaned over and vomited all over the floor. The doctor popped in and after a quick exam told the nurse to take her straight to the delivery room. When they got her on the table, the nurse told her *not* to push. Was she kidding? Every fiber of her being told her to push—push hard!

The doctor strode into the delivery room as he pulled on his gloves. He took one more, quick look. "We're not going to have any time to deaden her, the baby is crowning." He reached one gloved hand down and laid it on her abdomen, then told her to push. With teeth gritted, she grunted with the effort. Through a fog she heard the doctor say the baby's head was out of the birth canal. Her next major push brought out the baby's shoulders.

The doctor said, a smile in his voice, "You have a beautiful baby girl!" She opened her eyes and saw a dark-haired, red-faced baby who made a tiny squalling noise. Her Natalie Joann arrived, healthy, and beautiful. Kara's felt her face would break from her huge smile. She shook from the cold, so the nurse covered her with a blanket.

The doctor laid Natalie on across her chest. She admired the infant before the nurse took her to clean her up. "I'll show her to your family as I take her to the nursery. Once you're in your room, they'll be allowed a quick hello, but they'll have to leave until regular visiting hours."

April and Geoff were all smiles when they came to see her; excited at being a part of the miracle of birth. They pronounced Natalie perfect.

"Boy, you scared me. I thought you were going to deliver the baby before we could get you here!" Geoff chuckled. "I'll call your mom and dad right away. Do you want me to send a telegram to Fred to let him know he's a daddy?"

"Thanks, Geoff, I'd appreciate it. I'm not sure how fast he'll get a telegram, but it's sure to be faster than a letter." She wished she could hear Fred's voice when he got the news, but he was probably out in the jungle or slogging through rice paddies. She could hardly wait for him to see their baby. She needed a camera—soon. "Geoff, could you ask my parents to bring a camera? I want to create a photo record for Fred, so he'll feel a part of this."

Geoff laughed. "I doubt Aunt Joann or Uncle Pete need a reminder to bring a camera, but I'll ask them."

Geoff waited until they returned to her apartment to call Pete and Joann. He hoped the early hour wouldn't scare them, but they'd want to know as soon as possible. He dialed their number and waited as it rang four ... five ... six ... seven times. A groggy voice mumbled, "Hello."

"Hello yourself, Grandpa!"

There was total silence on the other end of the phone; then a voice said, "Joann, get on the extension. You're going to want to hear this." After a pause, her tentative voice said hello.

"Congratulations. You're the grandparents of a beautiful baby girl. Her name is Natalie Joann. She was born an hour ago. I thought you'd want to know as soon as possible."

"The baby is here? Is she healthy? Who does she look like? Does she have hair? How is Kara?" Joann's questions peppered the air, too excited to let Geoff answer.

He pulled out the stats on the new arrival. "Umm, she looks like a baby; red and wrinkly. She's seven pounds, three ounces; twenty-one inches long; lots of long, dark brown hair; and the doctor said she's healthy and Kara is doing fine, too."

"When you see her, tell her we'll be there as soon as we can make arrangements. Has anyone notified Fred?" Pete knew Fred was anxious for the news.

"I was going to send a wire later." He hoped to catch a couple hours of sleep first. At least there were no classes today.

"Don't worry about it; we'll send it. Geoff, thanks for helping Kara so much. You and April have been a real blessing—to Kara and us. Knowing you kept an eye on her relieved our minds."

"Hey, it's been fun and a reminder for April and me to wait." He chuckled, but it was no joke. He and April loved Kara, but her circumstances were a cautionary tale. "By the way, Kara wants you to bring her a camera so she can take loads of pictures for Fred. See you when you get here."

Chapter 19

All Fred wanted was a hot shower, clean clothes and a nap. Not necessarily in that order. Back from patrol, he was ordered to see the base chaplain. He growled "Yes, sir" to the officer of the day and stomped out the door. He knocked on the chaplain's door entered, and growled, "You wanted to see me, sir?"

The chaplain gave a warm smile. "I know you're looking forward to down time, but I have something you need to see." He held out a yellow Western Union envelope. Hands shaking, Fred took the envelope. Not waiting for an invitation he folded onto the closest chair. With clumsy fingers he tore the envelope open and unfolded the yellow sheet inside. He read each word slowly:

NATALIE JOANN ARRIVED THIS A.M. STOP 7 LBS. 3 OZ. STOP MOTHER AND DAUGHTER FINE. STOP CONGRATULATIONS TO THE NEW DAD STOP PETE AND JOANN.

Fred covered his face with trembling hands. To his embarrassment, tears streaked down. The chaplain sat quietly. As his tears slowed, the chaplain lifted his teakettle off the hot plate, poured two cups of water and added tea bags. He turned and sat on the edge of the desk and handed Fred a box of tissues.

As he wiped his eyes and runny nose, the chaplain handed him a cup of tea. "Bad news, son?" His question was gentle.

"No, sir. It's good news. My wife had a baby—a little girl. They're both fine." He gave a watery smile. "It's been hard being away, worrying about them ..." He heaved a sigh, shook his head wearily. "This whole pregnancy thing has been hard on both of us. Uh, she was pregnant when we got married. She's had to face a lot of wagging tongues. I don't know what you've heard from the chaplain at boot camp. Do they send you information about us?"

The chaplain didn't answer; he just lowered his head. "The baby isn't mine, biologically." Fred continued, "But I plan to be the best daddy possible for our little girl. Did I tell you it's a girl?" The cup turned around in his hands. "Kara's a wonderful girl; she got messed up with this guy. He's not a bad guy either, but they were wrong for each other. They agreed to go their separate ways before Kara knew she was pregnant. Kara and I were close. I loved her from the first time we met. When he took off, I was there for her as much as possible. We're the perfect fit. While I was in boot camp, she found out she was pregnant. She wrote asking for advice before my leave came up. I went home and talked her into marrying me. It was the happiest day of my life. You can see why it's hard being so far away."

"I wish I could give you emergency leave, son. It's not possible right now. Conditions are beginning to escalate here. Tell you what, though, you can try to call her from my office. It's difficult to get calls through, so you might prefer to write. Use my office if you'd like. I'll make sure it goes out as a priority."

"Thank you, sir. I'll write a letter. She's in the hospital. I doubt if I could reach her by phone anyway."

The chaplain handed him pen and paper, clapped him on the shoulder and left the office. He sighed as he walked toward the USO. So many boys with so many problems. He could do so little for them.

> *Dear Kara,*
>
> *Hey little momma, you did it! I heard from your parents that you're both fine. I wish I could have been there for you. Who took you to the hospital? How long were you in labor? There is so much I want to ask you. I want to hear your voice. I want to hear my little girl cry and coo and whatever else babies do.*
>
> *Tell me all about my little Natalie. Is she as pretty as her momma? I hope you can send me pictures of the two*

of you soon. The telegram didn't have too much informa-
tion in it. Of course, if they'd written a book, it wouldn't
be enough.

When I got back in from the bush today and was told
to report to the chaplain's office, I was grumpy because
I'm dirty and tired. Suddenly, it didn't matter anymore.
I feel like I am walking on air—in combat boots no less!

Chaplain says he'll get this out right away, so I'm
going to close. Write me soon and often. Tell Natalie her
daddy loves her and can't wait to hold her.

I can't wait to hold you either. You are so precious to
me.

I love you,
Fred aka Daddy

Fred placed the completed letter in an addressed envelope in the middle of the chaplain's desk. He knew Kara would write as soon as she was able. He also knew he might not get the letter for weeks. Mail was uncertain. That fact, along with the news his platoon was going out again soon, made for the long delays. He smiled as he thought about Kara and the wonder of being a daddy to a tiny girl halfway around the world. Right now, a hot shower and his bunk were a siren's call. He followed that call.

He woke to the sound of his friends calling his name. "What is this about you being a new daddy? ... When did you plan to tell us? ... Let's go celebrate!" Their excited voices ran over the top of each other in the pleasure of shared good news.

He left the telegram out, knowing someone was bound to read it. In a constant state of boredom, mail left unattended was fair game. He grinned up at them. Throwing his legs over the edge of the bed, he sat rumpling his hair. "What do you have in mind? A movie? The closest bar to drink and dance?" It was fine with him. He'd drink one beer and switch to coke. When he danced with a bar girl, he'd close his eyes and imagine Kara.

Nate set out on his journey well before dawn. The moon remained high in the sky after the eastern horizon showed streaks of pink, and then gold. It was a beautiful morning for running. As fast as he could run, it was still a two-day trip. While he wanted to hurry, he also wanted time for contemplation. He wanted to say the right words the right way. But he wasn't exactly sure what the right way was.

Deciding to spend the night in Needles before he crossing into Arizona, he stopped mid-afternoon. He'd cross the rest of the Mohave Desert after he rested and rehydrated. It was barren and dry land.

He checked into a room, showered and put on clean clothes. He'd wear the dirty clothes in the morning. An hour in the desert and his clothes would be filthy anyway. He hadn't brought many changes.

When he reached Flagstaff he planned go to a Laundromat before his search for Kara. She must live on campus, but he had no idea which dorm. Wherever she was, he wanted to wear clean clothes.

There was a twenty-four hour diner next to the motel. He ambled over. It had a good selection of food; breakfast served all twenty-four hours. Burgers, steaks, pork chops with all the fixin's. He ordered a rare T-bone, baked potato, salad and apple pie. "Just trot the cow over the coals for me, would you, Ma'am? Oh, make that pie a la mode, too." He grinned at the overworked waitress.

The steak was perfect, raw enough to dampen his need for blood until he hunted again. When he finished eating, he pulled out his wallet and left a substantial tip for the waitress. He figured she could use the extra money. Her job wasn't easy, especially in a place as busy as this.

He left early the next morning. The sun crested the horizon when he caught the scent of a coyote. They were plentiful no matter where he went. Leaving the road to chase it down, he caught another scent—the scent of milk. The coyote was a lactating female. Darn it, he couldn't kill her, not when she had pups to feed. He'd have to wait for something else. He let her loose and caught the scent of wild rabbits. He wasn't choosy about them. He drank their blood then tossed the carcasses to the coyote mother. The rabbit blood was a mere snack to him, but their flesh would help the coyote out. He'd continue to hunt.

As he reached the road, a pickup slowed and stopped. A man called out, "Where ya headed?"

"I'm on my way to Flagstaff."

"I'm only going as far as Williams, but if you'd like a ride, I'd appreciate the company. By the way, I'm Buddy." He offered his hand while he gave Nate in a speculative once-over. "Doesn't look like your backpack is large enough to hold the water you'd need to cross the desert."

"The ride would be great, Buddy. I'm Nate. It'll sure get me there faster! Thanks. You're probably right about not having enough water. I didn't plan too well for this trip." The truth was that he didn't need much water as long as he found a source of blood—something he'd never confess to this affable stranger. "Are you headed home?"

"Yep, it'll be good to get back into my own bed. My mom died a month ago. I've been in California settling her affairs. I sold her house in Temple City and sold off most of her stuff at an estate sale. I donated the rest. My sister kept a few small items. So did I. Neither of us needed much in the way of furniture, but we wanted a keepsake or two to remind us of her and dad."

"That's nice—to have something to remember your parents. My parents and our house were lost in a flood. There was no sense trying to find anything. It was long gone." Nate frowned with remembered pain.

Seeing his expression, the man changed the subject. "What has you headed to Flagstaff? A new job?"

"No, sir. I'm hoping to reconcile with my girlfriend. I know it's a long shot because it's been awhile since I've seen her. But, I have to try." Nate worked at a grin.

"She must be pretty special."

"That she is, sir; that she is." A faraway look in his eyes.

"I need to fill my tank. Would you be willing to drive while I nap?" Buddy asked, yawning hugely. "I sure could use forty winks."

"Absolutely. I'm not tired at all. I'd be happy to drive." The station was a mile down the road. Nate got out, pretended to use the men's room, returned to the pickup and slid behind the wheel. Buddy paid for the gas, made use of the facilities, returned to the truck. Slamming the door hard.

Buddy slid down in the seat and closed his eyes. His breath deepen into the rhythm of sleep in a matter of moments.

It would be easy to kill this man and dump his body along this stretch of road. Nate shook himself. What was he thinking? The words "deliver me from evil" popped into his head. He repeated them under his breath as a prayer until he regained control.

The hum of the tires relaxed Nate and allowed his mind to wander over the possibilities of his trip. The drive was peaceful since there was little traffic this early. He watched the sky turn golden and then brighten. A new beginning for the world and a new beginning for Kara and him.

It seemed only moments later when he saw the sign that announced Williams was five miles away. "Hey, Buddy." He paused as the man continued the deep breathing of sleep. He reached over and gently nudged the man.

"Buddy, we're on the outskirts of Williams."

The man snorted then gave a muffled groan as he straightened in the seat.

"Sorry to wake you, but I figured you'd want to know."

Buddy stretched his arms as far as he could in the interior of the truck cab and yawned. "I didn't think I'd do more than doze; sorry."

"No need to apologize. I got a ride, which I appreciate and drove a while in return."

"Why don't ya drive over to the truck stop? Ya might be able to pick up another ride to Flagstaff."

"Thanks, the closer I get, the more anxious I am to see Kara. God willing, I'll talk to her soon." He had to make her understand he'd changed.

When they got to the truck stop, Buddy hopped out of the truck and yelled to a trucker he knew, "Hey, Allen, ya headed to Flag?" The man nodded, so Buddy gestured for Nate to come forward. "Can you give a ride to my new friend here? He's headed to see a girlfriend, so you'd be helping out young love."

The trucker gave a genial harrumph. "I can't stand in the way of young love. You ready to leave now?" At Nate's nod, he signaled him to hop on board. Nate turned to thank Buddy for his kindness. Buddy slapped him on the back and wished him success.

The trucker played a country music station so loud it limited much conversation. That was okay with Nate. He sang along with a few of the Hank Williams and Johnny Cash songs. The genial trucker joined in on ones that he knew too, so the time quickly passed.

When he got to Flagstaff the first thing Nate did was change his clothes in the men's room of the truck stop. The dirty clothes were shoved in his backpack while he searched for a Laundromat. It was hours before he could check into a motel, so there was time to wash his clothes and take a stroll around the campus to get the feel of it—and watch for Kara.

When he finished the laundry, he carefully folded the clothes to fit neatly into the backpack, and slung it over his shoulder. He headed out the door toward the campus. As he neared the campus, he spotted a young woman sitting on a bench across the street. At first glance, he thought it was Kara. He gasped in surprise. Could he be that lucky?

After a more critical look, he noticed the dark circles under her eyes, hair that needed washing, and clothes looked like she slept in them. That couldn't be Kara.

The woman stood, turned toward a baby stroller parked in the shade. She reached down and picked up the baby inside. The baby was wrapped head to toe in something green, which gave the baby the look of an enormous caterpillar. She gave the baby a few quick pats before she returned it to the stroller. Pushing the stroller, she trudged toward one of the campus buildings. This poor drudge was definitely not his Kara who was always neat and tidy. In addition, this girl had a baby. His imagination had run wild. From now on he'd take his search slowly and not assume every female he saw was Kara.

As he wandered around the campus, he realized he'd no idea which dorms were girls' dorms. He approached a couple of laughing girls in front of an old dorm. One of the girls was tall and skinny with a cloud of curly hair, the second a darker-haired girl with straight hair. "Excuse me ladies, I'm here to visit my girlfriend. The problem is I don't remember the name of Kara's dorm."

The two girls glanced at each other; the darker-haired girl responded. "It would depend on if she's in a sorority or not. There are three sororities on campus: the Tri Deltas, AO Pi's, and the Gamma Phi's. If she's not in a sorority, there are several girls' dorms. You should be more specific if you want to find her."

"I don't think she joined a sorority, I assume it must be one of the dorms." Nate drew his brows together in thought.

"Well, this is one. We'd like to be of help, but it's time for class. Good luck."

As the two girls walked around the corner, April turned to Jillian. She whispered, "I'm sure that's Nate, the guy Kara broke up with and never wants to see again. She told me he was incredibly good-looking—he certainly fits that bill. We'd better pass the word not to help him find her. Warn Kara that he's here."

Jillian looked askance at April. "I can't imagine why she'd dump him. He is *unbelievably* gorgeous. I'll help her avoid him if that's what she wants." The girls hurried off to warn every friend they saw and ask others to do the same. Jillian hastened to warn Kara.

When the girls left, Nate had an uneasy feeling they were hiding something. But why? The dark-haired girl examined at him like he was dirt. He'd never met her. There was no way those girls could know anything about him—unless Kara told them. But they said they didn't know her. He shrugged his shoulders and continued to walk around the campus.

April found Geoff. "I'm positive Nate is here looking for Kara. Natalie is with her and she wouldn't want Nate to find either of them. Can you pick them up and take them to her apartment?"

"Yeah. Nate may not remember my name, but we've met several times. He's bound to remember my face. It'll be better if I stay out of sight, too."

"You're right. If he sees you, he's bound to ask about Kara. You can't claim not to know her."

More dejected by the minute Nate wandered the campus. One helpful student suggested he check with the Registrar's Office. He thought it was a great idea until he got there.

The registrar glowered at Nate like a criminal. "We do not give out personal information regarding our students to anyone. If this young woman wished to see you, I am sure you would know exactly where to find her—assuming she is on this campus. I suggest you check with her family as to her whereabouts."

Nate struggled to be polite. "Thanks, I'll do that." He wanted to grab that pompous jackass by the neck and rip out his throat. As angry as he was, he had the good sense to turn and walk away. He took a deep breath and blew it out between clenched teeth, in an angry hissing sound. Who did that guy think he was? Why did he think it necessary to treat Nate like some low-life pervert?

He had enough. He'd leave for Payson in the morning and talk to the Carson's. They were sure to understand and tell him where Kara was. The thought put him in a better mood. Maybe she dropped out and was living back in Payson working for her dad again. That could be the reason no one knew her—maybe she didn't stay. Whistling a cheerful tune he walked to the motel.

The following morning he returned to the student center to hang out for a while in case he might see her. There were few students around. After an hour of little activity, he checked out of the motel. Next stop, Payson. Kara was there; she had to be. The thought put a dreamy smile on his face. Maybe he could catch a ride and be home in little over an hour. He trotted straight for the highway.

Funny, he never thought of it as home until Kara came along. He'd never thought of any place as home since his parents drowned. He and Josh moved so often they never bothered to put down roots. Now he was tied to Kara in a very specific way. He didn't understand the bond, but he understood she represented love, hearth, and home to him. He longed those things.

He got lucky and picked up a ride in the first five minutes. As he got close to Payson, his nervousness increased. The trucker dropped him off near the road to his old cabin. He'd check on the cabin, then go to the Carson's and take a look around their house. They'll be at work for hours, so he'd have time to look around the town and hunt.

The cabin sat as it had when he'd left. Its remote location left it unmolested the many months he and Josh were gone. He shook the dusty bedding out in the yard and left his backpack on the foot of his re-made bunk. After he shut the door behind him, he trotted across country on the familiar route to the Carson's.

Emerging from the trees which skirted the property, he paused to sniff the air. Something was different. He eased around the side of the house to the back to Kara's room. There was no fresh scent of her. In fact, there were no fresh human scents at all. He went back to the front to check for anything he might have missed. A sign lay in the dirt. He picked it up and read "For Rent" followed by a local phone number. Why weren't they here? Did they leave Payson or moved to another house? He'd go the store to check later.

After the episode with Buddy and his struggle not to kill the Registrar, he decided it was wise to hunt. Hunting would give him time to process the changes. Kara wasn't on campus. Her parents moved; perhaps out of town. What if he never found her?

He was too nervous to eat; so rather than hunting he ran to his old fishing hole. It was a great spot to think as well as fish. He needed time to consider his future. How would he live—with or without Kara? He laid out his pain, and the potential for grief before the one who knows all things. The one who'd walk with him whatever path lay ahead. As the shadows lengthened, he drew himself up and marched to the Carson's store.

Chapter 20

Pete Carson prepared to lock the store for the night. He was thinking about dinner when he heard the bell over the entrance jingle. When he stuck his head around the corner he saw a familiar young man standing with hands shoved in his pockets. Though the man stood over six feet tall, he looked like a little boy who'd gotten into mischief and had to face the music.

"Nate Whitworth, what on earth are you doing here, son? I haven't seen you in a month of Sundays," Pete greeted jovially.

"Yes, sir, I know. Not since ...Well you know. I was wondering if you could tell me where Kara is at. I went to Flagstaff. I couldn't find anyone who knew her—where she might be."

Pete's eyes held a world of sadness. "Come back to my office, son. Let's talk." He reached inside a mini-refrigerator and pulled out two of bottles of pop. "Would you like a cold drink?"

Nate nodded, so Pete tossed one to Nate, who caught it one-handed with natural grace. Pete opened his, but Nate held his turning it in his hands.

"Nate, I like you and I'd like to help. But Kara made us promise never to tell you anything about her."

Pete watched Nate's surprise slowly twist into grief. "Why? Pete, I have to see her. There are things she should understand. I ..." His voice broke in a muted sob.

Pete sat back in his chair; waited in silence while Nate struggled to regain his composure. "Look, Nate, I never found out what happened between the two of you. Kara never said. Frankly, at first we feared the worst. We wondered if you *had* been the one to hurt her after all—perhaps raped her."

In a split second Nate's expression changed from grief-stricken, to horrified, to angry. He continued before Nate could respond. "Joann asked her point-blank if that was the case. Kara screamed at her mother not to be ridiculous—you'd never hurt her."

"No, I never would. I love Kara!" Was Nate's fervent reply.

"Whatever happened, Kara made us swear if we saw you again, we wouldn't tell you where she was or what she was doing."

Nate sat and stared at the floor for several minutes. He set the cold drink aside. Rubbing his hands over his face and through his hair, he asked. "Could you tell me if she's happy?"

Pete grimaced. "I wish I could tell you for sure. She seems happy enough. She smiles, she laughs, she sees her friends, but I don't know. She's changed in some fundamental way I don't understand. She is not my same little girl."

Pain shot through Nate. His shoulders slumped, he mumbled, more to himself than to Pete. "Josh told me to leave her alone. He said it would never work out, but I had to try. I loved her from the first moment I saw her but I should have listened to Josh. I should have walked away."

"Can you tell me what did happen between you?"

What could he say that wasn't a full-out lie? His mouth worked as he struggled to get the words out. "There were several things, but one of the fundamental reasons was I wouldn't go to church with her. I couldn't believe in God. If there was a God, why did he let my parents die? I didn't think he'd accept me because I haven't lived a good life. That's all changed now. I believe in God. I wanted to tell her how it came about. If she knew, she might be willing to give me a second chance." He pleaded, "I know I promised I'd stay away from her, but I only half meant it. I thought she'd change her mind—especially now." Pete sympathized with the boy's suffering, but what could he do?

Pete put his chin on his fist in thought. After a long pause he said, "Look, Nate. I promised Kara I'd tell you nothing, but it's not fair to let you go on like this. Kara's married. You have to let go for the sake of your own sanity."

"She's married? So soon?" He whispered in pain. "I was wrong. She never loved me at all. God, oh God." He sat with his face buried in his hands. The shrill ring of the telephone jarred him back to awareness of his surroundings.

Pete picked up the phone. "Hi, honey. Sorry, I had something to take care of, but I'll be there soon. Hold on a second ... Nate would you like to join us for dinner?" Nate shook his head. "Okay, see you soon. Love ya." He ended the call. "That was Joann."

"I figured it was. How is she doing and how are Don José and Fosdick?" Nate asked listlessly, slowly getting to his feet.

"Joann's just fine, but we lost Don José. He was hit by a car. Kara was right. I never should have let him out by himself. Now Fosdick won't stay home. We moved, but he keeps going back to the old place. He sits on Donnie Boy's grave out back. The cat misses Donnie and he misses Kara. She's pretty much his world." The large man obviously mourned his little dog and held himself responsible for the dog's death.

"I'm sorry to hear that. I liked Donnie. He was a funny little guy. There's something unique about Fosdick, too. He understands people more than most animals." He took a slow step toward the door. "I don't want to keep you from your dinner. Could you tell Kara you saw me?"

Pete sighed. "No, I don't think I can. It would only cause her pain. I hope you understand."

Nate nodded without speaking. Shoulders slumped, he shuffled out into the night. Outside on the steps, his thoughts returned to Fosdick. The poor cat was as sad and lonely as he was. Maybe he'd see if he could find him and lure him out. It was a long time since the cat saw him. He might not remember Nate. A plain hamburger should work as bait for the cat.

When he approached the counter of the Burger Hut, he heard an unwelcome, but familiar voice.

"Well, well, well. Look who's here. Kara's cast-off boyfriend, Nathen."

He looked around. Behind the register sat Joyce Anderson or Andrews—something like that—the nasty one Kara didn't like.

"Hi Joyce. How are you?"

"More to the point: How are you, lover boy? Lost your girlfriend? Imagine her getting knocked-up by Fred—of all people—and having to get married. What a joke. That must have been a blow to your ego." She looked him up and down and smirked.

Nate wanted to smack the smile off her hateful face. He just received the painful news Kara was married. To discover she was pregnant when she married was another knife in his heart. Fred. Fred, who he trusted. Fred was the baby's father? It was another stab to his dead heart.

As much as he wished to hurt the girl, he said, "I need a plain burger to go." He kept his voice and face expressionless.

"Don't want to talk about your love life, sugar? Maybe you need to try someone new. I'd be happy to take you on for a little while. I'm sure we could have a *real* good time." She smiled seductively.

"Sorry I'm busy," he growled at her. "Can you get me that burger? I need to go. I have a friend to meet." He smiled inwardly as he thought about his little four-legged friend. This girl was a sleaze.

Joyce slammed the burger in front of him, grabbed his money from the counter. "Have fun with your *friend.*" In the single word she implied the meeting was an assignation.

"I'm sure we will." Unsmiling, he turned from the girl. He shook himself off as he tried to rid himself of the accumulated filth, then he turned, "What time do you get off work? Maybe I can stop by for a few minutes."

Her eyes brightened. "I get off at midnight. Here, I'll give you my address." She wrote on a small paper bag and handed it to him. "See you later, honey."

As he turned away, his lip turned up to reveal his fangs as he whispered, "You'll wish you didn't." Now, to find Fosdick.

He hurried to the empty house, ghosted to the back. He didn't see the cat and there was little scent. He fingered the name carved in the trunk of a ponderosa. It read "Donnie." He smiled sadly, as he summoned the memory of the little dog whose tail waved like a banner in the breeze.

He searched, but saw no sign of Fosdick. He whispered, "Fosdick, where are you, old son?" He thought he heard a faint meow. He called out again. A filthy, emaciated cat limped into view. Apparently, the victim of an animal attack, he'd come out the loser.

"Hey buddy, what happened?" His voice gentle as he squatted down. "Look, I brought you some dinner." Nate opened the bag and broke a piece of meat into tiny pieces for the starving cat. He fed him, bite by bite, a quarter of the patty. In his condition the cat needed time before he ate more. Fosdick ate hungrily, looked into Nate's eyes and meowed his thanks.

Nate picked him up and cradled him in his arms. "You miss her, too, don't you, boy?" The cat let out a mournful yowl that seemed to hang in the air. "If it's all right with you, I'll take you to the cabin. See if I can clean these wounds." Fosdick purred and rubbed his head against Nate's chin and chest. "All right, mister. Let's go. I'll give you more to eat when we get there."

Nate held the cat with firm, but gentle hands. Held him against his chest as he ran the distance to the cabin. He didn't have any antiseptic or gauze on hand, so he gave the cat water and another small amount of food. "Okay, buddy, you stay and eat while I get what I need to make you better. I'll get more food, too. Don't worry, I'll be right back."

The cat gazed up with complete trust, and then drank from the water dish. Nate made sure the door closed and hurried to the store for his purchases. When he returned, Fosdick sat on the foot of Nate's bed, watching the door expectantly.

Nate dug through the sack and pulled out a pet brush. "Let's get some of this dirt off of you before I clean your wounds." Carefully, he brushed the cat's matted and dirty hair until he looked a slightly cleaner. Next, he pulled out cotton balls, dampened them with hydrogen peroxide, and began to clean the myriad cuts on Fosdick's face and body.

There wasn't much he could do about the cat's torn ear other than clean it and apply an antibiotic ointment. The dead piece would fall off given time. He was able to clean and bandage the deep wounds on the cat's broken tail and front paw. He hoped the bandage would keep the wounds clean while the ointment did its work.

"I need to hunt, old son, so make yourself at home. I won't be gone long." Even though the cat might not understand the words, he couldn't bear to tell him he was going to kill that slimy girl. He fed the cat the last of the burger and filled the empty water dish.

Blanking his mind to the evil of his plan, he pulled out the small bag with Joyce's address. He reached her house a few minutes before she'd get home, so he stood in shadows watching. He saw the lights of her car and let his rage and hurt grow to a pitch.

Her head lights flashed over him as she turned in the driveway. Bouncing out of the car she called, "Don't be shy. Come in and let's get this party started." Barely, in the door she turned and reached for the buttons on his jeans. He didn't stop her, instead he reached for her blouse.

This was better. His clothes wouldn't carry the scent of what he planned. Dressed only in her underwear, she turned to lead him to the bedroom. He clamped a hand over her mouth and jerked her off her feet. Once outside, he carried her miles into the mountains before he threw her to the ground. Here no one would hear her screams. He saw the raw fear on her face, smelled it on her skin. It gave him pleasure. He growled, "Run."

She whimpered, "I don't understand."

Loosening his animalistic nature, he screamed, teeth exposed, "Run!"

Stumbling to her feet, she tried to run, but the rocks bruised her bare feet. He let her gain fifty yards, time enough to hope for escape. Then he ran her down and attacked. Throwing her to the ground, he savaged her in ways he never had before. He took his time, wanting to cause as much pain as possible before he finished her off. Maybe he wouldn't kill her. Maybe he'd leave her broken and bloody, for the other predators. Yeah, he didn't want to drink her revolting blood anyway.

She moaned as he pulled away from her. "That was for Kara, you piece of trash." He moved away with a sense of completion.

"Please. Don't leave me alone," she croaked, barely able to form words.

"You won't be alone long. Bye, *honey*," he sneered. He heard the stealthy paws of a cougar. It ignored him while heading for the easy kill. Moments later he heard her scream and heard the scream break off.

Before retrieving his clothes, he hopped into an icy stream to wash away signs of what he'd done. As he returned to the cabin the full import of his action hit him. Horrified by what he'd done, he fell on his knees and cried out to God. Bent over, forehead touching the ground, he wailed out his distress and disgust for his actions. Had he really chewed away an ear and broken many of her bones? Had he ... He couldn't acknowledge the next thought. How could he perform such disgusting acts? He'd committed unspeakable sins out of love for Kara? She would be horrified and disgusted.

All he managed to do was prove to himself he was not worthy of Kara's love. She'd made the right decision when she rejected him. He prayed for hours questioning if God could forgive this night's actions.

When he struggle to his feet, he shuffled to the cabin, a broken man. Emotionally exhausted, he lay on the bunk, Fosdick limped over and stared at Nate, his limpid eyes shining.

"Okay, I know Kara let you sleep with her. I heard her talk to you. Come on up." He put his hand around the cat's belly and lifted him to the bed. The cat nestled next to Nate and began to purr.

"How are you getting along without Kara? Me? I'm not doing so hot. I found out tonight that she never loved me—not like I loved her. I mean, I was barely out of the picture when she goes and gets pregnant. Then she turns right around and marries Fred. She wouldn't give up school for me, but I doubt if she's going to school now. Not with a baby. Don't get me wrong: Fred is a straight-up guy—except he stole my girl. I know I'm rambling, but thanks for listening to me.

"Now I've done something terrible. I hope God forgives me, because Kara won't, not for this. I'm not sure I can ever forgive myself."

He grew silent, lost in thought as the volume of the cat's purr increased. Muscle by muscle, Nate relaxed. His eyes drooped as he pulled the cat closer. "Maybe since we're both alone, you'd be willing to live with me." Nate was lulled into sleep.

When he awoke, refreshed and—all things considered—in a good mood, he opened the door to let Fosdick out to perform his necessaries. Nate joined the cat in the early morning sun and waited while the cat explored his surroundings. When the cat returned to his side, Nate noticed a distinct improvement in the cat's looks. Still emaciated, he managed an almost jaunty step and there was a sparkle in his eyes. Nate marveled at what a little food and care had done for his furry little friend. "Come on, old son, let's get your breakfast." The care of the cat was the one good thing he'd done this trip.

After he put down the fresh food and water for the cat, he told him he'd be back shortly. He was desperate for blood, since all he had were those two small rabbits in the desert. A shudder passed through him as the image of Joyce's broken body flashed through his mind. Fresh blood was welcome, but the thought of human blood made him want to vomit.

Avoiding the area he'd taken Joyce, he followed a game trail into the mountains. When he picked up the scent of deer, he ghosted behind the herd keeping careful track of the wind direction. He'd get as close as possible to choose a target. He managed to move above the herd without being noticed. He selected a buck and took it down. While this kill was quick and painless he struggled to drink. Satiated, he left the carcass for other carnivores to devour, like he had Joyce. He wandered back toward the cabin, deep in thought.

Should he head back to Los Angeles or relax a few more days? Perhaps he should stay until Fosdick was in better shape to travel. But he'd need a way to carry the cat. One that was comfortable and had room for food and water. In his frail condition, he'd need plenty of both to survive the desert. That decided it. He'd stay a few more days to make preparations.

Nate went to the local sporting goods store to check out the latest backpacks. He wanted to find one larger than his current backpack. If he found one, he'd have room for his clothes, extra water for the cat and room for the cat in to ride in comfort. Food wouldn't be as much of a problem; he could hunt for fresh food for the cat along the way.

After finding a backpack that looked perfect for the job, Nate returned to the cabin to re-dress the cat's wounds. He decided three more days would be enough. He'd give Fosdick short rides in preparation for the long trip.

The evening of the third day, he checked Fosdick's wounds. Except for the loss of part of his ear, a permanently crooked tail, all were healing. Nate fed him several small meals every day. The cat began to move from emaciated to very skinny, a step in the right direction.

"Okay, old son, now's the time to decide. Do you want to hang out with me from now on?" The cat leaped up on the bunk next to Nate and crawled in his lap. Nate's eyes lit with pleasure. "I guess that's a definite yes. We can travel together and talk about Kara. We'll try to figure out how to get along without her. Does that sound okay?" The cat made a noise somewhere between a meow and a purr. Nate chuckled. He hugged the cat, stretched out on the bed, as he held Fosdick in his arms.

Chapter 21

Fred received regular mail from Kara—as regular as mail ever got in Vietnam. He loved getting letters that included pictures. The first pictures he received after the baby, Kara looked exhausted. The baby was a bundle of blankets with a chubby face. Natalie's dark hair stood straight up in her newborn picture. More recent pictures of Kara matched his memory of her. The baby developed into a tiny little being complete with visible arms and legs and hair long enough to comb into a curl. Sometimes Natalie wore goofy expressions, but he could see she was a beautiful little girl. She looked a lot like Nate, Fred decided with a pang of jealousy. He gave himself a shake to remind himself that he, Fred, was her daddy and always would be.

Dear Fred,

I got some interesting news the other day. Geoff went home for the weekend and Dad told him Nate was in town. Mom and Dad haven't mentioned it to me so I haven't asked them anything.

The less said the better, as far as I'm concerned. Geoff saw Joyce, too. She was her usual charming self and made him mad. Big surprise there. Apparently, she missed work the next day. Sick? More likely she's hung over.

Guess what? Natalie can sit by herself now! That is she can sit if I put her in a sitting position; she can't get herself into a sitting position yet, but it's a start. She smiles all the time. She laughed out loud the other day. It was a real belly laugh, too. She found my hiccups very funny.

She loves the bear you sent her, too. It may end up bald because she chews on its ears and nose all the time.

My classes are going well, thanks to the girls. They have my schedule down pat, so someone is here to watch Natalie while I go to class. She is going to be confused about who her real mamma is soon. Even Bridget watches her once in a while, When her busy social schedule doesn't interfere. She's quite the social butterfly.

I miss you so much, and Natalie wants to meet her daddy. I show her your picture and tell her about you, but I'm anxious for the day when you get home.

We both send hugs and kisses.

Love,
Kara

The news Nate was in Payson upset Fred. He'd hoped this time he was gone for good—totally out of their lives. Kara hadn't mentioned if anyone in Flagstaff spotted him. Maybe Nate overlooked Flagstaff. He didn't like Nate on his mind when he headed out into the bush. It was important to be on the alert at all times out there. He re-read the letter and smiled over Kara's description of the baby laughing. It must have been funny. She was beginning to sit up now. Geez, it wouldn't be any time before Kara would tell him Natalie was crawling—then walking. He was missing so much.

The next day his platoon trekked through the jungle. Each man took a turn at point. Fred couldn't decide if he hated rice paddies or the jungle more. The rice paddies meant slogging through the water, fully exposed to enemy fire. The jungle meant poisonous snakes and booby traps. Wherever they were, the point man watched for traps. In the jungle, the point hacked a path through undergrowth with a machete, so the men switched often. The use of a machete while a man carried 130-pound packs was exhausting.

With no warning, explosions left a small craters beginning where the point man stood seconds ago. A daisy chain of mines surrounded the platoon catching the men in a trap. The sound of the explosions left Fred's hearing muffled. He felt a burn as a bullet skimmed his arm. Men fell all around, some almost sliced to pieces by a vicious crossfire. His friend Alabama fell steps away. Fred stood and in a crouching run tried to reach him. But his world tilted—he felt no pain, his body was numb.

He lay on the ground, staring into the treed canopy—tried make sense of the nightmare. Men in black pajamas crawled through the bush. VC! They slashed at the fallen men with machetes or sent multiple rounds into them. *Please, God, make this a nightmare. Let me wake up.* He prayed to wake in his own bed wrapped in Kara's arms with Natalie safe in her crib. He heard screaming punctuated with the sound of M16s as they shot round after rapid round. His vision faded.

"Medic! This one is still breathing! Do what you can to stabilize him and we'll pack him out. It's too dense for the copters. Carry survivors to the clearing a half a klick back. I'll call in the coordinates ASAP. I hope they've got a good supply of body bags back at base. This is damn near a massacre." He used a number of expletives.

"All I can do with this one is pack his wounds and hope he stops bleeding, sir. There's a little morphine, but the shape he's in—he's kind of a mess. There's one flesh wound, but the rest ... Sweet Jesus; I hope somebody is praying for this boy."

Fred was vaguely aware of a whumping sound and the hum of voices. He tried to open his eyes, but it took too much effort. He let himself drift back into the darkness.

The MASH unit where Fred was sent was a top-notch facility despite a frequent shortage of supplies. "God must be smiling down on this boy;

we just got in a major blood supply and he's gonna need a lot of it." Two nurses went to work cutting away his clothing and dousing him with Betadine. A third searched for a vein for the IV.

Fred lay in a coma his entire time at the MASH unit and his transfer to Manila. While in Manila, he had brief moments of consciousness before he faded into blackness again. He heard whispered voices, but he didn't care; it was too hard to listen and open his eyes. Oblivion was better.

One day a whispered voice spoke two names, "Kara" and "Natalie." He struggled to wake. He croaked one word. "What?"

A Red Cross worker sat by his bedside. She smiled. "Welcome back, soldier. I said you just got a letter from your wife, Kara, and she writes about your baby daughter, Natalie. Would you like me to read it again?"

With his long unused voice, he croaked another single word, "Yes."

> *Dear Fred,*
>
> *I got the scare of my life today when a military car pulled up by the apartment and two men got out. I almost fainted, but the chaplain, one of the men, grabbed my arm and helped me inside. Geoff was there visiting us. He turned as white as a ghost when they walked me inside.*
>
> *They told me you've been seriously wounded and at first had not been expected to live. However, you were showing signs of improvement daily and now they think you'll be okay.*
>
> *It was a good thing Geoff was here because at first I couldn't put a coherent thought together. He asked the questions and we both listened to the answers.*
>
> *They said you'd be in the hospital for another month before you can come home to fully recuperate!*
>
> *You'll meet your baby girl at long last. She is creeping along like a little inchworm right now. It is so cute. I hope she is still doing it when you get home. I've been told you'll fly into Fort Lewis; then they'll send you on to Phoenix. I can't wait to hold you in my arms. Geoff and I will come to get you. (Natalie, too, of course!)*

Know you are in our thoughts and prayers more than ever before. I love you so much and I can hardly wait to see you.

Hugs and kisses from both Kara and Natalie.

Love you much,
Kara

Fred's lips turned up in a weak smile. "I can go home?" he asked in a whispery croak.

"That you can, soldier. You can kiss your pretty wife and your pretty baby girl. Oh, I almost forgot—here's a picture." The Red Cross lady grinned at him. "I suppose you want to see it."

Fred tried to reach for the picture, but his arm was strapped down to prevent him from pulling an IV loose from his arm. The lady held it up for him. "How about I tape it up right here where you can see it all the time?"

Fred gave a weak nod and smiled his thanks. The impact of the picture coupled with a chance to go home gave him the motivation to get well. The picture proved life and hope continued in the world. He asked the Red Cross lady to read the letter a second time before he dozed off again.

The next day, the nurses raised the top of the bed to raise Fred's head a few minutes. More minutes were added each day. It made him dizzy after laying flat for such a long time. At the end of the week, two orderlies came to help Fred from his bed and into a chair during his meals. The effort to sit upright left him wet with sweat and exhausted. He slept until it was time for his next meal.

As the days past he pushed himself, exceeding the staff's expectations, Fred was scheduled to leave early. His physical therapist lectured him to continue his work-outs while he was on leave. "Work on your upper body strength when you get home. Go for walks every day. Get in a weight-training program. We don't do this to torture you, but to help you. You need the desire to help yourself after you leave here."

"I understand, sir. I intend to do just that. I don't want my wife married to a cripple. She's been through enough as it is. I want to be able to actually play with my little girl."

The doctor eyes tightened as he stared straight into Fred's eyes. "You're one of the lucky ones. We send all too many of our boys home as paraplegics or quadriplegics. Their wives and families are happy they're alive."

Fred's face reddened. "I apologize, sir; that was a thoughtless and stupid thing to say. I've seen them in action during physical therapy. What they're able to accomplish is amazing. Those boys are true heroes."

"I'm glad you understand. They *are* heroes—every single one of them."

꙰

As soon as he was loaded for the final leg of his flight home, Fred fell into a fitful sleep. No longer drugged, he had occasional nightmares— flashbacks— about the firefight. A deep but gentle voice wakened him, "Are you all right, soldier? You're having quite a dream there."

"Oh, sorry. I hope I didn't disturb you." Fred was wet with sweat. His heart pounded as he sucked in air.

The man smiled and offered his hand. "My name is Adam and I'm an ex-GI myself. That was a very vivid dream."

Fred rubbed his hand over his face and grimaced. "Yeah, it was. I lost most of my patrol awhile back. I relive the firefight in my dreams."

"Talk to the doctors at the VA. They can help you work past it. They helped me. I wasn't in Nam; it was Korea, but it's all the same thing. We go through a living hell and see things no man should ever see. Think about it, son, there's no shame in getting help when you need it."

"Thanks. If it keeps happening, I'll do that. I appreciate your suggestion." Fred was about to comment further when the stewardess approached pushing the cart.

"What would you like for lunch? Would you prefer a chicken or a beef sandwich?" she asked politely. Fred gave his order; then she asked his drink choice. He asked for a coke; then she turned to Adam and got his choices.

As she moved on, Fred grinned at Adam. "Man, I'd eat almost anything as long as it's not C-rations or hospital food. I've had my fill of both!"

"So you were wounded. How long were you in the hospital?"

Fred looked blank. "I'm not exactly sure, to tell you the truth. I have to say 'too long'. They're sending me home to finish recuperating. I have to check in at the VA hospital in a month for evaluation."

"It sounds like it was pretty serious."

Fred nodded and turned away, his hands trembling. He didn't want to talk anymore. Talking forced him to remember terrible things. His friends cut down in the prime of life—screams—smoke—gut-wrenching fear. Alabama's head half blown off. Demons in black pajamas coming closer with machetes and rifles. Fred began to hyperventilate.

"Tell me about your family. You said they're coming to pick you up." As he watched Fred melt down, Adam became more concerned. He tried to distract Fred from where his thoughts led.

Fred took a deep breath, held it a moment, and blew it out. As he gained control, he told Adam about Kara and Natalie. He pulled out his recent pictures and passed them across the aisle to Adam.

"No wonder you're anxious to get home—beautiful wife and a new baby. You're a lucky man!"

Fred smile was genuine. His body relaxed again. "That I am. Kara is the most special girl in the world. I'm lucky she chose me."

When the stewardess brought his food, it ended the conversation while he ate. He savored each bite of the food. He finished as the stewardess returned to pick up trays. They'd start the descent very soon. He sat forward in his seat staring out the window. He had the foolish thought he'd glimpse his family at this altitude. He leaned back, his knees bouncing up and down.

"Hold on, son. It'll be a few minutes before we land. Try to relax." Adam chuckled. "Why don't you tell me where home is now?"

"Kara's at Arizona State College in Flagstaff, so that's home right now. We have a little apartment up in Campus Heights—that's married couples housing. But I'm from a little town called Payson. It sits just under—"

"The Mollogon Rim, right?" Adam continued, cutting Fred off.

Fred was enormously pleased. "You know it?"

"I was interested in paleontology when I was young. I spent many a day camped out, searching for fossils up there. It's a beautiful area. In fact, I should take my sons up there. I think they'd enjoy it." Adam nodded at his idea. "It's hard to believe all that was under water at some point, isn't it?"

As Fred opened his mouth to reply, the captain's voice announced the final approach to Phoenix. His heart pounded, soon he'd hold Kara in his arms.

Chapter 22

As the passengers disembarked, Fred shook Adam's hand. "I hope we meet again."

"I do, too. Have a wonderful time with that pretty wife of yours. Enjoy your baby girl."

"Thanks. I plan to do that." Fred made his careful descent to the tarmac. He limped his way toward the building, walked inside as his eyes swept the waiting crowd. He spotted Kara and pushed forward to meet her. She was at the back of the crowd of people waiting to meet arrivals. She elbowed through the crowd toward him. They stopped inches from each other. Mesmerized, their eyes held eagerness and pain. Oblivious to the surging crowd, they embraced as if the other was a lifeline. Loosening his hold, Fred whispered, "Where's Natalie? Where's our baby?"

Kara turned her head, gestured to where Geoff waited. In his arms nestled their baby girl. One arm wrapped around Kara, Fred moved with hesitant steps toward them, his face unreadable. He reached for the bundle in Geoff's arms—cradled her to his body. Gazing in awe at baby's face, emotion overwhelmed him. "She's beautiful, Kara," he breathed out. Geoff stepped back to give them privacy, but remained near enough not to miss what was said. He'd give a full report to April later.

Off to the side, Adam paused to watch the young couple. When he saw Fred greet his wife and baby, he smiled; lost in memories of his return from Korea, his own wife waiting.

"Mom and Dad wanted us to come spend the night, but I told them we'd need a few days to ourselves. I hope that's okay." Kara looked for his approval.

"Yes, it's okay. I don't want to share you with anyone. We have plenty of time to see them later." He turned toward Geoff. "Thanks for picking me up, buddy. I appreciate it, but I don't want to see you for the next few days either." He grinned at his longtime friend, and slugged him playfully on the arm. "I think you understand."

Geoff laughed out loud. "Got the message loud and clear. April will be disappointed, but she'll get over it. Do you want to give us the all-clear or shall we wait until next weekend?"

Fred threw his free arm around Kara, pulled her to his side. "Friday's okay. But, we have a lot of catching up to do."

If there'd been a forest fire on the return trip to Flagstaff, Fred wouldn't have noticed. He, Kara, and Natalie shared the back seat while Geoff chauffeured. Fred's eyes bounced between Kara and the baby—his little girl.

He thought of the horror he'd been through. The miracle of birth softened the pain he'd experienced. He unwrapped her blanket and examined her little fingers with their perfect tiny nails. She wrapped her little fingers around his and grasped it. "Look, Kara, she's got quite a grip. She'll be doing pull-ups before long."

Kara laughed. "She already does. Wait 'til you see her in action! She's a busy girl." At that, their busy girl yawned, pulled Fred's finger in her mouth. After a few fruitless sucks, she cried. Kara reached for her. She tossed a blanket over herself and pulled up her blouse to let the baby nurse. Fred's eyes widened in surprise. He hadn't realized Kara nursed the baby.

An odd twist of jealousy shot through him. He was instantly ashamed of his reaction—confused, too. Why should he be jealous of a baby? There were many for changes for him to absorb over the next few weeks.

Even with Fred home, she had classes to attend. He watched Natalie while she went to class. It gave the girls a break. Some days it was hard to leave him. But, she liked occasional girl-time away from him. She needed time with April to discuss certain situations. They planned to meet at the Student Center between classes.

"Kara, over here!" April sat in a comfy chair in an alcove, waving her direction. She plopped down on the chair next to April.

"How's it going with Fred?"

She wasn't sure how to answer. Glad to have him home, certainly. But as days passed, she saw changes in him that scared her. "In the past, he was a peaceful sleeper. Now he thrashes around and moans during the night. I worry he's in pain. He doesn't mention it and I haven't seen any pain medication. But, he limps and he has trouble walking distances."

"Hmm."

"His restlessness doesn't bother my sleep much. I'm up with Natalie so often when I sleep, I sleep hard. I notice it when I'm up with her. It's getting worse, too. I don't know what to do to help him."

April frowned in concern. "Have you asked him about it?"

"I have. He gives vague answers or acts as if he has no idea what I'm talking about. If I press him, he changes the subject. I think there's something he's not telling me." April's forehead creased, perplexed.

"Another weird thing, sometimes he acts jealous of Natalie, then the next minute he's holding her. He'll sing silly songs like the *Itsy Bitsy Spider* and *Patty Cake* for hours on end. She giggles and coos the entire time. He changes her diaper at least half of the time. The only time he acts jealous is when I nurse her."

"Maybe he's jealous you can feed her and he can't." April thought a moment more. "Or—maybe he's jealous the baby has a part of you he can't share. The act of nursing itself."

Kara screwed up her face. "That's creepy."

"Think about it. He had you to himself for such a short time. Now he's forced to shares you in a very intimate way. When you think of it that way it's not so creepy." April reached out her hand and squeezed hers reassuringly.

"You don't think his jealousy has anything to do with Nate, do you?" She whispered the horrible thought.

"Nah, not with the way he acts around her the rest of the time. I'd say *you're the* one with a reason to be jealous." April chuckled at Kara's incredulous look.

"Umm, I don't have any reason to be jealous because ... never mind." Her voice trailed off as her face reddened. April chortled.

She felt better after talking to April. She didn't know what she'd do without her. She helped clarify her thoughts, as Fosdick used to do. Her thoughts strayed to the cat.

Mom wrote her cat, Fosdick, wouldn't stay at the new house. He missed her and must expect her to return to the old house. Maybe if she got him and took him to the new house, he'd stay. He'll understand she'd return to that house sometime. She'd get him next weekend, when they saw Mom and Dad.

Two days later, she was up at five thirty to feed Natalie. When she came out of the bathroom, Fred thrashed in the bed. She tiptoed over, touched his arm to calm him. Fred screamed and shouted, "Get away from me!" He shoved her so hard she fell against corner of the dresser.

He came fully awake the instant she hit the dresser. He leaped from the bed taking her arm he helped her up.

"Kara, dear God. Are you okay? I am so sorry. I didn't mean to hurt you. I had a bad dream, I thought you were one of them!"

Drawing a ragged breath, she tried not to cry. "I'm okay. One of whom?" She wasn't okay. Her back hurt where it hit the corner of the dresser. It was sure to bruise.

Hugging her to his chest he planted kisses on her face. He apologized a second time.

Needing time to compose herself, she pushed away from his embrace. "The baby is crying, let me get her." She picked up Natalie and sat in the rocking chair trying to disguise her shaking. Fred followed. He sat at her feet, his head in his hands.

"You never answered my question: One of whom?" She insisted. "You said you thought I was one of them."

Fred wrapped his arms around his knees and rocked back and forth. "I can't tell you."

"You have to, Fred. You can't go on like this. You have nightmares every night—toss, turn, and moan in your sleep. I'm worried sick."

Fred jumped to his feet yelling, "I can't, Kara! Don't you understand, I just can't!" He stomped off while she sat in shocked silence at his outburst.

She fought back tears by drawing in great gulps of air. Crying wouldn't help. Fred never yelled at her before. Not like that. She tried to calm herself so she wouldn't upset the baby. The baby pulled away from her and screwed up her face like she might cry. Kara held her to her shoulder and patted her back. She burped, so she tried to nurse her again. This time she was eager to feed.

⌒◌

When Fred came out of the bedroom, he carried his sketchpad and a box of colored pencils. He opened the curtains to let in the early morning light and then stood in front of her. "Do you mind?" He pulled off the blanket that cover Natalie and her and sat at her feet. He never said a word. In complete concentration, he drew on his pad. Drawing took him to another place. Agitation and pain flowed out of him with each pencil stroke.

She sat in silence and rocked as she observed Fred as he drew. Satisfied, he stood and soberly turned the pad her direction. It was an exquisite Madonna-like drawing. The colors were soft. He managed to show both shadow and light. Barring her embarrassment over her bare breast, she loved it. But she didn't want others to see it. It was too personal. "It's exquisite," she whispered in awe.

"The two of you are stunning." His eyes were luminous and she wanted to hold him. "Kara, be patient. Please."

"Let me put the baby down. I'll be right back." Fred followed her into the baby's room. He watched as she laid the baby in the crib and covered her with a light blanket. Turning, she wrapped her arms around his neck, and laid her head against his chest. His arms encircled her. Though neither said a word, volumes were spoken.

As she poured the coffee and fixed breakfast, Fred picked up his pad and began to draw again. If drawing took him to another place, this time it took him straight to hell. His strokes were furious attacks on the paper. He rocked back and forth as he drew, sweat beading his forehead. His breathing became rapid and ragged. When breakfast was ready, he slammed the pad down. "Can I see it?" she asked.

"No!" he snapped harshly. He leaped to his feet and marched into the bedroom with it. After a minute, he came back, face washed, hair combed. Calm, as if nothing unusual happened.

There stood Fred fully dressed, looking sharp and here she was, in pajamas with sleep in her eyes. She made a fast run to the bathroom to brush her hair and splash water on her face.

He'd poured more coffee by the time she returned. Fred was calm as they ate, so she didn't bring up the mystery drawing again. After they finished eating, Fred stood and grinned. "I'll wash; you dry."

"Deal." This was more like Fred. "Oh, hey, Geoff and April are coming to dinner. I invited them for spaghetti. I have to go to the store as soon as I shower." She heard Natalie stir. "Oops, I'll bet she needs changing. The shower will wait."

"Why don't I take the baby to the store and do your shopping while you get a shower? Give me the list. She and I will have fun together." Fred's offer was what she needed—time for a peaceful shower!

"Really? You don't mind? I'll love you forever," she joked.

"Didn't you already make that promise?" His smile came slow and sweet.

She gave a seductive look. "Now that you mention it, I believe I did. Maybe this will do instead." She pulled him into the bedroom. Natalie and the shower could wait.

After they left for the store, she hurried to the bedroom for clean clothes. As she opened the closet, she saw the sketchpad shoved to the side. It wasn't exactly hidden, but Fred didn't want her to see what he'd drawn. She was nosy and couldn't resist a peek.

She paged past the picture of Natalie and her to the second picture. If someone could draw a nightmare, Fred had. It was a vivid scene of a mass murder—bodies strewn everywhere. This didn't look like what she imagined a battle scene would be. This was a slaughterhouse. No wonder Fred couldn't talk about it. Now she understood. It was horrible and done with complete attention to detail. It sickened her to look at the picture with faces colored in agony. He might not be able to talk about what happened, but he drew it—graphically. Since he was unwilling or unable to talk about the firefight, maybe drawing would help dispel the demons that haunted his dreams.

Her chest hurt and tears threatened to overwhelm her. She thought of the promise she'd made after Fred left for Vietnam. She'd be a strong person. She had to gain control of her emotions and a hot shower might help. She wouldn't tell him she'd seen the picture, but she'd encourage him to continue to draw. When he went to see his VA doctor, she'd make sure he took the pad.

The dinner with Geoff and April was pleasant. They'd eaten their fill of spaghetti, played with Natalie, and played a round of cribbage. But after they left, they were eager for bed. Fred lacked stamina for late nights and she'd be up with the baby within a couple of hours. Her head barely hit the pillow when she heard the baby. As she blinked herself awake, she realized the muffled cries came from Fred. She slipped over the side of the bed as he thrashed around, moaning a terrified "Nooo ..."

She moved a safe distance from him and whispered his name repeatedly. "Fred? Fred? Fred ... it's all right. You're safe at home." He came awake, his breath ragged; his body covered in a sheen of sweat. Sitting next to him, she pulled him into her arms—rocked him back and forth as she rocked Natalie. "It's going to be okay, sweetheart, I promise you. We'll find a way. It's going to be okay."

As he calmed, she said, "I'm going to warm milk for you. It'll help you relax." As the milk warmed, she dampened a washcloth and gently washed the dried sweat from his face. After he drank the milk, she crawled back in bed and wrapped her arms around him. She rubbed his back until his muscles relaxed. Natalie began to stir. She wasn't going to get any sleep.

Taking Natalie into the other room, she sat in the rocking chair, lost in thought. What could she do to help Fred? What did the neighbors think was happening? She'd learned how thin the walls were by being forced to listen to the neighbors' arguments in full detail. She didn't care what they thought, but it would upset Fred if strangers heard his struggles.

Fred continued to draw virtually every day. He sketched her and Natalie sleeping, rolling around on the floor and eating. He sketched them on a blanket outside on a sunny day. When he drew them, there was a peace and joy around him that was almost palpable.

But when he sketched his nightmare scenes—his body language and the pictures gave testimony to the words he couldn't say—the air pulsated with hate and anger. As he drew those pastels, the fear which poisoned his nights was pulled from him and put it on paper.

The nightmares remained, but over time they'd become less violent, less vocal. His agitation and night sweats remained a part of his nightly terrors.

They planned to arrive in Payson on a Friday night. She prayed the familiar surroundings of home would calm him. Before they drove to the house, they drove past Fred's rented house to check on it. From what they could tell from the outside, the renters took good care of it. It relieved Fred's mind since he hoped to move back to Payson someday. They got to her parent's home in time for dinner.

When Mom saw how thin Fred was, she took it as a personal challenge to fatten him up. He politely refused seconds. At her encouragement, he took a second piece of chicken. But he explained if he ate too much at one time, he'd get sick.

"You feel free to dig around in the refrigerator whenever you'd like a snack then." Mom offered an alternative—smaller meals, but more often.

"Thanks Mrs. Carson, I'll do that," Fred said, pleased with her offer.

"What's this Mrs. Carson business? It's Joann or Mom now, whichever you prefer." Joann was emphatic. "You're part of the family, remember?"

Fred snapped to attention. "Yes, ma'am, Mom!" They burst out laughing.

After cleaning up the kitchen, she saw signs of fatigue around Fred's eyes. She begged off more conversation that night. She prayed Fred would have a peaceful night.

∽◦

Mom fixed a substantial breakfast in the morning. She couldn't keep from trying to fatten up Fred. She told him to eat what he wanted, when he wanted, though.

As they cleaned up the dishes, Mom said, "That girl, Joyce, is missing. She left work one night and never came back. I guess it wasn't unusual for her to be late or miss a day of work without calling. But, after a couple of days, her boss reported her missing. When the police checked her house, her car sat in the driveway. The door to the house was unlocked so they entered. No Joyce, but her work clothes were scattered around the room. Her purse sat untouched, with car keys and tips inside. No one has seen her since."

"Do they think she's dead?"

Fred snorted, "She probably took off with some Bozo who promised her some excitement. It's no great loss."

"It's too bad everyone held such a low opinion of her. I think the police agree with you. They're not actively searching for her. They did send out a bulletin with her picture to other agencies."

∽◦

Joann babysat while Kara and Fred drove to the old house to find Fosdick. She thought how she hated the homely brown house the day they moved in. Now the sight of it made her homesick. The house where her parents currently lived was nicer, but it was never *her* home. This small, plain house was her last real home before she moved. In a funny way, she missed it more than the house in Phoenix.

They got out of the car and wandered around to the back. Dad said Fosdick liked to sit where poor little Don José was buried. She didn't see her cat anywhere, so she called him. "Fosdick, here kitty, kitty. It's Kara. Fosdick, come here. I'm going to take you home." Nothing. They walked completely around the house while she called, hoping she'd see his large orange form appear out of the trees. The nearest neighbor waved, signaling for her to come closer. She hurried over to her.

"You and your man looking for that big orange cat? The one who keeps coming back here?" The old farmwoman's face held a worried frown. She must have come out from the ramshackle old barn where she kept her cow. Her boots covered in muck and gray hair had pulled loose from her bun and straggled down her neck.

"Yes, have you seen him?"

"He got hisself into a pretty big fight and got tore up bad. I tried to catch him, but he wouldn't let me anywheres near him. I put food out for him in the barn, but it sat in the dish." She wiped her hands nervously on her faded housedress. "Last I saw, he was real skinny and sickly looking. I ain't laid eyes on him in a coon's age. I sure am sorry to tell you this."

It was kind of her to talk to her at all. While Mom and Dad had been friendly to her, she couldn't remember ever speaking to her. She thought her name was Ruby.

"Oh, no," She drew a shaky breath. "Thank you for letting me know. Will you call my parents if you do see him, so they can take him to the vet?"

"Sure, honey, if'n I do, I'll let 'em know." Her voice was sad as she turned back to her rundown barn. Kara was positive Fosdick was dead.

"Oh, Fred, I let him down. I should have come home sooner. He probably felt deserted. He was my best friend and he counted on me. I should have come sooner; I thought I couldn't take the time. I am such a selfish person." She moaned more to herself than to Fred.

"No, you're not selfish. Face it, Kara; you've had a lot on your plate these past months. You told me once Fosdick always understood you. He must have known you'd come if you could." Fred put his arms around her pulling her to his chest.

"That's just it, Fred. He was always there when I needed him, but I wasn't here when he needed me." She knew in the depths of her heart what Ruby hinted was right. Fosdick was dead. She ached for the loss of her feline friend.

⌇⏾

The VA psychiatrist, Dr. Jones, appeared to be a nice man—if a bit over-worked. Fred didn't say much to him. At her prodding, he handed the doctor his sketchpad. Dr. Jones opened it, looked at the first picture then at her—much to her embarrassment. "This is an excellent like-ness." Adjusting his glasses his glasses over his large ears, he broke into a smile.

As he turned the page, his brows drew together in a "V". "Tell me about this picture." Turning the pad he gazed at Fred and waited. Fred legs bounced and he wiped sweaty hands on his pant legs.

"Umm, it's what I ... ah ... dream about. It's the last thing I remember from the patrol when I was injured." Fred refused look the doctor in the eye; instead he looked at his hands wrapped around his knees. "It's hard to talk about. I don't really like to talk about what happened."

"These are good and graphic drawings. I see they are interspersed with those of your home life. Can you tell me about those?"

Fred's whole demeanor began to change. He muscles relaxed as he talked about Natalie and her: their walks, picnics, and dinner with friends. His smile was joyful with the pleasure of happy memories.

"Fred, I'd like to have a few moments to speak to your wife. If you'd step outside for a moment, please." Fred's eyes widened, but immedi-ately complied. She was surprised, too, unsure of what to expect.

"Kara, can you tell me briefly about Fred's behavior from the time he came home to the present?" At her confusion he clarified what he'd meant. "Have you noticed any significant changes since he came home?"

She hoped Fred wouldn't be angry, because she told the doctor everything that happened from beginning to end. She included Fred's attack—the night he thought she was one of "them." Part of her felt disloyal, as if she betrayed Fred. The other part knew Fred had a mental wound festering inside which wouldn't heal until it was drained of its poison.

"From what you say, Mrs. Jacobs ..."

"Call me Kara."

He nodded and continued, "... his behavior's improved steadily since he began to draw his pictures. It appears he's searching for balance in his life as he draws the safe and ordinary occurrences along with the horrors of battle. He may never talk about what happened, but if he can use the medium of art to express his fears and his rage over what happened, it may be as effective. Do you have any questions? She shook her head, mulling over his words. "Let's call him back to the office." Doctor Jones walked to the door and invited Fred to re-join them.

"Fred, if you don't mind, I'd like to keep a few of your pictures here. Your work is excellent, and while not all of it might appeal to a general audience, I believe much of it is marketable. I'd like to keep a few of the battle scenes as well as a few that depict your daily life. Would that be okay with you?"

Fred's brows drew together, intent. "I guess, but why do you want them?"

"We have men in the hospital who, like you, who cannot face what they've been through. I think your pictures might open a window for them—let them see the ugliness that someone else experienced. Sometimes empathy for others allows an individual to begin the healing process. While family pictures allow them to remember how good ordinary life can be."

"I guess that would be okay." Fred paused then added, "You can't have the first picture though. I won't let you have that one."

"That's fine, son. That one's rather special, isn't it?"

Fred's face softened into a smile. "Yes, sir, it is. It is as special as my Kara." He reached for her hand.

Dr. Jones smiled back and bent over to write notations on a chart. He flipped back through the sketchpad and selected several prints. He checked for Fred's approval before he tore one from the pad. "Okay, son that will do it for now. I want to see you back here in one month, so take this card to the scheduling clerk. He'll set up your appointment. In the meantime, keep drawing. Bring your pad with you for the next appointment."

"Yes, sir, I will." Fred took a step back and snapped to a salute, which was returned, and they walked out the door of the office.

She offered to drive on the return trip to Payson. Fred looked exhausted.

Sure, but can we stop and get something to eat? I'm starving."

"Do you mind if we just go to a Jack-in-the-Box drive-through? I'm anxious to get back to the baby."

"Sure, that's fine. I'm anxious to get back, too." He reached over and touched her breast lightly. His touch caused an immediate reaction. The front of her blouse became instantly drenched.

"Darn it, Fred. Now look what you did," she yelled in dismay.

Startled, he roared with laughter. "I'm sorry, Kara." He choked through his paroxysm of laughter. "I didn't think ... I mean ... I knew when the baby cried, but ..." He couldn't stop laughing.

She allowed a small giggle.

⁓᥆

Natalie was awake and hungry when they arrived at her parents. She lay on the bed to feed her baby. Moments later, a whispered voice said, "Kara, dinner's ready." She'd fallen asleep, Natalie sated, slept next to her.

Fred brought her clean blouse and bra. He'd washed them. "Get dressed and come eat."

She walked into the kitchen moments later. "I'm sorry, everyone. I didn't realize I was so tired. You should have wakened me."

"No, you wouldn't have fallen asleep so quickly if you hadn't needed a nap." Mom smiled. "I remember what it was like when you were a baby. I was tired all the time!"

They ate a simple, but delicious dinner and drifted into the living room to watch TV. Her folks were big fans of *The Andy Griffith* show.

The comedy ran weekly, and it included very interesting characters. Andy was a widowed father raising an adorable son. His inept deputy, Barney, had her in stitches laughing. But Natalie stirred, so she went in, changed her diaper and fed her again before rejoining the family. By that time the show had ended.

"Why don't you let her sleep with us tonight? I'll come get you if she's hungry, but it'll be fun to take care of her tonight."

She happily agreed to let them take Natalie. Fred and she could have some much needed private time.

Chapter 23

The warmth of the welcome overwhelmed Nate when he returned to the mission following his trip.

"It's about time you got your ugly mug back here."

"Well look who's here, 'Mr. I Need a Vacation' is finally back!"

"Where's your toolbox? This place is falling down around our ears."

All the rough jesting came accompanied with grins and friendly pats on the back. This motley bunch had become a kind of family. Not in the same way he and Josh were brothers, but similar because they shared a mutual need of support.

"Can any of you losers tell me if Dale's in his office?" Nate grinned with the camaraderie he shared with the men.

"Yeah, man; he's in there. What do you want to talk to him about?"

Nate raised a finger to his lips. With a sly smile and a wink he left them to wonder. He knocked on the office door and received permission to enter.

"Welcome back, Nate. How did your trip go?"

He wasn't ready to address this particular question. Not yet. "Not as well as I'd have liked. Before I tell you about my trip, I have a favor to ask. He pulled off his backpack, set it on the ground. The big orange cat stepped daintily out and stretched.

Dale's mouth dropped open as he looked at the ratty, emaciated cat. "What in the world is that?"

"It's a cat, Dale," Nate said, exasperated. "Kara's cat. He was in a fight and was dying when I found him. I couldn't leave him. I doctored him up, fed him, and brought him home. I need a place to leave him for a few days," Nate pleaded.

"Why didn't Kara keep him?"

"Her parents moved. He wouldn't stay at their new house. I don't understand why. He's a good cat."

"I could be in big trouble if the health department knew I let you bring him." Dale looked skeptical. "Do you think you can keep him out of the kitchen?"

"Yeah. He's real smart. He'll stay with me as I work. He won't be any trouble."

"I'll probably be sorry. But I guess we'll try it. Does he have a litter box?"

"I didn't think about one. He didn't need one on the road. I'll buy one now. Can he stay in your office until I get back?"

"Okay, but you're responsible for any messes he makes." Dale said, unhappy with his decision. He'd never liked cats. He liked dogs. Dogs were loyal and friendly, while cats were ... not.

"Deal. I'll be right back." Nate sprinted out of the office, spun around and reentered. "Fosdick, I'll be back. You stay here and behave yourself." He shot out the door again.

Does Nate think the cat understands what he says? Dale watched as the big scrawny cat strolled over to the backpack, kneaded it a few times and lay down. Its golden eyes stared at Dale and purred.

"Hi, cat." The cat gave a small meow—almost a response. "I'll bet you're hungry. I'll get you something."

Dale carefully closed the door to his office as he went to the kitchen. "Bring a bowl of milk and some kind of meat—chopped small." Max's face held an unasked question, but brought the items to Dale. He watched Dale carry the bowls to his office.

"This should fix you up, cat. Here you go." Dale put the two bowls on the floor. Fosdick stood and strolled to the bowls. The cat looked up at him, meowed again before lapping the milk. Dale pondered the cat's response. Was the cat thanking him? Did he understand what he'd said? He might be forced to rethink his ideas about cats.

By the time Nate made it back to the mission, rumors spread an animal was in Dale's office. The men had little to do with their time. Any rumor provided high excitement. They'd chew it over to get every ounce of enjoyment from it. But when they discovered the animal was a cat, one man scoffed. "Oh ... a cute little kitty." The men guffawed.

Nate opened the office door and Fosdick came out; his head—with its ragged, partial ear and his crooked tail held high. He viewed the room as a despot surveyed his subjects—with utmost distain. He marched to the center of the group of men gazing at them in his imperious manner.

"Holy ... that ain't no 'cute kitty.' This guy's been around."

"Geez, Nate, where'd you get this cat?"

One of the other men voiced his amazement, "This cat looks like he's had all life could throw him and came out the victor. He's one of us."

Nate proceeded to tell them portions of how he came across Fosdick—his plan to keep the cat at the mission for a while. "You'll see how amazing he is after a while." He got his toolbox and strode upstairs to tackle the neglected work. Fosdick followed, his crooked tail held straight as possible. His bearing regal.

As Nate continued his work, the cat explored, never far from his side. Without warning cat stiffened, drop to a crouch—staring intently at something out of Nate's sight. With a mighty leap, he disappeared into the bathroom. Nate heard a loud squeak and the crunch of bones. The cat reappeared with a dead rat clutched in his jaws. "Hey, good boy." Nate reached to pat the cat, but the cat strode past him without a glance and trotted down the stairs.

Curious, Nate followed, laughing as he reached the bottom of the stairs. Fosdick took his kill directly to the man who'd made the "cute kitty" remark. He dropped the dead rat at his feet. The man yelped an obscenity as he flopped back in his chair. Fosdick stared at him, his golden eyes shone. He challenged the man to laugh again.

The man's eyes widened and his mouth dropped open. "Well I'll be—" was all the man managed before Fosdick turned away, bounded back to Nate's side. He left the dead rat at the man's feet.

The entire room broke out in laughter as the men joshed. "That'll teach you to insult a cat before you know him."

"Look at the size of that rat."

"Better not mess with him—he'll come after you next!"

"Way to go, Fosdick. I guess you showed them a thing or two," Nate whispered as he leaned over and patted the cat. "Let's get back to work."

By the end of the day, Nate had a good start on the neglected repairs. Fosdick killed another rat. "Shoot, old son, they should put you on the payroll, too. This old building will give you plenty of work. There are lots of rats."

He and the cat shared a bowl of stew with the men. Fosdick with his own bowl, ate at Nate's feet. Before they left, Nate spoke to Dale again. "You asked about my trip earlier. I didn't give you many details and I won't. But something happened that shook me up. I have to leave to sort things out. I'll stay until Josh returns, but I wanted to warn you, so you could keep your eyes open for a new handyman."

"Is there anything I can do to change your mind?"

Nate shook his head. "No, but I will ask for your prayer. I need to find a place to pray and meditate."

"I can help." He opened a file drawer and pulled out a sheet of paper. "This is a list of retreat houses. There's many faiths represented on this list, so you have choices. As far as my prayers go, you don't have to ask for mine." He pulled Nate into a one-armed hug and whispered a prayer. When Dale finished praying, Nate picked up his backpack, the cat inside.

A few days later Nate settled into bed when he heard a knock on the door. He raced across the living room, opened the door. Josh grabbed him in a big bear hug. He hugged him back. "Hey man, I've really missed you."

"Me too. Good thing I have Liz to keep me company." Josh grinned and wiggled his eyebrows suggestively. As Liz followed Josh through the door, an ear-splitting yowl ripped through the air. Nate glanced around. Fully puffed up; Fosdick gave Liz and Josh a warning snarl.

Nate grabbed the cat before Liz or Josh could react.

"Where did you get that? Are you keeping a cat for a midnight snack?" Liz questioned, plainly curious.

"He was Kara's cat and he's strictly off-limits." Nate glared along with the command. He proceeded to tell how he'd found the cat and part of the reason he'd brought him home.

"So did you talk to Kara? How is she?" Josh kept his tone neutral, but watched Nate with open curiosity. He could plainly see something was wrong.

"Let's not talk about it tonight. I'll tell you later. I don't want to deal with it now." Nate looked grim as he turned away from his brother's questions.

"Okay, Nate, whenever you're ready, I'll listen."

They visited as Liz nervously watched the cat glower at them. "I don't think that cat likes us," she concluded.

"Fosdick doesn't know you yet. He sees you as the enemy—something to be feared. When he understands you're not a threat, he'll calm down."

"Do you mean he knows we're vampires?"

"No. He understands you're predators. He was cautious around me until he realized Kara was safe with me. She trusted me, so we became friends."

"I drank a cat's blood earlier today," Liz volunteered. "You're not going to kill the cat for its blood?"

"No. I. Am. Not. Neither are you. Do I make myself clear?" Nate's voice threatened—his face a thundercloud.

Liz opened her mouth to speak, but Josh grabbed her hand. "Liz, it's time to go home and let Nate sleep." He turned to Nate—his expression a bid for patience. "I'll see you tomorrow. I'll be back to work. Liz is going to work a few hours at the library, too."

As they left, Nate wondered if Liz's return to work was a good idea. He hoped so, for Josh's sake. His brother displayed a new level of maturity. Apparently, work with the new family member gave him insights. He looked forward to a quiet talk with Josh. He had to explain why he was moving on.

Fosdick grumbled his way to bed next to Nate. "I know, old son. That was a bit of a shock, wasn't it? I know Josh won't hurt you and I'm sure Liz won't either. All the same, I'm glad we don't live with them." Nate sighed. "Life's never easy, is it, buddy?"

The cat grumbled one more disgruntled meow before he curled next to Nate.

"I pictured my life with Kara. We'd be so happy together. You'd live with us, too. I guess life didn't turn out like either of us thought, did it? I can't understand why Kara left you, hurt and all. Of course, I don't understand why she married so soon—as if I never mattered." He talked until he fell asleep; mid-sentence. The only sound was the purr of the cat at his side.

Nate and Josh weren't able to talk privately until after work. They walked home deep in conversation. Nate was right. Things hadn't been problem-free for Josh and Liz while they'd been gone. It was an on-going struggle to keep Liz from killing humans. Only recently was she ready to accept the limitations Josh imposed.

"Are you ready to talk about Kara now? If you're not, it's okay." Josh tried his hardest to be tactful. But tact was never his strong suit.

Nate sighed, rubbed his hands over his face then through his hair. "Putting it off isn't going to change a doggone thing. I'll just say it: Kara got married shortly after I left. She was pregnant at the time. I feel like I've been stabbed through the heart. I was positive she loved me. But, she couldn't have loved me and married so soon. Out of sight—out of mind." He tried to smile, but his expression was rueful.

"There's more bothering you, isn't there?" Nate came to a complete stop, his hands over his face, shoulders shaking. "What's wrong, Nate? Tell me. Let me help you."

"There's nothing you can do," he choked out. "Give me a minute and I'll try to tell you what happened and why I'm leaving." Staring at the ground, Nate began the tale of his encounter with Joyce. He didn't try to soften the impact of his words. He told Josh his hurt, how Joyce insulted Kara and him and how his anger escalated to the breaking point. "What's worse was the pleasure I got torturing her. I wanted her pain to last, so first, I broke her legs, so she couldn't run. I broke every finger, one by one. I bit every square inch of her body and chewed off her ear. I don't remember everything I did, but I left as she begged for help. The kindest thing I did was let a cougar kill her."

Josh enveloped his brother in his arms. "I am so sorry, Nate. What are you going to do?"

"Dale gave me a list of retreats—places I can go for spiritual healing. When I came to my senses, I prayed and God forgave me, but I can't forgive myself. Not yet. I'm sickened by what I did."

"Promise me you won't do anything rash and you'll keep in touch."

"I promise. I love you, Josh. I'm very proud of you. I hope someday you can be proud of me again." With another hug, they went their separate ways.

Chapter 24

The drive back to Flagstaff was quiet. Fred obviously didn't want to talk about the VA appointment. She didn't have anything positive to say. They knew the day would come, but they didn't expect it so soon. Fred had only been home seven weeks. Not only was he released for active duty, but his return was scheduled in two week. She wanted to cry, but overt emotions would not help.

His drawing were less horrific and violent lately, but he continued to whimper and moan in his sleep. She wasn't sure the doctor made the right decision by calling him fit for duty while the nightmares continued unabated. She was positive neither of them were ready to be separated.

April and Geoff kept Natalie while they made the trip to Phoenix. They had dinner planned for when they got home. As much as she loved them, she wished they weren't going to be there.

Fred reached for her hand and gave a crooked smile. "It will be all right, Kara; we'll make it through this."

She tried to smile in return, "I know we will, but ... I'll miss you."

"I know, as I'll miss you. It will only be approximately two years of active duty. We can tough it out that long."

She nodded, staring at the passing scenery, unable to look at him without losing her fragile grip. She thought back to the day they'd met. The laughing, teasing boy who didn't have a serious bone in his body, hid a serious, thoughtful side. When revealed this surprising dichotomy showed a depth of character she loved. But, now he had a secretive side, a side he wouldn't share with her or anyone else. Would that laughing, relaxed part of him ever fully return? She was afraid he might never be the same.

Dinner simmered on the stove when they got home. April fixed a fragrant beef stew, salad and dinner rolls. Geoff had provided a bottle of Merlot and a berry pie from the local bakery. They greeted Fred and Kara with warm smiles. They tried to return the smiles, but hers was a grimace. Perhaps they didn't notice. Fred passed on the news in a matter-of-fact manner, as she peeked in on the baby. Relieved the baby slept, so she didn't have to deal with her.

Before they ate the last bite of pie, Geoff said he had to be back at the dorm early. He and April left as soon as the food was put away and the dishes were done. It was his way to give them privacy to lick their wounds. He and April would move to a different location for the remainder of their date.

ᴄ⏤ᴏ

The night before he left, Fred wrapped his arms around her and pulled her to his chest. His heart beat against her cheek and his breath warmed her hair. He pulled her down on the couch. "Kara, I've been thinking; I don't want you to come to the airport when I fly out. I want you and Natalie to stay home, so my memory is here—in our home. I can't handle seeing you alone on the tarmac."

Before she answered, Natalie's cry came, demanding to be changed and fed. She tried to stand, but he pulled her back down. "Let me get her. I won't have too many more chances before I leave." She nodded her head in silent understanding.

He cooed as Natalie's sobs came to a shuddering halt. "Wow, sweetheart, you're a soggy mess. Let's get these wet things off Daddy's girl and get you into something dry. Then Daddy will feed you cereal. Would you like that?" He blew on her belly, the vibration bringing instant giggles from her and a smile to Kara's face. Moments later he returned carrying the giggling little girl who shared Nate's eyes and hair, but Fred's humor. They were a beautiful sight.

Placing her in the high chair, he tied a bib around her neck. He spoke her in a voice as soft as velvet. "Daddy is going to miss his little funny bunny, but don't worry—Daddy will never forget her." He glanced soberly at Kara, anguish in his eyes. "I hope my funny bunny doesn't forget me." Lifting her from the chair when she finished, he held her warm body to his face and drank in the sweet baby fragrance.

The baby cradled in one arm, he reached for Kara with the other. He pulled her along as he laid the baby in the crib and covered her. Wrapping his arms around his wife, he held her close to his side. Their cheeks touched as they watched their sleeping daughter; her mouth suckling as she dreamed.

He turned after silently watching the baby and rested his forehead on top of Kara's. With a deep sigh, he led her to the bedroom, sat on the edge of the bed and reached to unbutton her blouse. She reached to help him, but he stayed her hand. "No, not yet."

He undressed her, button-by-button, watching his own hands remove her clothes and drop them to the floor. She stared at his face, so serious in the half-light of the room.

Pulling her down on the bed next to him, he traced her face, his thumb gently moving over her eyes, down her nose and to the hollow of her throat. His hand continued to slide down her side with a touch so soft she could barely feel it. She thought of the way he drew; such gentle strokes. Was he drawing her in his mind's eye? Was he trying to memorize every curve of her body?

Her fingers slid to his chest to his beating heart. Her head on his chest, she listened to its rhythm—so strong, so familiar. The rest of the night was spent in tactile memories with gentle touches that grew in intensity. At long last, they drank in the love they shared with a passion born of fear.

Morning came too soon. With a final kiss, Fred rose from the bed and headed for the shower. She took Natalie from her crib, fed her while he showered and dressed. He brought his duffel bag into the living room and set it by the door.

He held Natalie while she fixed a hasty breakfast. A knock on the door announced Geoff. He was cutting his classes to take Fred to the airport.

Since she wasn't hungry, she offered Geoff her breakfast.

"Thanks. I figured I'd grab a roll or something, but this is better." He shoveled food in his mouth.

She made a valiant effort to remain calm. When the time came for them to leave, Fred kissed the baby, kissed her like he was off to the store, and then turned away. But, she'd felt the tension in his shoulders and hoped he didn't feel it in hers. *Dear God, it was hard to say good-bye not knowing if she'd ever see him again or if the old Fred would ever return.* She smiled and waved as they drove away, her face stiff with the effort. She watched as the car drove down the gravel-parking strip, down the road long after the trees obscured the view.

⤚⟲

Fred's plane touched down in Vietnam. As the door opened to disembark, he froze. The smells and the humidity brought back unwanted memories. He'd give anything to be home, but he had a job to do. When he finished that job, he could go home and leave this nightmarish country behind.

He had been told during a layover he was given a new assignment. He'd report to the base commander for duty instructions as soon as he arrived.

"Welcome back, Corporal Jacobs." The new commander had a gruff demeanor. Fred knew his reputation as one who brooked no insubordination from his men, but he was also known to be a fair man. "Take a seat. I have been looking over your records and I see that you've had a tough go of it. Most of your platoon was killed and the rest were injured?" He looked up at Fred.

"Yes sir, that's right."

"It also says you're a level-headed young man and easy to get along with. Would you say that is a fair assessment?"

"Yes sir, at least I believe I am."

"Good. I have a small group of men I plan to send out as liaison to the villages we think are friendlies. I want you to take charge of these men, Sergeant."

"Sir?" Fred was shocked at the unexpected promotion and assignment.

"You heard me. Most of these men are good men, but they have little experience. I want someone I can trust to lead them. I'll send an interpreter along. I want you to learn the language and the customs of these people. It's as important not offend them, as it is to make friends. Here's the dossier. Read it and commit it to memory. You and your men will carry extra food and gifts for the people in the villages. Be especially generous to the headman in each village. Understand?"

"Yes, sir." Fred stood and snapped a salute. At receiving an answering salute, turned smartly and left the office.

A corporal in the outer office glanced up and said, "I'll to show you where to bunk while you are here, Sarge." He grinned at the shock on Fred's face. "You're scheduled to meet your men and the interpreter in the morning."

As a sergeant, Fred got a small room to himself, complete with a desk and his own bunk He stored his gear and sat down to read the file. It would take several readings to commit it to memory so. He read twice. He'd read it again if necessary. He didn't want to let the Old Man down.

After he read the dossier, shook his head. How was he going to learn the names of the villages and the headmen when he couldn't pronounce them? Blowing a heavy breath through his pursed his lips, he laid the papers aside and grabbed paper and a pen.

He wrote Kara to tell her about his promotion and give general details on his new assignment. Although he missed his wife and child, he felt a sense of accomplishment as he reached his goal for the afternoon. The new assignment would be interesting.

In the early hours of morning, in a half-dream state—he reached for Kara. The emptiness brought him to full remembrance of where he was and what was ahead. He hoped a hot shower would wash the fuzziness from his head.

Once fully dressed, he pulled the dossier out of his desk drawer and re-read it in the few minutes before morning chow. With this reading, he paid particular attention to specific notations about each man:

Tran was the interpreter. A local, well-educated man, he'd taught school before he began his job with the military. He'd proved himself loyal.

Corporal Andrew Jackson, a southern boy whose family had a long military history. If he'd been a Marine, he'd be *gung ho*—ready and raring to fight. Sadly, he was a hothead who didn't care who he fought. One more screw-up and he'd lose his stripes.

Private Joseph Yoder raised in an Amish home, shunned by his community when he refused to follow their strict guidelines. He'd enlisted shortly after being shunned. Reading on, Fred was surprised to find Private Yoder excelled during his time in the military and was qualified as a sharpshooter.

Private Isaac Kleinman was a non-practicing Jew from a family of non-practicing Jews. No need to worry about a kosher diet. He was their radioman and had an excellent record.

Private Sam Rankin was an Oklahoma farm boy. Adjusting well to being away from home. Another sharpshooter.

Last—and to Fred's surprise—was Private James Begay. Fred knew without reading farther, the boy was Navajo. Begay was a common Navajo surname. Even better, he was from northern Arizona. Like many of the Navajo people, he was soft-spoken and intensely loyal to friends according to the notes.

The blast over the speakers announced chow. Drawing a deep breath, he prepared to meet his men. He walked out into the early morning light and with a firm steps, heading toward his destination. The corporal from the CO's office met him halfway and walked with him.

The corporal said, "Sarge, there are three jeeps ready and loaded with the extra food and gifts for the villagers. These are your men." He waved his hand to direct Fred to a nearby table.

The men began to stand, but Fred signaled them to remain seated. The men distanced themselves as far as possible from the interpreter. "Tran, please come closer so we can get to know each other," Fred requested.

"How do we know this guy isn't *Charlie*? I don't trust him." Corporal Jackson snapped with contempt.

Fred turned and gave him an icy stare. "We trust him because *I say* we can trust him, Corporal. Got a problem with that? Speak up if you have a problem with anyone here. I'll make sure I find a replacement for you."

"Uh, no sir, I guess not." He didn't sound particularly sorry. He'd bear watching.

"That's good. I only want team players on my crew. Our job is vital— not only for us, but for the entire military. We'll be leaving at 1100 hours to visit villages we think are friendlies. If they are vacillating, it's our job to bring them to our side. They can help give information on VC activity. Maybe tell us where the tunnels are hidden so our tunnel rats can go in and clear them out and destroy stored weapons."

"That is why, Corporal Jackson, you need to consider Tran your new best friend. We don't know the languages. He'll be our voice, got it?" He looked hard at Jackson, then at the other men.

"Yes, sir," they shouted in unison.

"Drop the sir; call me Sarge. I don't want to give anyone the mistaken idea that I'm an officer—I think you know why." The men understood all too well. Identified officers might as well have targets painted on their backs.

Tran show up early. His English was excellent, but heavy accented. It would take time to grow accustomed to the pattern of his speech, but Fred knew he could do it. He liked Tran. The man was a schoolteacher whose school had been bombed. Before a replacement site was found, Tran was recruited as an interpreter. As Tran told Fred, "I love teaching, but the military pay is much better. I was able to move my parents and wife to a safer area. When the war is over, I hope to return to my school."

The two mapped out the route they'd take and villages they'd visit. The drive to the first village was slow going over a rough dirt road. The

Army forces had gone over it the day before with heavy equipment that left the road rutted and potted. Tran assured him, it made their trip safer—less chance of snipers and landmines.

Tran explained the Vietnamese were a proud people. It was important to accept their hospitality before giving them gifts. It might mean eating unfamiliar foods and drinks with graciousness—even if they didn't like the offerings. If they were insulted, they'd be less likely to help. He was happy to eat rice and kimchi, a Korean dish, but he hoped he could avoid beetles and monkey brains rumored to be part of the local diet.

Fred decided Jackson should ride in the same jeep with him and Tran. Jackson needed to fully understand how his behavior might influence the villagers for or against them. Assuming he got the point, Fred would make him responsible to oversee some of the other men.

As they arrived at the first village, a handful of children ran out to greet them, chattering like a flock of magpies. The children reached out in anticipation of some small token. A man's voice called out and the eager children raced back to their huts or behind trees to peer out at the soldiers anxiously. This, Tran told Fred was the headman who waited with a stoic expression.

Fred ordered the men to get out of their jeeps but to wait next to them for the time being. As Fred and Tran approached the man, Tran bowed his head briefly, gestured toward Fred, and chattered something unintelligible. The small skinny man bobbed his head and chattered back. He smiled in welcome and gestured for them to enter his hut.

As they entered the dark hut, Tran whispered a reminder to eat and drink anything offered. They lowered themselves to bamboo mats on the floor as the man called to his wife. She came quickly, and after a brief exchange hurried off again. The man produced a bottle and poured small cups of liquid into them.

"Sip this slowly, sir," Tran told Fred. "It may be stronger than you think."

Fred took a sip. The clear liquid burned his throat and made his eyes water. He smiled, nodded his head in approval then said to Tran, "Thanks for the warning. This stuff would be great as paint remover."

Their host smiled in response to Fred's appearance of approval and poured more of the fiery liquid.

Fred lifted his cup. "Your health." Tran quickly translated. The headman laughed; offered his own toast.

Before the discussion could continue, the woman returned carrying a pot with a ladle in one hand and a stack of bowls in the other. She squatted down and rapidly filled the bowls. She handed each of the men a bowl and a spoon. She smiled as she gestured for them to eat.

The soup looked like nothing Fred had ever seen. Since the first time he had come to Vietnam all he had eaten was C-rations and food from the chow hall. This was a broth filled with leaves and odd black thin things floating in it. There were other unidentifiable items as well.

"What is this?" Fred asked as worked hard to keep a pleased look on his face.

Tran quickly translated something to their hosts and smiled at Fred. "It is called lau, a popular local soup. There's fish in it and maybe some chicken, tofu, mushrooms, lemongrass. Maybe other things as well. Eat it and act like you like it."

Fred took a mouthful of the soup. It was spicy—not like the spicy Mexican food he'd eaten all his life, but in an entirely new way. Fred began to sweat in a matter of moments. Though his tongue burned, he admitted it tasted good. He nodded his head and smiled appreciatively.

The woman rushed out and returned with what looked like small burritos. She gave them each one and placed a tiny bowl of an oily substance in front of them, indicating they were to dunk the little burrito into it. Tran tried to warn Fred to be careful—the sauce was extremely hot—but he was a moment too late. As soon as Fred took a bite, his eyes watered and his nose to ran. If he had thought the soup was spicy, this was like the fires from Hades.

Tran laughed. He rapidly explained to his hosts Fred never before had the oily substance and didn't realize how hot it was. His laughter brought laughter from his host, who slapped Fred on the back in a jocular manner.

Fred grinned in chagrin, pointed to the sauce and said, "Hot!"

That brought on another round of laughter. The woman handed him a piece of pineapple. The fruit helped cut the heat from the oil so Fred could finish what he discovered was a spring roll. The spring roll was stuffed with finely shredded vegetables, deep fried and delicious.

Fred's reaction to the hot oil broke the ice so completely they began to talk about VC infiltration in the area right away. When they finished, they went out to the jeeps and handed out needed items to the villagers, including food. The children got candy and packages of gum. The other villagers came forward to pass on information they'd heard about VC movement in the surrounding area.

Invited to stay the night in the shelter of the village, at Tran's direction they set up camp. Fred had Kleinman radio what they had learned back to base. They hoped the information would save lives.

The months past swiftly as they traveled from village to village. Occasionally they'd find a squad of injured, but mobile, soldiers who needed to be picked up and sent back to the hospital. Helicopters picked up the most severely wounded and the dead. Fred's men would load the wounded soldiers into the jeeps and take them to the next friendly village. They'd call in the location, so the next available trucks or an empty helicopter's could pick them up.

On a return trip to a village where they'd dropped off wounded soldiers two days before, they found total devastation. The village was a smoldering pile of burned huts and dead bodies. A searched for signs of life found every man, woman and child dead. On the edge of the village were the bodies of the soldiers, their bodies mutilated. Fred prayed they died before the mutilations.

Sick to his stomach, he heard his men curse what happened. The men played with the children of this village, kissed the babies, and grew attached to them. The villagers were as much brothers in arms as the dead soldiers. They had every right to be angry.

Kleinman called for helicopters to pick up the bodies of the mutilated soldiers as they dug a pit for the mass grave. It was slow and disgusting work, but his men handled the bodies with tenderness and care. With tears running down their faces—especially as they laid a child in the grave— they continued to curse the VC using every obscenity in their vocabulary. When they finished, each man prayed in his own way. Begay gave a Navajo blessing over the grave; sending the dead to the spirit world. Kleinman said the *Kaddish* and laid a handful of stones for remembrance on the grave site.

After they finished the unhappy work, they drove to the next village, afraid of what they might find. That village swarmed with US and Aussie troops. These villagers would be safe—at least for today.

Because of his friendship with the villagers, Fred stayed in a hut of his own. The hut soon swarmed with old women who tugged at his filthy clothes and indicated he needed to remove them. As he took them off, they were grabbed and taken outside until he was down to his skivvies. The old women were relentless, refusing to allow any privacy. He remembered Tran's words: "You must follow their lead. You cannot offend them in any way."

Embarrassed, he removed the last of his clothes, along with his dignity, in the face of the determined women. As soon as one rushed out with the last of his clothing, others returned with pots of warm water. The women proceeded to bathe Fred from the top of his head down to his feet. His is grandmother's adage when she sent him in for a bath was, "Wash up as far as possible, wash down as far as possible, then wash possible." That's exactly what the old women did. They didn't miss a square inch.

Clean water was brought in and ladled to rinse him. At last, he was handed a towel and a blanket. They brought a clean, dry mat for him as well as food. While Fred struggled to recover his dignity, he wrapped himself in the towel and sat on the mat to eat. They gave him a bottle of the fiery drink he'd had before.

He drank the entire bottle, trying to burn out the smell and the memory of the day. His vision fuzzy, and light headed, he shook, chilled to the bone. The women chattered. One brought a second bottle as a young girl entered the hut with another blanket. He drank half of the second bottle, collapsed on his back on the mat. The older woman chattered briefly then left as the young girl covered him with the blanket.

He continued to shake as he drifted into an uneasy sleep. The young girl eased beneath the blanket to share her body heat with him.

༄

In the early morning, Fred's dry clothes were returned to the hut, while he and the girl slept. When he awoke, his head pounded and his mouth tasted awful. As he turned, he felt the girl's body next to his. He jerked upright at the sight of the half-dressed girl. The motion shot pain through his head.

He moved slowly, partially not to wake the girl and also the pain didn't allow for faster movement. He dressed quietly, walked to the edge of the village, where he vomited. Holding his head in his hands, he squeezed and tried to remember what happened during night.

He ate and then drank too much; dreamed about Kara. In the dream he held her, kissed her, and made love ... Realization hit him like a blow to his gut; he turned, vomited again, and retched until there was nothing left in him. Appalled, he wondered if he raped that girl. Sweet Jesus—it would explain her half-dressed appearance. He whispered, "Dear God, Now what am I going to do?"

The only thing he could think to do was abort the mission immediately. He'd go back to base. Let the CO know what happened and turn himself in. Likely, he destroyed relations with this village forever. He couldn't tell his men. He was the one who was supposed to set the example. Could he ever tell Kara? She'd never forgive him.

He roused his men and told them to get ready to leave right away. They grumbled aloud; he wasn't the only one who'd drank too much the night before. They quickly passed out gifts and left the village.

When they reached base, Fred dismissed the men until the following morning. He headed directly to the CO's office. As he entered, the corporal looked up in surprise. "Sergeant Jacobs, aren't you supposed ..." His voice trailed off as he took a good look at the whey-faced man.

"I need to see the CO right away. Is he in?" Fred's voice sounded strained even to his own ears.

"Wait a sec. I'll check if he's available." The corporal picked up the phone and mumbled a few words into it. Fred only understood the last few, "Yes, I do, Sir." Then, "He'll see you now. Go right in."

Fred walked to the door, took a deep breath, straightened his shoulders and turned the knob. He walked forward; his jaws stiff from his clenched his teeth. "I came to turn myself in, sir. I've let you down. I think I raped a girl."

The CO leaned back in his chair, gave Fred an appraising look. "Sit down, sergeant. Tell me exactly what happened in your own words.

Fred sat and told the CO about the previous day's happenings, ending with his waking up to find the half-dressed girl by his side.

"I thought you weren't a drinker."

"I'm not sir, it's just ... sweet Jesus ...finding our soldiers ... mutilated. The villagers ... our friends murdered ... even the children and babies ... it was hard to take. I drank to try to block out what I saw." He squeezed his eyes trying to block out the invading images.

"If you were that drunk, how did you entice this girl into your bed?"

"I don't remember. All I remember is the old women taking my clothes, bathing me and bringing me the bottle and food. I remember being dizzy from the alcohol and falling on the sleeping mat. I had a nightmare. Then I dreamed about Kara, my wife. She has this way of relaxing me when I'm stressed ... Uh; anyway, when I woke up here was this girl, half-dressed. I must have raped her. All the signs were there ... even blood," he whispered, head in his hands.

The CO sighed and drummed his fingers on the desk. "You didn't let me down, son. Overall, you pulled together that squad of unruly men into a team—a team that gleaned a lot of strategic information. I can't send you back out. While I don't believe you raped the girl, I don't doubt you had sex with her. From what you say, it was consensual. We'll send another team out to get the feel of the village. If they know she is no longer a virgin, her family will consider her devalued. If she's kept it quiet, everything might be okay. That is, as long as she isn't pregnant. If she is ... we are in for it. I'm not going to send you to the stockade, if that's what you think, but I am going to break you in rank for disorderly conduct. Report to the office tomorrow morning for reassignment. Right now you may want to talk to the chaplain."

"Thank you, sir." He saluted turned and left the office in a fog. The words "if she's not pregnant," echoed through his mind. He trudged to the chaplain's office more sick at heart than he'd been before. He thought about Kara. She got pregnant her first time. This girl could, too. Maybe Kara would understand because of what happened with Nate, but she never cheated on him. What happened between her and Nate was before they got together. What would she think of him if she knew?

The chaplain listened to the entire story without comment. Then he said, "Sergeant, first of all, you know God forgives you of your sins, but he doesn't remove the consequences of your actions. One of those consequences is how it relates to your relationship with your wife. You need to write and ask her forgiveness. Otherwise, this will hang over you and eat away at your relationship. Will it change your relationship? Undoubtedly. But that change can forge a stronger bond between the two of you."

"Sir, I don't think I can tell her. She trusts me. I don't want to destroy that trust."

"If you don't tell her the guilt will continue to eat away at you. If the girl is pregnant? What then? Will you tell her then, or are you going to ignore your responsibility to the child? You've damaged the trust between you and your wife whether intended or not. You need to do damage control, son. The sooner the better."

After spending time in pray he wrote Kara. It was the hardest thing he'd ever done. He didn't sugar-coat his words. He laid out the ugly facts, and then begged her forgiveness.

Reading what he had written, he wanted to take the letter, ball it up and throw it in the trash. But he knew in his heart the chaplain was right. If he wanted a good life with Kara, it had to be built on trust. He hoped they could rebuild the trust they had—that it wasn't damaged beyond repair. With icy hands, he stuffed the letter in an envelope, addressed it. He intended to mail it. Instead, he shoved the letter in his pocket and took it to his room.

Unable to face his men, he opened C-rations in his backpack and ate it in the silence of his room. After he'd eaten, he searched for his pad and pastels. It'd been awhile since he'd drawn any pictures. Now he wished to honor his friends from the village. He put in every detail he could remember—visualizing the midst of the village in happier times. He drew old women squatting by a fire or washing clothes in a pot, children with laughing eyes at play, and babies tied to their mothers' backs. His eyes wet, he drew a picture of a young girl in another village, standing shyly in the shadow of a tree. His fingers flew of their own volition. As the picture took form, he recognized her. Always in the shadows, away from him and his men, her eyes following him. As small as she was, she was no child; she was the young woman in the hut.

Chapter 25

The morning coffee perked to a stop as Fred reached for two cups. He'd been at his position as clerk for the CO long enough to be comfortable in the role. He poured cups of the steaming coffee, when the sound of angry voices came closer as each second passed. Glancing through the blinds he saw a Vietnamese man appear dragging a reluctant young woman by the arm. As they made their way toward the office a young soldier tried to stop them, but the small man pushed on, determined.

"Sir, I think you'd better come here. It looks like trouble."

The CO stood beside Fred. He took in the situation at a glance "It looks like you're right. Get an interpreter and get right back."

"Yes, sir." Fred bolted out the door in search of the nearest interpreter to sort this out. As soon as Fred was out door, the small man bolted around the soldier and attacked him. Perplexed, he stopped in his tracks as the man continued to hit and scream at him.

He yelled to the soldier who stood eyes wide and arms at his sides, "Hey. Get an interpreter. Now." Fred held his arms over his face—tried to block blows in hopes of defusing violence. The girl collapsed in a huddle. He attempted to side-step the angry man to help her to her feet, but the man blocked his way. He kept yelling the same incomprehensive things and hitting Fred. Two guards ran up and pinioned the man's arms behind him. The CO came to the door and shouted, "Bring him into my office. Corporal Jacobs, help the girl inside. Someone get the chaplain, too."

Bewildered by the events, Fred went to help the fallen girl. He lifted her to her feet. With a sense of dread his eyes traveled from her obviously pregnant belly to her face. This was his worst nightmare come true. In spite of her bruised face and split lip, he recognized her. This was the girl he'd seduced while he was in a drunken state. Though several months passed, he had no doubt this was the girl.

The guards forced the man into a chair. They stood on either side of him, rifles pointing. Fred, white-faced, half-carried the girl inside and gently placed her in another chair. She glanced up and quickly looked away. She recognized him.

The chaplain and the interpreter came through the open office door at the same time. "Can you find out what the hell is going on?" The CO barked to the interpreter. They listened to the sound of angry gibberish from the man who turned and pointed at Fred. The CO's eyebrow rose as he looked back and forth from Fred to the interpreter. "Well, Corporal, remember the day I said if the girl was pregnant, we'd be in for it. Today is the day. You'd better grab a chair. We're going to be here awhile."

The old man's tirade boiled down to one thing. He wanted Fred to marry his daughter.

"I can't marry her! I'm already married. Sir, what else can we do?"

The translator spoke rapidly to the father. The man's voice rose in agitation while the girl wailed. "The father won't take her back home. He'll let her starve if she tries to return."

The CO heaved a sighed. "There's a group of local women who work on the base. Chaplain, see if you can find out if this girl could work to support herself. Corporal Jacobs, you have a responsibility here," he pointed his finger at Fred. "I understand you cannot marry this girl, but you will step up to the plate. Find a place for her to live and get her set up in a job. You're responsible to see to her and the baby's needs, before and after it arrives. Do you understand?"

"Yes, sir."

"Go with the chaplain and take care of business. Report back to me when you've got things under control."

Shell-shocked, Fred said, "Yes, sir." Taking the girl by the arm, he helped her to her feet.

Escorted from camp, her father received gifts for the family as payment for the loss of his daughter. The translator hurried them to the chaplain's office to find a suitable job for the girl. She'd have to work with women who spoke Vietnamese and at least Pidgin English.

It was all Fred could do to focus on the conversations around him. There was work at the base laundry. The workers were displaced and widowed Vietnamese women. A few spoke decent English, which would help her learn as she worked to support herself. Fred and the interpreter, the girl in tow, went to talk to the woman in charge.

The woman in charge wasn't thrilled with the idea of a pregnant worker, but she agreed to let her on, and suggested someone the girl could live with as she settled in to her new life.

Fred asked what the girl might need, since she'd come with nothing but the clothes on her back. The woman wrote out a list of necessary items. She patted Fred on the arm. "Bring these back here today. I take good care your girl," she assured him in her Pidgin English.

Fred's head jerked back as if she had slapped him. "Tell her she is not my girl."

"Let it go, Corporal; she won't believe me anyway," smiled the translator.

He couldn't face anyone. Rumors spread like wildfire throughout the camp, the bored men were worse than a bunch of gossipy old women. They'd elbow each other and laugh at his expense. His steps led him to the only place where he could find solace, the chapel.

He sat all night at the back of the chapel. He counted the months twice. Could it really have been seven months ago? If the girl went full-term, that left two months to prepare for her baby—his child too. His stomach lurched.

Why me? Why Kara? Ashamed of his thoughts; he and Kara were hardly the only ones affected by the coming baby. He sat on the cold floor all night, his knees drawn up to his chest, until the room began to lighten. Stiff from sitting in the same position, he stood, feeling no better than when he came to the chapel. He stretched and limped out the door to shower and prepare for the day.

Later, after a quick breakfast, he headed to the laundry to check on the girl. *I should find out her name since she's bearing my child,* he thought grimly. When he walked in, the head woman waved him over to where she worked.

"Your girl come right on time. She work hard. You no need to worry; I look out for her." She gave him a cheerful smile and patted his arm.

"Um, thanks. Can you tell me her name? Also, is there anything else she needs for herself or the baby?"

"You don't know her name? How come you don't know her name?" The woman was nothing if not persistent.

"Because, I never was introduced to her, okay?" He snapped, angry and embarrassed. "Now please answer my questions."

"Okay, okay. Her name Mai Pham. She need more clothes, but you need to take her—get right sizes. She need everything for baby."

Fred threw his hands in the air. "I'll bring an interpreter Saturday and take her shopping. Have her meet me here at 0900."

"Sure, sure. I make sure she here. You seem like good man. Why you no marry her?"

Fred turned his back and stomped away without answering. Even the women in the laundry were making him a topic of conversation. Great. He headed over to his office and reported to the CO. "Sir, the girl situated with a place to live and a job. I'll take her shopping Saturday morning for clothing and basic needs for the baby. I could use an interpreter along."

"I'll put one at your disposal, corporal. The chaplain tells me the girl is a Christian, so you'll escort her to chapel Sunday."

"Sir? You're telling me I have to take her to *church*?" Fred's voice rose an octave.

"That is exactly what I'm telling you. You'll escort her to other things as well; help her assimilate to her new life. I assume you don't have a problem with that, Corporal." The CO crossed his arms, his face darkening. He'd brook no argument.

Fred did have a problem with it, but he sure couldn't tell him. Orders were orders. "No, sir. Anything else, sir?" Anger wouldn't help the situation. He jaws clenched, he tried to keep his face impassive.

"Go about your regular duties. I'll let you know if I need you. You're dismissed." Fred snapped a salute, turned, and left the room.

The old man was going to rub his face in this mess—as if things weren't bad enough. He should write Kara, but the stack of papers in his inbox told him the letter would have to wait.

When he finished the stack of paperwork on his desk, he ambled over to the canteen and sat alone in a dark corner sipping a beer. He wanted to relax before he wrote Kara. He ordered a second beer, sipped it when he realized he was avoiding the letter. He didn't want to write it, but what good would it do to put it off? He stood, left the rest of the beer on the table. Might as well get it over with. It sure as hell wasn't going to write itself.

When he finished writing, Fred rubbed his eyes with the heels of his hands. He picked up the letter and re-read it. It was terrible, but what could he say to make it better? He folded it and shoved it in his footlocker along with another letter he couldn't bear to send.

Fred trudged down the dirt road to Mai's quarters. He was on his way to pick her up for the chapel service—reluctant as usual. She'd picked up English quickly. Although she wasn't yet fluent, she had a good grasp of the language. So good, in fact, that the CO wanted her enrolled in an advanced class. He'd suggested she be trained as an office assistant. He hadn't yet said how Fred would be involved, but that part was sure to come. He might not be married to Mai, but it sure as heck felt like it—except he had all of the responsibilities and none of the joys of a marriage. Not even the simple joy he shared with Kara doing the most mundane task. His lips curled into a smile as he pictured doing the dishes: one washing, the other drying.

Mai complained her back hurt last night, so he bought her aspirin. He wasn't sure what she did to it; maybe it was from carrying a large baby. However, she never complained about anything; not about hard work or long hours. There were few people who could say that—him included. If she said her back hurts she was in a lot of pain.

As he reached the small house where she lived he raised his hand to knock and heard a babble of voices inside. The door was jerked open by one of the women who worked at the laundry. "You go away," she shouted. "Baby coming!" She slammed the door in his face.

He stood dumbfounded; hesitated and turned to go to the chapel. He'd pray for an easy delivery and a healthy baby for Mai. Maybe since the baby was here, he wouldn't have to be so heavily involved in her life. After all, she'd be busy with her newborn.

Distracted throughout the sermon, he was aware enough to get the point: When one reached out to help another, he honors God. He didn't need a mirror to see himself. Every single thing he'd done for Mai was filled with anger and resentment. He'd focused on how people saw him—what Kara and his friends would think if they knew.

Never considering her shame and the forced separation from her family, only himself. The situation wasn't her fault—it was completely his, yet he'd been barely civil to her throughout this ordeal. Now her baby—their baby—was coming. Ashamed of his behavior he determined to change.

After the chapel service, he went to check on Mai's again. As he approached the door, he heard the sounds of celebration. He knocked tentatively. The door jerked open and he was welcomed inside. The group of smiling women reaching out to pat him on the arm or back—actually any body part they could reach.

"You have son—a fine boy! Come see your boy." Hands pulled him forward to the bedroom where Mai laid, a small bundle cradled in her arms. "Are you okay?" he asked.

Mai's face was streaked with sweat and tears. "Yes, I am just very tired. Here— see your son."

A frisson of fear went through him as he reached for the proffered baby. Gazing into the tiny face, his own face blinked back with unfocused eyes. The face was red and scrunched up with an odd baby expression, but it was undeniably his child. A wave of dizziness passed over him and the surrounding women laughed. "Get him chair, before he fall." A voice call out as several pairs of hands steadied him. Another placed a chair behind him. Hands worked in unison to help him sit.

Gazing in wonder at his son, he unwrapped the babe to see his tiny hands and feet; perfect, with tiny finger and toenails. His heart swelled, knowing in a moment he loved the infant in his arms—as he loved Natalie.

He'd watch him go through the early stages he'd missed in Natalie's life. He'd chronicle today so he'd always remember it. "I need to get something. Hold the baby. I'll be right back." He placed the baby in the nearest set of arms and took off running.

Fred raced back to his quarters to get his pastels and paper. He wanted the first pictures to include the crowd of celebrating women. He'd draw a picture of Mai, so the baby would know how his mother looked the day of his birth. He'd do one of—his steps faltered as a new thought came to mind. *What are we going to name him? We can't just call him "him" or "the baby."*

He burst back into the house and shouted the question, "What are we going to name our son." Mai looked surprised. It was the first time he'd said "our son." She smiled gratefully.

"I have thought of names for him, good names." She took a sheet of paper from between the pages of her Bible and began to read them to Fred. They were all Vietnamese names.

Why should he be surprised? Of course, she'd choose a name she was familiar with, but he wanted an American-sounding name. He wanted his son to speak English before he left for home. That was a stupid, though. The baby wouldn't talk until long after he was gone.

He rejected over half the names as sounding too foreign. They were down to the last four: Dahn, which meant love and prestige; Trang, which meant honored; Trung, which meant loyal; and Tuan, which meant bright and smart. He understood what she meant by "good names." She had chosen names by the characteristic they would bring the child. He scratched his head, trying to think of American names that he might substitute for these Vietnamese names.

Perhaps Dan or Don for Dahn. All that came to mind for Trang was train and that wouldn't do. He had the same problem with Trung ... truck? ... train? No. Tuan? He could call him John—not perfect, but it would do.

He left the final choice to Mai. She chose Dahn. Now his son had a name: Dahn or Don Jacobs. His face creased in a joyous smile. Now that his son had a name, he'd draw the pictures; paper memories he'd leave for his son and Mai.

The next morning he went to Mai's home and knocked. There was no answer, so he tried the door. It was locked. He walked around, tried to look through the windows when a friendly voice called out, "Mai not there; she go work."

"What did she do with the baby?" Surely, she hadn't left him alone in the house.

"She take baby with her," the woman replied. Her eyes asked, "What do you think she'd do with him?"

Fred couldn't imagine taking a baby to the laundry. He had seen toddlers there, but he'd never considered why they were there. Was there no nursery available?

He went directly to the laundry. "Mai, should you be back at work so soon?"

"Yes, I need work to make money for Dahn. I want him go to school and not be a lost child."

Fred didn't understand what she meant, so he shrugged it off and asked, "Can I take him to show the chaplain and the CO? I'll bring him back soon so you can feed him." She nodded her head.

It was strange to hold a baby this small. Natalie was a lot older the first time he held her. By comparison, Dahn felt like a moving doll. He was fascinated by every noise and movement the child made. He couldn't stop grinning when he walked into the chaplain's office to show him Dahn.

The chaplain eyed him speculatively. "Have you thought of what you're going to do when it's time to go home? I'm glad to see you're taking responsibility now, but have you thought about this boy's future?"

"What do you mean? He'll stay here with Mai. I'll send her money so he can go to school when he's old enough."

"I think you need to talk to Mai about that, son," the chaplain said sadly. "Come back here and talk to me after the two of you have talked."

Puzzled, he went to the CO's office and asked if he was free. As the old man looked up, he smiled with pleasure. "Is this who I think it is? Is this your baby?"

Fred smiled. "Yes sir, this is my son. His name is Dahn, but I think I'm going to call him Don."

The CO chuckled. "That reminds me of an old joke, but never mind. Your son, huh? So you're taking full responsibility for him? If you are, you need to get started on the paperwork ASAP."

"I don't understand, sir. Paperwork? What for?" Fred was clearly confused.

The CO searched Fred's face before answering. "If you plan to take him back to the USA, you need to start the process now. It takes a long time to work through all the bureaucracy."

"Take him back to America?" Horror written across his face, he said, "I don't plan to take him home. His mother will want him here."

The CO sat back in his chair, stared Fred straight in the eyes. "Have you talked to Mai about this at all? She doesn't plan to keep him."

"What do you mean not keep him? What else would she do with him?" Fred's stomach churned. His joy from the morning vanished.

"Son, do you remember what her father said they'd do with the baby?" The CO didn't pull any punches as he reminded Fred, but his face was tinged with sorrow.

When the full realization hit Fred, he jumped from his chair and yelled, "You can't mean Mai would leave our baby out in the jungle or put him in some dirty, overcrowded orphanage?"

"That's exactly what I'm saying, son. Mixed-race children are not wanted in this culture. As long as Mai works on base, neither of them will be mistreated. But what happens when the war ends and she's by herself? Or she wants to see her family? You need to talk to the girl."

"That's what the chaplain said, but I didn't understand. Dear God, dear God, what am I going to do?" Fred's agitation wakened the sleeping child and he began to cry.

"Let me see the little fellow." The CO took the crying baby from Fred's arms and held him to his chest, and patted his small back. "You're a fine little guy, aren't you? Good strong lungs, strong legs, all bright-eyed and bushy-tailed ... He looks like a keeper to me, Corporal. Think about it." He handed the crying baby back to Fred who understood he'd been dismissed.

He carried the baby back to the laundry. "Mai, we need to talk. Can I come over tonight?"

"Yes, of course you can. You come see your son again." She smiled sweetly, but her words conveyed a new meaning. When she said 'your son,'" it expressed a different message to his quaking heart.

He brought small gifts—a new blouse, for Mai and a teddy bear for Dahn—when he saw them. After handing off the gifts, he broached the subject of his son's future. "This morning you said you did not want Dahn to become a lost child. What did you mean by that?"

Mai's eyes drifted to her hands. "You do not wish to marry me. You have another wife?"

"Yes, you know I do. Her name is Kara and we have a daughter."

Mai started at the mention of Kara's name. "Ah, Kara. That is what you say ..." She looked away, but not before Fred read the pain in her eyes.

"Mai, I am sorry for what happened. If I could take it back, I would, but I can't. Now we have this beautiful baby boy and we need to decide his future. I don't understand what you mean about being a lost child."

Tears leaked slowly down her face. "I cannot keep him. I could never have a life if I did. No job, no marriage, no family. I would be as much an outcast as he will be. I will try hard to find an orphanage to take him—one where they won't beat him. One where he can go to school."

"If I send you money—" Fred began, but Mai shook her head vigorously.

"Money does not matter. Nothing would change."

Sick to his stomach, he said, "I can't let my son go to an orphanage if I can help it. The CO says it's possible for me to take him home, but there's a lot of paperwork involved. You'd have to agree to let me take him, and Kara would have to agree to adopt him. Then, I could begin the rest of the paperwork. There are no guarantees Kara will agree. Whatever happens, I want you to begin an advanced English class; train to become a secretary; prepare for your future, too."

"I can't take Dahn to class," Mai whispered as she looked at the baby in her arms.

"I'll watch him. I'll get permission from the CO. I'm sure he'd let me give up my lunch so I could help you. I'll check with him first thing tomorrow."

This could be the final straw with Kara. He'd put off mailing the letters which explained the situation. Now he'd blindside her by asking her to accept his illegitimate child. He'd ask in the most desperate way possible—plead to bring his son home. Begging might be the only way. How could he word a letter that broached such a painful subject? There was no way she'd be happy with his request. His heart was torn in two. He loved Kara with all his heart, but he loved his tiny son, too. He couldn't abandon him to the fate he'd have left in this godforsaken country. He couldn't.

He asked for the day off so he could figure out what to say. No matter what he said it would break Kara's heart. Would she be able to forgive him? As he sat in the chapel, head bowed in pray, he asked the Lord of his life for wisdom and courage.

He wrote a cover letter of apology, removed the unsent letters and laid them on the desk. Sighing with apprehension and regret, he wrote the final letter.

Chapter 26

In her fourth year of college, Kara loved the challenge of balancing school with Natalie. It wasn't simple to get babysitters any more. Several of her friends left school for other endeavors and other friends schedules no longer jibed with hers. By taking a smaller course load, she combined school with working in a day care. It allowed her to leave Natalie when she had a class. Splitting her days gave her extra money for school and free childcare.

She'd picked up her mail on the way home and decided to sort it at home. Once home she set Natalie down to let her play. She sorted through the mail. There was a fat envelope from Fred. Uneasy by the unusual thickness of the envelope, she opened it first. It was silly to be apprehensive. Letters were sometimes far between, so he'd written a longer letter. Why this feeling of dread?

With a deep breath, she mentally shook herself, and began to read. From the first line, her stomach knotted, but she read the phalanx of letters, dated months apart, to the bitter end. At least he didn't beat around the bush, but got straight to the point. She laughed bitterly. She should have expected this. After all, she got pregnant the very first time.

Was this God's idea of a joke? Some sort of celestial payback for her mistake—never being sorry for what had happened? After all, she ended up with a beautiful daughter and Fred. Maybe Fred wasn't as good a choice as she thought. For the short time they actually lived together, some of it had been magic. But most of it had been difficult. Now Fred fathered a child? He expected her to believe his far-fetched story and accept this child into her home. What a sick joke. "I love you with all my heart"? Did he expect her to believe him? The letter sounds like a veiled threat: "I cannot leave him." If she didn't agree, well, good-bye, because he won't leave his son. Is that what he's saying?

⌒♾

April and Geoff were coming for another night of a homemade spaghetti dinner and salad. It was good and it was cheap—and it usually tasted better eaten with friends. It was doubtful she could eat after the update on Fred.

Kara stumbled to the kitchen and threw up in the sink. After scrubbing and bleaching the sink, she mechanically began the spaghetti sauce

The sauce set to simmer, she made the salad. She glanced at the clock to time when Geoff and April would arrived. She filled a pot with water for the spaghetti and turned the heat low.

Wet and hungry, Natalie cried to get her attention. When she noticed, she changed her and gave her part of a banana, but the toddler continued to fuss.

"Shut up, Natalie; just shut up!" she screamed. The toddler stared with rounded eyes and then cried in earnest. Kara picked her up, patted her briefly, and tucked her into bed, unable deal with histrionics today.

By the time Geoff and April arrived, Natalie was asleep. Kara tossed the spaghetti noodles into the pot and turned to greet them. Her attempt to a smile was a grimace. April was by her side in an instant. "Kara, what's wrong? You look horrible! Here, sit down." She pulled Kara to the rocking chair.

Without a word, Kara picked up the letter and handed it to them, her eyes on the floor

"Oh, Kara," April knelt at her feet.

Geoff bent and put his arm around her. "Kara, I know what you must think, but I'm sure Fred is telling the truth,"

"Right. Some cute girl ends up in *his* bed and he knows nothing about it? He screws her, but doesn't remember until—surprise—she's next to him the next morning? Half-dressed and it's some big surprise? I don't think so. I can't buy that sorry excuse. Now he wants me to adopt the child from his liaison?" Angry and hurt, she didn't want to give him an easy out. But she was wrong to expect sympathy.

"What kind of mother would leave a child by the side of the road to let him die? That's outrageous. No wonder Fred wants to bring his son home," Geoff said.

"To think she'd be an outcast if she tried to keep her own son. How tragic," April added.

"So you think I should agree to let Fred bring his illegitimate half-caste child home with him?" She asked crossly.

Her friends stared in disbelief. "Kara, would you expect Fred to do any less than try to rescue his own son?" Geoff asked softly.

Damn him all to hell for being logical, so compassionate. She wanted anger and outrage—not this! Tears welled in her eyes. "No, I guess I don't," she whispered in defeat. "That wouldn't be Fred, would it? It just that... every time I looked at that baby, it would be a living reminder of what he did."

Geoff's words eased their way into her mind and heart, as he spoke about Fred's honesty. He forced her to remember the reason Fred married her—her own pregnancy with Nate's child.

He was right. Fred didn't have to marry her. He married her to give her baby a name. He loved her and he loved Nate's child. She dissolved in tears.

Geoff and April wrapped her in a cocoon of love as she struggled through pain. Pulled to the table, they placed dinner before her and encouraged her to eat. April took care of Natalie, so she didn't need to worry about the child.

"Kara, are you ready to hold Natalie? She wants her mama," April announced following dinner.

"Of course. Come see Mama, sweetheart." Natalie came forward dragging a doll by one arm. She pulled them to her lap.

"Mama cry?" she asked.

"Yes, but Mama is fine." She kissed her cheek gently. "How is your baby today?" The girl held up her doll. "Baby needs kiss." She kissed the doll's cheek and kissed her daughter.

After Geoff and April cleaned up the kitchen, he strolled over and picked up the letter again. "It sounds like his squad had a pretty rough go of it. Finding the villagers the soldiers they helped all dead." Geoff grimaced. She recalled his temporary student deferment. He could be called up immediately following graduation.

As she considered Fred's nightmares, the night sweats, how he cried out in his sleep, and the graphic drawings of his experiences, her heart softened.

"You know what, Geoff? Fred's actually lived with me such a short time, considering the length of time we've been married. Sometimes I don't feel married."

Geoff pulled her up and hugged her. "Remember the good times, Kara. Don't forget him. April and I will help you remember if you'll let us." She sighed, nodded her head.

He opened a bottle of wine and poured her a large glass. They began a night of remembering; first laughing over her abominable bowling on her first date with Fred. Then April brought up the day she discovered she was pregnant; when she realized Fred was the perfect person to advise her. She recalled the day he showed up on campus ready to propose. They laughed again over the "cattle chute" wedding ceremony. They discussed his health; the physical and mental wounds and how he healed. She remembered ... she remembered ... she remembered.

She'd write in the morning when her head cleared from the stress of the day and the wine.

> *Dear Fred,*
>
> *I've enclosed the signed paperwork so you can begin whatever is necessary to bring your son home. How could I do otherwise, knowing it could mean an unhappy life at best, or even the child's death?*
>
> *I would appreciate a few pictures so I know what he looks like. I'll prepare Natalie for her baby brother with the pictures.*
>
> *You must to know I'm upset. Jealous, I guess. That woman will have spent more time with you than I have in our entire married life. I feel cheated. I know it's not*

all your fault, but I hope you understand my frustration and anger.

I do love you, Fred. The very thing I love most is your willingness to reach out to rescue people. I remind myself of that daily.

Let me know if there's more I need to do at this end to facilitate your son's homecoming. I assume he has a name. What is it?

Love,
Kara

The letter was whiney and cold, but it was the best she could do. The other three drafts she'd written lay wadded on the floor. Cold or not, this letter, along with the official paperwork, would be sent. Hopefully, Fred would understand. If he didn't, well, they'd cross that bridge when they came to it.

The day the letter arrived, he warred with himself. Should he open it immediately or wait for more privacy? Anxiety won out over patience and he ripped it open. From the tone of the letter, he could tell how damaged she was by emotional pain and fear. He could do little from here. He wanted to wrap her in his arms and breathe in the scent of her hair. Kiss every inch of her face and neck and make love. Nothing could make him want Mai, as sweet as she was. Kara was his heart, his soul, his very hope for tomorrow. All he could do was write another letter to make his words convey his emotions. He'd never leave her as long as he had breath in his body.

Chapter 27

The bell rang over the door and alerted Amos a customer had come in. Wiping his hands, he hustled out of the kitchen and looked toward the entrance. The glare of sunlight made it hard for him to see the man's face.

"Are you just going to stare, or are you going to say hello?"

"Nate! Is it you, son? You finally came to see ole Amos? How long has it been?"

Nate laughed, "No, I came for a piece of sweet potato pie! It's been five years, so I'm ready for that pie!" This giant of a man grabbed him off his feet in a hug.

"Get on over here and sit yourself down. I just finished cleanin' up from the breakfast crowd, so I got me a minute to sit. Tell my about yourself, son, and tell me about Josh."

Nate sat and began to relate stories of his travels. He wouldn't tell Amos he killed Joyce or tell him about the two men he'd killed to save the life of an innocent young woman. He mentioned the monasteries, but didn't elaborate on the years spent praying for forgiveness and peace. Instead he explained his travels using Josh's marriage as an excuse.

Amos brought him up-to-date on how quickly his restaurant got off the ground. He was forced to hire another chef to help with dinner crowd. He came early to do the baking and prepare breakfast and lunch. He'd prepare many of the main dinner items while the second chef cooked the special orders. "I had me a dishwasher who's supposed to come and do the clean-up after lunch and dinner today, but he up and quit on me. I don't suppose I could get you to fill in for a few days, could I?"

Nate grinned. "My time is my own. I'd be glad to help. My only problem is a place to stay—someplace where I could have keep Fosdick."

"You still got that ole cat with you? I like what you wrote about that cat. I kept all your letters. As far as a place to stay, I own this building, thanks to my brother. There're two apartments above this place. I live in one, but you could sure use the other one."

"That would be great!"

"You may not think so when you see it. I never got around to cleanin' it up. It's real dirty and needs paint, but it's yours for the askin'."

"Sure. How much time do I have before I report to work? I could clean now." Nate was pleased to have a reason to stay and reconnect with his friend.

"You only got about an hour. Let me show you how to get up there; then I'll bring you up some soup and a sandwich. Maybe a little bit of chopped meat for that cat."

Amos put a "Back in ten minutes" sign on the front door, led Nate back through the kitchen and out the back door. A second door next to the back entrance led to a landing where two doors faced each other. Amos pointed to the one on the left and said, "That's my place; this'n will be yours." He took the keys from his pocket and unlocked the door.

The blinds in the room were closed. The gloom gave the room a depressing appearance. Opening them didn't help much. Dust lay thick over everything. A miasma of filth and grease hung over the room.

"I guess I'll need to buy cleaning supplies."

"Nah. I got loads of supplies down in the restaurant. I'll get my vacuum right now. You can get the dust off things first. Hold on a second." Amos hurried across the landing to his apartment to retrieve his vacuum and a handful of rags. "I'll bring you lunch in just a minute, so you may want to start with that table there."

As Amos hurried back down the stairs, Nate eyed the place again. "Real dirty" didn't begin to describe the apartment. It was filthy. Nate vacuumed the table and chairs before he tried to wash them. The accumulated filth of years covered every surface. He vacuumed the countertops. He ran water in the sink to rinse it of dirt and debris before he attempted to clean it. He ran downstairs, got a bucket and Lysol to wash down surfaces. Grateful he could move fast; he had the counters washed, the table and chairs spotless before Amos appeared with his lunch. Amos remembered the chopped meat for Fosdick.

"This ole cat looks jus' like I figured from the way you wrote about him." His huge hand caressed the cat. "He sure saw some hard times." His glance took in the kitchen.

"Whoa, boy. I forgot how fast you and your brother work. Your mama and daddy did a good job raisin' you boys."

Nate didn't correct Amos. He smiled and answered, "Yeah, they did."

"You can get your pie when you come on down. The crowd is startin' to come for their lunches, so I gotta go." Amos patted Nate's back and hurried down the stairs.

"Will you be okay until I get back, buddy?" Fosdick looked at Nate, meowed his answer before he strolled off to the explore bedroom. Nate picked up the lunch dishes to take downstairs. He laughed hearing Fosdick give an explosive sneeze from the other room.

Amos hadn't exaggerated over the size of the lunch crowd. It was three in the afternoon before it cleared out. More people followed for pie and coffee.

When there was a pause, Nate approached Amos about another necessary item. "I need a litter box and cat litter. Where's the nearest store?"

Amos directed him to a supermarket two blocks south and one east. This town was built in a grid, with the city hall and town square built in the center of the town. The grid made it easy to find his way around.

He found the supermarket and picked up the litter and box, plus cat food for Fosdick. As he wandered through, he noticed small kitchen items he could use, so he added them to his cart before he checked out. As they bagged the items, he realized he had more than the average person could carry, "Do you think I could borrow a cart for a few minutes? I'm only three blocks from here."

The clerk hesitated until he mentioned Amos; he smiled and said, "Oh that's fine. Any friend of Amos' is a friend of mine." He held out his hand to shake Nate's.

The clerk laughed as Nate described the condition of the apartment. "You know what they say about a gift horse. But, I can't complain. Amos is letting me use it rent free for while I'm here."

"I'll look forward to seeing you again. I'm Mike Michaels." He raised both hands into the air. "I know, I know ... I have no idea what my parents were thinking either." He shrugged his shoulders self-depreciatingly.

"I'm Nate Whitworth. I'll look forward to seeing you again, Mike." Nate grinned at the affable man. "I'd better get a move on. Amos is going to need me back at the restaurant and I have to bring the cart back."

"Bring it back tomorrow sometime; it will be okay," Mike suggested.

Nate hurried back to the apartment. He poured litter into the box, put down water in a small bowl he had purchased then hurried downstairs to ready himself for the next round of diners.

If he ran the dishes through the large commercial dishwasher as fast as he could rinse and load them, Nate could barely keep up. Amos hadn't been kidding; he had a going operation. It gathered a large base of regular customers since the day it opened.

The other chef proved to be almost as fast as Amos and Nate. He was also amazingly good-humored, given the rate at which he was forced to work. "I don't mind; as long as I'm cooking, I'm working. As long as I'm working, I'm taking care of my family." His name was Albert Bacon. Amos called him Albee. Albee liked his new nickname. He liked it so much he encouraged everyone to call him that.

After work, Nate vacuumed the remainder of the apartment giving it what his mama would call a lick and a promise. He'd laid his sleeping bag over the mattress until he had time to wash the sheets. Fosdick continued to sneeze. He insisted on attacking the hoard of dust bunnies under the bed.

Nate paused long enough to feed the cat dinner to get him out of the way. Then he attacked the bathroom. He finished the tub at one in the morning and fell into bed next to the sleeping cat. He was satisfied when he could wash up in a clean sink and take a shower without the nasty muck on the bottom of the tub.

Sunday came before Nate knew it. He tapped on Amos's door, wondering if he could go to church before work. "Son, you won't see a soul here today. This is the Lord's Day, so I'm not open. Get your clothes on, come on down, and I'll cook us up a mess of breakfast."

Nate shuffled through his meager clothes before he picked out a clean pair of jeans and a clean white shirt. He hoped no one would mind if he didn't wear a suit. He didn't own one. He'd only been inside a church a few times since he was changed. He'd been to chapel at the mission and at camp, but dress was casual in both places. At the monastery, he'd worn a robe, when he'd gone to pray. He fed Fosdick then headed downstairs for breakfast with Amos.

"Amos, I'm not comfortable wearing jeans to church, but I don't own a suit or slacks.

"Son, the good Lord don't care who you are or what you got on. He jus' wants you to come. Those people that'll be there, well, most of them feel the same way I do. But a few got their noses stuck in the air. I been judged all my life, for the clothes I wear or the color of my skin. You do like I do—ignore them."

Amos was right. A few people scowled at Nate and Amos when they walked in the door of the church, but most of the people welcomed them.

As they sat down in the pew, Nate looked around at the people in the congregation. The minister wore casual khaki slacks and a sport shirt. He recognized many of the faces from the restaurant. Mike Michaels was there with his family, all dressed casually. A little girl with pigtails stood on the pew in front of him and gave a shy gap-toothed smile before her mother pulled her into her lap. He sighed, let his muscles relax as he sat back to listen to the music and the sermon.

This was the kind of place he'd love to call home, but that was impossible. He could stay a few years at most, then he'd be forced to move on.

He'd been in the town for almost nine months when one night he jerked awake. He reached out to pet Fosdick, but his cat's body lay still and cold. Nate lurched into a sitting position, turned on the bedside lamp and took a close look at his old friend. His beloved cat was dead. Nate picked up the body and cradled it close to him as he cried out in the pain of loss.

Fosdick had been his best friend since he'd rescued him from certain death. The cat stayed with him after he'd let him down by savagely killing those men. If there was anything good, it was the cat died in his sleep.

He held his beloved friend knowing what he'd do. He'd take Fosdick home to Arizona—bury him next to Don José. It was where he belonged. He'd tell Amos in the morning

He got out of bed, found a roll of gauze bandages and wrapped Fosdick as he'd seen in pictures of mummified cats in a book on Egypt. He didn't believe cats were gods as those ancients did; nor did he know anything about mummification. He did know Fosdick was too special to toss in a hole in the ground.

After he finished tightly wrapping him in the gauze, he wrapped him in foil. He'd look for a box for his cat in the morning. Was he acting weird? Perhaps he was, but he didn't care.

The drive to Arizona went quickly since Nate didn't feel much like sleeping. Still, the long hours in the car brought back the painful memories he'd face in Arizona. So many thoughts flickered through his mind. The first time he saw Kara, so sweet and innocent. Don José with his tail waving like a banner in the breeze. Pete and Joann who welcomed him into their home. Kara fishing. Fred. Kara's kisses. Josh's attack. Sneaking Fosdick into the hospital. Kara. Kara. Kara. He and Kara together in the hospital bed ... Worst of all, his savage attack on Joyce.

He wished to lay Fosdick to rest in a place where he'd been happy— where Don José waited at rest. Since, going to Payson brought back painful memories, he wouldn't stay longer than necessary. He was glad the return trip would take him back the way he'd come, through the White Mountains and into New Mexico. He didn't want to travel over the Rim to Flagstaff. He wasn't sure he'd stop at the cabin either.

He hunted in the plains and the desert for blood most nights along the route. The final night he'd stopped in Star Valley, a tiny town east of Payson, to grab a burger and a cola. He wanted to avoid everything connected with his past. There were too many ugly memories. He arrived at the café shortly before closing and ate slowly to extend the time for the last leg of his journey. He paid for his meal and left a sizeable tip for the waiter since he'd kept him well past closing.

Most people would be asleep in their beds before he dug Fosdick's grave. The crushed granite made a lot of noise. There was no way to avoid the scraping sound of the shovel. Whoever lived there better be a sound sleeper.

The house was dark when he drove past. After he parked off-road, Nate grabbed his shovel, the box that contained Fosdick's remains and ghosted down the road. Slipping quietly into the backyard, he dug with what to him was normal speed. The hole was completed in moments. As he placed the box into the hole he whispered a brief prayer.

He gathered pine needles, spread them under the tree to disguise the freshly turned soil and then pulled a knife from his pocket. Under the name Don José, Nate carved "Fosdick." Then he carved two more words: "Friends Forever." He whispered words of thanks for the gift of friendship they shared and ghosted back to the waiting car.

Memories of Joyce made him anxious to shake the dust of this town from his boots. As much as he loved Amos, he wanted to go to another place of prayer and contemplation. Guilt and pain resurfaced and he longed for peace.

Nate left Payson and drove an hour east then slept in the car for the rest of the night. Having delivered Fosdick to his final resting place, he felt a sense of completion. It was time for his next step—time to move on.

Chapter 28

Natalie and she stood to watch planes take off and land while they waited for Fred to arrive. The plane was late and Natalie grew impatient. "When is my daddy and my baby bubba gonna be here?"

Glancing at the announcement board she said, "They'll be here soon now. Let's take you potty and wash your pretty face, okay?"

Natalie scowled, but reluctantly agreed. Kara took her time washing the girl's face and sticky hands. It was a mistake to offer her candies to pass the time. The candy made Natalie more active than ever. She crawled off the chair and ran down the hall and then jumped up and down shouting, "I want my daddy! I want my bubba!"

Frazzled by the time they announced Fred's plane landed; her stomach was a knot of dread and anticipation. She'd been on an emotional roller coaster since she received the letter asking her to adopt his son. Reams of papers came to sign and notarize. Each page she signed brought up questions of her relationship with Fred.

She never doubted they should bring his infant son out of harm's way. He wasn't responsible for any of this. He was a victim of circumstances. Her doubts stemmed from jealousy and anger.

"Let's go to the window and watch Daddy and Don get off the plane, okay?"

"Yea! Where are they? Where are they?" Natalie yelled.

"Shhh. Look, right there. There's your daddy and he's carrying your baby brother."

"My bubba, my bubba! I want to hold him."

"Natalie, you need settle down or you'll scare your brother." She longed for a drink. Just one—to calm her nerves. Ah well, it wasn't going to happen.

The passengers came through the gate and were greeted by family and friends. "There they are, Natalie. There's your daddy and your new baby brother." Her back ached, so she put Natalie down, but she kept a tight grip on her hand.

Fred's eyes searched, and then looked in their direction. In an instant he was by her side, a hesitant smile on his face. His eyes held doubt and fear. "Kara."

"Welcome home." While she said the words, there was no warmth in them.

"Daddy!" Natalie wrapped her arms around Fred's knees. Reaching forward, Kara took the baby from his arms so he could free his knees and pick up Natalie.

"You've gotten so big since I saw you." Fred and Natalie began to chatter.

Sitting down she pulled the blanket away from the baby's face. He was awake. As she gazed into his sober eyes, he stared at her, she felt a pull in her heart. His eyes had a slight Asian cast, but they were undeniably Fred's eyes. His hair was laughable in the way it stood straight up, but the color was the same as Fred's. "Hello, there, Don. I'm your new mommy," she whispered. With a smile of incredible sweetness, he won her heart.

Fred held Natalie as he sat beside them. Natalie leaned over and patted the baby's head. "Hi bubba. We're going to be best friends and I gotta new toy for you in the car. You get to sleep in my old bed 'cause I got a big girl bed now."

"Shall we get your bags and go?" At Fred's nod, she stood and turned away. Disappointment flashed in his eyes. As she walked ahead she realized she hadn't kissed him.

"Mom and Dad have dinner planned for tonight. I figured we might as well get that out of the way." It didn't come out the way she meant, but she didn't know what to do about it.

"I thought we'd have time alone first." Fred stared at the floor, but she saw his hurt and disappointment.

"They're anxious to see you, too. We'll only be there overnight. We have plenty of time to be alone." Again, her words didn't come out right. They were cold. Things were getting worse and worse.

The drive to Payson was quiet. Both Natalie and Don fell asleep in the car. So did Fred. The exhaustion from the long flight with the baby was written on his face even while he slept. She wanted to touch him, but she was afraid to let down her guard. Her heart ached in confusion. Could she make things right between them?

Her parents planned an early dinner knowing they'd be tired. Dinner was awkward, since Dad played with Natalie, but completely ignored Don. He hardly spoke to Fred. Mom tried to make up for it by feeding Don and chatting with Fred.

After the dishes and leftovers were put away, Fred took the babies for a walk. The new stroller was roomy enough for both of them. Mom left to buy milk and ice cream at the store.

She went into the bedroom to set up a portable crib for Don and fix a pallet on the floor for Natalie. That done, she went into the living room, her back aching, and fell into the chair across from her dad.

"How are you dealing with all this, Kara?"

"With all what?"

"With the fact that Fred can't keep his pants zipped, and then has the gall to bring home his bas ..."

Dad raised his voice, but she shocked him into silence as she leaped up, and shouted, "Don't you dare say that! What happened was an accident. Fred was drunk. You know Fred doesn't drink. He dreamed the girl was me. Her voice an octave higher than usual.

"Right." Pete's tone was sarcastic. "I'm surprised you bought that story. He cheated on you, Kara, and now he expects you to raise his little half-caste brat! He's no damn good!"

"Not good?" she shrieked. "You want to know how truly good he is?" She grabbed a framed picture of Natalie that sat on the end table and shoved it in his face. "Look carefully at this picture, Dad. Who do you think Natalie looks like?"

He looked confused, but took the picture in his hands and studied it.

She shouted, "Does she look like me? No? Does she look like Fred? No? I'll tell you who she looks like. She looks exactly like her father, Nate Whitworth—that's who she looks like!"

By the color of her father's face, she was afraid she killed him—sure he was having a stroke. He'd turned a deep puce, and then turned white.

"Nate?" He gasped, "How?"

"How?" She gave a humorless laugh. "The usual way, Dad—the usual way. Don't blame Nate either. It was entirely my fault. I was the one who seduced him."

Her voice softened. "That's why you're wrong about Fred. I wrote to ask him for advice when I realized I was pregnant. He came to help me. I didn't know how to tell you and Mom and I didn't want to hurt you. But I didn't want to drop out of school or give up my baby. He married me so I wouldn't have to hurt you—so I could keep Nate's baby. He didn't have to do that. Then you have the nerve to tell me he's no good and insult his character? You are so wrong, Dad. He is nothing but a truly good person. Yes, I believe his story. Fred *always* tells the truth."

Fred stood outside, his hand on the knob when he heard the shouting voices. He froze in place at the angry words and then reached for the doorknob a second time. Another hand closed over his. Joann stood behind him holding a finger to her lips. She'd driven up unnoticed. She whispered, "Let them get this out in the open before we go in."

As Kara made her angry confession to her dad, Fred turned away to avoid Joann's disappointment, but she reached out and placed her hand on Fred's shoulder.

"Fred, I've known for a long time Nate had to be Natalie's father. She looks exactly like him. I think Pete knew it in his heart, but he didn't want to admit Kara's not his perfect little girl." She reached up and touched his cheek. "Thank you for all you've done for us."

They waited outside until Pete regained his normal voice. Joann pushed the door open with a loud bang and said cheerfully, "What great timing. Fred, the babies, and I got back at the same time. Who's ready for ice cream?"

She walked into the living room and paused. "Did we interrupt something?"

Pete stood up, agitated. "Yes. Uh, no. We're through talking." He turned toward Fred, his face a mask of conflicting emotion. "I guess I owe you an apology, Fred. I didn't realize you saved my daughter's honor when she got pregnant. I was angry, assumed you were at fault. Now with this new child, well, again I ... I guess I thought you were ruining my daughter's life. I'm sorry." He offered his hand to Fred.

"I understand how you feel, Pete. I'm afraid I'll ruin your daughter's life, too. All I've ever wanted was to make her happy, but I'm not doing too well at it."

"Yes you are." Kara spoke softly. Moving to his side, she wrapped her arms around him. "We've hit a few bumps, but we'll get past them. One thing I know to be true is that I love you, Fred Jacobs. I want to spend the rest of my life with you." Tears sparkled in her eyes as she stood on tiptoes to kiss Fred.

"How about that ice cream now?" Joann asked.

"I'll help you fix it," Kara said as Don began to cry. "Oh, I guess he's ready for a bottle."

"You warm it up, but I'll feed him. It's about time I get to know my new grandson." Pete reached down and lifted the baby from the stroller. Don looked at his grandfather's face and gave him the same sweet smile he'd given Kara when she first held him. "Huh, you're not such a bad-looking little fellow, are you? You're pretty cute, but we're going to have to do something about that hair."

That evening, Joann asked, "Why don't you let us watch the babies tonight? You can have privacy and get a good night's sleep."

Kara was quick to agree. The storm over, she planned to give Fred the welcome he deserved.

❦

Getting a wild idea to clean closets, she found a stack of sketchbooks. Fred had been home for several months, so she was curious to see if he still drew nightmares. As she thumbed through the books, she came across several pictures of the same young woman. She was sweetly pretty with a distinct look of fragility. She wasn't on every page, but appeared far too often for her not to guess who she was. A page where she was distinctly pregnant confirmed Kara's guess. This had to be Mai Pham, Don's biological mother. She knew Fred drew pictures of her at the time of Don's birth, but why so many before he was born?

At war with herself, she shoved the sketchbooks back in the closet. Did she trust Fred? He'd always been honest to the point of the ridiculous, never telling as much as a white lie. She believed he loved her, so why couldn't she let this go? He explained his responsibility in Mai's pregnancy and how he was required to look after her. He explained everything, even though it was painful. Shouldn't that count for something?

The kind of marriage she aspired to have was based on love, respect and trust. Traits lived out in her parents' marriage. Not to say they never argued. That wasn't realistic. In fact, they could get pretty hot sometimes, but they always worked out their differences together.

As she tried to think through her emotions, she listed the facts. First, she loved Fred—that's a given. Second, she respected Fred— another given. She trusted him, but why then was she upset and betrayed by the pictures? She didn't understand herself. She wanted security for herself and the children. God knows the children had rough starts in life.

Should she ask him about the pictures? Tonight was takeout pizza night, so there wouldn't be much to clean up. After they ate, she'd put the kids to bed so they could talk. A bottle of wine with dinner should help calm her nerves.

Fred got the kids in their pajamas and read them a story. As he turned out the lights, she asked him to pour the wine. She slipped in and grabbed the offending sketchbooks. Puzzled, when she returned with the armload of books, he asked, "What's going on?"

Without a word, she sat and opened the first book. "Here's a picture of Mai, right?" He nodded his head, more confused than ever. "Yes it is."

"Here's another and another, and oh look, here's another one. It's a lot of pictures of one girl." Her tone was accusing, but she couldn't help herself.

"Your point is ... what? That I shouldn't have drawn any pictures of Mai?" Fred's jaw tightened.

"It seems to me you have more pictures of her than anyone or anything else. I want to know why. Are you sure you weren't in love with her?"

Fred's shoulders slumped and his voice dropped to a husky whisper. "Kara, are we back to that again? Are you never going to forgive and forget?"

"Yes ... No ... I don't know. I'm confused. I thought I let this go, but when I saw all these pictures ..." Her words slipped away in choked silence.

"I drew most of these pictures to help Mai with her English. I'd point to a picture. She'd tell me about what she saw in the picture. She was supposed to clearly explain what she was doing and where she was at the time: at work in the laundry, shopping for food, whatever. When I came home, I kept the pictures for Don to have later. I never thought they'd upset you or I'd have told you about them right away. They aren't significant in any other way."

He sat in silence as he stared down at the books.

"I'm sorry, Fred. I try not to be jealous, but I still resent the fact that she had all those months with you. I know I'm a jerk." She looked at him pleading for him to understand and forgive her.

When he looked up it was with a wry smile on his face. "You do remember, don't you, we have the rest of our lives together?"

She threw her arms around his neck. "Are you sure you can put up with me that long?"

Hi voice husky, he whispered, "I can give it a try." His soft and warm lips pressed against her neck.

Ashamed of her streak of jealousy, she determined to work to overcome it. She was her own worst enemy and came close to damaging their relationship yet again. Glad she decided to confront him, instead of further damaging their relationship. Making up was much more fun.

Part Two

Chapter 29

2008—She woke from a dream about Fred. Dreams of him didn't come often these days. In the dream, they'd done nothing extraordinary—sat outside in the sunshine, talking companionably. It was funny how something as insignificant as a dream could bring both joy and pain. He's been dead long enough that most of her days were good days—happy days. But, there were other days where the pain sliced to her heart like a razor.

They had a good life together. There were bumps in the road of life, but they'd overcome each struggle one by one. People use the term Yin and Yang; it was a good way to describe their relationship. They'd fit together, though they were so different. Fred was sweet, understanding, and honest to a fault. Despite her best intentions, she was jealous and a practitioner of 'creative truth telling' which Fred called lies. With his encouragement, she'd overcome those faults. They complemented each other in all they did, their two parts made a whole. She focused on the wholeness they shared on the dark days. If it hadn't been for the children she wouldn't have wanted to live after he died. But, she had a responsibility to help them through the grieving process. In fact, they helped each other.

The wreck shortened their time together, but God allowed time to raise their kids. Don was a sophomore in college when his dad was killed. Natalie had begun her first full time job. They are wonderful kids. Don was blessed with his dad's good temperament. He's good, kind, and honest—all the positive things that Fred personified. Natalie was more like her. She was sarcastic and challenging, but also good and honest. They filled her life with joy.

Natalie was an excellent teacher. Her traits serve her well in the school where she works. It's an inner-city school where students challenge teachers in every possible way. She makes them toe the line and work hard in her classes, and yet they love her.

Don is in international business. While he was in high school, they took the kids to Vietnam to search for Don's biological mother, Mai. However, records were lost or destroyed, so that aspect of the trip was a failure. Don was disappointed they were unable to find his birth mother, but they visited her home village. Fred said the village hadn't changed in the intervening years.

The trip and Don's interest in finding Mai, developed into an interest in international business, especially in the Pacific Rim countries. He travels a lot, spending as much time in Asia as in the Pacific Northwest. She didn't see him much, but while in Oregon he spent time with her. With Skype, she didn't feel the miles between them as much.

If there was a disappointment in their lives, it was never returning to live in Payson. After Fred graduated, he applied at Payson High School. Because it was a small town with a small school, there weren't any openings. In fact, there were no jobs available in Arizona that year. As he expanded his search for work in his field of expertise, a good job opened up in Salem, Oregon. They bought a home in the small town of Keizer. Contiguous to the capital city, it had a small-town feel. It was a family oriented community where everyone knew everyone. They came up in the summer and found it beautiful, green and lush, so Fred applied for and was offered the job.

Obviously, she wanted a job nearby. As she checked openings, she found one that was tailor-made. They wanted someone experienced. Her five years of teaching was enough to get her the job. She was delighted and so was the school.

The difficulty lay in saying good-bye to family and friends. They'd assured them they'd move back at the earliest opportunity. It never happened. Not to live. For years they checked to see what jobs were available, and every year there was nothing. Finally, they had too much tenure to leave.

When they accepted the reality they'd never live in Payson again, they notified the renters. The renters were eager to buy the house since it suited their needs and they wouldn't have to move. They applied for a loan, qualified, and the deal was made.

Except for the interminable rain in the winter, they loved Oregon. It's a good place to raise kids. Natalie and Don both played baseball and soccer in school and both were in scouting. They camped, hiked, and fished—she was the one who taught them to fish and how to clean their catch. The family loved to whale-watch and play on the beach and search the tide pools, everything within an hour's drive. Yes, it was a very good life until the car wreck.

Nietzsche once said, "That what does not kill you makes you stronger." He was right, but he neglected to mention before you get stronger, you want to die. You question why God allows a man, so young and beloved, to die while the streets teem with low-life people of every ilk. At least, that was the case for her.

She'd spent many nights screaming her loss into the pillow so she wouldn't disturb the kids when they were home. She slept with one of Fred's unwashed flannel shirts for over a year—just to have his familiar scent with her.

Time passed and she came to acceptance. It was not up to her to judge others; each man and woman has their own story. An editorial helped her understand her life had purpose, even without Fred. The author, a man named Leonard Pitts, writes for the *Miami Herald*. His commentary appears in the local paper. He wrote in part:

But the tendency to focus on the end is like looking through the wrong end of a telescope. It suggests mortality is a thing to be feared.

Granted, one would never think this, much less say it when death breaks hearts and overflows eyes, when it strikes without warning or lingers above a sickbed, when it takes away the very young or the very loved, but a case can be made that mortality is really a gift of sorts.

The understanding that life is finite lends a bittersweet urgency to this business of living. Seasons change, years pile upon years, hair turns to silver, then to memory and in all of it, there is an undercurrent: get done what you came here to do, give the gifts you meant to give, do the good you're able to do, say what you need to say, now, today, because everything you see is temporary, the clock is ticking and the alarm could go off at any second.

So what were her gifts? These days she volunteered. She worked at the food bank at church; lunched with former coworkers to provide a listening ear; and she gardened and donated fresh produce to those in need; and walked her dog. Perhaps not everything she did was a gift, but her life had purpose.

She pulled herself from her musings at the thought of her dog. It was past the usual time to take Rocky to the park to play. Dressed in layers because of the fog and cold, she called the dog. There wouldn't be many walkers out today. People avoided the trail when it was foggy, but she never worried. A 20-pound guard dog accompanied her. He's not much protection, but he could bark up a storm! Besides, there's something mystical about a fog covered park, when the edges of the world became soft and blurred. She'd let her imagination run wild, wondering if fairies or unicorns danced outside of her vision. It was silly for a woman of her years to hold such thoughts, but the world held things most people didn't believe existed—some of them frightening. At least her musings were pleasant ones.

The two mile drive to the dog park from home forced Rocky to whine with excitement. She watched for the drivers without their lights on. Fred's death made her over-cautious. Obviously, the lights didn't help anyone see any better, but they alerted other drivers to her location.

As she predicted the parking lot was virtually empty. No matter. She liked quiet, mystical walks.

Nate crouched in the branches of a filbert tree with a good view of the access road to the park. He'd thought about throwing in the towel since he'd seen few people. It was thick with fog so she might not come. He sighed in frustration. In three months, he'd never had the nerve to approach her. He'd run various scenarios through his mind repeatedly, yet none seemed right. Josh thought he should forget trying to make contact. It's been a long time. He mentioned Kara was older now. She was, yet she was still his Kara, the bond that bound him to her was as strong as ever. He never stopped loving her.

A car pull into the parking lot. It looked similar to hers, but the fog made the color unidentifiable. As she stepped out of the car, he knew without doubt it was her. The little dog bounced at her side, eager to explore today's new wonders. He grinned as he watched her walk down the path with frequently stops for the dog to sniff the grass or lift a leg. At last, she turned on to the paved loop. He hastened through the trees to be near her as she bent to remove the dog's leash. She picked up her pace. The dog trotted by her side, but he paused for an occasional sniff at the ground.

Fog shrouded the area, so if other walkers came, it was doubtful they'd see Kara or him. She spun on her heels, walking backward while she called the dog as he fell behind. He made his move. Without a sound, he dropped from the tree, vaulted the fence, and stopped a foot behind her. As she called her dog; she backed into him.

༄ᴑ

"Oh, I'm terribly sorry, I should have been—" As she turned, her voice trailed off in the shock of recognition. "Nate?" She slipped to her knees. Sucking in a breath and shook her head, as she tried to decide if she was hallucinating or simply out of her mind.

"Hey Kara, I've been waiting for you."

༄ᴑ

As if she weighed nothing, he lifted her in his arms. A smile lit his face at the feel of her body next to his. A lone picnic table sat where the fog was thickest, near the river. He carried her as the dog trotted by his side.

This past three months he'd tracked her—Josh, never one to mince words—said he stalked her—Nate knew where she shopped, where she lived, and where she went to church. Her dog not only knew him, they were friends. Many a night, after she slept, he'd gone into her backyard with a treat for the dog. He'd tossed his ball for him, too. One night he found a way inside. The door had been left unlocked.

Now Rocky didn't hesitate to follow him. When they reached the picnic table, Nate sat her down. "Kara, are you okay?" He knelt on the ground in front of her.

⌒♉

She blinked her eyes and took a shaky breath before repeating, "Na ... Nate? Is it really you?"

He gave the same crooked smile she remembered. Yep, it's me. I've searched for you for a very long time." He was cheerful.

"But, why?" She whispered, fearing he'd discovered the secret she'd kept hidden from him.

"You *must* know why. I've never stopped loving you. I want to be a part of your life." His coffee brown eyes gazed into hers. "I've worked all over the country in various jobs, while I searched for you and Fred. A few months back, I traveled to Payson to pay my respects to a special friend. While I was there, I went to the cemetery to see if I recognized any new names. I found your parents' headstones and then I spotted Fred's. I'm sorry about your parents. I liked them. I'm sorry about Fred, too. He was a good man."

She closed her eyes and took another deep breath, as she tried to compose herself. "I don't know what to say or to think." Her voice cracked.

"Let me take you home. You can rest better there."

"No, I've got my car here. I can't leave it just sitting here."

Nate grinned. "That's okay. I don't have a car. I'll drive yours."

"I ... um ... I guess that's okay." She struggled to garner a coherent thought; decide if this was a mystical adventure in the fog or reality. Nate was as beautiful as she remembered. He still wore a western shirt and jeans. The only change was he wore tennis shoes instead of his boots. He picked her up and carried her at a steady trot as if she weighed nothing.

"Come on Rocky; we're going home," Nate called over his shoulder.

He knew the dog's name. *How does he know Rocky's name? How long has he watched her?* Her stomach clenched with anxiety. How would she keep her secret with him in her life again?

When they reached the car, he set her gently on her feet and asked for the keys. He unlocked the car, turned and lifted her and set her on the passenger seat. She gawked at him. His smile was beautiful.

"Hey Rocky, buddy, I got your treat right here," he said as he lifted the dog and put him on the back seat. He reached into his pocket and pulled out a dog biscuit. "Hope you don't mind if Rocky eats in the car."

She shook her head. "No, that's fine. I give him cookies all the time in here."

They drove in silence until she told him to turn north at the corner.

"It's okay, Kara; I know how to find your house."

Nate beamed, not at her surprise, but at the fact she sat in the same car with him and spoke to him. Sort of spoke—he talked she listened. At the moment, she was speechless with shock. She must have many questions, but then he had questions, too.

The rest of the trip passed in silence as Nate concentrated on the things he wanted Kara to know about him—how he'd changed and how he tried to make up for the evil he'd done. Changes he'd made for her as he tried to live the life the Creator originally designed for him. Everything he planned to say would take hours. When he pulled into the driveway, he let Rocky out of the car and then opened Kara's door. Her face was milk white. As he began to lift her, she said querulously, "I can walk, you know." She slipped from the car and staggered. He slipped his arm around her waist and led her to the door.

"Would you like a cup of tea?" he asked as he sat her gently on the couch. "I'll fix you a cup."

"You've been in my house, too?" She demanded.

"I ... uh ... you left the back door unlocked one night, so I ... uh ... sort of came in and looked around."

He looked so very much like Natalie when she had tried not to lie but didn't tell the whole truth. She chuckled hearing the nervous ring in his voice. "Oh Nate, what am I going to do with you? Yes, I'll have a cup of tea. I'll have the Earl Grey. On second thought, make it chamomile—it's calming."

In some ways it felt natural to have him here, yet her mind was at war. Was it a huge mistake to allow him inside? Whatever would she tell the children if they showed up?

While Nate heated the water for tea, he brought his own thoughts into focus. He knew he couldn't tell her he'd taken her key to copy, nor of the countless nights he'd wandered the house while she slept.

Before he told her about his life, he had to know if she'd ever loved him. If she hadn't, he'd be foolish to say he'd spent his life in an effort to please her. It would be a pathetic attempt to win something which never existed; her love.

Recalling a mongrel dog from the past; a dog that was badly mistreated by his drunken master. He'd been regularly kicked and beaten; yet when the man called him, he'd slink on his belly and lick the man's hand. The kindest thing the man had done was put a bullet between the dog's eyes to end its suffering. Killing that man was one death Nate didn't regret.

While Kara wasn't deliberately cruel, he didn't want to be like that pathetic dog. If she rejected him, he wouldn't be the dog, begging for love that never existed.

When he brought the tea, he sat next to her on the couch, drew in a deep, if unneeded, breath. He spoke in a rush of words. "Kara, I have to know—in all these years did you ever *once* think of me? Did you *ever* love me, or was I just a way to pass the summer?"

She hid her face in her hands as she attempted to answer his question. "I can honestly say I thought of you every ... single ... day ... of my life."

Nate got up and paced the room. "How can you say that, when you and Fred got married so fast after I left?" He growled, barely hiding his pain, "I saw Joyce. She told me you were pregnant with Fred's child before you married." He growled, unable to hide his pain. "I saw Joyce and she told me you were pregnant with Fred's child before you married. You didn't let any grass grow under your feet did you?" He turned and pointed an accusing finger at her. She stared askance in his eyes, which slowly changed from accusing to hurt.

"Sit down, please, while I get something," She sighed, not sure if she should do this. She didn't want to, but she couldn't stand his pain. Standing abruptly, she squared her shoulders, walked to a large bookcase, and retrieved a brown photo album. She sat stiffly beside him and opened the album to the first page.

"These are pictures of that summer in Payson. Pictures of you and me, of my cousin Geoff, and the friends I made." She pointed and named each one before turning the page. "These are my dorm friends. This one, April, my best friend. She was my maid of honor when Fred and I married. Later I was her matron of honor. She's married to Geoff."

A crease appeared between Nate's brows, "What does this—"

She held up her hand, interrupting him. "Please be patient and you'll understand." He nodded his head. She turned another page. "This is our daughter, Natalie."

He looked at the pictures and smiled, albeit reluctantly. "She's a beauty." He paused, studied the pictures of the little girl. "Who does she look like? I don't see much of you or Fred in her."

They were close to the truth. "She looks exactly like her father," she whispered.

He frown again, "Huh? She doesn't look at all like Fred."

"No she doesn't. Fred was, and always will be, her daddy. Natalie looks exactly like her father—her biological father."

A heartbeat later Nate's head jerked up. He shot her a look and slammed back against the back of the couch. He grabbed the book out of her hands and stared at the pictures. It would have been funny, the way his head jerked back and forth between the pictures and her, if it wasn't so painful to reveal. Stunned, he lost all power of speech.

In a choked whispered, he asked, "Are you telling me that I have a child? Natalie is *my* daughter?"

"That is exactly what I am telling you. You asked if I ever thought of you." She paused, thought carefully about her words. "Nate, no woman ever forgets her first love, especially when he's the father of her child."

He stood up, sat back down, and then stood again as a smile played across his lips.

"I have a daughter," he said slowly, wonderingly. "I have a little girl. Does she know about me?" He rushed on before she answered. "Of course not, how would you tell her something like that?'

He came back over, pulled her from the couch and wrapped his arms around her. "Can I meet her, Kara? She won't have to know her father is a monster."

Frowning, she said, "I never thought of you as a monster, but how could I explain who you are? I don't know, Nate. Natalie believes Fred is her father."

"Please, Kara." He held out his hands pleadingly. "Years ago I met a little girl named Grace. I watched her grow for a few months. There wasn't a day that went by, I didn't wish I had a little girl like her. How was I to know I had a daughter? I never thought it was a possibility for me to father a child."

"You would have liked her, Kara." He smiled at the memory. "We became friends because she liked Fos—"

He hesitated, a guilty look spread across his face. "I guess I should mention I took your cat. I came to Payson to find you, but no one knew where you were. I thought Pete might tell me. While he was kind, he flat out refused to tell me anything. He mentioned Fosdick wouldn't stay at their new house—he kept wandering back to the old house. I got a burger to tempt him out of hiding and went to look for him. When I found him, he was badly injured. One ear half chewed off and a broken tail and an infected leg. His was all ripped up and dying. I couldn't leave him in that condition."

She leapt up, and willingly threw her arms around him and hugged him. "You found Fosdick and took care of him? Did he get better?" Nate didn't get a chance to answer since she spoke so rapidly. "When I couldn't find him, I thought he'd died, alone and afraid. He must have thought I'd deserted him. I was so ashamed. I cried for days."

"Yeah, when I found him, I took him to the cabin and doctored him up. When he was well enough to travel, I took him with me. He lived with me several years before he passed. He was one of the friends I went to pay my respect to—Fosdick and Don José. I buried him under the same tree."

Tears glistened in her eyes as he finished talking. She grabbed a tissue and blew her nose. "Thank you for being there when I wasn't. I felt so guilty when I couldn't find him. So much happened so fast; he fell through the cracks. I'm glad you took care of him."

"He was my buddy." Nate smiled. "He made friends all around the country, too." He launched into the story of the mission. How Fosdick proved his worth to the calloused men by killing rats. He went on to tell of his own gradual coming to terms and accepting the offered forgiveness from God for his many failings.

She shared a few stories, too. She explained how Fred came to her rescue from the quandary of being an unwed mother before he left for Vietnam. How Fred insisted they name the baby in honor her real father. She told him about Don's birth and her jealousy. The joy-filled years watching the two children grow up. She shared a piece of her heartache when Fred died.

He told of the time he faced down his deepest fear to rescue friends from a forest fire. "Fire is one of the few things that can kill vampires. Josh and I lost our foster family in a horrific fire."

"Speaking of Josh, he fell in love with a human girl," Nate laughed wryly. "What an about face. I repeated the list of problems of loving a human he'd given when I dated you. It was difficult when Josh found his happy ending with the Liz. I realized I'd have to leave and let them be a couple. I miss him. He was my only family."

A faraway look in his eye, he burst out, "Kara, could I meet Natalie? She doesn't have to know who I am." He was desperate.

"I promise to think about it, but you have to accept my answer."

"I'll try to be patient. Kara, I have one more question. Can I spend the night with you?"

She froze to statue stillness. *What is he asking? He surely couldn't expect to sleep with her.*

Before she unfroze, he said, "Look, I don't have any expectations. I know you loved Fred and I don't want to dishonor him in any way. It's just..." He paused, staring down at his feet. "It's just," he repeated quietly, "I'm lonely. I miss not having family around. If I could stay tonight, more if you're willing. I swear I won't be in your way or ask more than you're willing to give. Please, Kara." When he looked at her with those pleading eyes, her defenses broke.

"You can stay in the guest room, but I need to figure out what to tell the neighbors and kids." She gestured for him to follow her down the hall and stopped halfway down the hall.

"Maybe I can be a long-lost nephew or something. We can make up a tale tomorrow. Thank you for letting me stay." He leaned over to plant a kiss on the forehead. "Sweet dreams, Kara."

She smiled in memory of those words. "Good night, Nate." As he closed the door she realized they hadn't eaten. Her stomach was in such a knot she couldn't eat, but she should have fed Nate. Maybe he was full of blood. She went into her bedroom as memories of that long-ago summer flooded her mind. As she changed into her pajamas and crawled into bed, she wished Fosdick was by her side.

There was no cat to whisper her shock at seeing Nate after all these years. No one to express her fears what this might mean. No cat to bathe her in his comforting purr. Neither could she lay her head on Fred's comforting chest—listen to the regular rhythm of his beating heart. His arms no longer wrapped around her, assuring her everything would work out as it should. She drifted into a fitful sleep.

⁓᳁

The door cracked open as he crept into her room. He knew this room as he knew his own face. Since he'd found her, he'd spent many nights watching her sleep. Sometimes she slept quietly, but many nights her sleep was restless. He'd listened to her soft moans; hear her cry out in her sleep. He wanted to comfort her on those nights—to wrap his arms around her and hold her until she relaxed back into peaceful sleep—but he didn't dare. Now he'd promised he wouldn't push her. He'd try to keep that promise.

At the moment, it was enough to breathe the same air she breathed. It was enough to watch as she slept. Light filtered in behind her shades when he crept back into the guest room and lay on the bed. He prayed she'd let him stay, even if it meant as a friend.

He had a daughter. A smile slowly curled his lips. A daughter who is now grown up. He had to meet her. He didn't care who she thought he was; he had to see her face and hear her voice.

He heard Kara stir. He dressed and went down the hall to make coffee. Rocky jumped around underfoot, so he pulled out his food and fed him first. As he heard the sounds of the shower, he pulled a skillet from the cabinet. Got out the eggs, spinach, and mushrooms from the refrigerator. He hoped she liked omelets. He smiled as he thought back to time when Amos taught him to make a decent omelet. While she didn't have the right pan, her skillet was well seasoned and should do fine. He quickly set the table, so he'd drop the beaten eggs in to cook as soon as he heard her shower turn off.

As she walked into the kitchen, he turned the omelet out on to a plate. "What's all this? Did you cook this yourself?" *That was a stupid question. Who else could have done it? Rocky?* It came as a surprise; something more she didn't know about Nate. He could cook. "What a nice surprise. And you've made coffee!" His face lit with pleasure.

"I hope you like it," he said, looking from under his long lashes, like a bashful little boy.

"It smells wonderful. If it tastes half as good as it smells, I'm going to love it. I'm so spoiled."

"I always wanted to take care of you, remember?" The comment made her uncomfortable. She blushed at the wistfulness it conveyed.

There were decisions to be made and today was the day to make them. But first, she was going to enjoy breakfast.

Nate was helpful and accommodating, so it was easy to begin the day without giving it much thought. He fixed breakfast, so she cleaned up the dirty dishes. While she did that, he made the beds. He accompanied her when she walked the dog. All the while, her mind whirled with unanswered questions from the previous night.

They sat at the picnic table by the river at her request. The spot would give more privacy than they'd get at home. They were bound to run into her friends, but the phone wouldn't interrupt them. Nor would her cell which she deliberately left home.

It was a beautiful fall day with a light fog that would soon burn off. The hardwood trees were beginning to change into shades of red, gold, and yellow, so they discussed the weather, avoiding the inevitable. However, they couldn't avoid it indefinitely, so she squared her shoulders. "Nate, I can't introduce you to Natalie."

He opened his mouth to protest, but she interrupted. "I'm not saying never—just not yet. After we figure out a plausible reason you're here and the relationship we're supposed to have. I might be comfortable allowing an introduction then."

His eyes closed and his chin dropped to his chest. She almost felt guilty, but her first obligation was to her children—to protect them and the memory of their dad.

"Why can't I be the grandson of your distant friend come for a visit?" he suggested after a momentary pause. "I could work for my keep while I'm here. You know, help you with yard work and stuff."

They tossed around several scenarios before fine-tuning his original suggestion. "It might work, but you'll have to leave if the kids come to spend the night. You could meet them—have dinner together, but then you'd have leave." He agreed.

Nate was a willing worker. Her windows sparkled, her gutters clean of debris, and her floors were spotless in no time at all. Even the cabinets were cleaned and organized. She'd love to claim things were always that way, but she'd rather not lie.

A few days later, he invited her out to dinner. "I have a surprise planned. The place we're going isn't fancy, so dress is casual."

She hesitated, but said, "We have to create a public story eventually, so I guess now is as good a time as any. They went local bar that served burgers and held karaoke nights. No soon were they seated, when he popped back up.

"Can you hold the fort? I'll be right back." He gave a mysterious smile. As he walked away, two couples, who'd taught at the same school as she, came through the door and spotted her. They came over and chatted, so she wasn't able to see where Nate went. They chose the table next to hers. She wouldn't be able to avoid introducing Nate. *Ah well, "in for a penny, in for a pound,"* she thought nervously.

The emcee for the karaoke announced, "We have the first singer for the night! Give it up for Nathan Whitworth!"

Her head jerked up and the blood drained from her face. Nate smiled her way and belted out Trace Adkins' song *Ladies Love Country Boys.* Following the applause, he said, "I'd like to dedicate this next song to a very special lady." He proceeded to sing a George Strait love song; *I Cross my Heart.* What was he thinking? Her face suffused with blood. Throughout the song, he smiled her direction as she sat frozen in place.

"Kara, do you know him?" her friends at the next table asked. "He's staring right at you."

With a parody of a smile, she said, "He's the grandson of a dear friend. He's staying with me for a while."

"A likely story," one of the women teased. "He is every woman's dream lover. I didn't know you were such a cougar." They all chuckled.

She was right. He was every woman's dream. Every woman in the audience went wild, clapping and screaming his name. For her it was more of a nightmare. She tried to joke back, "Oh darn, my secret's out."

As the song ended, Nate could tell she was upset. He refused offers of drinks and lewd suggestions, pointing out he was with a lady friend. He wended his way to the table while she waited, a frozen smile on her face. "Did you like the songs?" he asked tentatively.

"I didn't know you could sing," she replied evasively. "Nate, I'd like you to meet my friends."

No wonder she's upset. If the crowd held strangers, the song wouldn't have upset her. He never thought this could happen. She'd hate him for putting her through this situation.

Nate turned and with a warm smile, held out his hand. "Hi there, I'm Nate." The two couples introduced themselves and complimented his singing. "Thanks. I enjoy singing. Although I usually confine it to the church choir or the shower. This was fun. My best girl here agreed to come with me tonight."

"Yep, Kara's a peach," one of the men responded.

"She sure is. I've known her most of my life and I've never known her to be anything other than a kind and generous person," Nate noted.

"You can say that again," one of the women enthused. "I team-taught with her for two years. I learned more about dealing with troubled kids than in all my years in college."

The food came, so Nate was able to gracefully return his attention to Kara. He whispered, "Can you forgive me? I didn't mean to upset you."

Her response was wooden. "I know you didn't. You did a good job of defusing any rumors from my friends; so yes, I can forgive you this time." But she couldn't relax.

On the drive home, Nate apologized again. "I let my excitement control my behavior. I promise I won't do it again."

"You need to understand this is difficult for me. I don't want to look like some old fool who took on a young lover. It's not who I am, Nate. No matter that you're older than I am. You look exactly like you did the day we met."

She paused to clarify her thoughts. "I love the memory of our time together. It's precious to me. I love the *memory* of you. I like you, but I don't know you anymore and you don't know me. Too much time has passed. If we can keep the façade of you as a grandson of an old friend, you can stay. If you slip up again, you'll have to leave."

Nate pulled to a stop at the side of the road. A look—something like grief—passed over his face. He rubbed his eyes and when he looked up, the look was gone. He gave a wry smile. "I promised I'd take what you were willing to give. If it's strictly friendship, I'll take it." He'd choked his answer and they drove home in silence.

Things looked brighter by morning. Though they lived in a precarious circumstance, it didn't change the fact it was a beautiful fall day. Most people love the spring or summer, but there's something about fall that called to her. Perhaps it was the poignancy of the dying year, or perhaps the autumn colors and rich smell of the fallen leaves. Whatever the reason, she loved it.

Nate had gone hunting during the night and hadn't returned. It was odd he could eat regular food but had to supplement his diet with blood. It was easy to forget blood was a major factor of his nature. In fact, it was easy to forget he was a vampire.

After she finished a bowl of cereal, she took her coffee outside to soak in the autumn sunshine.

Nate hadn't pressured her about Natalie, but she'd caught him numerous times staring at the family pictures that lined the hallway. He spent the most time staring at pictures of Natalie, especially at collage of her pictures: one of her gapped-tooth smile when she was in the first grade, her first fish, her senior prom, and her graduation pictures from high school and college. He'd raise his hand as if reaching to touch her. Was he trying to experience her life through photographs? It hurt to see his quiet desperation.

She settled in with a newspaper and a second cup of coffee when the back gate opened. She turned and watched him walk around the short hedge privacy barrier. "Want a cup of coffee?" Deep in thought, he hadn't noticed her. She'd startled him with her question.

"Huh? Oh, coffee. Yeah, that would be good," he said absently.

"You look lost in thought." She handed him a mug.

"I was thinking about Fred." His brows drew together, a faraway look in his eyes. "I know why he married you and that he was a good guy. I actually hoped you'd marry someone like him. I know what you told me about Vietnam and Don's birth and all, but that's all I know about your life with him. Could you tell me more about him?"

She loved her memories of Fred, but they brought the pain of loss along with the joy of the past. Did she want to share that with Nate? It was deeply personal. She wasn't sure she could. Nate stroked her arm. "If it is too hard to talk about, Kara, you don't have to tell me." Her expression said what words had not.

Managing a smile, she whispered, "It's okay, but I may not be able to tell you everything." He nodded, understanding. "Let's go back into the house. I don't want the whole neighborhood listening."

She began at the beginning, explaining how their friendship blossomed after he left. How Fred begged her to marry him—to give the baby his last name when she was unsure if she loved him.

She told about the terrible Vietnam years and her love-hate relationship with him spawned by jealousy. How they forgave each other and learned to love again.

When Nate asked if she had the sketchbooks, she pulled them from the closet where they were buried under the detritus of years. He looked soberly at them, and asked an occasional question. His single comment was, "It is amazing he came out of the war with any desire to live."

The intervening years were easier to share. Both of them taught, raised the children, and played with them and with each other. Those were the happy years with a few minor bumps to mar the way.

It came time to talk about the accident. "Fred was on his way to school early that morning. He'd planned to help one of his students prepare for his SATs. It was our date night—the two of us planned to go out for dinner and a movie after school.

"I was ready to leave for work when a police car pulled in front of the house. An officer and a police chaplain got out of the car. They asked my name. The chaplain led me back into the house and told me Fred's car had been T-boned by a drunk driver—hit on the driver's side.

"They'd come to take me to the hospital. The chaplain asked if he could notify anyone to be with me. I gave him the name and phone number of Anita, a long-time friend. He called and asked if she could meet us at the hospital. She was the one who notified the children and the church.

"Natalie was at school when she got the news. She came down as soon as she arranged for a substitute. Don was at a conference in Japan at the time; so it took many hours before he could arrive home.

"When I got to the emergency room, an aide led me straight back to where Fred was." The tears rolled down her face.

"He looked awful, bruised and bloody—tubes everywhere. They had to intubate him, so a ventilator breathed for him." Her hands bunched into fists. "I hated that damn machine as it whooshed air into his lungs, but I loved it for the same reason. It kept him alive. I wanted to throw myself on his bed—hold him in my arms. But there was no place I could touch him that wasn't damaged or where an IV wasn't in place.

"The doctor came in and asked how soon the rest of the family would arrive. I told him Natalie was on her way, but Don wouldn't arrive for another day. He took me out to the lobby and gave his prognosis. Surrounded by Anita and friends from church, I learned Fred had severe head trauma. His brain swelled rapidly. He wasn't expected to live. I asked the doctor to call Karl for a second opinion. Do you remember Karl?" Nate nodded with a wry smile.

"He became a renowned brain surgeon. He called after he received the test results and agreed with the doctor here. They could attempt surgery to allow the brain to swell; however, his eyes were fixed and dilated—a sign he was brain dead."

"'Since your son won't be here until tomorrow, we'll keep him on the ventilator. We can't guarantee his heart won't stop, though.'" The doctor spoke in the gentlest manner. He held my hand and looked in my eyes. A thought flitted through my mind: *He recognizes death, this man.*"

As she'd done when she'd first heard this news, she jumped to her feet and sobbed. Nate leaped up after her and carefully wrapped her in his arms. "Kara, I am so sorr ..."

A voice interrupted him. "Surprise! I came down earl ... Mom, what the hell is going on here? Wh ... who is this ...this child!" Natalie's voice was strident in shock and anger.

Wasn't it Robbie Burns who spoke of the best-laid plans of mice and men? Kara wished she could laugh at the situation. Here she stood, tears streaming down her face, in desperate need of a tissue. And here stood Nate, his arms around her, his mouth agape; still as a statue. Across the room Natalie shrieked like a fishwife.

Chapter 30

*D*ear *God, take me now, please. If I'd ever had a plan to tell Natalie, it's in that proverbial hand basket on its way to the nether regions.*

Kara pulled gently away from Nate who stood frozen in place, his arms stayed midair, mouth agape. She grabbed Natalie's arms and shook her.

"Natalie Joann, sit down and shut up. If you want answers, you'll have to listen. This is Nathan Whitworth."

Natalie perched on the edge of the couch, eyes glaring at Nate. Kara gave Nate a hard poke. "Nate, this is Natalie." He blinked his eyes as one who wakes from a dream.

"Hello, Natalie." His voice was a whisper. Kara led him to the opposite end of the couch and sat him down. His ability for coherent thought and movement apparently gone.

Plan or no plan, this was it. Kara had no choice in the matter. She couldn't let Natalie think there was something *illicit* going on, but she had no idea how she'd explain the situation. Her one idea—though weak—was the one she'd used to tell Nate about Natalie. Kara got the photo album.

"Natalie, you know how much your daddy loved you."

"Of course I do. That is what makes this ... so ... obscene" She gestured toward Nate.

"You know your daddy picked your first name. Have you ever wondered why he chose that particular name?"

"I don't know; he liked it?" she guessed grumpily.

Kara shook her head and continued. "Your daddy and I met in Payson the summer I moved there." Kara opened the photo album. "These are the pictures from summer—all my friends and family."

"What does this have to do with my name? I've seen all these," she protested.

"I know you have. Be patient and look again. Look closely at them and tell me what you see."

With a sigh of disgust, Natalie looked at the pictures, naming them in a kind of litany. "Here's Grandma and Grandpa; here's Uncle Geoff; here's Daddy; here is you with some guy ..."

Kara held her breath as she saw something click in Natalie's brain. She frowned and looked over at Nate. "This looks like him." She jerked her head in Nate's direction. "Is he a relative or something?"

Nate turned his face away from Natalie, unable to face her dawning discovery. "You might say that," Kara responded. "Do you notice anything else about the picture?"

Natalie looked again—more closely this time, her eyes widened in shock. "He looks like me." Natalie gasped in shock. "Why does he look like me?"

Kara hesitated. "I'll tell you everything. But you must swear you will tell no one what I tell you now. Do you promise?"

Wordlessly, she nodded her head. "When I moved to Payson I fell head over heels with a very handsome man. He was my first true love. Without going into every single detail of that time, we decided it was best to break up. We had significant differences, so we agreed to end it. I didn't find out I was pregnant until later. Your dad was a good friend of mine. He asked to marry me when he knew I was pregnant."

Natalie was horrified over the details of her conception. She tried to speak, but Kara waved her down and continued. "You're probably wondering what this has to do with your name. Your blessed dad wanted to name you after your biological father. Natalie was the closest name we could come up with for Nathan. Nate's your biological father."

"That is the stupidest thing I've ever heard in my life—and an insult to my intelligence! You," she shouted at Nate. "Look at me."

Nate slowly turned his head and looked his daughter in the eyes. His eyes held the depth of sadness borne of a life of tragedy. "If you're supposed to be my father, then how come you look the same today as you did then?"

His voice a whisper, he said, "You remember the differences your mother mentioned? You might say they were irreconcilable differences. See, for her to stay with me, I would have had to kill her. I didn't want to hurt her or her family nor did she want me to hurt them. You see, Natalie, I *am* your father and I'm also a vampire." Nate spoke softly and sadly, expecting his daughter to run from the house screaming. Instead, she sat there and studied him.

"You're just some nutjob and Mom—" At a temporary loss for words, she waved her hands in the air. "I don't believe in vampires." She scowled at Nate. "So if you're a vampire, you're going to have to prove it."

"I'm not going to suck anyone's blood if that's what you suggest. All the stuff you may have read about vampires or seen in movies—most of it is not true."

"Okay, then, show me your fangs," she said sarcastically, sure this was some ridiculous tale.

Nate smiled, then his smile widened, his fangs bared in all their dangerous glory.

The disbelief and sarcasm was wiped from Natalie's face in a single instant. She turned an ashy white and she began to gasp, hyperventilating. Kara ran to her side while Nate dashed to the kitchen for water and a damp towel. "Here, drink this." He shoved the glass into Natalie's hand. He placed the cold, damp towel around her neck.

As her color returned, she stared at her mother, "Mom, why would you date a vampire?"

"I didn't know he was a vampire, not at first. All I knew was that he was a gorgeous guy and he liked me. He was a gentleman and fun to be around." Kara blushed at a long-ago memory.

"Did you know he was a vampire when you got pregnant with me?"

Kara stared at her hands her lap as she answered Natalie. "First, you have to realize it was another time. I was ignorant about birth control.

Birth control pills were relatively new on the market and had many negative side effects. Other choices weren't reliable. But it never even occurred to me that I could get pregnant if I had sex one time."

In the background, Kara heard a snort and heard Nate mumble, "Huh, I remember doing it more than once."

She shot him a scathing look. "Shut up, Nate, you know what I mean. In our defense, neither of us thought vampires could reproduce. A few months later, I learned the truth. Nate only found out about your birth a couple of weeks ago."

"Why didn't you get rid of me or put me up for adoption?"

"Natalie Joann, I'd never do either one. I wanted you, even though it came down to difficult decisions. I wanted you from the beginning. First, because you were Nate's baby and then, because you were mine. I thank God every day for your dad. He was willing to take a lot of abuse for us. He made it possible for me to keep you and finish school."

"This is all true, isn't it? It's not just some terrible nightmare where I'm going to wake up soon?" Natalie's voice seemed to come from faraway.

"It's true. I hope you're brave like your mother. Brave enough to allow me get to know you." Nate's voice was soft and low. Even Natalie couldn't ignore the longing in his voice.

She sat quietly for a moment, her face in her hands. When she took down her hands she said, "I guess I can try, but how are we ever going to tell Don?"

Don proved much easier to convince than Kara or Nate expected. He'd long suspected Fred wasn't Natalie's biological father. As a young teen, he'd spent a lot of time combing through the family photo albums. He saw what Natalie hadn't. A photo of a tall, handsome young man—a man who bore Natalie's face. It wasn't an exact match. The man's face was distinctly masculine while Natalie's was feminine. That aside, feature by feature he saw the strong resemblance. The same dark hair and eyes. The long dark lashes. They both had a slightly half-smile. The same perfect features. Don chose not to tell his sister his suspicions fearing she'd be upset. Nor did he mention his discovery to his parents. While he didn't understand why they'd never told Natalie, he trusted their decision.

As to his own parentage, it was obvious. He looked like his dad, except for the slight slant to his eyes and his skin color. Not exactly Asian, but not completely Caucasian either. There was the matter of his unruly hair which got from his biological mother's side of the family. While he'd loved to meet his biological mother, she'd never replace his mom in his heart. His mom loved him from the beginning, as did his sister. They were a very tightly knit family.

Now this tall, handsome stranger in front of him looked exactly like he did in the picture. That's what he couldn't comprehend. This guy should be the grandson of the one in the picture, yet his mother and Natalie swore it was true. They explained why the man appeared ageless. He was a vampire.

"If you're a vampire, how can you go out in daylight without burning up?" Don challenged.

"Your sister asked me the same question. First, let me say most of the stories you hear about vampires are not true; they are fables. Many of us only go out at night because it's safer to hunt in the dark, not because they must avoid the sun." Nate remained patient as he answer the inevitable question.

"Is it a fable you kill people for their blood?" Don took a deep breath in an effort to calm his own heart.

"No, that's not a fable. However, we can exist on animal blood supplemented with human food. That's what I consume."

Don challenged, "Are you telling me that you've never killed a human—never drank human blood?" He wiped his sweaty hands on his pant legs.

Nate examined his hands. When he looked up and spoke, his voice was sad. "No, won't lie and tell you that. There was a time when I enjoyed the kill, enjoyed the warmth of the blood going down my throat, I had reason to hate humans. That all changed when I met your mother. I promised Kara I wouldn't kill again. I would like to say I never have since I made that promise, but that, too, would be a lie."

Kara's head jerked sharply in his direction. She was about to ask, when Nate gave a warning glance. He was going to lie by omission. He couldn't tell them what he'd done to Joyce. "Fosdick and I were traveling down a back road when I heard voices. Two men had a young woman tied up. They planned to rape and kill her.

"Fosdick was your mom's cat, but he traveled with me at the time," Nate said by way of explanation. "He flew at the man who held the girl, scratched and bit him badly. When the man turned to chase the cat, I attacked him and his partner. I took the young woman to safety and returned to dispose of the bodies. I would like to pretend what I did was simply to rescue the girl, but Fosdick and God forced me face the truth. I enjoyed the blood. I broke a promise to both them and your mom. I spent the next month in prayer for forgiveness. I asked the Lord to help me be the man he wanted me to be."

"Huh, you're sort of like an alcoholic, then?" Don asked. "Hi, my name is Nate and I'm a blood-aholic?"

Nate smiled wryly. "I guess that would be as good a way as any to describe the hunger. I always have to be on my guard and never let myself get too low on blood in my body."

Don frowned. "So ... you're really a vampire—not just some psycho nutcase."

"He really is; I've seen his fangs," Natalie offered.

Don looked over at his mother then back to his sister. "You both trust him?" They nodded in unison. He shrugged and said, "Well, okay then. What am I supposed to call you?" There was a collective sigh of relief from everyone.

"Call me Nate, if you want. Kara, can I invite Josh and Liz here to meet Natalie?"

She was incredulous. He wanted Josh to come here? After what happened in the past, he wants to invite his explosive brother here? No.

Was he mental? "Ahhh ... Josh? I don't think—" was all she managed before Nate jumped in.

"He's not like you remember him, Kara. He's not the same wild child he was when you saw him last. He gave up human blood when I did and became a believer before me. He has turned into a settled, responsible person. You'd like him now."

Her hesitation and Nate's comment brought a round of questions from her children. She'd never tell them about the attack. Her children would find it an unforgivable offense. Instead, she said, "Josh was a hot-tempered and impetuous young man. If I let them come, it will be for an afternoon only. I'll hold you personally responsible for his behavior, Nate. If there are problems, you'll have to get them out of here immediately."

"That's fair. He's going to be thrilled to know he has a niece and nephew. I hope you don't mind being included, Don." Nate pulled out his cell phone and punched in a number. "Hey, bro. Can you and Liz make it up here for a barbeque? I found Kara. You're not going to believe this, I've got a daughter."

Don sat bemused. *It's hard to make sense of this. It's as if reality made a 180-degree turn. I have ... what? A stepfather and step-uncle and aunt who're vampires? Now I know how Alice felt when she fell down that rabbit hole.*

As Don focused back on the phone conversation, he heard Nate say, "There's no room here ... Call me when you get close ... Yeah, I know ... I'll tell you all about it when you get here ... Okay, I will. Bye."

Smiling, Nate turned to Kara. "Josh sends his love. He's excited to see you again and meet Natalie. They'll be here soon."

A frisson of fear went through her at the memory of the last time she'd seen Josh. Nate came and put an arm around her shoulder. "I promise you, Kara, he's different; you'll like him now."

Nate was honest and protective, so she'd be safe. She tried to relax. *With one vampire living here, what problem could two more be?* She didn't want to think about it.

The weekend came too fast. When the doorbell rang, Nate raced to the door. She stood back while the two brothers gave each other hugs that would break anyone else's back. "Please come in," she offered formally.

"Kara," Josh said, as he gently took her hand between his big paws. "It's good to see you again. Nate said Fred died. I'm sorry for that and so many other things," he said sincerely. "Can you ever forgive me?"

His sincerity made it easy to say yes. But she held doubts on the wisdom of having him here. She was glad Natalie and Don were out in the backyard setting up lawn chairs. She wouldn't have to explain why he asked for forgiveness.

It was a glorious fall days of a true Indian summer. After the rain and the fog, this was a treat. They'd eat outside and soak in the beauty of the day. It was perfect weather for the planned a barbeque.

"Who is this charming young woman, Josh?" His smile was huge as he pulled the young woman forward.

"Kara Jacobs, this is my wife—my Liz." He spoke with a mix of sweetness and pride as he introduced the girl. It was easy to see he loved her. She looked at him with adoring china-blue eyes. She was a porcelain doll—almost too pretty to be real. Kara reached out and gave her a gentle hug.

"I'm pleased to meet you. There's a couple of other people out in the backyard you'll to want to meet. Nate, why don't you make the introductions? I'll bring out the lemonade."

Don moaned, "Geez, aren't any of you ... people ... skinny with bad hair and pimples? Look at you. All of you look like supermodels with great hair." In mock disgust, he ran his hands through his own unruly hair.

"It comes from clean living and a healthy diet," Josh quipped, with a wink. With that, the ice was broken. All the questions and distrust her children may have had, faded like the morning's mist amid the laughter.

By the end of the day, her own doubts faded. Liz and Josh were bright and articulate. Conversation and horseplay, common at our family gatherings, appeared natural and our guests joined in wholeheartedly.

The men stood around the barbeque and watched the meat cook. The women brought out salads and side dishes. Don said grace before they ate, thanking God for the new family members. She was touched as pure joy bloomed on Nate, Josh, and Liz's faces at Don's words.

The meal passed in spates of amiable conversation while they ate. Rocky, ever the opportunist, waited under their chairs, hoping for a dropped bite of food or a furtive treat to come his way. As evening drew near, Josh stood and said, "We need to go soon. What time is church in the morning?"

"You want to go to church?" Incredulous, the words burst from her mouth. Neither Nate nor Josh would step into a church in the past.

"If it's all right with you, yes, we'd like to go with you," Josh said cautiously.

"Of course, it's all right!" Pleased by the turn of events, but she questioned how she'd introduce them.

Natalie intervened. "I've got an idea. Let's meet at seven thirty and go to the pancake house for breakfast."

The words were scarcely out of her mouth when Don jumped to second her idea. A plan was set to meet here, proceed to the pancake house, and then attend church.

Things couldn't have gone smoother. When the server brought the food, Josh asked if he could say grace. His words were soft and warm as if he talked to a dear friend. Kara understood—he did.

Natalie handled things at church so well it would never be a problem to have them with her again. They were warmly welcomed.

When time came for Josh and Liz to return home, she realized she'd enjoyed the visit. She invited them to come visit again.

Natalie and Don would be up at the crack of dawn to return to their jobs. Natalie to her to her classroom and Don for an international flight to Tokyo. The house would be quiet with them gone. For the first time, she was glad Nate was here. It wouldn't be as empty with him here.

Chapter 31

If Nate had a problem Kara, it was her rule the bedroom was off-limits. He understood her reasoning, but celibacy was difficult when they lived in such close proximity. After three years, they lived as man and wife in countless ways, but not in the bedroom. He lied when the pressure overwhelmed him. It wasn't what he wanted, but he excused himself by saying *he had needs.* Feeding became his excuse to be gone.

He'd heard the term "booty call" used by young people in the taverns he visited. They were casual about sex. He could go to any watering hole and find a willing female. Most of them were nice girls, too. The advantage of hooking up with nice girls was he didn't have to fight the urge to kill them. But he didn't understand their lack of self-worth.

It was strange to take a girl to bed with no expectations of seeing her again. He made sure he didn't. He traveled up and down the valley, never going to the same place twice. He was guilty on many levels: taking advantage of these girls, lying to Kara, disobeying the commandments. *I'm a weak man. Why can't I learn to control myself? How would Kara handle it if she found out? Would she kick me out of her life again?*

That night in Philomath he met a cute college girl full of hopes and aspirations. For the price of a beer and a few peanuts, they enjoyed the time together. Since he found out about Natalie, he was careful not to mess up another girl's life. He carried and used protection, wondering if he'd fathered other children in the past. It was pleasant to think he might have other sons and daughters. But a sickening thought crossed his mind. Disgusted at the thought, he grimaced. *Natalie looked like him. However, if he hadn't seen her pictures compared with his, would he have realized he was her father?* The thought of incest made him cringe. It gave him an iron-clad reason to use self-control.

As eager as he was to see Kara, he couldn't tell her what he'd been doing. Perhaps he'd ask her opinion on the odds he had other children.

The house was unusually quiet when he came in the door. It was barely ten, so Kara should be awake. Most nights she'd be watching the news or reading a book. Rocky padded down the hall from the bedroom. He wasn't his usual ebullient self; instead, he was sober, almost sad. Nate froze in his tracks.

"What's the matter, Rocky? Where's Kara?" The dog whined and turned back toward her bedroom. He hurried after him.

The odor of stale sweat and vomit filled the bedroom. *Dear God, I've only been gone two days. What happened?* He grabbed a wash-cloth, dampened it to wash her face. She burned with fever and was dehydrated. He carefully lifted her, placed her on the shower seat, and turned on the taps. He stripped her filthy clothes from her and washed her clean. She roused slightly. "Nate?"

"I'm here, Kara. Can you sit by yourself for a second? I'll get clean clothes."

"Yes." Her voice was weak. She leaned against the shower wall and closed her eyes.

Nate found a clean nightgown and brought it over. He toweled her dry, dressed her, and carried her to the living room. When he laid her on the couch, he brought a glass of water. "Try to drink this. I'm going to change your sheets. I'll be right back."

He moved so fast he made her dizzy, so she closed her eyes as he blurred down the hall. The soiled sheets went directly into the washing machine. He raced back to the bedroom, and returned in moments.

"Your bed has clean sheets again. Can you tell me what's wrong with you?"

"Flu. I got sick right after you left." She couldn't speak above a whisper.

"When was the last time you ate anything?"

"I don't remember—maybe before you left."

"I'm going to fix you something. What do you feel like eating?"

"Nothing. I don't want anything."

"You have to eat... I'll be right back." Nate returned with a half-cup of chicken broth and a small individual cup of Jell-O. "Here, take a sip of this." He held the cup with the broth to her lips, encouraged her to sip and spoon-fed her a few of bites of Jell-O. He got her to drink another sip of the broth before she balked.

"I can't eat any more."

"Kara, you're dehydrated; you need fluids."

"I can't right now. I'll throw up again."

Nate worried. "Would you rather stay up or go back to bed?"

"I want to go to bed." Her eyes closed as she answered him.

When Nate carried her to the bed, he gently laid her down. Finding aspirin, he gave her two tablets, forcing more water into her. If he left her uncovered she might cool down. He checked the sheets to see if they were ready to go in the dryer. Like it or not, he'd sleep next to Kara tonight. Someone had to take care of her; get her water, or tea. Gaunt and frail, her condition frightened him. It brought to mind her mortality. He knew with a bitterness of spirit he'd lose her one day, but it wouldn't be tonight if he could help it.

She was asleep when he returned to the bedroom. He sat on the far side of the bed, and watched her restless sleep. Pulling off his boots, jeans, and shirt, he laid next to her. A feeling of rightness washed over him. This was where he should be.

When she woke during the night, she felt him next to her. It felt safe with him there, knowing he'd take care of her. She pushed herself closer and her movement woke him. He leaped up and brought her water. She took a sip and managed a smile. "Stay with me tonight." He didn't answer, just gazed at her with his dark, enigmatic eyes, and wrapped her in his arms. She fell asleep with her head on his chest.

The next morning Kara's fever broke. Her gown and sheets were soaked with sweat again. Nate put her in the shower and bathed her with the efficiency of a nurse. He dressed her in loose clothing and put slippers on her feet. He laid her on the couch, her head rested on the cushioned arm. He brought a cup of green tea, stripped and remade her bed, and then put eggs on to boil and dropped toast in the toaster. He prepared a tray for her. *A soft-boiled egg, dry toast and tea should be enough to start with today. I hope she'll eat it.* He sat by her side, fed her small bites and offered sips of tea until she put her hand in the air. "No more. That's all I can eat for now."

"Are you tired? Do you want to go back to bed, or would you rather sit up for a while?"

"I'd like to sit for a while. I wish it were sunny, I'd sit outside and watch the birds."

"I'll move a chair near the big window. You can bird-watch from there."

Touched by Nate's eagerness to do whatever possible for her comfort, she began to understand his love. Until that moment, she assumed he loved the eighteen-year-old girl of his memory; when he looked her, he saw that girl. But he'd cleaned her up when she'd puked all over herself, stunk to high heavens with vomit and sweat; his eyes held nothing but tenderness and love ... love. He loved her—changed though she was. No longer naïve and trusting—no longer a nubile young woman. He loved her as she was now. The barricade she'd built around her heart collapsed.

She bird-watched for an hour. Nate pressed her to drink more green tea, more water. As she watched birds, she surreptitiously watched Nate. He buzzed around doing chores: cleaned the kitchen, and chopped vegetables for soup with amazing dexterity. As he chopped, he began to tell stories about his friend, Amos. Amos, who taught him about cooking and more about life. He'd become Nate's surrogate father. She wished she'd met him.

She tried to walk back to bed without Nate's help, but she was too weak. He scooped her up. Hesitantly, he asked if she needed help to use the bathroom. She laughed. This man who'd stripped her filthy clothes from her and showered her twice, was embarrassed to ask the question.

"Put me down and stay close, if I need you, I'll call." She managed nicely on her own, but Nate waited outside until she came out. Tucking her into bed, he offered another sip of water. "Will you stay with me until I fall asleep?"

"Sure. Would you like me to read to you?"

"Would you sing instead?" She recalled his beautiful voice from the karaoke bar.

He smiled and began to sing *I'll Fly Away* ... With a smile she drifted off. He'd remembered the gospel song was a favorite of hers.

When she woke that afternoon, she felt almost human again. She rolled over to greet Nate. His laid hands tucked behind his head and his brow furrowed. "You're deep in thought this afternoon." He turned his head, surprised she'd spoken.

"Sorry, Kara, I've had something on my mind. Are you ready for soup?"

It was obvious something was bothering him. "The soup can wait. What's wrong?"

"Not now. We'll have lunch first; then we can talk. How do you feel?"

"I'm much better, thanks to you."

He'd pulled on his jeans and tee shirt. As she answered, he padded down the hall barefooted. Odd. It appeared he'd never heard her answer. She pulled on slippers and trailed to the kitchen. Nate had a pot of tea brewing. A cup of soup waited on the table along with cheese and crackers. He was his usual efficient self, but he'd never looked directly at her since she sat down. She didn't know what to think, but he'd made it clear he wasn't going to talk until after they'd eaten.

After the dishes were in the dishwasher, Nate poured more tea and sat. He looked as if he'd lost his best friend.

"What is going on? Tell me what's bothering you." She began to think it was serious.

"Let me start with a question. Do you think I might have fathered children other than Natalie?"

"Assuming you didn't kill all the girls you slept with, I would say it is a distinct possibility," she said wryly. "Why?"

"You are going to hate me, but I've slept with *hundreds* of girls I didn't kill."

"Nate, you've had many years to accomplish those numbers. Even with those numbers, there's only a small percentage who may have gotten pregnant," she said pragmatically.

Nate put his face in his hands again. "That's what I was afraid of. What percentage? Ten—fifteen percent? Even five percent is too many."

"Is that what's bothering you? Nate, you didn't know you could father children until you found out about Natalie. While your behavior may not be exactly honorable—"

Nate interrupted. "That's only a part of it, Kara. The worst of it— those long hunting trips I go on? I hunt, but I also look for willing girls. I don't have to look too far, either. Go into any bar and there are nice girls willing to hook up with complete strangers. I'm ashamed to admit this, Kara. I hope you can forgive me."

"Nate, I knew." She reached out and laid her hand on his arm. His head shot up, surprised. "I went to see if you had any dirty clothes I could wash while you were away on one of your trips. A pair of jeans you'd left folded on the foot of your bed held a telling foil packet in the pocket. At least you're being safe," she said with a wry smile.

"You never said anything," he whispered.

"I don't have the right to question your behavior. I might not approve, but I understand you have needs. You're still very young."

"I'm *not* young. I am close to a hundred years old now. I can't help how I look, but—needs or not—it's got to stop. I put all this out of my head when you were sick because I was worried about you. But Kara, think about it. I could have slept with my own daughter or granddaughter and wouldn't have known it. God in heaven, the thought of incest sickens me. I wish I was dead." He buried his face in his hands and refused to look up.

"First, if that happened it was in innocence. If I know you, you've asked God for forgiveness. We both know you have it." She pulled a hand away from his face. "As for me, you don't have to ask for my forgiveness. I'm a part of the problem, but I don't know what to do about it. We'll find a solution together. But, Nate, I could never hate you, no matter what."

He shuddered, then slowly raised his head. "Together?" He managed a half-smile.

⌒⟲

Natalie called that evening. When Nate took the call, he told her how sick Kara had been before he passed the phone to her.

"Why didn't you call me?" she demanded.

"I was too sick to get out of bed. It was a good thing Nate came home when he did. He took such good care of me. He stayed with me day and night." She wanted to jerk the words back as soon as they left her mouth. Natalie would pick up on the fact Nate spent the night in her bed. She never missed a trick.

"All night, huh?" She heard the hint of a chuckle. "I'm coming down this weekend. There's something I want to talk to you about."

"We can talk now," she offered hopefully.

"Nope, it can wait for the weekend," she said annoyingly. This time Kara was positive she heard a loud chuckle. "Bye, Mom."

⌒⟲

Saturday morning Nate and she barely sat down for breakfast, when Rocky barked a greeting an instant before the front door banged open. "We're here." A familiar male voice called. *Don? Natalie said nothing about Don being back.* She jumped up to greet them, surprised.

"Can I fix you breakfast and pour some coffee?" Nate smiled his greeting to them.

"No breakfast. We already ate, but coffee would be great." Don answered. "Hi, Mom. Surprise! I'll bet you didn't know I was coming." He bent to kiss her cheek.

"No, I didn't, but it's a welcome surprise. When did you fly in?"

"I flew in to PDX at four this morning. My lovely sister was on hand to pick me up," he said with a flourish. We stopped and ate pancakes on the way down." He grinned, licking his lips with relish.

They joined her and Nate at the table while they finished eating breakfast. While they ate, Don gave an update on what he'd done since his last visit. Natalie kept grinning like the cat that ate the canary. Something was definitely up.

As they finished, Natalie turned toward Don and Nate. "I need to talk to Mom. Why don't you two make yourselves scarce?"

Nate looked nonplused, but Don hit him on the shoulder. "Come on big guy. Let's you and me go for a run at the park." Nate nodded in agreement.

As they left, Kara turned to Natalie. "What is going on? I know the two of you have something up your sleeves. What is it?"

"I'll get right to the point. Do you love my father?"

"What a silly question. You know how much I loved Fred." She didn't have a clue where Natalie was going with this.

Irritated, she said, "Not Daddy, Mom. I know you loved him, but what about my father—Nate. Do. You. Love. Him?

Natalie's emphasis on each word made her uncomfortable. "I ... uh ... well, I *am* very fond of Nate."

"How fond? I repeat my question: 'Do you love him?'" She was always tenacious and today was no exception.

If she answered honestly, would Natalie see it as a betrayal? She hadn't done much lying for many years. If she tried to lie or tell a half-truth, her daughter would see right through her.

"Yes. I think I do."

Her face broke into a huge smile. "I know you've slept with him. You said so yourself."

"Natalie!" She broke in, shocked and embarrassed. "That is *all* that has happened. We slept!"

"Why? You said you loved him."

"I could never ... not with a man I'm not married to," shocked at what her daughter suggested. "Besides he is much younger than I am."

"No he's not. He's older than Grandpa Pete. Quit making excuses, Mom. If you won't have sex unless you're married, then marry him!"

"What about your dad? What would Fred think?"

"Oh for Pete's sake, don't use Dad as an excuse. If there was anything Dad wanted, it was for you to be happy," Natalie said in an exasperated tone.

"But ... how could I stand up in front of my friends and marry him. I'd look like an old fool!"

"So it's your pride that keeps you from marrying him?"

Kara was completely flustered. When Natalie put it that way, it did sound foolish, but she couldn't deny the truth of it. "I ... um ... well, I ... guess so."

"Marry him privately, here, with just the family; with God and us as witnesses. You could keep your public face with Nate as your helper; but in fact, he'd be your husband. I know he wants to marry you, Mom. Be happy—both of you. Oh, by the way, Don is talking to Nate about this, too."

God, why did you give me such interfering children? "We'll see, Natalie; we'll see."

As if on cue, the front door crashed open. "We're back! Did we give you enough time?" Don bounced in, wearing a big grin.

Natalie smirked. "I think so."

Nate came on slow feet. Chewing on the side of his lip, he stumbled to her and dropped to his knees. As he gazed up into her eyes, she saw her fears and doubts matched by his own. With gentle hands, he took hers. "Kara, will you marry me, now, today?"

What could she say but yes. He laid his head in her lap and whispered, "Thank God, thank God."

Leaning over she put her arms around him and pulled him closer to her. Stretching up, his lips found hers for a long, sweet kiss. In the background she heard a cheer. *My two children have carried their plan to fruition,* she thought. Wrong—their plans had just begun.

"Okay you two; enough of the lovey-dovey stuff for now. We've got things to do. Mom, you need to get your hair done and a manicure. You have to buy a new dress. Nate, do you have a suit or a nice sports jacket?

Oh, we need to shop for rings, too. Don, go with Nate and get him set up. I'll go with Mom. Did I tell you Don got his license to perform weddings? He got it through the internet, so we're all set."

Natalie snapped out orders like a general preparing for battle. They set off in different directions—Kara with Natalie in her car. Nate with Don in hers. Her head spun with all the quick plans.

It seemed an eternity when they returned home. Natalie ordered her to the bedroom and brought a late lunch to her there. The little general told her to stay there until time for the ceremony. She promised to come back to help her dress. Later, she heard Don repeat the same orders to Nate as he escorted him to the guest room. The doorbell rang a few times and there was a flurry of activity. *What was going on?*

As she waited, she tried to decide if she was making a colossal mistake. She and Nate worked side-by-side in harmony for the past three years and she enjoyed his company. When she was sick, his presence was a comfort. She sighed over her fears and doubts—every fear was about her, not one about Nate.

Out of boredom, she picked up a book she'd been reading, but it was hard to concentrate while in such suspense. *What are the children doing?* She laid the book aside and looked down at her hands.

Her nails were a wreck from gardening. Though she owned three pair of good gardening gloves, she'd have her hands in the soil before she remember to wear them. Today they looked nice with the soft mauve polish. She was pleased Natalie insisted on the manicure.

Pleased, Natalie encouraged her to get her hair done, too. She planned to get it cut and styled for weeks, but there was always something else to do, so she'd put it off. The new style was flattering and soft around her face.

After hours—actually the clock said an hour and a half—of waiting, though it seemed much longer—Natalie returned to help her dress and to change her own clothes. The guest room door creaked open, so Nate was free from his captivity.

The dress she wore was a soft rose-beige. It was dressy, but not so dressy she'd never wear it again. It was a good color for her; in fact, she loved it. She'd never have bought it for herself, but Natalie insisted.

With the final touches, Natalie released her to go down the hall. Soft classical music came from her CD player. Candles burned around the room and on either side of the stone fireplace stood two bouquets of flowers. Between the bouquets stood her son—serious in his dark suit ... and Nate. He was beautiful. He stood in a dove gray jacket and dark trousers, waiting, his hands clasped together. Serious one second and a smile the next. He stepped forward to greet her. They clasped hands; gazed into each other's eyes and turned to face Don.

She always loved weddings. She loved the idea of two disparate people joining together to make a cohesive unit—a family. The vows, spoken by countless people throughout the centuries, were beautiful. Don did a wonderful job reading them. The final line he used was *until death separates us*. Nate flinched as he heard those words. But neither of them flinched when they heard "you may kiss the bride." His kiss was gentle and sweet. She smiled shyly as their children grabbed them in a massive hug of congratulations.

"Now we have another surprise," Natalie said as she opened the door to the dining area. All her good crystal and china decorated the table, which was covered with her best damask cloth. To top off the surprise, a catered dinner sat ready to be served. The children must have planned today's events before they showed up this morning. They must have been positive of the outcome.

There was a small wedding cake. Kara shook her head in wonder at all they'd accomplished. They ate, drank a glass of champagne, laughed, and thoroughly had a wonderful time. She looked at Nate then down at her wedding band. A simple gold band, one she could easily switch to her right hand in public.

The ring she selected for Nate was a heavy gold band set with hematite. It could second as a simple man's ring. No matter which hand they wore them on—they knew their significance.

"One last thing," Natalie said as she and Don stood in front of them. "We pooled our money and got the use of a cabin for the week." Don pulled a set of keys from his pocket and dangled them in front of them as Natalie retrieved a paper with directions to the cabin. "Go packed while we clean up and don't worry about Rocky. I'll take care of him until you get back. We wanted you to have a honeymoon—just the two of you—no interruptions."

Both Nate and she thanked them profusely until Don protested. "Enough already, you're wasting time. Go, be happy; that's all we want." So they did.

⌒◯

The cabin was set high in the Cascades. It offered plenty of privacy and plenty of wild game for Nate. They hiked and recalled the trails they'd traversed in Arizona and the discoveries they'd made. They fished and laughed about their first fishing trip.

Nate chuckled as he reminded her how she looked gutting her first fish. Now, thanks to him, she fished with the best of them. Each night, before bed, they sat companionably before the fire.

Nate was the same gentle lover she remembered. Patient and undemanding, he never asked her to go beyond her comfort zone. Understanding her nervousness, he was everything she could have wished. She wished their life wouldn't have to be hidden from the judgment of others. The week ended all too soon, but the thought of leaving this little hideaway was eased by the knowledge they would be together for whatever time she had left on earth.

The kids were there to greet them when they returned home. They brought Rocky back and had a hot meal waiting. After a quick visit, they made excuses and left them alone. Don was flying back to Japan in the morning. Natalie would be back in her classroom a few hours after she dropped him at PDX.

As they drove away, Nate said, "You know, we have a couple of fine kids there."

She smiled and nodded. Now they'd begin their real life together. It was ironic how she'd worried about how to deal with Nate's fears; how he'd handle the "no more sex" rule. She told him they'd figure it out together. Who'd have thought the children would give them the answer they needed.

Chapter 32

The quote "time flies when you're having fun" was on her mind as she wakened. It was true. It was a shock to realize fifteen years passed since she and Nate married. Today the entire family was coming to celebrate their anniversary. As she lay in bed, she recalled the past few years.

Natalie met and married another teacher. Jackson taught in the same school district, but at another school. They met at a training conference, both assigned the same discussion group. They met later for lunch and the rest became history. They have two adorable boys—named, not surprisingly, Fred and Nathan. Fred began middle school this year. Nathan joins him next year.

Don met Anna, who worked for another Pacific Rim company. Originally, from Louisiana she has a charming southern drawl. She's a stay-at-home mom taking care of Belle, who is almost five, and Fredrick Peter, called Pete by his playmates. Pete is almost three. Belle's real name is Annabelle, after her mother. Don and Anna chose to distinguish them to prevent confusion. She laughed as her children explained the difficulty in picking a name. Like the ball player, Yogi Berra, said all those years ago, "It's déjà vu all over again."

None of the grandchildren know about Nate's situation, although Fred and Nathan are suspicious. We'll have a talk with them before long.

Jackson and Anna were told and understand the importance of secrecy. She hated the day she first met them—their shocked expressions when they realized Nate and she were a couple. They told Jackson just after he and Natalie married. Don flew over for the wedding and stayed for moral support. Explanations are a painful, if necessary, routine.

To say Jackson was disconcerted would minimize his reaction. He leaped from his chair, stalked around the room, shouting, "You people are sick and twisted." Stomping out the front door, he slammed it behind him. Natalie cried when he walked out. While they tried to calm her down; she gave her tissues and Nate brought chamomile tea, Jackson returned.

"I don't understand what you're trying to make me believe," he growled. He pointed to Nate. "You're telling me this guy is Natalie's father? That doesn't make sense. He looks years younger than she does. Maybe you'd better explain it again."

Of course, the old photo album was put into service again. He stared at the pictures and concluded what they'd said was true. She could see he was shocked, but knew he'd eventually come around, if for no other reason than he loved Natalie. It took time, but she was right.

Anna, on the other hand, proved easy to convince. She was comfortable with them from the very beginning. The Cajuns in her family had a few strange beliefs of their own. While Kara wondered what strange things they might be. Anna never explained, so she never asked.

If she was shocked at the apparent age difference between Nate and her, Anna, being the proper Southern Belle, never verbalized it. The pictures convinced her. Nate, who looked so young, was older than her grandfather.

Nate moved beside her, so she rolled over and kissed him as he stretched his long frame. He said, "You're up early."

"I know. I thought I'd take a hot shower to get me moving. The older I get the harder it is to get moving."

"You get showered and dressed; I'll feed Rocky and start breakfast." He pulled her to his chest and kissed the top of her head down to her neck before he moved away.

"Come on, buddy, rise and shine!" Rocky groaned as he pulled himself out of his basket. She wasn't the only one who moved slowly these days. It's really no surprise. In dog years, Rocky was older than she was. They were old.

⌢⚲

As much as she loved the family visits, she hoped they wouldn't stay late. When they came, she couldn't catnap in the afternoon. She'd be exhausted by evening. No matter. She could sleep anytime.

The smell of breakfast drew her down the hall. The scent of the coffee alone, was a strong motivator. After they finished breakfast, she rose to clear the table and load the dishwasher.

"Kara, you look tired. Why don't you take a short nap while finish. I'll come join you as soon as I'm done."

"I might do that. I want to be well-rested when the kids arrive." She had no worries about dinner because the kids were bringing the food for the celebration.

It felt like she'd barely closed her eyes when the door banged open and a cacophony of voices filled the room.

"Oh, did we wake you? Sorry Mom."

"Kara woke early this morning, Natalie. I talked her into a nap," Nate explained. "I wanted her to enjoy the day." He extricated himself from under her head and pulled her to her feet.

Armed with containers and sacks, they made their way into the kitchen. They put the food in the refrigerator and preheated the oven. That done, the small army surrounded them, each wanting hugs and kisses.

Nate poured coffee for everyone, including the kids. The kids' "coffee" was a mixture of hot chocolate and coffee. Don and Anna's little one's get a dollop of coffee in their hot chocolate. Fred and Nathan get a half-cup of coffee and half of the chocolate. No seconds for the kids—one cup only.

The effect of the coffee on the children is amazing. It's not the coffee so much as being treated as adults. She watched the children take careful sips and gently set their cups back on the saucer. She wished she'd done it with her children.

Dinner was pleasant; filled with good conversation. The rain let up so after the kitchen was cleaned, they grabbed their coats. The air was fresh and clean and the pavement sparkled. Since they had the little ones, they didn't go far—a couple of blocks. By the time they reached the second block, Pete was ready to be carried, so they headed home. Pete was passed from man to man. Though only three, he was going to be a big boy. When they reached home, her children packed their offspring into their respective cars. After a protracted good-bye, they waved them off.

She sighed, collapsing into a chair. "The kids are growing so fast. Don't you love the way Fred and Nathan entertain their little cousins." She loved watching Nate around the kids, too. He was such an integral part of the family and she couldn't imagine it any other way.

"Come here and sit next to me." He patted a spot on the couch, and then tucked her under his arm. His familiar body relaxed her. She melted into his shoulder. She awoke in the bedroom with Nate removing her clothes. He helped dress her for bed. It was early—only eight thirty, but she couldn't rouse herself to protest. He tucked her in; picked up a book he was reading, stacked pillows and lay next her. "Don't come to bed if you'd rather stay up," she whispered drowsily.

"I want to be with you." He reached over and stroked her cheek with the back of his hand. A flash of a question lit his eyes, but she was too tired to wonder why. Her lids grew heavy and she closed her eyes; lost in the arms of Morpheus.

Nate watched Kara as she sank into sleep. Something wasn't right. Perhaps she's overtired. He'd make sure she ate, exercised, but didn't overdo as she often did. His book forgotten, he watched her dreamless sleep. It was midnight when he reached over and turned off the bedside lamp. He wrapped arms around her and held her through the night.

The next day he prepared her meals with the careful calculations of a nutritionist, making sure she took her vitamins. He took her for a walk as Rocky tagged along behind them. After a few days of this routine, she was more her old self and he began to relax. He took over all the chores. She loaded the dishes into the dishwasher after meals, but he did everything else. She didn't have the stamina to do more than that simple task.

Three months later, Kara awoke in surprise one morning to find Nate's face inches from her belly. "What in the world are you doing?"

"Kara," he said seriously, "I want you to make an appointment for a physical. I'll go with you when you see the doctor. Something's wrong. I can smell it."

"It's your imagination; I feel fine. I probably spilled something on myself last night. That's what you smell."

"I'm serious. Indulge me. If not for yourself, do it for me. Please."

She nodded her head with reluctance. "It's foolish, but I'll do it for you. Besides, I'm due for a physical soon."

Nate kissed her. "Thank you. What do you want for breakfast? The coffee's on."

Kara grimaced. "I don't want coffee today—maybe a cup of herbal tea. Cook what you like; I'm not particularly hungry."

Nate fixed tea and toast. He sat peanut butter and an assortment of jams on the table. She automatically reached for the peanut butter, but was nauseated the moment she smelled it. "You know, Nate, the last time I had an aversion to coffee and peanut butter, I was pregnant with Natalie." She grinned wickedly at him. "You don't suppose ..." She let the words dangle in the air while she watched his look of complete horror. Laughing at his expression, she won a chagrined smile from him.

She scheduled an appointment with her doctor. It was a month before she could see him, but he scheduled the lab work prior to her visit. The usual routine: a twelve-hour fast, the blood draw and urinalysis a week before the appointment. Maybe she was anemic. It would explain why she was tired so much of the time.

〜つ

When they arrived at the doctor's office on the appointed day, the nurse frowned in Nate's direction. "He needs to wait in the lobby."

"No, he doesn't," she said firmly. "He's my helper and the primary person on my advanced health care directive. Mr. Whitworth and I have no secrets. I want him with me."

Her eyebrows shot high and her lips tightened, but the nurse nodded. Dr. Jackson would get an earful before he saw her.

Dr. Jackson entered the room without any comment on Nate's presence. He pulled up his stool. Without wasting a breath he said, "Kara, I'm concerned about these tests. Tell me how you feel."

She tried to make light of her symptom, but Nate jumped in and interrupted. "She doesn't have an appetite. She refuses foods she usually loves. She is tired all the time even though she sleeps through night."

The doctor nodded. "Here are the results of the lab tests. Your blood sugar is very high. Your A1c is 12.6. It should be below 6.5. Your urinalysis also shows abnormally high sugars. Since you've never had a problem with diabetes, I'd like to run further tests—specifically a MRI scan. I hope to rule out a few things. The MRI will give more information. If necessary, I'd like to do a biopsy.

"In the meantime, I want you to test your blood sugar two hours following every meal, before breakfast and just before bed. I'll give you a prescription for Glucophage. Be sure you take it as prescribed. It will help control your blood sugar level until we know what we're dealing with."

Nate asked, "What do you want to rule out?"

The air left the room as the doctor answered, "Pancreatic cancer." She glanced at Nate, whose lips were drawn in a straight line as he fought for control.

"Assuming it is pancreatic cancer, how do we treat it? What kind of odds can you give me?" Her voice was hollow.

"There are too many variables to say. Without the tests, I can't give a realistic answer. It depends on if the cancer's metastasized—spread, and where it is located. Also, if surgery is a viable option ... I need more information. I can schedule the MRI right away. The radiologist will call you with your appointment time. Come back in when it's complete."

"All right, I'll have the MRI. Beyond that, I make no promises."

He handed her the prescriptions and order forms to leave at the desk. They left in silence.

The test came back positive. Because it was determined inoperable, her choice was easy, she'd go home to die. No hospital—no hospice.

She agreed to start insulin. She asked the doctor if she'd have a lot of pain.

"You'll get progressively sicker, but there won't be much pain until near the end. I'll order morphine at that point to keep you comfortable."

"No morphine. I've seen people on morphine. They're out of it—sleeping away the last days of their life. I want to be fully present with my family as long as possible."

Nate and she discussed her decision. He took it calmly. He claimed he needed to hunt that night. When he came home, his voice was hoarse. She had no doubt it was from screaming out to God.

There's something about a deadline that gave her new purpose. What was it Leonard Pitts had said? Something about "knowing we are finite that lends a bittersweet urgency to life." The commentary was filed away, but she'd have to read it again.

Loose ends to tie up—phone calls to make, letters to write, friends to whom she must say good-bye. Her own memorial service to plan. It should be joyful, not depressing and sad. All her plans made it appear she wasn't afraid, but she was. Not of the afterlife. She was fully assured where she'd be. Her fear was leaving her children and her beloved Nate when she took the final step no one can take with another—the step from life into eternity. Plans helped her focus on the positive and provided closure for those she'd leave behind.

Nate told Kara he needed to hunt, but nothing was further from the truth. There was no way he could feed. He thought about an option. He could change her, but she would never forgive him, nor would Natalie and Don. So he ran. He ran as fast as he could run—east to Silver Falls. There in the middle of the forest, as far from habitation as he could manage and yet return to her side quickly, he fell to his knees in tears.

Next to Winter Falls, he screamed out his pain and fear. He was going to lose Kara. He known this time would come, but he'd chosen to ignore the facts. Now he couldn't ignore the truth. It was no longer possible.

After a while a quietness entered his soul. He realized he was not alone. He began to talk to the spirit that enveloped him and thanked him for the years he'd shared with Kara. He thanked him for the days they'd yet share until she went to her final home. His strength slowly returned as he asked for the courage to make her days good ones.

He guessed she'd be asleep when he returned, but she was awake. Without a word she opened her arms as he sat beside her. Kara wrapped her arms around him and pulled his head to her chest. He thought he was cried out, but he wailed again. Kara held him and rocked him as she'd rocked the children. Her tears mingled with his. They sat entwined the remainder of the night. All that needed to be said was spoken. They'd face tomorrow with the rising of the sun.

Epilogue

It was late afternoon when he drifted through the trees. The sun was up but hidden under the heavy cloud cover. The rain hadn't begun, but the electrical storm drew closer. It was doubtful he'd be disturbed here in the cemetery. No one wanted to be outside when the storm hit. He'd have all the time he needed to prepare.

He recalled his last days with Kara as he cleaned the grave sites. As she got steadily weaker, he increased the amount of insulin she needed as her pancreas failed. Days when the pain got the best of her, she'd squeeze his hand for hours on end. When the weather allowed, he'd wrap her in blankets and take her out to sit in her beloved yard. She'd watch the birds, smile and say, "Remember Nate, 'His Eye is on the Sparrow.'"

He didn't need a reminder, but he smiled hearing her say it. There was little she said or did that didn't make him smile—even her stubborn refusal to give in to her pain. She lived life on her own terms—the terms she said God allowed. She'd even told him when it was time to call the children for their final good-byes.

Don had taken a temporary transfer to Portland so he could be as close as possible during those dark days. Nate called him first with the news and asked him to call Natalie. It was the coward's way out, but he couldn't be the one to tell his daughter that today was her mother's last day on earth.

They gathered their families together and came down to say good-bye to their mother and grandmother. The children behaved remarkably well. Though in their teens and early twenty's none of them had dealt with death of a family member. Nate suspected they'd been thoroughly coached by their parents. They kissed Kara's hand, careful not to jostle the bed, said good-bye. Quietly crying, they left the room. Jackson and Anna thanked her for being a loving person who accepted them wholly into her life. Finally, only Natalie and Don were left. It was painful to watch as they said their farewell, but Kara smiled, told them how much she loved them. "Death is temporary, I'll see you again in eternity." Sighing she said, "I think I want to sleep now."

As the others left the room, Nate gathered her into his arms; she smiled up into his face and told him she loved him. She looked past his shoulder. Her eyes and smile widened as if she saw a friend. Closed her eyes—and just like that, she was gone.

She was buried in the plot next to Fred's. It was ironic how Fred wanted to move back to Payson, but only came home to this small plot of ground. Kara purchased the plot next to him at the time of his death. Somehow, it was fitting for her go back to the place where their lives intertwined.

He'd been a wanderer since she died. Recently, he visited his kids and saw Josh and Liz. They were as happy as ever, even though they were forced to move every five years.

Most of the friends he'd made through the years were gone. Dan ... Amos ... Dale, only little Grace still lived. She'd lived a successful life and raised a family. Now she was a great-grandmother.

No one needed him anymore. He'd written letters to Don and Natalie to tell them he wouldn't be back. He kept a copy of the letter in his possession, though no one else would read it. He had pictures of them and the grandkids. No one else would see the pictures. He carried the New Testament Kara gave him all those years ago. It was ragged and the pages were loose. It was held together with a rubber band. But it didn't matter. He needed these, his most precious possessions, to give him courage.

He'd accrued a fair amount of money through the years. His needs were few, so money he made was invested in trust funds for the family.

They should never want for anything they needed. Like Kara he tied up his loose ends.

Within the final minutes before the storm was directly overhead, he cleaned the gravestones that marked Fred and Kara's final resting places. He thanked Fred for all the happy years he'd given Kara. He thanked him for loving his daughter so fully. He thanked him for raising Don to be the fine man he became. As for Kara, he'd said all he needed to say while she lived, so laid his hand on her gravestone. Then he turned his attention to the one who has power over all things.

The thunder and lightning moved directly overhead. Nate cried out, "Lord, I am alone and lonely. The eternity I live has no point or value. I am tired, Lord. I want to come home. I want *your* eternity; please let me come home."

Nate raised his hands in supplication as lightning struck the tree next to him. It split the tree and caught the branches on fire. He smiled as he reached up and embraced the burning branches.

Made in the USA
Charleston, SC
09 October 2014